BLOOD
MEMORY

BLOOD MEMORY

GREG ILES

POCKET BOOKS

NEW YORK   LONDON   TORONTO   SYDNEY

POCKET BOOKS
A Division of Simon & Schuster, Inc.
1230 Avenue of the Americas
New York, NY 10020

This book is a work of fiction. Names, characters, places, and incidents either are products of the author's imagination or are used fictitiously. Any resemblance to actual events or locales or persons, living or dead, is entirely coincidental.

This Pocket Books trade paperback edition November 2008

POCKET and colophon are registered trademarks of Simon & Schuster, Inc.

For information regarding special discounts for bulk purchases, please contact Simon & Schuster Special Sales at 1-800-456-6798 or business@simonandschuster.com

Manufactured in the United States of America

9   10

Library of Congress Cataloging-in-Publication is available.

ISBN-13: 978-1-4391-2826-8
ISBN-10:   1-4391-2826-X

This novel is dedicated to those women who realize in the dead of night that something is wrong, and has been for a long time. More than most, they know that Faulkner's words are true: "There is no such thing as *was*—only *is*. If *was* existed, there would be no grief or sorrow." You are not alone.

BLOOD
MEMORY

Memory is the guardian of all things.

—Cicero

Evil being the root of mystery,
pain is the root of knowledge.

—Erasmus

CHAPTER

1

When does murder begin?

With the pull of a trigger? With the formation of a motive? Or does it begin long before, when a child swallows more pain than love and is forever changed?

Perhaps it doesn't matter.

Or perhaps it matters more than everything else.

We judge and punish based on facts, but facts are not truth. Facts are like a buried skeleton uncovered long after death. Truth is fluid. Truth is alive. To know the truth requires understanding, the most difficult human art. It requires seeing all things at once, forward and backward, the way God sees.

Forward and backward. . .

So we begin in the middle, with a telephone ringing in a dark bedroom on the shore of Lake Pontchartrain in New Orleans, Louisiana. There's a woman lying on the bed, mouth open in the mindless gape of sleep. She seems not to hear the phone. Then suddenly the harsh ring breaks through, like defibrillator paddles shocking a comatose patient. The woman's hand shoots from beneath the covers, groping for the phone, not finding it. She gasps and rises onto one elbow. Then she groans and picks up the receiver from the bedside table.

The woman is me.

"Dr. Ferry," I croak.

"Are you sleeping?" The voice is male, taut with anger.

"No." My denial is automatic, but my mouth is dry as a cotton ball, and my alarm clock reads 8:20 P.M. I've been out for nine hours. The first decent sleep I've had in days.

"He hit another one."

Something sparks in my drowsy brain. "What?"

"This is the fourth time I've called in the past half hour, Cat."

The voice brings up a well of anger, longing, and guilt. It belongs to the detective I've been sleeping with for the past eighteen months. Sean Regan. An insightful, fascinating man with a wife and three kids.

"What did you say before?" I ask, ready to bite off Sean's head if he asks me to meet him somewhere.

"I said, he hit another one."

I blink and try to orient myself in the darkness. It's early August, and the purple glow of dusk filters through my curtains. God, my mouth is dry. "Where?"

"The Garden District. Owner of a printing company. Male Caucasian."

"Bite marks?"

"Worse than the others."

"How old was he?"

"Sixty-nine."

"Jesus. It is him." I'm already getting out of bed. "This makes no sense at all."

"Nope."

"Sexual predators kill women, Sean. Or children. Not old men."

"We've had this conversation. How fast can you get here? Piazza's hovering over me, and the chief himself may be coming down for a look."

I lift yesterday's jeans off the chair and slip them over my panties. Victoria's Secret, Sean's favorite pair, but he won't be seeing them tonight. Maybe not for a long time. Maybe never again. "Any gay angle on this victim? Did he use male prostitutes, anything like that?"

"Not even a tickle," Sean replies. "Looks as clean as the others."

"If he's got a home computer, confiscate it. He might—"

"I know my job, Cat."

"I know, but—"

"Cat." The single syllable is a probing finger. "Are you sober?"

A column of heat rises up my spine. I haven't had a sip of vodka for nearly forty-eight hours, but I'm not going to give Sean the satisfaction of answering his interrogation. "What's the victim's name?"

"Arthur LeGendre." His voice drops. "Are you sober, darlin'?"

The craving is already awake in my blood, like little teeth gnawing at the walls of my veins. I need the anesthetic burn of a shot of Grey Goose. Only I can't have that anymore. I've been using Valium to fight the physical withdrawal symptoms, but nothing can truly replace the alcohol that has kept me together for so long.

I shift the phone from shoulder to shoulder and pull a silk blouse from my closet. "Where are the bite marks?"

"Torso, nipples, face, penis."

I freeze. "*Face?* Are they deep?"

"Deep enough for you to take impressions, I think."

Excitement blunts the edge of my craving. "I'm on my way."

"Have you taken your meds?"

Sean knows me too well. No one else in New Orleans is even aware that I take anything. Lexapro for depression, Depakote for impulse control. I stopped taking both drugs three days ago, but I don't want to get into that with Sean.

"Stop worrying about me. Is the FBI there?"

"Half the task force is here, and they want to know what you think about these bite marks. The Bureau guy is photographing them, but you have that ultraviolet rig . . . and when it comes to teeth, you're the man."

Sean's admiring misstatement of my gender is typical cop talk, and it tells me he's speaking for the benefit of others. "What's the address?"

"Twenty-seven twenty-seven Prytania."

"Sounds like an address with a security system."

"Switched off."

"Just like the first one. Moreland." Our first victim—one month ago—was a retired army colonel, highly decorated in Vietnam.

"Just like that." Sean's voice drops to a whisper. "Get your lovely ass down here, okay?"

Today his Irish intimacy makes me want to jab him. "No 'I love you'?" I ask with feigned sweetness.

His reply is barely audible. "You know I'm surrounded."

As usual. "Yeah. I'll see you in fifteen minutes."

* * *

Night falls fast as I drive my Audi from my house on Lake Pontchartrain to the Garden District, the fragrant heart of New Orleans. I spent two minutes in the bathroom trying to make myself presentable, but my face is still swollen from sleep. I need caffeine. In five minutes I'll be surrounded by cops, FBI agents, forensic techs, the chief of robbery homicide, and possibly the chief of the NOPD. I'm accustomed to that kind of attention, but seven days ago—the last time this predator hit—I had a problem at the crime scene. Nothing too bad. A garden-variety panic attack, according to the EMT who checked me out. But panic attacks don't exactly inspire confidence in the hard men and women who work serial murder cases. The last thing they want is a consulting expert who can't hold her mud.

The word got around about my little episode, too. Sean told me that. Nobody could really believe it. Why did the woman that some homicide detectives call "the ice queen" suddenly lose her composure at the scene of a not-very-grisly murder? I'd like to know that myself. I have a theory, but analyzing one's own mental condition is a notoriously unreliable business. As for the sobriquet, I'm no ice queen, but in the macho world of law enforcement, playing that role is the only thing that keeps me safe—from men and from my own rogue impulses. Of course, Sean gives the lie to that little strategy.

Four victims now, I remind myself, focusing on the case. Four men between the ages of forty-two and sixty-nine, all murdered within weeks of each other. In a single thirty-day period, to be exact. The pace of the killings is virtually unprecedented, and if the victims were women, the city would be gripped by terror. But because the victims are middle-aged or older men, a sort of fascinated curiosity has taken hold of New Orleans. Each victim has been shot in or near the spine, mutilated with human bites, then finished off with a coup de grâce shot to the head. The bites have increased in savagery from victim to victim, and they've also provided the strongest evidence against any future suspect—mitochondrial DNA from the killer's saliva.

The bite marks are the reason for my involvement with the case. I'm a forensic odontologist, an expert on human teeth and the damage they can do. I acquired this knowledge in four boring years of dental school and five fascinating years of fieldwork. If people ask me what I do for a living, I tell them I'm a dentist, which is true enough and all they need to know. *Odontologist* doesn't mean anything to anybody, but in post-*CSI* America, *forensic* prompts questions I'd just as soon not answer in a grocery store. So, while most acquaintances know me as a dentist who's too busy to accept new patients, an assortment of government agencies—including the FBI and the United Nations Commission for the Investigation of War Crimes—knows me as one of the leading forensic odontologists in the world. Which is nice. I take my identity where I can find it.

The task force wants my expertise on bite marks tonight, but Sean Regan wants more. When he sought my help on a murder case two years ago, he soon learned that I knew about a lot more than teeth. I completed two years of medical school before I withdrew, and that gave me a strong foundation for self-education in forensics. Anatomy, hematology, histology, biochemistry, whatever a case requires. I can glean twice as much information from an autopsy report as any detective, and twice as fast. After Sean and I became closer than the rules allowed, he began using me unofficially to help with difficult cases. And *used* is the proper word; Sean Regan lives to catch killers, and he'll exploit anything and anyone to help him do it.

But Sean isn't simply a user. He's my comrade-in-arms, my rabbi, and my enabler. He doesn't judge me. He knows me for what I am, and he gives me what I need. Like Sean, I'm a born hunter. Not of animals. I've hunted animals, and I hate it. Animals are innocent; men are not. I am a hunter of men. But unlike Sean, I have no license to do this. Not really. Forensic odontology brings only tangential involvement with murder cases; it's my involvement with Sean that puts me into the bloody thick of things. By allowing me access—unethical and probably illegal access—to crime scenes, witnesses, and evidence, he has put me in a position to solve four major murder cases, one of them a serial. Sean took the credit every time, of course—plus the attendant promotions—and I let him do it. Why? Maybe because telling the truth would have exposed our love affair, gotten Sean fired, and freed the killers. But the truth is simpler than that. The truth is that I didn't care about the credit. I'd tasted the pulse-pounding rush of hunting predators, and I was addicted to it as surely as I am to the vodka I need so terribly at this moment.

For this reason, I've let our relationship run long past the point where I would usually have sabotaged it. Long enough, in fact, for me to have forgotten one of my hardest-won lessons: *the husband doesn't leave.* Not the husbands I pick, anyway. Only this time it's different. Sean has gone a long way toward convincing me he really means to do it. And I'm very close to believing him. Close enough to find myself hoping desperately for it in the most vulnerable hours of the night. But now . . . the situation has changed. Fate has taken a hand. And unless Sean really surprises me, our relationship is over.

Without warning, a wave of nausea rolls through my stomach. I try to tell myself it's alcohol withdrawal, but deep down I know better. It's panic. Pure terror at the idea of giving up Sean and being alone. *Don't think about it,* says a shaky voice inside me. *In two minutes you're onstage. Think about the case . . .*

As I decelerate down the interstate ramp to the surface streets at St. Charles Avenue, my cell phone rings out the opening notes to U2's "Sunday, Bloody Sunday." I know without looking that it's Sean.

"Where are you?" he asks.

I'm still fifteen blocks from the stately Victorian houses of Prytania Street, but I need to calm Sean down. "A few blocks from the scene."

"Good. Can you handle your gear okay?"

My dental case weighs thirty-one pounds fully loaded, and tonight I'll also need my camera case and tripod. Maybe Sean is hinting that I should ask him outside to help me. This would give him an excuse for a private talk before we find ourselves together in front of others. But a private talk is the last thing I want tonight.

"I've got it," I tell him. "You sound strange. What's going on down there?"

"Everybody's uptight. You know the history."

I do. There have been three serial murder cases in the New Orleans–Baton Rouge area in as many years, and serious investigative mistakes were made in all of them.

"We got some Sixth District detectives down here," Sean goes on, "but the task force has taken over the scene. We'll be running our investigation out of headquarters, just like the others. Captain Piazza's already busting my balls."

Carmen Piazza is a tough, fiftysomething Italian-American woman who came up through the ranks of the detective bureau and is now the Homicide Division commander. If anyone ever fires Sean for his involvement with me, it will be Piazza. She likes Sean's record of arrests, but she thinks he's a cowboy. And she's right. He's a tough, devilish Irish cowboy. "Does she suspect anything about us?"

"No."

"No rumors? Nothing?"

"Don't think so."

"What about Joey?" I ask, referring to Sean's partner, Detective Joey Guercio. "Has he blabbed to anybody?"

A millisecond's hesitation. "No way. Look, just be cool like you always are. Except for last time. You feeling okay about that? Your nerves or whatever?"

I close my eyes. "I was until you asked."

"Sorry. Just hurry down here. I'm going back in."

A rush of anxiety blindsides me. "You can't wait for me?"

"Probably better if I don't."

Better for you . . . "Fine."

Focus on the case, I tell myself, checking the house numbers on Prytania to be sure where I am. *They expect you to know your business.*

The facts are simple enough. In the past thirty days, three men have been shot by the same gun, bitten by the same set of teeth, and—in two cases—marked by the saliva of a man whose DNA shows him 87 percent likely to be a Caucasian male. The NOPD crime lab did the ballistics that matched the bullets. The state police crime lab did the mitochondrial DNA match. And I matched the bite marks.

This is much more difficult than it appears to be on television. To explain my job to homicide detectives, I often tell them about the forensic researcher who used an articulated set of teeth to try to create perfectly matched bite marks on a corpse. He couldn't do it. The lesson is clear, even to street cops. If matching two bite marks known to have come from the same set of teeth can be difficult, then matching marks that might have been made by any teeth among millions is next to impossible. Even comparing bite marks on a corpse with the teeth of a small group of suspects is more problematic than many odontologists pretend.

Saliva left in a bite mark by a killer can simplify things enormously, by providing DNA to compare against that of suspects. But four weeks ago, when the first victim was discovered, I recovered no saliva from the two bite marks on the body. I figured the killer for an organized offender who washed the saliva out of his bites to prevent recovery of DNA evidence. But a week later, when the second victim was found, my theory was blown out of the water. I recovered saliva from two of four bite marks left on the corpse. This raised the possibility of a different—and disorganized—killer. But by using reflective ultraviolet photography and scanning electron microscopy on the bite marks, I concluded that the same killer had indeed murdered both victims. Ballistic analysis of the recovered bullets supported my conclusion, and six days later, when the third victim was murdered, my opinion was confirmed beyond doubt by DNA recovered from the bite marks left on that body. The same killer had murdered all three men.

The importance of this cannot be overestimated. The baseline criteria for classifying a serial murderer are three victims killed by one person, each victim killed in a different location, and a cooling-off period between the crimes. I had helped prove what I'd known from the moment I saw the first victim. New Orleans had another predator on the hunt.

My official responsibility ended with matching the bite marks, but I wasn't about to stop there. As the New Orleans Police Department joined the FBI in the uneasy marriage of a task force, I began to analyze other aspects of the case. In sexual homicide, the murderer's selection criteria for his victims hold the key to every case. And like all serial murders, the NOMURS killings—so dubbed by the FBI for "New Orleans murders"—are at root sexual homicides. Something *always* links the victims in these cases, even if it's nothing more individual than geographic location, and that link draws the predator. But the NOMURS victims have ranged widely in age, physical type, occupation, social status, and place of residence. The only similarities are that they're white, male, over forty, and have families. These four facts combined exclude them from the known target profiles for serial killers. Moreover, none of the victims is known to have had habits that might draw a predator to an atypical target. No victim was gay or had a known sexual paraphilia. None was ever arrested for a sexual crime, reported for child abuse, or known to frequent strip clubs or other sleazy establishments. For this reason the NOMURS task force has made no progress at all in finding a suspect.

As I slow the Audi to read a house number, my skin itches with fear and anticipation. The killer was on this street only hours ago. He may be here *now,* watching the progress of the investigation, as serial murderers often do. Watching *me.* And herein lies the thrill. A predator is not prey. When you hunt a predator, you place yourself in a position to be hunted yourself. There's no other way. If you follow a lion into a thicket, you step within reach of his claws. And my adversary is no lion. He's the deadliest creature in the world: a human male driven by anger and lust, yet governed—at least temporarily—by logic. He stalks these streets with impunity, confident in his prowess, meticulous in his planning, arrogant in his execution. The only thing I know about him is this: like all his brothers before him, he will kill again, and again, until someone unravels the riddle of his psyche or he self-destructs from the intensity of conflict in his own mind. A lot of people don't care which way it ends, so long as it ends soon.

I do.

Sean is standing on the sidewalk, waiting. He's walked a block up from the victim's house to meet me. He always did have guts. But does he have enough to face our present situation?

I park behind a Toyota Land Cruiser, get out, and start to unload my cases. Sean gives me a quick hug, then unloads the cases himself. He's forty-six years old but looks forty, with the easy, confident grace of a natural athlete. His hair is mostly black, his eyes green with a bit of a twinkle. Even after being his lover for eighteen months, I half expect a lilting Irish brogue to emerge when Sean opens his mouth. But it's the familiar New Orleans accent instead, the Brooklynesque drawl with a hint of crawfish.

"You doin' okay?" he asks.

"Changed your mind?"

He shrugs. "I felt bad."

"Bullshit. You wanted to see for yourself if I was sober."

I see the truth of it in his face. He gives me a penetrating survey with his eyes and makes no apology for it.

"Go on," I tell him.

"What?"

"You were about to say something. Go ahead."

He sighs. "You look rough, Cat."

"Thanks for the vote of confidence."

"Sorry. Are you drunk?"

Anger tightens my jaw muscles. "I'm stone sober for the first time in more years than I can count."

I see skepticism in his face. Then, as he studies me, belief comes into his eyes. "Jesus. Maybe a drink is what you need."

"Worse than you know. But I'm not going to."

"Why not?"

"Come on. Let's do this."

"I still need to go in ahead of you." He looks embarrassed.

Exasperation makes me look away. "How long? Five minutes?"

"Not that long."

I wave him off and get back into my car. He steps toward my door, then changes his mind and walks down the block.

My hands are shaking. Were they shaking when I woke up? I grip the steering wheel and force myself to breathe deeply. As my pulse steadies and my heart finds its rhythm, I pull down the vanity mirror and check my face. I'm not usually compulsive about my appearance, but Sean has made me nervous. And when I get nervous, crazy thoughts flood into my head. Disembodied voices, old nightmares, ancient slights and mistakes, things therapists have said . . .

I consider putting on some eyeliner to strengthen my gaze in case I have to stare somebody down inside. I don't really need it. Men often tell me I'm beautiful, but men will tell any woman that. My face is actually masculine in structure, a vertical series of V's, simple and to the point. The V of my chin slants up into a strong jaw. My mouth, too, curves upward. Then comes the angular bottom of my nose; my prominent, upward-slanting cheekbones; my tilted brown eyes and sloping eyebrows; and finally the dark widow's peak of my hairline. I see my father in all of this, twenty years dead now but alive in every angle of my face. I keep a picture of him in my wallet. *Luke Ferry, 1969*. Smiling in his army uniform, somewhere in Vietnam. I don't like the uniform—not after what the war did to him—but I like his eyes in the picture. Still compassionate, still human. It's how I like to remember him. A little girl's idea of a father. He once told me that I almost got his face, but at the last minute an angel swooped down and put enough softness in mine to make me pretty.

Sean sees the hardness in my face. He's told me I look like a predator myself, a hawk or an eagle. Tonight I'm glad for that hardness. Because as I get out of the Audi and shoulder my cases and tripod, something tells me that maybe Sean is right to be worried about my nerves. I'm going in naked tonight, without benefit of anesthesia. And without the familiar chemical barrier that shields me from the sharp edges of reality, I feel more vulnerable to whatever it was that panicked me last time.

Walking down the dusky street lined with wrought-iron fences and second-floor galleries, I sense a human gaze on my skin. I stop and turn but see no one. Only a dog lifting its leg beside a lamppost. I scan the galleries overhead, but the heat has driven their owners inside. Christ. I feel as if I've been waiting all my thirty-one years to see the corpse in the house ahead of me. Or maybe it's been waiting for me. *Something* is waiting for me, that's for sure.

A crystal image rises into my mind as I resume walking, a sweating blue Dasani bottle with three inches of Grey Goose sloshing in its bottom, like meltwater from a divine glacier. If I had that, I could brazen my way through anything.

"You've done this a hundred times," I tell myself. "You did Bosnia when you were twenty-five and didn't know shit."

"Hey! You Dr. Ferry?"

A cop in uniform is calling to me from a high porch on my right. The victim's house. Arthur LeGendre lived in a large Victorian typical of the Garden District, but the vehicles parked in the cross street around the corner are more commonly found in the Desire and St. Thomas housing projects—the coroner's wagon, an ambulance, NOPD squad cars, and the FBI Suburban that carries the Bureau's forensic team. I see a couple of unmarked NOPD cars, too, one of them Sean's. Climbing the steps, I think I'm fine.

Ten feet inside, I know I'm in trouble.

CHAPTER

2

A brittle air of expectancy fills the broad central hallway of the victim's house, and curious eyes track my movements. A forensic tech moves through with an alternate-light source, searching for latent fingerprints. I don't know where the body is, but before I have to ask the patrolman standing inside the door, Sean steps into the rear of the hall and beckons me toward him.

I go, taking care to keep myself balanced with my cases. I wish Sean would squeeze my arm as I reach him, but I know he can't. And then he does. And I remember why I fell in love with him. Sean always knows what I need, sometimes even before I do.

"How you doin'?" he murmurs.

"A little shaky."

"Body's in the kitchen." He takes the heavy case from my right hand. "This one's a little bloodier than the last, but it's just another stiff. The Bureau forensic team has done its thing, all but the bite marks. Kaiser says those are your show. That ought to make you feel pretty good."

"Kaiser" is John Kaiser, a former FBI profiler who helped solve New Orleans's biggest serial murder case, in which eleven women disappeared while paintings of their corpses turned up in art galleries around the world. Kaiser is the Bureau's point man on the NOMURS task force.

"The scene's more crowded than it should be," Sean says softly. "Piazza's in there. Plenty of tension, if you're looking. But that's not your problem. You're a consultant. That's it."

"I'm ready. Let's do it."

He opens the door to a gleaming world of granite, travertine, shining enamel, and pickled wood. Kitchens like this always feel like operating rooms to me, and this one actually has a patient in it somewhere. A dead one. I sweep my eyes over a blur of faces and nod a greeting. Captain Carmen Piazza nods back. Then I look down and see a blood trail on the floor. Someone has crawled or been dragged across the marble floor to a spot behind the island at the center of the kitchen. *Dragged,* I decide.

"Behind the island," Sean says from my shoulder.

Someone has set up a floodlight. When I round the island, I see a stunning Technicolor image of a naked corpse lying on its back. The details of the upper body hit me in a surreal rush: livid bite marks on the chest, bloody ones on the face, one bullet hole in the center of the abdomen, a contact gunshot wound to the forehead. The superfine blood spatter of a high-speed-impact wound has dotted the marble tiles like a monochrome Pollock painting behind the victim's head. Arthur LeGendre's face is a frozen shriek of horror and pain, shocked into permanence when part of his brain was blown out through the back of his skull.

I force my eyes away from the bite marks on the chest. The lower body has its own tale to tell. Arthur LeGendre isn't nude after all. He wears black nylon socks, like a man in a 1940s porno loop. His penis is a pale acorn in a nest of gray pubic hair, but I can see blood and bruising there. I take a step forward, and my breath catches in my throat. Scrawled in blood across two cabinet doors on the wall of the island opposite the sink are five words:

MY WORK IS NEVER DONE

Rivulets of blood have dripped down the cabinet doors, giving the message an almost comical Halloween look. But there's nothing comical about the pool of separated blood and serum under the elbow of the dead man. LeGendre's antecubital vein was sliced to provide the blood for this macabre message. The tip of his right forefinger was obviously dipped in blood. Did the killer write the words with his victim's dead finger to avoid leaving his own fingerprint in the blood? Or did he force LeGendre to write the message prior to death? Free-histamine tests will answer that question.

I need to start working, but I can't take my eyes off the message. *My work is never done.* It's a common phrase, so common I can hear my mother's voice saying it in my head—

"You need any help, Dr. Ferry?"

"What?"

"John Kaiser," says the same voice.

I look over at a tall, lanky man of about fifty. He has a friendly face with hazel eyes that miss nothing. He's left off his title. *Special Agent* John Kaiser.

"You need help with your lights or anything? For the UV photography?"

Feeling oddly detached, I shake my head.

"He's getting more savage," Kaiser observes. "Losing control, maybe? The face is actually torn this time."

I nod again. "There's subcutaneous fat showing through the cheek."

The floor shudders as Sean sets my heavy dental case beside me. Too late I try to conceal that I jerked when the vibration went through me. I tell myself to breathe deeply, but my throat is already closing, and a film of sweat has coated my skin.

One step at a time . . . Shoot the bites with the 105-millimeter quartz lens. Standard color film first, then get out the filters and start on the UV. After that, take your alginate impressions . . .

As I bend and flip the latches on my case, I feel like I'm moving at half speed. A dozen pairs of eyes are watching me, and their gazes seem to be interfering with my nerve impulses. Sean will notice my awkwardness, but maybe no one else will. "It's the same mouth," I say softly.

"What?" asks Agent Kaiser.

"Same killer. He's got slightly pegged lateral incisors. I see it on the chest bites. That's not conclusive. I'm just saying . . . my preliminary assessment."

"Right. Of course. You sure you don't need some help?"

What the hell am I saying? Of course it's the same guy. Everybody in this room knows that. I'm just here to document and preserve the evidence to the highest possible degree of accuracy—

I'm opening the wrong case. I need my camera, not my impression kit. *Jesus, keep it together.* But I can't. As I bend farther down to open my camera case, a wave of dizziness nearly tips me onto the floor. I retrieve the camera, straighten up, switch it on, then realize I've forgotten to set up my tripod.

And then it happens.

In three seconds I go from mild anxiety to hyperventilation, like an old lady about to faint in church. Which is unbelievable. I can breathe more efficiently than 99 percent of the human population. When I'm not working as an odontologist, I'm a free diver, a world-class competitor in a sport whose participants commonly dive to three hundred feet using only the air trapped in their lungs. Some people call free diving competitive suicide, and there's some truth to that. I can lie on the bottom of a swimming pool with a weight belt for over six minutes without air, a feat that would kill most people. Yet now—standing at sea level in the kitchen of a ritzy town house— I can't even drink from the ocean of oxygen that surrounds me.

"Dr. Ferry?" says Agent Kaiser. "Are you all right?"

Panic attack, I tell myself. *Vicious circle . . . the anxiety worsens the symptoms, and the symptoms rev up the anxiety. You have to break the cycle . . .*

Arthur LeGendre's corpse wavers in my vision, as though it's lying on the bottom of a shallow river.

"Sean?" asks Kaiser. "Is she all right?"

Don't let this happen, I beg silently. *Please.*

But no one hears my prayer. Whatever is happening to me has been waiting a long time to happen. A slow black train has been coming toward me for a very long time, from very far away, and now that it's finally reached me, it plows over me without pain or sound.

And everything goes black.

CHAPTER

3

A female EMT is kneeling over me, reading from a blood pressure cuff strapped to my arm. The deflating cuff awakened me. Sean Regan and Special Agent Kaiser are standing over the EMT, looking worried.

"A little low," says the tech. "I think she fainted. Her EKG is normal. Sugar's a little low, but she's not hypoglycemic." The tech notices that my eyes are open. "When was the last time you ate, Dr. Ferry?"

"I don't remember."

"We should get some orange juice into you. Fix you right up."

I look to my left. The stockinged feet of Arthur LeGendre's corpse lie beside my head. Its legs and torso extend away from me at a right angle, down a different side of the kitchen island. I glance in that direction and see the bloody message again: *MY WORK IS NEVER DONE.*

"Any OJ in that fridge?" asks the EMT.

"Crime scene," says Agent Kaiser. "Can't disturb that. Anybody got a candy bar?"

A reluctant male voice says, "I got a Snickers. It's my supper."

"You on Atkins again?" Sean quips, and nervous laughter follows. "Cough it up."

Everybody laughs now, grateful for the release of tension.

As I get to my feet, Sean reaches out to steady me. A paunchy detective steps forward and hands me his Snickers bar. I make a show of gratitude and accept it, though I know I have no blood sugar problem. This charade is witnessed by a rapt audience that includes Carmen Piazza, commander of the Homicide Division.

"I'm sorry," I say in her direction. "I don't know what happened."

"Same thing as last time, looks like," Piazza observes.

"I guess so. I'm okay now, though. I'm ready."

Captain Piazza leans toward me and speaks softly. "Step out here with me for a moment, Dr. Ferry. You, too, Detective Regan."

Piazza walks into the hallway. Sean gives me a warning glance, then turns and follows her.

The captain leads us into a study off the central hall, where she leans back against a desk and faces us, arms folded, jaw set tight. I can easily imagine this olive-skinned woman facing down armed street punks during her years in uniform.

"This isn't the place to talk about complications," she says, "so I'm not going to. I don't know what's going on between you two, and I don't want to know. What I do know is that it's jeopardizing this investigation. So here's what we're going to do. Dr. Ferry is going to go home. The FBI will handle the bite marks tonight. And unless the Bureau objects, I'm going to request that a new forensic odontologist be assigned to the task force."

I want to argue, but Piazza has said nothing about my episode in the kitchen. She's talking about something for which I have no defense. Something about which Sean told me not to worry. But why am I angry? Adulterers think they're discreet, but people always find out.

A patrolman steps into the study and sets my tripod and dental cases on the floor. When did Piazza tell him to pack them? While I was unconscious? After he leaves, Piazza says, "Sean, walk Dr. Ferry back to her car. Be back here in two minutes. And be in my office tomorrow morning at eight sharp. Clear?"

Sean's eyes lock with his superior's. "Yes, ma'am."

Captain Piazza looks at me, her face not without compassion. "Dr. Ferry, you've done some remarkable work for us in the past. I hope you get to the bottom of whatever this problem is. I suggest you see a doctor, if you haven't already. I don't think a vacation's going to do it for you."

She walks out, leaving me alone with my married lover and the latest mess I seem to have made of my life. Sean picks up my cases and starts for the front door. We can't risk talking here.

Warm water drips from the oak leaves as we walk down the block in silence. It rained while I was inside, a typical New Orleans shower that did nothing to cool or cleanse the city, only added more water vapor to the smothering humidity and washed more filth into Lake Pontchartrain. The air smells of banana trees, though, and in the darkness the street has a deceptively romantic look.

"What happened in there?" Sean asks, not looking at me. "Another panic attack?"

My hands are shaking, but whether from my episode inside, alcohol withdrawal, or the confrontation with Captain Piazza, I don't know. "I guess. I don't know."

"Is it these particular murders? It started with the third victim, Nolan."

I can tell by Sean's voice that he's worried. "I don't think so."

He looks over at me. "Is it us, Cat?"

Of course it's us. "I don't know."

"I told you Karen and I are talking about seeing a lawyer now. It's just the kids, you know? We—"

"Don't start, okay? Not tonight." My throat tightens, and a sour taste fills my mouth. "I'm in this situation because I put myself in it."

"I know, but—"

"Please." I make a fist to stop my right hand from shaking. "Okay?"

This time Sean heeds the hysteria in my voice. When we reach the Audi, he takes my keys, unlocks the door, and loads my cases into the backseat. Then he looks back up the block, toward the LeGendre house, probably to make sure Piazza isn't watching us. That he has to do this, even now, is like a knife in my belly.

"Tell me what's really going on," he says, turning back to me. "There's something you're not telling me."

Yes. But I'm not going to play that particular scene here. Not now. Not like this. Even I cling to some fairy-tale dreams, and this wet street after a murder isn't part of them. "I can't do this," I tell him. It's all I can manage.

His green eyes widen in a silent plea. They have a remarkable intensity sometimes. "We have to talk, Cat. Tonight."

I don't reply.

"I'll get away as soon as I can," he promises.

"All right," I say, knowing it's the only way to get out of here. "There's Captain Piazza."

Sean's head whips to the left. "Where?"

Another knife thrust. "I thought I saw her. You'd better get back in there."

He squeezes my upper arms, then opens the door of the Audi and helps me inside. "Be careful driving home."

"Don't worry about me."

Instead of leaving, he kneels in the open door, clasps my left wrist, and speaks with genuine urgency. "I *am* worried about you. What is it? I know you, damn it. Tell me!"

I crank the engine and pull slowly away from the curb, leaving Sean no choice but to let go of my wrist.

"Cat!" he yells, but I close the door and drive on, leaving him standing in the wet street staring after my taillights.

"I'm pregnant," I tell him, far too late.

Two miles from my house on Lake Pontchartrain, I realize I can't go home. If I do, the walls will close around me like suffocating pillows, and I'll pace the shrinking rooms like a madwoman until Sean pulls into the garage and lets down the door with his remote control. Every word he says after that I will hear against a ticking clock that marks the time remaining before he has to go home to his wife and kids. And I absolutely cannot endure that tonight.

Normally, after working a crime scene, I stop at a liquor store and buy a bottle of vodka. But not tonight. The little agglomeration of cells growing inside me is the only pure thing in my life right now, and I will not do it injury. Even if it means the screaming heebie-jeebies and a rubber room. That's the only thing I'm sure of this minute.

I tried to go cold turkey in the beginning, thinking it was best for the baby. Twenty hours into that particular mistake, I got the shakes so bad I couldn't unzip my jeans to pee. A couple of hours later, I started seeing snakes in the house. A small rattler in a corner of the kitchen, curled into a deadly spiral. A fat cottonmouth moccasin hanging from a fern planter in the living room. A brilliantly hued coral snake sunning itself in the painful glare by the glass doors in the den. All lethal, all planning to slither up to me, bury their fangs in my flesh, and not let go until every drop of poison in their venom sacs had been injected into me.

Hello delirium tremens . . .

Cold turkey wasn't going to cut it. I hit my medical books, which told me that the first forty-eight hours of withdrawal would be the worst. Addiction specialists prescribe Valium to blunt the physical symptoms while the psychological addiction is cured, but Valium can cause cleft palate in a developing fetus, the risk depending on dosage and duration of use. The full-blown d.t.'s, on the other hand, can cause seizure, stroke, and death in the mother. This choice of evils was ultimately no choice at all. I know a dozen oral surgeons who can repair a cleft palate; I know no one who can bring back the dead. When the coral snake began slithering toward me, I climbed onto a table, called the Rite Aid pharmacy, and self-prescribed enough Valium to get me through forty-eight hours.

The Audi's tires squeal as I wrench it into a U-turn and stop at the base of the Interstate 10 on-ramp. Cars and trucks roar by, angrily blasting their horns. An hour of driving west on I-10 would put me in Baton Rouge. From Baton Rouge, Highway 61 follows the Mississippi River northward for ninety miles to Natchez, Mississippi, my childhood home. I've begun that journey many times without completing it. Tonight, though . . .

Home, I say silently. *The place where, when you have to go there, they have to let you in.* I can't remember who said that, but it's always seemed apt to me. On the face of things it shouldn't. My family has always begged me to visit. My mother actually wants me to move back into the house where I grew up. (*House* isn't exactly accurate. It's an estate big enough to hold me and about twelve other families.) But I could never move back to that house. I can't even move back to Natchez. And I don't know why. It's a beautiful city, more so than New Orleans in many ways. Certainly safer and more peaceful. And it's drawn back many who've tried to leave it over the years.

But not me.

You leave a place young and you don't know why, only that you have to get out. I graduated high school when I was sixteen, left for college, and never looked back. The one or two interesting boys I knew wanted out as badly as I did, and they made it, too. I returned for Christmases and Thanksgivings but little else, and this deeply wounded my family. They never understood, and they never let me forget it. Looking back across fifteen years, I think I fled my home because elsewhere—anywhere—Cat Ferry was only what I could make of her. In Natchez, she was heir to a suffocating matrix of expectations and obligations that I couldn't bear to face.

But now I've wrecked my carefully constructed sanctuary. It was inevitable, of course. I've been warned by the best. As predicted, my troubles here now dwarf those I left behind me, and my options have dwindled to one. For a moment I consider going back to my house and packing a bag. But if I do that, I'll never leave. The pregnancy scene with Sean will be played out, and then . . . maybe the end for us. Or perhaps only for me. I'm not going to walk myself up to that ledge tonight.

My cell phone rings out "Sunday, Bloody Sunday" again. The screen reads *Det. Sean Regan*. I'm tempted to answer, but Sean isn't calling about the case. He wants to see me. To question me about my "episode" at the crime scene. He wants to hash out what Captain Piazza might or might not know about our affair. To decompress after the frustration of dealing with the task force.

He wants sex.

I switch the ringer to silent and drive up the ramp, joining the night traffic leaving the city.

CHAPTER

4

In the South you are never far from the wild. In less than ten minutes, I-10 leaps off terra firma and sweeps over a fetid marsh filled with alligators, pit vipers, wild hogs, and panthers. All through the night they will stalk and kill, enacting the ritual of death that preserves their lives. Predators and prey, an eternal dance. Which am I? Sean would say hunter, and he wouldn't be wrong. But he wouldn't be quite right, either. I've been prey in my life. I carry scars Sean has never seen. I'm neither predator nor prey now, but a hybrid creature who knows the minds of both. I track predators to protect the most endangered species of all—the innocent.

A naive term these days, perhaps. *The innocent.* No one who reaches adulthood with his sanity intact is innocent. But none of us deserves to be prey for the truly damned. The older men dying back in New Orleans did something to draw their killer to them. Something innocuous, perhaps—or maybe something terrible. I'm concerned with that only insofar as it helps me find the killer who took their lives. But of course, I shouldn't be concerned with it at all. Because Captain Piazza has excluded me from that hunt.

No, you excluded yourself, chides the censor in my head.

My cell phone lights up green on the passenger seat. Sean again. I turn over the phone so I won't have to see the glow.

For the past year, when anxiety or depression has become unbearable, I've run to Sean Regan. Tonight I'm running away from him. I'm running because I'm afraid. When Sean learns that I'm pregnant—and that I intend to keep the baby—he will either honor the promises he's made to me or betray them. And I'm terrified that he won't give up his family for me. This fear is so tangible that the outcome seems a foregone conclusion, something I've known all along and was foolish to ever lie to myself about.

Sean has never hidden his doubts. He worries about my drinking. My depression. My occasional manic states. He worries that I can't be sexually faithful. Based on my history, these are legitimate concerns. But at some point, I believe, you just have to go for it, to risk everything for the other person regardless of your fears. Besides . . . can't Sean see that if he doesn't have faith in me after coming to know me so intimately, it's so much harder for me to have faith in myself?

My hands are shaking on the wheel. I need another Valium, but I don't want to risk falling asleep on the interstate. *Suck it up,* I tell myself, the mantra of my youth and the unwritten motto of my family. After all, it's not as if my present dilemma is new. I never got pregnant before, but pregnancy is merely a new wrinkle in an old habit. I've always chosen unattainable men. In some ways, my whole life has been a series of inexplicable decisions and unresolved paradoxes. Two therapists have thrown up their hands in despair over my ability to function at my present level despite self-destructive behavior that keeps me dancing on the edge of disaster. My relationship with my present therapist, Dr. Hannah Goldman, has survived only because she allows me to skip my scheduled appointments and call her whenever I feel I need her. I don't require face time. Just an understanding voice.

Actually, it's about time I gave Hannah a call. She doesn't know about my pregnancy. She doesn't know about my panic attacks, either. After four years with her, I still find it difficult to ask for help. I come from a family that believes depression is a weakness, not an illness. I didn't see a therapist as a child, when one might have done me some real good. My grandfather, a surgeon, believes psychiatrists are sicker than their patients. My father, a Vietnam vet, saw several VA therapists before he died, but none was able to alleviate the symptoms of his post-traumatic stress disorder. My mother also discouraged therapy, saying shrinks had never done her older sister any good, and that one had even seduced her. When suicidal impulses finally convinced me to seek treatment—at the age of twenty-four—neither the MDs nor the psychologists were able to control my mood swings, ease my nightmares, or slow my drinking and occasional reckless sexual behavior. For me—until Hannah Goldman and her laissez-faire style—therapy was pretty much a washout. And yet . . . though my present situation would qualify as a crisis in Hannah's book, I can't quite bring myself to call her.

As the night landscape changes from wet bottomland to hilly forests of oak and pine, I sense the great river out to my left, rolling southward as it has for millennia, oblivious to human travail. The Mississippi River links the town of my birth to the city of my adulthood, a great winding artery connecting the two spiritual poles of my existence, infancy and independence. Yet how independent am I? Natchez, the upstream city—older than New Orleans by two years, 1716 versus 1718—is the source of all that I am, whether I like it or not. And tonight, the prodigal daughter is returning home at eighty-five miles an hour.

Forward and backward . . .

Hurtling around curves in the dark forest, I feel a sort of emotional gravity sucking at my bones. But until the sign that reads ANGOLA PENITENTIARY flashes out of the night, I'm not sure why. Then I know. Just south of the razor-wire-enclosed fields known as Angola Farm, a great island rises out of the river. Owned by my family since before the Civil War, this atavistic world hovers like a dark mirage between the genteel cities of New Orleans and Natchez. I haven't set foot on DeSalle Island in more than ten years, but I sense it now the way you sense a dangerous animal stirring from sleep. Only a dozen miles to my left, it sniffs for my scent in the humid darkness.

I step on the gas and put the place behind me, slipping into a driving trance that carries me the remainder of my journey. I slip out of it not on the outskirts of Natchez, but on the high-banked, curving drive that leads through the woods to my childhood home. Once surrounded by two hundred acres of virgin forest, the antebellum estate where I grew up now occupies only twenty landscaped acres hedged around by St. Catherine's Hospital, a residential subdivision, and a stately old plantation called Elms Court. Nevertheless, the tunnel of oaks that arches over the drive still gives tourists the sense of approaching a cloistered European manor.

A high wrought-iron gate blocks the last fifty yards of the driveway, but it's been unlocked for as long as I can remember. I stop and press a button on the gatepost. The iron bars retract as though pulled by unseen hands. As though the gods themselves have opened my way home.

Why am I here? I ask myself.

You know why, replies a chiding voice. *You have nowhere else to go.*

After dry-swallowing a Valium, I drive slowly through the gate.

The bars close behind me with a clang.

CHAPTER

5

In a vast clearing ahead, moonlight washes over a sight that takes most people's breath away. A French palace rises like a specter out of the mist, its limestone walls as pale as skin, its windows like dark eyes glassy from fatigue or drink. The scale of the place is heroic, projecting an impression of limitless wealth and power. Viewed through the prism of a modern eye, the mansion has a certain absurdity. A French Empire palace nestled in a Mississippi town of twenty thousand souls? Yet Natchez contains more than eighty antebellum homes, many of them mansions, and the provenance of this one perfectly suits the town, a living anachronism of grand excess, much of it built by the hands of slaves.

My family arrived in America in 1820, in the person of a Paris financier's youngest son, sent to the wilds of Louisiana to make his fortune. Cursed with a cruel father, Henri Leclerc DeSalle worked like a slave himself until he surpassed all paternal expectations. By 1840, he owned cotton fields stretching for ten miles along the Mississippi River. And in that year, like most of the cotton barons of the time, he began building a regal mansion on the high bluff across the river, in the sparkling city called Natchez.

Most cotton planters built boxy Greek Revival mansions, but Henri, fiercely proud of his heritage, broke tradition and constructed a perfect copy of Malmaison, the summer palace of Napoléon and

Josephine. Designed to humble DeSalle's father when he visited America, Malmaison and its attendant buildings became the center of a cotton empire that—thanks to my family's Yankee sympathies—survived both the Civil War and Reconstruction without mortal damage. It endured until 1927, when the Mississippi overran its banks in a flood of biblical proportions. The following year came crop fires, and in 1929 the stock market crash completed the proverbial "three bad years" that even wealthy farming families dreaded.

The DeSalles lost everything.

The patriarch of that era shot himself through the heart, leaving his descendants to scrape out a meager existence alongside the blacks and poor whites they had so recently exploited. But in 1938, fortune reversed herself again.

A young geologist with Texas backers leased a huge tract of former DeSalle land. Through a quirk in Louisiana law, landowners retained the mineral rights to their property for ten years after it was forfeited. My great-grandfather was ecstatic just to get the lease money. But nineteen days before his mineral rights expired, the young geologist struck one of the largest oil fields in Louisiana. Christened the DeSalle field, it produced over 10 million barrels of crude oil. My great-grandfather eventually bought back every acre of DeSalle land, including the island. He also bought back Malmaison and restored the house to its pre–Civil War splendor. Its present owner, my maternal grandfather, keeps Malmaison in pristine condition, worthy of the *Architectural Digest* cover it graced ten years ago. But the city that surrounds the mansion, though as well preserved as Charleston or Savannah, seems as doomed to slow decay as any other Southern town bypassed by the interstate and abandoned by industry.

I pull around the "big house" and park beside one of the two brick dependencies behind it. The eastern slave quarters—a two-story edifice larger than some suburban houses—was my home during most of my childhood. Our family's maid, Pearlie, lives in the western quarters, thirty yards across the rose garden. She helped rear my mother and aunt from infancy, then did the same with me. Well over seventy now, Pearlie drives a baby blue Cadillac, the pride of her life. It sits gleaming in the darkness behind her house, its chrome polished more regularly than that on the cars of any white matron in the city. Pearlie often stays up late watching television, but it's past midnight now, and her windows are dark.

My mother's car is nowhere in sight. She's probably in Biloxi, visiting her elder sister, who's embroiled in a bitter divorce. My grandfather's Lincoln is gone, too. At seventy-seven, Grandpapa Kirkland still possesses remarkable vitality, but a stroke a year ago ended his driving days. Undeterred, he hired a driver and resumed the pace he'd always kept up, which would exhaust a man of fifty. Grandpapa could be anywhere tonight, but my guess is that he's on the island. He's an avid hunter, and DeSalle Island—which teems with deer, wild hogs, and even bear—has been a second home to him since he married into the family a half century ago.

When I get out of the Audi, the summer heat wraps around me like a thick jacket. The whine of crickets and the bellow of frogs from the nearby bayou fills the night, but this soundtrack from my childhood brings mixed feelings. As I glance toward the rear of Malmaison proper, my eyes lock onto a gnarled dogwood tree at the edge of the rose garden that separates our house from Pearlie's, and my throat seals shut. My father perished under that tree, shot dead by an intruder he confronted there twenty-three years ago. I can't look at the dogwood without remembering that night. Blue police lights flashing through rain. Wet, gray flesh. Glassy eyes open to the sky. I've asked Grandpapa many times to cut down that tree, but he's always refused, claiming it would be foolish to mar the beauty of our famed rose garden out of sentimentality.

Sentimentality.

I stopped speaking after my father was murdered. Literally. I didn't utter a word for over a year. But in my eight-year-old brain, I ceaselessly pondered what the intruder had come looking for that was worth my father's life. Cash? The family silver? Grandpapa's art or gun collections? All were possible targets, but no money or property was ever discovered missing. As I grew older, I wondered if it could have been my mother that drew the prowler. She was scarcely thirty then and could easily have caught the attention of a rapist. But since the intruder was never caught, this theory couldn't be tested.

After my first depressive episode—I was fifteen—a new fear crept into my mind: *that there had been no intruder at all.* My father was shot with his own rifle, and the only fingerprints found on it belonged to family members. I couldn't help but wonder whether my daddy—scarred within and without by a war he'd wanted no part of—had chosen to end his own life. Whether, even with a wife and daughter who loved him, he'd felt he had no choice but to stop his pain with a bullet. I'd been close to that point myself by then, so I knew it was possible. I've reached that point again in the years since, and more than once. Yet something has always kept me from accepting suicide as my father's fate. Perhaps it's my belief that the strength that kept me alive during those terrible nights was a gift from him to me, the only legacy he left behind.

I hate the fucking rose garden. Patterned on the Malmaison gardens tended by Josephine herself, where every variety of rose in the world was represented, it fills the air of Malmaison with scents that make tourists gasp with pleasure. But for me the smell of roses will always be part of the stench of death.

I turn away from the garden and, with paranoia born from years of urban living, unload my dental cases from the backseat. Only when I'm halfway to the door of our slave quarters do I remember that in Natchez I could leave my cases in the unlocked car for a month and find them just as I'd left them when I returned.

The front door is locked. I have no key. Trudging around to the window of my old bedroom, I set down my cases and slide up the pane. The closed-in smell that wafts through the curtains hurls me fifteen years back in time. I lift the cases over the sill, set them inside, then climb through and make my way through the dark to the light switch on the wall. It's an easy journey, because my bedroom looks exactly as it did in May of 1989, when I graduated high school.

The walls are brown 1970s paneling, the carpet the same navy blue installed the year I was born. Silk dragonflies of myriad colors hang from filaments tacked to the ceiling, and posters of rock stars adorn the walls: U2, Sinead O'Connor, R.E.M., Sting. Shelves of photographs and swimming trophies line the wall opposite my closet, chronicling a competitive career that began at five and ended at sixteen. The older photographs show my father—a dark, handsome man of medium height—standing next to a gangly little girl with long bones but no apparent muscle. As the girl's body begins to fill in, my father vanishes from the photos and an older man with silver hair, chiseled features, and piercing eyes takes his place. My grandfather, Dr. William Kirkland. Studying the photos now, it seems odd that my mother is in so few of them. But Mom never took much of an interest in my swimming, an "unsocial" activity that consumed vast amounts of time that could otherwise have been spent in more "appropriate" pursuits.

Glancing into the closet, I see clothes I wore in high school hanging there. Beneath the clothes, a wicker laundry basket filled with Louisiana Rice Creatures. The sight of the clothes doesn't affect me, but the colorful stuffed animals bring a lump to my throat. Originally stuffed with dried rice, Rice Creatures were local precursors of the Beanie Babies that later became a national craze. There must be thirty of them in the basket, but the only one that really matters to me is missing. Lena the Leopardess. Lena was my favorite, and I'm not sure why. Maybe because she was a cat, like me. I loved Lena's spots, I loved her whiskers, I loved how she felt pressed against my cheek while I fell asleep. I carried her everywhere I went, including my father's funeral. It was there, surrounded by adults in the visiting room prior to the service, that I saw my father lying in his coffin.

He didn't look like my father anymore. He looked older, and he looked very alone. When I pointed this out, my grandfather suggested that Daddy might not feel so lonely if he had Lena for company while he slept. The idea of losing Lena *and* my father on the same day frightened me, but Grandpapa was right. Lena made me less lonely every night, and I was sure she could do the same for Daddy. After asking Mom if it was okay, I reached over the high side of the coffin and nestled Lena between my father's cheek and shoulder, just as I did with her every night. I missed her badly after that, but I comforted myself with the thought that Daddy had a little piece of my heart to keep him company.

Standing in this bedroom is creeping me out, as it has on each of the occasions when I've returned home. Why does my mother preserve it this way? She's an interior designer, for God's sake. Practically manic in her desire to transform every space over which she's given dominion. Is it an homage to my childhood? To a simpler past? Or is it an open invitation to me to come back and start over at a point before I "veered off track"? Just when that was—my personal failure as a "DeSalle woman"—is a point of contention within my family. In my grandfather's eyes, I didn't screw up until I was asked to leave medical school, which precluded my following in his footsteps as a surgeon. But in my mother's eyes, my failure began long before, at some indeterminate point during adolescence. Though I'm not a DeSalle by name—my father was a Ferry—I am very much considered a DeSalle woman, which carries with it a legion of traditions and expectations. But a thousand small choices have taken me ever further from this predestined road, onto one that hasn't led me within a stone's throw of a husband, a fact my mother never lets me forget. I'm actually thankful I arrived tonight to find her gone.

As I stare at a photograph of my father holding my hand high in triumph, the Valium enters my bloodstream, and a blessed calm comes over me. Because my father died when I was eight, it was he alone that I never disappointed. I like to think that, had he lived, he would be proud of what I've accomplished. As for my problems . . . well, Luke Ferry had problems of his own.

I pull back the spread on my permanently made bed and take my cell phone from my pocket. A pang of guilt hits me when I see thirteen missed calls. Punching 1 to check my voice mail, I listen to the first message. Sean called me even before he left Arthur LeGendre's house. In a reassuring voice he tells me to stay calm, that Piazza is his problem not mine, and then he begs me to keep myself together until he gets there. "There" being my house on the lake. I skip ahead several messages. The change in Sean's voice is astonishing.

"It's me again," he says angrily. "I'm still at your house, and I have no fucking idea where you are. Please call me back, even if you don't want to see me. I don't know if you're drunk in some dive in the Quarter or lying dead in a ditch somewhere. Have you stopped taking your meds? Something's wrong, Cat, I know it, and I don't mean the murders. Look . . . you have to trust me, and you know you can." There's a crackling pause. "Damn it, I love you, and this is bullshit. This is why we're not together already. I'm sitting in this empty house and—" There's a click, then nothing. This message exhausted the phone's available memory.

I slip off my pants and draw the bedcovers up to my chest. I want to call Sean and tell him I'm all right, but the truth is, I'm not. In fact, I might be losing my mind. But there's nothing he can do about that.

As the cell phone drops from my hand, I see an image of Arthur LeGendre lying dead in his gleaming kitchen, black socks pulled up on his white, sticklike legs. Above his corpse floats the killer's message, painted in blood: *My work is never done.* Again I see the bite marks on LeGendre's bloodless flesh, one more set in the endless train of scars and mutilation I've witnessed over the past seven years. *Is this really my job? How can someone's life's work be the analysis of something so brutal, so small, so irritatingly specialized?* There has to be more to my choice of career. But what? My father's mysterious death? Too obvious. "My work is never done," I murmur, feeling the Valium course through my veins. Earlier today, the sedative I'd swallowed to combat my alcohol withdrawal gave me an unexpected gift: dreamless sleep. I haven't known such relief for years.

"Thank you," I whisper to the drug, as though to the god of sleep. My left hand slides over my hip and comes to rest on my lower tummy. My right hand slips out of the covers, reaching for a hand that isn't there.

"Daddy?" I whisper. "Is that you?"

He doesn't answer.

He never does, but tonight the aching loneliness that accompanies thoughts of my father isn't so severe. Valium pads the edges of the pain, easing my descent into sleep. For years I've suffered from nightmares, and lately the alcohol I use to deaden them seems to have made them worse. But the Valium is an unfamiliar drug, as fresh and potent as the first drink I ever swallowed.

Tonight sleep enfolds me like the ocean depths on a free dive, a bright upper layer that deepens in color and density as I descend, swimming down, down, down, away from the chaos of the surface, into the blue cathedral of the deep. My sanctuary from the world and from myself. No thoughts here beyond the exigencies of survival. Only peace, the bliss of entering a place where but a handful of humans can go without bottled air, where death is a constant companion, where life is sweeter for the awareness of its fragility.

Here I am weightless.

Shapeless.

An astronaut drifting through deep space without a tether, unconcerned that her life support systems have shut down, that her body must sustain itself or die. Anyone with a lick of sense would kick madly for the surface.

Not me.

Because here I am free.

I don't know how long I float this way, because time means nothing here. What I do know is that I must be sleeping, because on a real free dive, time means everything. Time is the remaining oxygen dissolved in your bloodstream, the only currency that can buy you depth, and depth is the holy grail, the point of the whole mad exercise. Or it's supposed to be, anyway. That part confuses me, actually.

Because you can never reach the bottom. Not in the real ocean. It's only back on land that you can do that.

Surfacing now. I know because the sea has slowly stopped trying to drive my wet suit into every opening in my body, and blue-white lightning is flashing above me. A sudden storm? I tense against the inevitable clap of thunder, but it doesn't come. When the lightning flashes again, a strange sound registers in my mind. Not thunder—not even the lap of waves against the dive boat. It's the *snick* of a camera shutter. When I finally break through the surface, I smell acetone, not the ozone that follows a lightning strike. Blinking in confusion, I call out, "Sean? Sean, is that you?"

A dark brown forehead and saucer eyes rise above the footboard of my bed. A nose and mouth follow, the mouth agape in wonder. I'm looking into the face of a black girl of about eight. She has the frozen look of a child who has entered a familiar yard only to find a strange dog waiting for her.

"Who are you?" I ask, half wondering if the girl is real.

"Natriece," she says, her voice almost defiant. "Natriece Washington."

I glance around the room, but all that registers is the sunlight pouring through a crack in some curtains. "What are you doing here?"

The girl's eyes are still wide. "I be here with my auntie. I didn't mean to make no mess."

"Your auntie?" The smell of acetone is stronger now.

"Miss Pearlie."

Suddenly it all comes rushing back. The phone call from Sean. The corpse in the house on Prytania Street. The zoned-out night drive to Natchez. What an irony to find that you do crazier things sober than you ever did drunk.

"What time is it?"

The child gives an exaggerated shrug. "I don't know. Morning time."

Pushing down the covers, I crawl to the foot of the bed. The contents of my forensic dental case are spread across the floor in disarray. Natriece is holding my camera; its flash must have caused the "lightning" that awakened me. Among the instruments and chemicals on the floor lies a spray bottle of luminol, a toxic chemical used to detect latent bloodstains.

"Did you spray any of that, Natriece?"

She solemnly shakes her head.

I gently take the camera from her grasp. "It's all right if you did. I just need to know."

"I might've sprayed a little bit."

I get out of bed and pull on my pants. "It's okay, but you need to leave the room while I clean it up. That's a dangerous chemical in that bottle."

"I'll help you clean up. I knows how to clean."

"Tell you what. Let's go visit your auntie, and then I'll come back and deal with this. I haven't seen Pearlie in a long time."

Natriece nods. "She told me nobody was out here. She just unlocked the door to get Mrs. Ferry's wash."

I take the little girl's hand and lead her to the door, then flip off the light and walk into the hall. Natriece lingers behind, standing with her back to me, looking into the dark room. "Did you leave something?" I ask.

"No, ma'am. I just looking at that."

"What?"

"That there. Did I do that?"

I look over the girl's head. On the floor near the foot of my bed, a greenish blue glow hovers in the darkness. The luminol has reacted with something on the carpet. The chemical registers false positives with several compounds, one of them household bleach.

"It's all right," I tell her, dreading my mother's reaction to the mess Natriece has made.

"Freaky," she says. "That looks like *Ghostbusters* or something."

Stepping around Natriece, I look down at the luminescence on the floor. It's not diffuse, as I had thought, but well defined. Suddenly, an eerie numbness spreads through my body.

I'm looking at a footprint.

I felt the same numbness twenty-three years ago, when my grandfather turned away from the first corpse I ever saw, knelt before me, and said, "Baby, your daddy's dead."

"Natriece, stay back."

"Yessum."

Actually, it isn't a footprint at all, but a boot print. I only register this fact because now another ghostlike image has taken shape beside it. The image of a bare foot, much smaller than the boot.

A child's foot.

With slow insistence, a percussive hiss intrudes into my concentration. Subtly at first, but growing steadily to a soft roar. It's the sound of rain drumming on a tin roof. Which makes no sense, because the slave quarters has a shingle roof—not tin—and I'm standing on the first of two floors. But I've heard this sound before, and I know it for what it is. An auditory hallucination. I heard the same metallic patter a week ago, at the Nolan murder scene. Just before my panic attack. I was staring down at the retired CPA's naked corpse and—

A rapid beat of footsteps startles me from my reverie. Natriece has bolted down the hall. A scream cuts the air in the bedroom.

"Nanna! Nanna! Nanna!"

Checking my watch, I wait for the glowing footprints to fade. False positives generally fade quickly, while the luminescence caused by the hemoglobin in blood lingers like an accusation.

Thirty seconds pass. I look around the bedroom, this strange shrine to my childhood. Then I look back at the floor. A minute now, and the glow shows no sign of diminishing.

"Come on," I whisper. "Fade."

My hands are trembling. I want to run for Pearlie, too, but I'm no longer a child. My eyes blur from the strain of focusing so hard. Could that be the imprint of my own foot? Bloodstains can endure for decades on some surfaces.

"Fade," I plead. But my plea does no good.

I've been drinking for over fifteen years. I've been sober now for forty-eight hours. I've never needed a drink so badly in my life.

CHAPTER

6

Inside my mind, instinct is at war with itself. As I stare down at the two glowing footprints, half of me wants to run, the other half to lock the door. I want photographs of the prints, but to get them I'll have to act quickly. Once the chemical reaction that causes the blood hidden in the carpet to luminesce is complete, it can't be repeated.

The front door of the house bangs shut. *Pearlie.* I cross the bedroom and lock the door. Then I open my camera case, bring out my SLR, and fit a standard 35mm lens and cable release to it. *Damn.* I forgot to unload my tripod from the trunk of my car.

Someone raps sharply on my bedroom door. A rush of déjà vu tells me that rhythm belongs to Pearlie.

"Catherine Ferry?" calls a throaty voice as familiar to me as my mother's. "You in there, girl?"

"I'm here, Pearlie."

"What you doing home? Last time you came back was . . . I don't know when. Why you didn't call ahead?"

I can't waste time trying to explain the situation. "I'll be out in a few minutes, okay?"

Grabbing my car keys, I slide up the window, climb out, and run to my car. Tripod in hand, I climb back into the bedroom, close the curtains, and set up the tripod almost directly above the footprints. Pearlie is still knocking on the door. After mounting the camera and aiming it downward, I switch on the lights and shoot a reference photo of the floor. Then I close down the lens aperture by two f-stops, take a ruler from my dental case, and switch off the overhead light. The ruler has copper wire wrapped around the inch markings. The copper will fluoresce when sprayed with luminol. Laying the ruler alongside the glowing footprint, I spray both ruler and blood-stain with more of the chemical and wait.

"What you doing in there?" Pearlie demands. "Did Natriece mess up something?"

"I'm all right!" I snap. "Just give me a minute."

I hear the muted chatter of Pearlie interrogating the little girl.

As the greenish-white glow begins to increase in intensity, I open the camera shutter with the cable release and look at my dive watch. To capture the faint glow of luminol in the dark, I need a sixty-second exposure. My hands are shaking badly, but the cable release will keep the camera from vibrating. This time the tremor isn't from medication or alcohol withdrawal. It's fear. The same sickening panic I felt at the LeGendre crime scene, and at the Nolan scene before that. If it weren't for the child's footprint, I'd assume the boot print was made with deer blood. Whitetail often wander onto the grounds of Mal-maison, and my grandfather has been known to shoot a buck now and again, sometimes from the window of his study. But the child's footprint *is* there . . .

When my watch hits the sixty-second mark, I close the shutter. Then, to be sure I capture the prints, I open the lens aperture by one f-stop and repeat the procedure. By then Pearlie is squawking through the door.

"Catherine DeSalle Ferry! You open this door!"

The familiar ritual of crime scene photography is calming my nerves. Habits have great comforting power—even bad habits, as I discovered long ago.

"Answer me, girl! I can't read your mind like I used to. You've grown up too much and been gone too long."

I smile in spite of my fear. The year after my father died—the year I stopped speaking—only Pearlie was able to communicate with me. The stoic maid could read my emotions in a glance, from the curl of a lip to the angle of my downcast eyes.

"I'm coming!" I call, going to the door.

As soon as I turn the knob, Pearlie pushes open the door and stands with her hands on her hips. Over seventy years old, she is tall, thin, and tough as gristle, with chocolate brown skin and clear traces of Caucasian ancestry in her facial features. Her eyes still flash with intelligence and wit, and her bark—though intimidating to strangers—is considerably worse than her bite. Around my grandfather and my mother, Pearlie displays the quiet dignity of a nineteenth-century servant. She can vanish as silently as a ghost when certain whites enter a room, but around me she is much more animated, treating me as she might a daughter. She still wears a starched white uniform, which you don't see much anymore, and a shiny, reddish brown wig to cover her grizzled white hair.

I've missed her more than I realized. For her part, I see a mixture of pique and excitement in her eyes, as though she doesn't know whether to hug me or spank me. Were it not for Natriece's fear and the odd scene in the bedroom, Pearlie would undoubtedly crush me to her chest.

"Answer me this minute!" she demands. "You ain't been home since your grandmother's funeral, and that's been a year now."

"Fifteen months," I correct, fighting a new wave of emotion that I can't afford to face right now. Last June, my grandmother drowned on DeSalle Island. Part of the sandbar she was standing on simply slid into the Mississippi River. There was no warning. Four people saw it happen, yet no one could save her. No one even saw her surface after the bar collapsed. Catherine Poitiers Kirkland was an excellent swimmer in her youth—she taught me to swim—but at seventy-five, she'd been no match for the mighty current of the Mississippi.

"Lord, Lord." Pearlie sighs. "Well . . . why didn't you call to say you was coming? I would have cooked for you."

"It was an impulse."

"Ain't it always with you?" She gives me a knowing look, then pushes past me into the bedroom. "What's going on in here? Natriece told me they's a ghost in here."

I see the little girl standing just outside the door. "There is, in a way. Go look at the carpet by the foot of the bed."

Pearlie walks over to the tripod, bends at the waist, and examines the floor with the eagle eye of a woman who has spent decades eradicating the slightest specks of dirt from "her" house.

"What's making that rug look like that?"

"Blood. Old bloodstains hidden in the carpet fibers. It's reacting with a chemical that Natriece sprayed on it by accident."

"Blood?" Pearlie says skeptically. "I don't see no blood. That looks like them Halloween teeth you used to wear when you was a child. Vampire teeth, like Count Dracula."

"It's the same principle. But there's blood there, you can count on that."

"Blood the only thing make that stuff glow?"

"No," I concede. "Some metals will do it. Household bleach can do it. Have you spilled Clorox in here? Or in the laundry room and then tracked it in here?"

Pearlie purses her lips. "Can't say I have. Can't say I ain't either. Could have done, I guess."

"I've seen lots of stains like this. Blood has a particular kind of glow with luminol. And I'm ninety-five percent sure I'm looking at blood."

"Well, I don't hardly see nothing now."

"It fades pretty quickly. That's why I took pictures of it."

Pearlie always minimized the negative aspects of any situation. Part of what she was paid for, I suppose. I even used to hear her sing an old Johnny Mercer song to that effect while she worked: *You got to ac-cent-uate the positive, e-lim-i-nate the negative . . .*"

"Could be deer blood," Pearlie suggests. "Or armadillo maybe. Dr. Kirkland shoots armadillos round here all the time. They always digging up the yard, nasty things."

"There are tests that will tell me whether the blood's human. You know, it would take a lot of blood to make prints this well defined. There's a boot print, and also the print of a child's bare foot."

Pearlie stares down with mute skepticism.

"Have there been any children around here since I left?" I'm an only child, and my aunt Ann, despite three marriages, has no children. "Has Natriece been around here much?"

Pearlie shakes her head. "My kids live in Chicago and Los Angeles, you know that. And Natriece only been to this house two times before this. She never been out here that I know about." She turns and glares at Natriece. "You ever been in this room before, child?"

"No, ma'am."

"Answer me straight, now! I ain't one of them soft teachers you got at school."

"I'm telling you true!"

As Natriece pooches out her lower lip, I kneel and study the fading image of the bare foot. Pearlie's right; it's nearly vanished. "Natriece, will you take off your flip-flop and put your foot over here?"

"In *blood*?"

"Not in it. Just hold your foot above the rug."

The little girl slips off her yellow flip-flop and places a callused foot in my waiting hands. I hold it just above the dying glow of the footprint. It's almost a perfect match.

"How old are you, Natriece?"

"Six. But I be big for my age."

"I think you're right." I had guessed her age as eight, so her foot is probably about the size of a normal eight-year-old's.

Pearlie is watching me with a worried look.

"Where's Mom, Pearlie?"

"Where you think? Gone to Biloxi again."

"To see Aunt Ann?"

"What else? That Ann draws trouble like my Sheba draws tom-cats."

"What about Grandpapa?"

"Dr. Kirkland gone off on another trip. He supposed to get back later today, though."

"Where has he been? The island?"

"Lord, no. He ain't been down there in a good while."

"Where, then?"

Pearlie's face closes. "I ain't supposed to say."

"Not even to me?"

"I don't know."

"Pearlie . . ."

The maid sighs and cocks her head at me. She and I have kept each other's secrets for years. Pearlie kept quiet about my sneaking in and out of the house as a teenager, which she usually witnessed while smoking on her porch in the wee hours. I kept quiet about occasional male guests staying over at Pearlie's house. Pearlie was never officially divorced, but she's been alone since she was thirty, and as she often said, she might be old, but she wasn't dead.

"You won't say I told?" she asks.

"You know I won't."

"Dr. Kirkland gone to Washington."

"Washington, Mississippi?" Washington is a small town about five miles east of Natchez, and at one time the territorial capital of Mississippi.

Pearlie snorts. "Dr. Kirkland wouldn't waste five minutes out there, unless there was timber to buy out that way."

"Then where?"

"Washington, *D.C.*, girl. He go up there all the time now. I think he must know the president or something."

"He does know the president. But that can't be who he's seeing. Who is it?"

"I can't tell you what I don't know. I don't think anybody knows."

"Not Mom?"

"She act like she don't. You know your grandfather."

I want to ask more questions, but Natriece doesn't need to hear them. I cut my eyes toward the child, who is trying to reach one of the silk dragonflies hanging in the corner of the room. Pearlie gets the message.

"Run outside and play for a few minutes, Treecy."

Natriece pooches out her lip again. "You told me I could have a sno-cone if I was good."

I laugh despite my sense of urgency. "She promised me the same thing lots of times."

"Did you get it?" Natriece asks with severity.

"If I was good, I did."

"Which wasn't too often," Pearlie snaps, taking a step toward Natriece. "If you don't go play right this minute, you ain't getting *no* kind of cone. You'll be eating brussels sprouts for supper."

Natriece makes a face, then darts past Pearlie, just out of reach of the old woman's spanking hand. I close the door. Pearlie is again studying the carpet where the bloodstains are hidden.

"How is Natriece related to you? Granddaughter?"

Pearlie laughs, a deep, rattling sound. "*Great*-granddaughter."

I should have guessed.

"That's what's wrong with black peoples round here nowadays," she says. "These little girls getting theirselves pregnant at twelve years old."

I can't believe my ears. "They don't do that alone, do they? What about the men who get them pregnant?"

She waves her hand dismissively. "Oh, mens gonna be mens no

matter how many shows Oprah runs about child mamas. It's up to us old ones to teach these girls how to act. But they all too far from the church now, these young people. Mm-*mm*."

The last two syllables carry such finality that I know it's fruitless to argue. "Pearlie, I want to talk to you about the night Daddy died."

She doesn't turn away, but neither does she say anything. She doesn't respond in any overt way, though I detect a deepening in her dark eyes. There are different levels of awareness in Pearlie's eyes, the way there are in the eyes of most black people of her generation. In Natchez prior to 1965, a black person could witness a fatal shooting between two white people and see nothing at all. Such an event was "white folks' business," and that was that. I hate to think what sins lie concealed beneath that outdated rubric. Instead of prodding her further, I wait in silence.

"You done asked me about that a thousand times, baby," she says, closing her eyes against my scrutiny.

"And you've put me off a thousand times."

"I told you what I saw that night."

"When I was a child. But I'm asking you again. I'm thirty-one years old, for God's sake. Tell me about that night, Pearlie. Tell me everything you saw."

At last the eyelids open, revealing dark brown irises that have probably seen more of life than I ever will. "All right," she says wearily. "Maybe it'll finally settle you down."

CHAPTER

7

Pearlie sits on the edge of my old bed and looks at the wall, her eyes cloudy with remembrance. "The truth is, I didn't see much. If I'd been sleeping in my house, I might have, but I was in the big house tending to your grandmother."

She stops talking, and for a moment I fear she means not to continue. But she swallows and goes on.

"Mrs. Kirkland was having pains that turned out be her gallbladder. She had to have it cut out the next night. Your granddaddy wanted to do it, but she wouldn't let him. Anyway, I heard a gunshot."

"What time?"

"About ten-thirty, I guess. Rifle, I thought. That cracking sound, you know? It woke up your grandmother. I said Dr. Kirkland probably just shot a buck that wandered up out of the woods, but Mrs. Kirkland told me to call the police."

"Did you?"

"Yes."

"How long did it take them to get here?"

"Ten minutes. Maybe a little longer."

"And you only went down to the garden after the police got here?"

She nods slowly. "But I phoned down here to make sure you and your mama was okay."

"Who answered?"

"Dr. Kirkland. He told me everything *wasn't* okay, but that I should stay with Mrs. Kirkland. I panicked and made him tell me you was all right. That's when I figured out something had happened to Mr. Luke."

Mr. Luke . . . Pearlie's term of address for my father.

"He was supposed to have left for the island about nine, but I just had a feeling. I went out to the back gallery of the big house and looked down. When I saw Mr. Luke lying under that tree, it broke my heart. Lord, let's don't talk about that."

"Did you speak to Mom when you phoned down?"

"No."

I close my eyes. Blue police lights flash behind them, illuminating the great U created by the rear of Malmaison and the two slave quarters, painting the streaking rain with a sapphire glow. Tall men wearing uniforms and caps stand talking to my grandfather amid the roses, deferring to him like soldiers to a senior officer. I open my eyes before the memory can go any further.

"This is what I remember being told," I murmur. "Daddy and Grandpapa both heard someone prowling the grounds. Daddy was in here, Grandpapa in the main house. They met outside, talked a few seconds, then started checking the grounds separately. Both had guns, but Daddy was surprised by the prowler. They fought in the dark, and Daddy was shot with his own rifle."

Pearlie nods sadly. "That's what Dr. Kirkland told me."

"Is that what he told the police?"

"Course it is, child. That's what happened. Why you ask me that?"

Without realizing it, I've already formulated an answer to her question. "Because I think that bare footprint on the carpet is mine. And I think I put it there on that night."

Pearlie shakes her head. "That's nonsense, child. You ain't never got over losing your daddy, that's all. You been trying to make sense of it for twenty years, but there *ain't* no sense to things like that. Not unless you God hisself. Then you understand everything. But that's the only sense there is. Ain't none for you and me."

I ignore Pearlie's simplistic philosophy, however accurate it might be. "Talking to Mom about that night was like pulling teeth. When she did talk, she told me conflicting stories. She heard the shot, she didn't hear it. She saw one thing, then she didn't see it. What do you think about that?"

Pearlie gives me a rare unguarded look. "You say you're grown up now . . . and I guess you are. Old enough to hear this, anyway. Your mama didn't see anything that night, baby. She was taking your father's sleeping pills back then. Or his pain pills. Whatever he took for his war wound and his nerves."

Nerves . . . Pearlie's euphemism for post-traumatic stress disorder. "You're saying that was a habit?"

"Girl, your mama swallowed most everything Mr. Luke got from the doctor back then. She had nerve problems herself. Your daddy went to Dr. Tom Cage back then, and I think Dr. Cage prescribed enough for the both of them. Your mama wouldn't hardly go see a doctor."

I make a mental note to find out if Dr. Cage is still alive. "So Mama was unconscious when Daddy was shot?" I close my eyes and try to visualize something—anything—before the blue lights appeared, but nothing will come. "So it was only when you came down to the garden that you saw me walk up to the body?"

"That's right."

"Where did I come from?"

Pearlie hesitates. "From this house, I think. Or behind it, maybe. I'm not sure."

I try again to recall something fresh from that night, but the impassable gate that guards that information from my conscious mind remains locked. "Pearlie, who do you think that prowler was? What was he doing here?"

The maid sighs with bone-deep fatalism, and then her dark eyes settle on mine. "You really want to know?"

"Yes."

"I think he was a friend of your daddy's. Either that, or somebody who came here to kill Dr. Kirkland."

For a moment I can't speak. In all the years since my father's death, I've never heard anyone voice either of these theories. "Kill Grandpapa? Why would someone do that?"

Pearlie sighs heavily. "Nice as your granddaddy can be, he's a tough businessman. He's ruined some people, and in a town this small, that can catch up with you."

"Has anybody tried to hurt him since that night?"

"Not that I know about." She gives a little shrug. "I'm probably wrong about that. But now he's got that driver, that Billy Neal. I don't like that boy at *all*."

I've met my grandfather's driver only once, and then briefly. Thin-faced and muscular, Billy Neal reminds me of the men who relentlessly hit on me in bars. Quiet men who assume too much. Their silence is not solicitous but threatening, almost belligerent. "Do you think Billy Neal is a kind of bodyguard?"

Pearlie snorts. "I know he is. He too mean to keep around for anything else. Specially just driving."

The idea that my grandfather should need a bodyguard seems ridiculous, yet that was the impression I got when I saw him in New Orleans with his new driver. But it's Pearlie's first theory that has my heart thumping. "Why do you say the prowler might have been a friend of Daddy's?"

"I think it would have had to be," she says firmly. "To get close enough to your daddy to shoot him with his own gun like that?"

"Why?"

"I never saw a man so alert, child. Mr. Luke slept with both eyes open. Always looking for danger. I guess the war made him that way. Dr. Kirkland think he's a big hunter, but your daddy . . . he could walk through the woods without bending a blade of grass. First couple of years he was back from the war, he walked this property all hours of the night. The island, too, I heard. 'Bout scared me to death sometimes. He'd just appear in front of you, like a ghost. Couldn't nobody slip up on Mr. Luke without him knowing. No way, no how. That's one thing I know."

"A friend," I murmur, trying to get my mind around the idea. "I don't remember Daddy having friends."

Pearlie smiles with regret. "They wasn't friends, really. Just boys like he was. Boys who'd been in the war. Not *with* him, but like him. They was good boys, but a lot of good boys come back from Vietnam hooked on that dope. Black and white the same. My nephew was one. Anyway, them friends would've known your daddy had pills around. Plus, they probably figured Dr. Kirkland kept drugs here. Not hard to figure the rest, is it?"

I gaze around the forlorn bedroom. A child's room without a child in it. I'm not claustrophobic, but sometimes certain places get to me, and in those times I have to move. Move or freak out. "Let's go outside."

Pearlie takes my hand. "What's the matter, baby?"

"I need some air."

"Well, let's get you some then."

I let Pearlie exit first, then close the door behind us. "Don't go back in there anymore," I tell her. "I still have work to do inside."

"What kind of work?"

"The same work I do in New Orleans. There may be more blood in there."

Anxiety tightens her shoulders.

"What's the matter?" I ask.

She stops in the kitchen and lays a hand on my forearm "Baby girl, it don't do no good to dig up the past. Even simple folk know that. And you ain't simple."

"I wish I were sometimes."

Pearlie clucks softly. "There's one thing we can't change in this world. Our natures. We come into the world with them, and they stay with us all the way through."

"Do you really believe that?"

A terrible wisdom seeps from her eyes. "I believe it, all right. I've watched too many children from the cradle to the grave not to."

I don't agree, but neither do I argue. Pearlie Washington has lived a lot longer than I have. We walk out into the sunlight of the rose garden.

"I have one more question," I tell her. "And I want you to tell me the truth."

The maid's eyes deepen again, like a stilling pool. "I'll try, baby."

"Do you think Daddy might have killed himself?"

She draws back. "What you talking 'bout, girl?"

"I'm asking you if there was really a prowler here that night, or whether everybody's been lying to me all these years to protect my feelings. Whether what Daddy went through in the war was just too much for him. So bad that . . . that even Mom and me weren't enough to keep him wanting to live."

Pearlie lifts her long brown fingers to my cheek and wipes away tears. "Oh, baby, don't you ever think that. Mr. Luke thought the sun rose and set in your eyes. That's a fact."

I try to blink away the wetness in my eyes. "Did he? I don't remember."

She smiles. "I know you don't. He got took from you too early.

But Mr. Luke didn't go through all he did in that war just to shoot hisself when he got back home. He loved you more than you'll ever know. So you get that foolishness right out of your mind. All right?"

"Yes, ma'am." I'm surprised by the childlike sound of my own voice.

"I better find Natriece," Pearlie says, squaring her shoulders and looking toward Malmaison. "You holler if you need me."

CHAPTER

8

As Pearlie walks toward the rear of Malmaison, I take my cell phone from my pocket and check the screen. Eight more missed calls, all from Sean. He won't give up.

I open my digital phone book and dial my mother's cell phone. She answers through a crackle of static.

"Cat? What's wrong?"

"Why do you think something's wrong?"

"Why else would you call me?"

Good God. "Where are you, Mom?"

"About thirty miles south of Natchez, coming back the Liberty Road way. I've been to see your aunt Ann."

"How is she?"

"Not good. It's too long a story to tell on a cell phone. Where are you?"

"Home."

"Are you working on those murders down there? I saw the news."

"Yes and no. I'm actually in Natchez right now."

Static never sounded so empty. "What are you doing in Natchez?"

"I'll tell you when you get here."

"Don't you dare do that to me. Tell me now."

"When you get here. Good-bye, Mom."

I hang up and look back at our house. I want to work the rest of my bedroom for latent blood, but I don't have the right chemicals. Luminol can damage the genetic markers used to identify the person who lost the blood. Some rapidly evaporating solvents neither dilute nor damage bloodstains. I have some in New Orleans, but not here.

My cell phone rings again. I answer by saying, "I'll tell you when you get here, Mom."

"This isn't Mom," says Sean. "But I guess I know why you finally answered."

I feel a rush of guilt. "Hey, I'm sorry about the missed calls."

"It's okay. I wouldn't have kept bugging you today if it weren't important."

"What is it?"

"Are you sitting down?"

"Just tell me, damn it."

"We've finally connected the NOMURS victims."

My heart stutters. "How?"

"You won't believe it. It's the women."

"Women? What women?"

"Female relatives of the victims."

I look around the gardens of Malmaison, my mind too filled with thoughts of the past to make sense of what Sean is saying. "Tell me from the beginning. I'm not there with you, remember?"

"When a low-risk victim is murdered, you have to look at the family, right? And these were all low-risk victims. The task force has been taking apart the lives of every family member, moving out in concentric circles. Well, this morning we learned that female relatives of two of the victims go to the same psychiatrist."

My skin feels hot. "Which victims?"

"Two and four. Riviere and LeGendre."

"What's their relation?"

"Riviere's daughter, LeGendre's niece."

"Holy shit. What's the shrink's name?"

"Nathan Malik."

I run the name through my memory. "Never heard of him."

"I'm surprised. He's pretty well known, and fairly controversial. He's written a couple of books."

"On what?"

"Repressed memories. Bringing back repressed memories, I guess."

This pricks something in the back of my mind. "That's usually related to sexual abuse."

"I know. Are you thinking what I am?"

"Revenge killings. Our victims are child abusers being killed by their victims. Or by a male relative of the abuse victims. From that angle, the sex and advanced age of the victims suddenly makes all the sense in the world."

"That's what I thought," says Sean. "We're checking every relative of every victim for visits to Nathan Malik or any other therapist. It's not easy, though. The two women we've linked to Malik were hiding the fact that they were seeing him. Paying in cash and lying to their families about where they went. The only reason we figured it out is because they were obsessive about keeping up with their money. They had amazingly detailed private records.

"The FBI psychiatrist at Quantico says there's a strong possibility that Dr. Malik could be doing the murders himself. There's something called countertransference, where a shrink vicariously experiences the pain of his patients. The FBI shrink says that could trigger Malik to commit revenge murder just as if he'd been abused himself. And Malik would have the knowledge to stage the scenes to look like garden-variety sexual homicide."

"Has anyone talked to Dr. Malik yet?"

"No, but he's under surveillance."

"How old is he?"

"Fifty-three."

This is outside the age range of the FBI's standard serial-killer profile, but well within the bounds of possibility, based on the literature. I can't believe the adrenaline flowing through my veins. "What happens next?"

"That's what I'm calling you about. We want you to check Nathan Malik's dental records. See if they match the bite marks on the bodies."

"You already have them?"

"No."

"When will you?"

"I'm not sure yet."

"I don't get it. What's going on, Sean?"

"We've got the name of Malik's dentist. And since you know damn near every dentist in the New Orleans area, we were hoping you could have an informal chat with this one. Maybe get a look at some faxed dental records. Just enough to tell if Malik is the killer or not."

A red flag goes up in my mind. "An 'informal' chat? You're shitting me."

"No."

"Who wants this, Sean? The task force? Or you?"

The resulting pause is long enough for me to guess the answer. "Are you out of your mind? There's no way a dentist is going to let me see his records without a court order. Not with all the new HIPAA regulations. When can you get a court order?"

"The task force is debating that now. The problem is, as soon as we ask for those records, we tip Malik to our interest in him."

"So? If his dental records match the bite marks on the victims, that won't matter. But if I break the law to get an 'informal' look at those records—or Malik's dentist breaks it—and that's brought out at trial, couldn't that get Malik off?"

"If it came out at trial, yes. But you're part of the old boy network in this town. In dentistry anyway."

"You're wrong about that, Sean. I'm tolerated—maybe grudgingly respected. But if I—"

"*Cat.*" His voice is filled with presumptuousness.

"Do you really want to stop this guy that badly? Or do you just want the glory of catching him?"

"That's not fair."

"Bullshit. This killer's been hitting one victim a week. It's only been twenty-four hours since his last strike. We have some time. The task force does, I mean."

Sean doesn't reply. In the silence, I try to divine his true motivation. He likes glory, but there's something deeper at work here. He's speaking again, but I don't catch what he's saying, because suddenly I understand.

"You're trying to save your job."

I know from the silence that I'm right. "Does Captain Piazza want to fire you because of us?"

"Piazza will never fire me," he says with bravado. "I make her look too good."

"Maybe. But she'd damn sure yank you off the task force. And bringing in a positive ID on the killer before the Bureau can would put you back into her good graces, wouldn't it?"

More silence. "I need this, Cat."

"Maybe so. But jailing this killer is more important than your job."

"I know that. I'm just—"

"No way, Sean. I've broken a lot of rules for you, but I've never put a conviction in jeopardy. I won't do it now."

"Okay, okay. But look . . . at least tell me if you know the dentist. His name is Shubb. Harold Shubb."

I feel a quick rush of excitement. Harold Shubb is part of the disaster identification unit made up of volunteer dentists across the state of Louisiana. I organized that unit. Shubb took one of my seminars in forensic odontology, and he would love a call from me.

"You know him. I can tell," Sean says.

"I know him."

"Is he an okay guy?"

"Yes, but that doesn't change anything. Get your court order, and Shubb will do you right. You should also be trying to find out if this Malik had any orthodontic work done as an adolescent, or even later. Orthodontists keep their patient models for a very long time, as a defense against future lawsuits."

Sean sighs heavily. "I'll tell them that."

"Kaiser probably knows already." I picture the former FBI profiler in my mind. I can't imagine much getting by him.

"I know you won't make the call," Sean says in a wheedling tone, "but at least let me fax you what I have on Malik. You want to see that, right?"

I don't answer. My thoughts have wandered back to the bloody footprints in my bedroom.

"Cat? Are you there?"

"Send me what you've got."

"Give me a fax number."

I give him the number of my grandfather's fax machine. I know it because we sometimes have to exchange documents dealing with my trust fund.

"I'll get it to you as soon as I can," Sean promises.

"Fine."

There's an awkward pause. Then he says, "Are you coming back tonight?"

I actually hear loneliness in his voice. "No."

"Tomorrow, then?"

"I don't know, Sean."

"Why not? You hardly ever go home, and when you do, you don't like it."

"Something's happened up here."

"What? Is somebody sick?"

"I can't explain now. I have to go."

"Call me later, then."

"If I notice anything interesting in the stuff you fax me, I'll call. Otherwise, it'll be tomorrow at least before you hear from me."

Sean is silent. Then, after a few moments, he says, "Good-bye, Cat."

I hang up and look back at the slave quarters, then up at the rear of Malmaison. I want to talk to my mother, but she's still twenty minutes away. Suddenly, from the roiling mass of thoughts that is my mind in this moment, a clear image rises. Breaking into a trot, I head into the trees on the east side of the vast lawn, following a path first beaten by my own feet fifteen years ago.

I need to be underwater.

As I jog through the trees, I spy a dark figure standing in the shadows about forty yards ahead. A black man in work clothes. I bear left so that I won't pass him too closely, but as I near the figure, I recognize Mose, the yardman who has worked at Malmaison since before I was born. Once a strapping giant who could carry railroad ties on his back, Mose now has a bent spine and white stubble that grows almost up to his watery yellow eyes. He lives alone in a small house at the back of the property, but once a week he commands an army of younger men who groom the grounds like a crack army platoon. I wave as I pass to his left. The old man lifts his arm in a vague way. He doesn't recognize me. Probably thinks I'm one of the suburban housewives from Brookwood. The scary thing is that I'm old enough to be one now. I quicken my pace, my mind racing ahead to a place I haven't visited in far too long.

Years fall away as I run.

CHAPTER

9

Pounding through the trees at the eastern border of Malmaison's grounds, I suddenly emerge behind the houses of Brookwood Estates, a subdivision built on DeSalle land sold to a developer during the 1930s, when Malmaison was out of the family's hands. The homes in Brookwood are mostly single-story, 1950s ranch houses, but a few at the back are two-story colonials. I came here countless times during my youth, and always for the same reason. One of the colonials belonged to the Hemmeters, an elderly couple who owned a swimming pool.

I came because my grandfather, despite his enormous wealth and my fanatical dedication to swimming—three consecutive state titles—refused to build me a practice pool. My request was not that of a spoiled child. My high school, St. Stephen's, had no swimming pool, so our team was forced to practice wherever we could get permission at different times of the year. My mother and grandmother gave my suggestion their usual shaky support, but since the original Malmaison had no pool, my grandfather refused to desecrate "his" grounds with one. To remedy this, I did my daily laps in the Hemmeters' pool in Brookwood. The old couple always sat on their patio to watch, and they became my biggest fans at local meets. Mr. Hemmeter died a couple of years ago, but his widow kept the house.

Something about the place looks different as I approach, but that's only to be expected after the man of the house has died. At least the pool is being kept up. Mrs. Hemmeter stopped swimming several years ago, so the clear water sparkling in the sun strikes me much as my bedroom did—something maintained in the hope that I will return to it someday. Vanity, perhaps, but I suspect I'm right.

I jog around the house and check the garage. Empty. Returning to the pool, I strip off my jeans and blouse and dive cleanly into the deep end, leaving hardly a ripple behind me. The dive carries me halfway to the far wall. I breaststroke to the shallows, then get out and search the flower bed until I find a flat, heavy rock about the size of a serving platter. This I carry down the steps into the shallow end. After a period of pre-immersion meditation, during which my heart slows to around sixty beats per minute, I lie down on my back beneath the water and set the rock on my chest.

The water is just under ninety degrees, like the sea under an equatorial sun. I lie on the bottom for three minutes, until my chest spasms in its first "physical scream" for oxygen. Free divers train themselves to ignore this reflex, which would send a normal person into full-blown panic. After enduring a varying number of these spasms, humans can move into a far more primitive mammalian state, one the body dimly remembers from its genetic heritage as a waterborne animal. In the beginning, I endured as many as twenty spasms before entering the primitive dive state. Now the miraculous transition is almost painless. Once in the dive state, my heartbeat decreases dramatically, sometimes to as low as fifteen beats per minute. My blood circulation alters to serve only my core organs, and blood plasma slowly fills my lungs to resist the increasing pressure of deep water.

I can feel it now, the steady descent to a state of relaxation I can find nowhere else in my life. Not in sleep, where nightmares trouble me. Not in sex, where frantic urgency drives me to numb a pain I cannot even name. Not in the hunt for predators, where the triumph of trapping my quarry brings only transitory peace. Somehow, when I am submerged in water, the chaos that is my mind on the surface discharges itself, and my thoughts either go flat or pattern themselves into a comprehensible order that eludes me in the air. With the pool water gently swaying my body, the crazed events of the past week begin to come clear.

I'm not alone today. A child is growing in my belly, eating what I eat, breathing my air. Being pregnant doesn't seem as frightening down here. The child's conception is no mystery, after all. A simple combination of carelessness and lust. Sean's kids were gone to summer camp, his wife was visiting her mother in Florida . . . he stayed over at my house from a Thursday to a Sunday. By Saturday morning I'd developed cystitis from too much sex—what they called honeymoon syndrome in medical school—so I took a brief course of Cipro to cure it. The antibiotic interfered with my birth control pills, and that was that. I was "with child," as my grandmother used to say.

The mystery is why I haven't yet told Sean. I love him. He loves me. Up to now, we've shared every thought and feeling. We've even confessed our secrets, which was painful but the only way to maintain sanity in a relationship conducted in the shadows. There has to be some honesty amid the lies. My fear—when I'm brave enough to face it—is that Sean will think I got pregnant on purpose. That I trapped him. And even if he believes the truth, will he leave his family to be with me? Will he want to father a child with me when he already has three of his own? Sean is obsessed with his work, so much so that it takes time away from his family now. Will the fact that we could work together persuade him that our relationship could succeed if it were out in the open?

I wonder if part of my zeal for solving Sean's cases has been an effort to make myself indispensable to him. Pathetic, if true. Yet if it is . . . this time I've failed at even that. With the NOMURS victims connected at last, finding the killer is only a matter of time. If Nathan Malik's teeth match the bite marks on the victims' corpses, it's all over but the lethal injection, ten years down the road. . . .

The idea of a psychiatrist-murderer intrigues me. There are similar cases in the literature. I wonder if Dr. Malik is aware of that. I've had therapists I suspected of deep-rooted weirdness. There was Dr. DeLorme, a soft-spoken psychologist of sixty whose eyes glittered whenever he questioned me about sexual matters. His best efforts went in vain, but I at least found a diversion from my problems during the sessions, by trying to read what went on behind those eyes. What would DeLorme make of my panic attacks at the crime scenes? He'd probably attribute them to my pregnancy. But I experienced the first attack two days before I discovered I was pregnant. Unless slightly elevated hormones can precipitate panic, the cause must lie elsewhere. Alcohol is another possible culprit—too much or too little—but I had the first attack while floating comfortably on Grey Goose and the second while stone sober. I've always suffered occasional blackouts from drinking, but never panic attacks. In fact, alcohol gives me a surplus of courage. Dutch courage, they call it in old movies.

As the level of oxygen in my tissues continues to fall, deeper questions bubble up from my subconscious. What's the significance of rain on a tin roof? Why am I hearing that? And why at the times that I do? The only tin roof at Malmaison is on the barn my father used for a studio, and my memories of that space are so precious as to be sacred. Nothing about the barn elicits panic. And my nightmares? For years my sleep has been haunted by terrifying scenes of creatures—sometimes human, other times half human, half beast—trying to break into my house and kill me. This scenario comes in a thousand variations, all of them as "real" as my experiences in the waking world. I also have recurring dreams, as though my subconscious is trying to send me a message. Yet neither I nor my therapists have been able to decode the imagery. Two weeks ago, before my first panic attack, I began dreaming of a summer day on DeSalle Island. I'm riding in the old, round-nosed pickup truck that my grandfather used for work on the island. Grandpapa is driving, and I'm just tall enough to see over the dashboard. The truck smells of old motor oil and hand-rolled cigarettes. We're riding across a pasture, up a gentle hill. On the other side of that hill lies a small pond where the cows drink. Each time the dream recurs, we make it a little farther up the hill. But we never reach the crest.

The glowing footprint from my bedroom fills my darkening mind. Did my eight-year-old foot leave that track? Who else could have left it? That bedroom was mine alone for sixteen years. The carpet was installed the year I was born, when the whole room was remodeled. No other child lived at Malmaison after me, and as far as I know, no other child has ever stayed in that room. The conclusion seems inescapable. But why am I using logic? The overpowering wave of déjà vu that hit me when I first saw that glowing print is all the proof I need.

That bloody track is mine.

The question is, whose blood was on my foot? My father's? If enough genetic markers survived Natriece's luminol bath—and if I can get a sample of my father's DNA from somewhere—a hair from an old brush, perhaps—then a DNA test can tell me whether it was his blood or not. Big ifs. And even with my contacts at the crime labs throughout the state, a DNA comparison could take several days. In the meantime, I have only my memory—or the lack of it—to go on.

I remember almost nothing from the night my father died, nothing before I walked through the rain to the dogwood tree and saw his body lying motionless on the ground. It's as though I simply materialized from the grass. Without my voice. And it was more than a year before I spoke again. Why? Where was I when my father died? Asleep? Or did I witness something? Something too terrible to recall, much less speak of? Pearlie knows more about that night than she's told me. But what is she holding back? And why? Once she states something to be true, she rarely goes back and adjusts her version of events. But maybe I don't need Pearlie. For the first time in my life, I have a witness to that night's events that cannot conceal or distort events: blood. The oldest sign of murder, Abel's blood crying out from the ground—

"Mayday!" cries a voice in my head. "Mayday! Mayday!"

That voice is the product of five years of dive training. It tells me when I'm nearing the crisis point. The level of oxygen in my tissues has fallen to a point where most people would be unconscious. In fact, most people submerged for the length of time I have lain here would be dead by now. But I still have a margin of safety. My thoughts have condensed from a bright stream of consciousness to a single line of pulsing blue light. The message carried in that blue light has nothing to do with my past. It's about my baby. She is here with me, cosseted in the sheltered pool of my uterus, a core organ if anything qualifies as one. Most women would excoriate me for risking my baby's life this way. In another situation, I might do the same. But I'm not in another situation. A lot of women, finding themselves pregnant by a married man, would already have scheduled an abortion. But I haven't done that. I will not. This is my baby, and I intend to have her. I risk her life only by risking my own. As for my motive . . . the pulsing blue thread of light in my mind tells me this: my baby can survive this. When we rise from this water, we will be one, and nothing Sean Regan says or does will have any power over us—

My body tenses. Opening my eyes, I see a dark figure hovering above the water. Slowly, a golden spear separates from the figure and descends toward the surface, directly above me. I shove the rock off my chest and burst up into air and light, sputtering in terror. A tall man stands at the side of the pool, a ten-foot-long net in his hands. He looks more frightened than I.

"I thought you'd drowned!" he cries. Then he blushes and turns away.

I cross my arms over my breasts, only now remembering that I went into the pool in my underwear. "Who are you? Where's Mrs. Hemmeter?"

"Magnolia House." He's still looking away. "The assisted-living home. She sold the house to me. Do you want to put on some clothes?"

I kneel so that the water covers me to my neck. "I'm decent now."

The man turns around. He has sandy brown hair and blue eyes, and he's wearing khakis and a blue button-down oxford shirt. Several tongue suppressors protrude from his shirt pocket. He looks to be in his early thirties, and something about him strikes me as familiar.

"Do I know you?" I ask.

He smiles. "Do you?"

I study him but can't make the connection. "I do. Or I did."

"I'm Michael Wells."

"Oh my God! Michael? I didn't—"

"Didn't recognize me, I know. I've lost eighty pounds in the last two years."

I survey him from head to toe. It's difficult to reconcile what I see before me with my memories of high school, but there's just enough of the old Michael left to recognize. It's like meeting a man in the real world whom you first encountered as a cancer patient on steroid therapy—bloated and soft then, but now miraculously recovered, healthy and hard.

"My God, you look . . . well, *hot.*"

Michael's blush returns, redder than before. "Thanks, Cat."

He was three years ahead of me at St. Stephen's, then at the University Medical Center in Jackson. "Did you stick with pediatrics?" I ask, searching my mind for details.

He nods. "I was practicing in North Carolina, but St. Catherine's Hospital came up and recruited me. This town was desperate for more pediatricians."

"Well, I'm glad you came back. You own this house now?"

"Yep."

"I used to swim here all the time."

He smiles. "Mrs. Hemmeter told me."

"Did she? Well, do you like it? The house, I mean."

"I do. I like being at the back of the neighborhood. It's no Malmaison, of course."

"Be glad it's not. You don't want the upkeep on that place."

"I can imagine. Did you ever live anywhere else in Natchez?"

"No. My dad came back from Vietnam with post-traumatic stress disorder. He couldn't hold a job, so my mom came home from college, and they moved into one of the slave quarters. I was born four years later. We never left after that."

"What did your father do before the war?"

"He was a welder."

"Is that where his sculpting came from?"

"Yes." I'm surprised Michael remembers that. After two years of wandering the woods and watching television, my dad fired up his welding equipment and began sculpting metal. In the beginning he produced huge, horrid pieces—Asian demons cut from steel and iron—but as time passed, his work mellowed and became quite popular with some collectors.

"Is that a rock down there?" Michael asks, pointing into the water.

"Yes. Your rock. I used it to keep me submerged. I'm a free diver."

"What's that?"

"I dive deep in the ocean using only the air in my lungs."

Michael looks intrigued. "How deep?"

"I've been to three hundred and fifty feet."

"Jesus! I scuba dive a little, and I've only been to ninety feet with tanks."

"I use a weighted sled to help me get down quickly."

"That's one extreme sport I've never heard of."

"It's pretty intense. As solitary as you can be on this planet, I think."

He squats beside the pool, his eyes filled with curiosity. "Do you like that? Solitude, I mean?"

"Sometimes. Other times I can't stand to be alone. Literally."

"I learned to fly five years ago. I've got a little Cessna 210 out at the airport. That's where I get my solitude."

"Well, there you go. Flying scares me to death. If I got into your Cessna, I'd need a doggie bag in the first two minutes."

Michael laughs and blushes at the same time. "You're just trying to save my pride."

"I'm not. Flying scares me, especially small planes." I look toward the trees that conceal Malmaison. "Have you met my grandfather yet?"

He smiles in a way that's hard to read. "The lord of the manor? Yeah. He still comes to the occasional staff meeting at the hospital, even though he's more of a wheeler-dealer than a surgeon these days, from what I hear."

"For a lot of years now. By the time he was forty, surgery was just a prestige hobby for him."

Michael glances toward the woods, as though my grandfather might be watching us. "I saw him out running one day. He didn't recognize me. I tell you, he's a tough old man. He's what, seventy?"

"Seventy-seven."

"God. He can run me into the ground. And he doesn't have that old-man jog, either, you know? He *runs*."

"He's strong."

"I haven't seen him much lately. He's apparently out of town a lot." Michael bends and dips his hand into the pool. "There's a rumor that he's buying up most of downtown Natchez."

"What?"

"When the paper mill closed, the real estate market here crashed. But then a front company started buying up downtown by the block. Like it's boom times again. Word is, the front company is really your grandfather."

I can't fit this into my frame of reference about my grandfather. "Why would he do that? Where's the profit in it?"

This time Michael shrugs. "Nobody seems to know. But some people say he has some grand plan to save the city."

I shake my head. "He's always done a lot for the town, but that seems a bit crazy, given the local economy."

"Maybe he knows something we don't."

"He always does."

We look at each other without speaking. Michael doesn't feel compelled to fill every silence, as some men do. But then this is his property. I'm the interloper.

"You know I didn't finish med school, right?" I say cautiously.

"I heard."

"What did you hear?"

He replies in a neutral tone, careful to keep any judgment out of his voice. "Depression. Nervous breakdown. The usual."

"Nothing else?"

"Something about an affair with an attending physician. Or a professor, something. He flipped out over you and lost his job, you got booted, something like that. I don't care much about gossip. Everybody's got a past."

I smile. "Do you?"

"Sure." He chuckles softly. "Maybe not as colorful as yours."

We both laugh.

"I had a terrible crush on you in high school," he says. "I have to tell you that. I didn't have the nerve to back then. The most beautiful girl at St. Stephen's . . . my God."

"And now I'm standing in your swimming pool in my underwear. How do I look?"

He doesn't answer immediately. I'm surprised by the anxiety I feel about his answer. Why do I care so much what a virtual stranger thinks?

"You haven't changed at all," Michael says.

"Now I know you're lying. You should have told me about the crush back then."

He shakes his head. "Nah. You only dated jocks or bad boys."

"What were you?"

"The chubby geek. You know that."

I don't insult him by arguing. "You seem to have reinvented yourself."

He nods, his eyes reflective. "Sometimes you have to. It's not easy, either."

"You're married, of course."

"Nope. One girlfriend all the way through med school, but we ended up splitting."

"You must be the most eligible bachelor in Natchez."

Michael expels a lungful of air with obvious frustration. "The local matrons and divorcées certainly treat me that way. It's a new reality for me."

My cell phone rings in my jeans pocket on the side of the pool. I slide over to it on my knees and check the screen. My mother is calling again.

"Mom?"

"I'm home now, Cat. Where are you?"

"Swimming at the Hemmeters' house."

"That's not the Hemmeters' house anymore."

"I know. I just met Dr. Wells."

"Did you? Well, get home and tell me what's going on."

I hang up and look at Michael. "I need to get out."

He retrieves a towel from his back porch, hands it to me, then turns away. Walking quickly up the pool steps, I strip off my underwear and dry my skin. Then I put on my outer clothes and wring out my bra and panties to carry home.

"All covered up again."

Michael turns around. "Please feel free to use the pool anytime."

"Thanks. I won't be in town long, though."

"That's too bad. Do you . . ." As question fades into silence, color rises into his cheeks.

"What?"

"Do you have someone in New Orleans?"

I start to lie, then decide honesty is best. "I really don't know."

He seems to mull this over, then nods with apparent contentment.

I turn to go, but something makes me turn back to him. "Michael, do you ever have patients who just stop speaking?"

"Stop speaking altogether? Sure. But all my patients are kids."

"That's why I asked. What causes a child to stop speaking?"

He bites his bottom lip. "Sometimes they've been embarrassed by a parent. Other times it's anger. We call it voluntary mutism."

"What about shock?"

"Shock? Sure. And trauma. That's not voluntary, in the strictest sense."

"Have you ever seen it last for a year?"

He thinks about it. "No. Why?"

"After my father was shot, I stopped speaking for a year."

He studies me in silence for several moments. There's a deep compassion in his eyes. "Did you see anyone about it?"

"Not as a child, no."

"Not even a family doctor?"

"No. My grandfather was a doctor, you know? Mom said he kept telling her the problem would be self-limiting. Look, I need to run. I hope I see you again sometime."

"I do, too."

I walk backward for a few steps, give Michael a last smile, then turn and sprint off through the woods. When I am deep into the trees, I stop and look back.

He's still staring after me.

CHAPTER

10

My mother is waiting in the kitchen of the slave quarters, sitting at the heart-pine breakfast table. She's dressed impeccably in a tailored pants suit, but she has dark bags under her eyes, and her auburn hair looks as though she drove all the way from the Gulf Coast with her windows down. She looks older than when I last saw her—a brief lunch in New Orleans four months ago. Still, Gwen Ferry looks closer to forty than fifty-two, which is her true age. Her elder sister, Ann, once had the same gift, but by fifty Ann's troubled life had stolen the lingering bloom of youth. At one time the two sisters were Natchez royalty, the beautiful teenage daughters of one of the richest men in town. Now only my mother carries what's left of that banner, occupying the social pinnacle of the town: president of the Garden Club, a deceptively courteous organization that once wielded more power than the mayor and the board of aldermen combined. She also owns and operates an interior design center called Maison DeSalle, which caters to the small coterie of wealthy families that remain in Natchez.

She stands and gives me a side hug, then says, "What in the world is going on? I've always asked you to come home more often, and now you show up without even a phone call."

"Glad to see you, too, Mom."

Her face wrinkles in displeasure. "Pearlie says you found bloody tracks in your bedroom."

"That's right."

She looks perplexed. "I went in there and didn't find a thing on the floor. Just a bad smell."

"You went into my room?"

"Why wouldn't I?"

The coffeemaker bubbles on the counter, and the aroma of Canal Street coffee hits me. Trying to suppress my exasperation, I say, "I'd appreciate you not going in there anymore. Not until I'm finished."

"Finished with what?"

"Testing the rest of the bedroom for blood."

Mom interlocks her fingers on the table, as though trying to keep from fidgeting. "What are you talking about, Catherine?"

"I think I'm talking about the night Daddy died."

Two splotches of red appear high on her cheeks. "What?"

"I think those footprints were made on the night Daddy died."

"Well, that's just crazy." She's shaking her head, but her eyes have an unfocused look.

"Is it, Mom? How do you know?"

"Because I know what happened that night."

"Do you?"

She blinks in confusion. "Of course I do."

"Weren't you knocked out from taking Daddy's pills?"

Her cheeks go pale. "Don't you talk to me like that! I may have taken a sedative or two in those days—"

"You weren't addicted to Daddy's medicine?"

"Who told you that? Your grandfather? No, he's out of town. You've been talking to Pearlie, haven't you? I can't believe she'd say something so hurtful."

"Does it matter who I've been talking to? We have to tell the truth around here sometime."

Mom straightens up and squares her shoulders. "You need to take some of your own advice, missy. There's no doubt about who's told the most lies in this house." With trembling hands she turns and pours a cup of coffee from the carafe. Maybe the hand tremor is a family trait.

I take a deep breath and slowly let it out. "We got off on the wrong foot, Mom. How's Aunt Ann doing?"

"She's married another bastard. Third time in a row. This one's hitting her."

"Did she tell you that?"

"I have eyes. God, I don't want to talk about it. I don't even want to *think* about it. I need sleep."

"Maybe you'd better skip that coffee, then."

"If I don't drink this, I'll get a caffeine headache." She takes a steaming sip and makes a face. "You ought to know about addictions."

I fight the urge to snap back. "I've been sober for nearly three days."

She looks up sharply. "What's the occasion?"

I cannot tell her that I'm pregnant. Not yet. As my eyes seek out the floor, I feel a soft hand squeeze my upper arm.

"Whatever it is, I'm with you," she says. "When we know better, we do better. That's what Dr. Phil says. Like me and those sleeping pills."

"Dr. Phil? Mom, please."

"You should watch him, honey. We'll watch this afternoon. Before my nap. Dr. Phil always relaxes me."

I can't listen to any more of this. I need to be out of the kitchen. "I've got a fax waiting in Grandpapa's office. I'll see you in a few minutes."

"He should be home soon," she says. "You know he doesn't like people in his private office when he's not there."

"When's he due back?" I ask, heading for the door.

"Today is all I know."

I start to leave, then stop at the kitchen door and turn back. "Mom, do you have anything personal left of Dad's?"

"Like what? Pictures? What?"

"Like an old hairbrush."

"A hairbrush? What on earth for?"

"I was hoping you might have some of his hair. Sometimes people keep a lock of hair when they lose a loved one?"

She's suddenly frozen in place, her eyes wide. "You want it for a DNA sample." A statement, not a question.

"Yes. To compare to the blood on the floor of the bedroom."

"I don't have anything like that."

"The carpet is the same one as when I lived here, isn't it?"

The two red circles have darkened on her cheeks. "You don't remember it?"

"I just wanted to be sure. Is the bed the same?"

"For God's sake, Catherine."

"Is it?"

"The frame is the same. I had to get rid of your mattress."

"Why?"

"Urine stains. You wet the bed so often when you were a child."

"I did?"

Puzzlement in her eyes now. "You don't remember that?"

"No."

She sighs wearily. "Well, it's best forgotten. Just part of being a child."

"What did you do with the mattress?"

"The mattress? I'm sure Pearlie had Mose take it to the dump."

"I saw Mose outside earlier. I can't believe he still works here."

"He refuses to quit. He's not as strong as he used to be, but he's still going."

I hate to push her, but what do I have to lose now? "I know it's a long shot, Mom, but do you think Daddy ever donated to a sperm bank or anything like that?"

My mother stares at me as though she can't believe I'm her child.

"I'm sorry," I whisper. "I have to do this. I have no choice."

After a long look, she turns away and takes a sip of coffee.

Knowing that no words from me will make her feel better, I walk outside and make my way across the garden to the rear of Malmaison's left wing. My grandfather's study is on the ground floor.

Entering the mansion, I walk with bored familiarity past priceless antiques, eventually making my way to the library, which functions as my grandfather's study. Patterned after Napoléon's library, it's a world of dark wooden columns, rich upholstery, and broad French doors that open onto the front gallery. Civil War muskets are mounted on the ceiling beams, and twin crystal chandeliers light the room. Leather-bound volumes line the shelves, with paintings suspended on velvet cords in front of them. A few of the canvases show English hunting scenes, but most depict Civil War battles—Confederate triumphs all. The room's only concession to modernity is a long cypress table beside my grandfather's rolltop desk. On it stand a computer, printer, copier, and fax machine. The fax tray is empty. I take out my cell phone and speed-dial Sean.

"Cat?" he says over the chatter of the squad room.

"I'm standing by the fax machine," I tell him. "Nothing's come yet."

"I'm sending it through now. There's a decent amount of public information on Malik, but it's mostly scholarly stuff. When you get right down to it, it's hard to get a feel for what makes this guy tick."

"When is the task force going to talk to him?"

"They still haven't decided. Like you said, they feel they have some time before he hits again. Nobody wants to screw this up."

"Okay. I'll get back to you if I notice anything interesting."

"Hey?" Sean says.

"Yeah?"

"Get back to me anyway. I miss you."

I close my eyes as a wave of heat runs up my neck. "Okay."

I hang up, then sit at my grandfather's desk and wait for the fax to come through. The room smells of fresh cigars, old leather, good bourbon, and lemon oil. Intrigued by Michael Wells's story of a front company buying up downtown Natchez, I consider poking through my grandfather's desk, but it's locked.

Tired of waiting for Sean's fax, I pick up the phone, dial information, and get the number of Dr. Harold Shubb in New Orleans. Before second thoughts can stop me, I let the number automatically connect, then identify myself as a fellow dentist to Dr. Shubb's receptionist.

"Just one moment, Doctor," says the woman.

After a brief pause, a man who sounds excited to be taken away from his operatory chair comes on the line. "Cat Ferry! I always knew this call would come. I look forward to it and dread it at the same time. Has there been a plane crash?"

Dr. Shubb has naturally assumed that I'm calling to activate the volunteer disaster identification unit. "No, Harold. I'm calling about something just as serious, though."

"What's going on? What can I do for you?"

"Have you been following the recent murders in town?"

"Sure, yeah, of course."

"There's a bite mark angle to the case."

"Really? I hadn't heard that."

"The police are keeping it from the public. What I'm about to tell you, you can't mention to a soul."

"Goes without saying, Cat."

"We—that is, the task force working the case—we have a suspect. He's one of your patients, Harold."

Stunned silence on Dr. Shubb's end of the line. "Holy God. Are you kidding me?"

"No." I hear his breathing, shallow and irregular.

"May I ask who it is?"

"Not yet. This is an informal call, Harold."

Another pause. "I'm not sure I understand."

"The FBI is probably going to contact you today—officially—to get a look at any X-rays you might have on this patient. The NOPD, however, wants you and me to have an informal conversation a little sooner than that."

Dr. Shubb processes this. "I'm listening."

"I'm worried that any specific discussion we have about X-rays or teeth could later wreck the chance of a conviction."

"You might be right. If you don't have a court order, I mean. All this HIPAA privacy crap is driving me insane."

"I'm sure. Look, what I was thinking was that we could have a general conversation about this patient, but without getting into his mouth. Would you have a problem with that?"

"Fire away. I won't tell a soul."

I pray this is true. "The suspect's name is Nathan Malik. He's—"

"A shrink," Shubb finishes. "Holy *shit*. He's a psychiatrist, not a psychologist, and he makes sure you know that in the first five seconds. I've seen Malik quite a bit. Done two root canals on him so far this year. MDs hardly ever take care of their teeth, you know that. I just . . ."

Harold Shubb falls silent. Then he whistles long and low, as if only now realizing the implications of our conversation. I fight the urge to describe the bite marks on the victims. In less than a minute, we could probably confirm or eliminate Nathan Malik as the killer of the NOMURS victims. But in a case this sensitive, procedure must be followed to the letter.

"What kind of guy is he, Harold?"

"An odd duck. Smart as hell. A little intimidating, if you want to know the truth. Knows something about everything. Even teeth."

"Really?" It's rare for MDs to know much about dentition.

"I know you're going to think your call influenced me to say this, but the guy makes me a little uncomfortable. Not much for small talk, though he has a smart-ass sense of humor. But what he really gives off is intensity. Total intensity. You know the type?"

"I think so. Has Malik talked about his background?"

"Not much. I think he's from Mississippi originally. Like you."

"Really? Does fifty-three years old sound right?"

"About right. He's in good shape, except for his teeth. I could check my records—"

"Don't do that," I say quickly.

"Right . . . you're right. Shit, I'm getting nervous just talking to you."

"We're almost done, Harold. Do you know anything about Malik's modes of therapy? What he specializes in? Anything?"

"Repressed memories. Physical and sexual abuse of women. Men, too, I think. We've had several conversations about it. He's an expert at helping people recover lost memories. Uses drugs, hypnosis, everything. It's controversial stuff. Lots of litigation in that area."

"That's what I thought."

"I'll tell you this. If Nathan Malik is your guy, I hope you have some rock-solid evidence on him. He won't be intimidated by the FBI or anyone else. When it comes to things like patient privacy, he'll go to jail before he'll tell you a damn thing. He's a fanatic about it. Hates the government."

I jump as the fax machine beside me hums to life. "That rock-solid evidence may be sitting in your X-ray files right now, Harold."

He whistles again. "I hope so, Cat. I mean—"

"I know what you mean. *If* it's him."

"Exactly."

"Look, the FBI doesn't need to know about this conversation."

"What conversation?"

"Thanks, Harold. I'll see you at my next seminar?"

"Can't wait."

I ring off and watch the paper spool out of the fax machine. Someone has typed a detailed summary of the available information on Dr. Nathan Malik. I have an almost overwhelming urge to go to my grandfather's sideboard and pour a quick shot of vodka before reading it, but I manage to strangle the impulse. As the second sheet emerges from the fax machine, I glance down, then grip the table to stay on my feet.

At the bottom of the page is a black-and-white photo of Nathan

Malik, a bullet-headed, bald man with deep-set black eyes. On some men, baldness conveys an image of weakness or advancing age, but on Nathan Malik the bald pate seems more a challenge than a weakness, the way it did on Yul Brynner. Proud, piercing, and defiant, his eyes silently order you back a step. Malik's nose was broken at some point in his life, and his lips curl in a wry smile that expresses only contempt for the camera. He has the arrogant disdain of an aristocrat, but that's not what has taken my breath away. What did that was the eyes. I first saw them—and this face—nearly a decade ago, at the University Medical Center in Jackson, Mississippi.

Grabbing the first page from the fax tray, I scan the psychiatrist's CV. Born 1951. Two years in the army, a tour of duty as a medical corpsman in Vietnam. Undergraduate education, Tulane University. Graduated Tulane Medical School in 1979. A residency at Ochsner Hospital. Several years of private practice followed, after which—I feel my heart pounding against my sternum—Nathan Malik took a position on the psychiatric faculty at the University of Mississippi Medical Center in Jackson.

"Jesus Christ," I whisper.

Malik *was* at UMC during the two years I was there. I *did* know him. But something is wrong. I didn't know the man in this picture as Nathan Malik, but as Dr. Jonathan Gentry. And Gentry wasn't bald, not even close. Higher up the page, I find what I'm looking for. Nathan Malik was born Jonathan Gentry in Greenwood, Mississippi, in 1951. He legally changed his name in 1994, one year after I was asked to leave medical school. I pick up my cell phone and speed-dial Sean, sweat breaking out on my face and neck.

"You got something?" Sean says without preamble.

"Sean, I know him! *Knew* him, I mean."

"Who?"

"Malik."

"*What?*"

"Only his name wasn't Malik then. It was Gentry. He was on the faculty at UMC in Jackson when I was there. He had hair then, but it's the same guy. I couldn't forget those eyes. He knew that professor I had the affair with. He actually hit on me a few times. I mean—"

"Okay, okay. You need to get—"

"I know. I'll leave as soon as I can get out of here. I should be there in three hours."

"Don't wait for anything, Cat. The task force is going to want to talk to you bad."

The calm I experienced in the pool has fled me. I can hardly keep a logical thought in my head. "Sean, what does this mean? How could this be?"

"I don't know. I'm going to call John Kaiser. You call me when you get on the road. We'll figure it out."

Though I'm alone in the room, I nod thankfully. "I will. I'll talk to you soon."

"Bye, babe. Hang tough. We'll get this straight."

I put down the phone and gather the sheets from the fax tray. There are three now. As I turn toward the study door, it suddenly opens as though of its own volition.

Towering in the doorway is my grandfather, Dr. William Kirkland, his angular face lined with care. His pale blue eyes survey me from head to toe, then take in the room.

"Hello, Catherine," he says, his voice deep and precisely measured. "What are you doing in here?"

"I needed your fax machine, Grandpapa. I was just about to head back to New Orleans."

A shorter man in his thirties peers around my grandfather's broad frame. Billy Neal, the unpleasant driver Pearlie complained about. His eyes flick up and down my body, making private judgments that produce a smirk. Grandpapa gently but forcefully pushes his driver backward, then walks into the library and closes the door. He's wearing a white linen jacket and a necktie. On the island he dresses like a laborer, but in town he is unfailingly formal.

"I'm sure you don't want to leave before we've had a chance to visit," he says.

"It's pretty urgent. A murder case."

He smiles knowingly. "If it was that urgent, you wouldn't be in Natchez in the first place, would you? Unless someone was murdered here while I was gone?"

I shake my head.

"That's a relief. Though I can think of a few locals I wouldn't mind seeing hurried along to their final reward." He walks to the sideboard. "Sit down, Catherine. What are you drinking?"

"Nothing."

He raises a curious eyebrow.

"I really have to go."

"Your mother told me you found some blood in your old bedroom."

"That's right. I found it by accident, but it's definitely blood."

He pours himself a neat Scotch. "Human?"

"I don't know yet." I glance longingly at the door.

Grandpapa removes his jacket, revealing a tailored dress shirt with rolled-up sleeves. Even at his advanced age, he has the corded forearms of a man who's worked all his life with his hands. "But you're assuming that it is."

"Why do you say that? I never assume anything."

"I say that because you look agitated."

"It's not the blood. It's the murder case in New Orleans."

He hangs his jacket on a rack in the corner. "Are you being completely truthful about that? I just spoke to your mother. I know how much the loss of your father hurt you, how it's haunted you. Please sit down, Catherine. We should talk about your concerns."

I look down at the faxed pages in my hands. The hypnotic eyes of Nathan Malik stare up at me, prodding me to leave for New Orleans. But then an image of glowing footprints comes into my mind—one tiny and bare, the other made by a boot. A work boot, maybe, or a hunting boot. The NOMURS killings have a claim on me, but I cannot leave Malmaison without knowing more about those footprints.

I take a deep breath and force myself to sit.

CHAPTER

11

My grandfather sits in a leather club chair and regards me with interest. He's an imposing figure, and he knows it. William Kirkland looks the way people want their surgeons to look: confident, commanding, untroubled by doubt. Like he could operate ankle-deep in blood and only get calmer as the situation deteriorated. God endowed my grandfather with that magical combination of brains, brawn, and luck that no amount of poverty could hold in check, and his personal history is the stuff of legend.

Born into the hard-shell Baptist farmland of east Texas, he survived a car crash that killed his parents while they were traveling to his baptism. Taken in by his widowed grandfather, he grew into a boy who worked from "can see to can't see" in the summers and in the winters managed to score so highly in school that he attracted the attention of his principal. After receiving a full athletic scholarship to Texas A&M, he lied about his age and enlisted in the marines at seventeen. Twelve weeks later, Private Kirkland was on his way to the Pacific islands, where he won a Silver Star and two Purple Hearts as he fought his bloody way toward Japan. He recovered from his wounds, then used the GI Bill to graduate from A&M, where he won a scholarship to Tulane Medical School in New Orleans. There, he met my grandmother, the demure princess of Tulane's sister college, H. Sophie Newcomb.

A Presbyterian and a pauper, my grandfather was initially regarded with suspicion by the Catholic patriarch of the DeSalle family. But by sheer force of personality, he won over his future father-in-law and married Catherine Poitiers DeSalle without changing his religion. They had two daughters before he finished his medical training, yet still he managed to win top honors during his surgical residency. In 1956 he moved his young family to his wife's hometown—Natchez— and joined the practice of a prominent local surgeon. The future seemed set in stone, which, as a believer in the Calvinist doctrine of predestination, suited my grandfather just fine.

Then his wife's father died. With no male heir to take over the DeSalle family's extensive farming and business interests, my grandfather began to oversee those operations. He showed the same aptitude for business that he had for everything else, and before long he'd enlarged the family holdings by 30 percent. Surgery soon became almost a hobby, and he began to move in more rarefied business circles. Yet he never left his rural past behind. He can still split a fifth of cheap bourbon with a group of field hands without their guessing he's the man who pays their wages. He runs the DeSalle empire—his family included—like a feudal lord, but without sons or grandsons to carry on his legacy, the weight of his frustrated dynastic ambitions has devolved onto me.

"Where have you been?" I ask, having endured all the silent scrutiny I can stand.

"Washington," he replies. "Department of the Interior."

The candid answer surprises me. "I thought that was a big secret."

He sips judiciously from his Scotch. "To some people it is. But unlike your mother and her sister, you know how to keep a secret."

I feel my cheeks flush. My status as my grandfather's favorite has always been more of a burden than a blessing, and it frequently causes jealousy in my mother and aunt.

"I want to show you something, Catherine. Something no one else has seen outside Atlanta."

He stands and goes to a large gun safe built into the wall, which he unlocks with precise twirls of the combination lock. I feel a great urgency to get to New Orleans, but if I want to find out anything about the night my father died, I'll have to humor my grandfather for a few minutes. Grandpapa Kirkland doesn't hand out anything for free, especially information. He's a quid pro quo man. *This for that*, I recite, mentally translating the Latin he insisted I study in school.

As he works at something in the safe, I recall what Michael Wells said about how strong Grandpapa seems. Most men age first in their shoulders and chests, their muscle mass waning as their middles thicken, the bones slowly becoming brittle like those of their wives. But my grandfather has somehow retained the shape of men twenty-five years his junior. He's a member of that rare brotherhood that seems to age at half the rate of mortal men—epic figures like Charlton Heston and Burt Lancaster.

Instead of the priceless antique or musket I expect him to bring out of the gun safe, he produces a large architectural model. It looks like a hotel, with two grand wings framing a central section done in the Greek Revival style so common to the antebellum homes of Natchez.

"What's that?" I ask, as he carries the model to a poker table in the corner.

"Maison DeSalle," he says with pride.

"Maison DeSalle?" That's the name of my mother's interior design business. I walk over to the table. "That looks way too big to be a new building for Mom's store."

He chuckles with rich amusement. "You're right. I just liked the name. This Maison DeSalle is a hotel and casino complex. A resort."

"Why are we looking at it?"

Grandpapa sweeps his arm over the model like a railroad baron taking in a map of the continent. "Sixteen months from now, this will be standing in downtown Natchez, overlooking the Mississippi River."

I blink in disbelief. By law, every Mississippi casino—even the Vegas-style palaces on the Gulf Coast—has to be built on some kind of floating platform. Natchez has its own riverboat casino permanently docked at the bottom of Silver Street. "How can that be? Doesn't state law restrict gambling to casinos on water?"

He smiles slyly. Michael Wells was right: my grandfather knows something no one else does. "There's a loophole in the law."

"Which is . . . ?"

"Indian gaming licenses."

"You mean reservation gaming, like in Louisiana?"

"Louisiana and about twenty other states. We have one in Mississippi already, up at Philadelphia. Silver Star, it's called."

"But there's no reservation in Natchez."

Grandpapa's smile becomes triumphant. "There soon will be."

"But we don't have any Native Americans here."

"Who do you think gave this town its name, Catherine?"

"The Natchez Indians," I snap. "But they were massacred by the French in 1730. Slaughtered down to the last infant."

"Not true, my dear. Some escaped." He runs his long fingers along the roof of one of the model's wings, then caresses the casino's central section. "I've spent the last four years tracking down their descendants and paying for DNA tests to prove their lineage. I think it would interest you. We're using three-hundred-year-old teeth to get the baseline DNA."

I'm too stunned to speak.

"Impressed?" he asks.

I shake my head in bewilderment. "Where did the survivors escape to?"

"Some vanished into the Louisiana swamps. Others went north to Arkansas. Some got as far as Florida. A few were sold into slavery in Haiti. The survivors mostly assimilated into other Indian tribes, but that doesn't affect my venture. If the federal government certifies their descendants as an authentic Indian nation, every law that applies to the Cherokee or the Apache will apply to the descendants of the Natchez."

"How many of these people are there?"

"Eleven."

"*Eleven?* Is that enough?"

He taps the model with finality. "Absolutely. Tribes have been certified with fewer members than that. You see, the fact that there are so few left isn't the Indians' fault. It's the government's."

"The *French* government, in this case," I say drily. "And by the way, they're called Native Americans now."

He snorts. "I don't care what they call themselves. But I know what they mean to this town. Salvation."

"That's why you're doing this? To save the town?"

"You know me well, Catherine. I'll grant you, the cash flow from this operation could run twenty million a month. But no matter what you may think, that's not my reason for doing this."

I don't want to listen to one of my grandfather's righteous rationalizations for his ambition. "Twenty million a *month*? Where will the people come from? The gamblers, I mean. The nearest commercial airport is ninety miles away, and we still have no four-lane highway from it."

"I'm buying the local airport."

"*What?*"

He laughs. "Privatizing it, actually. I've already got a charter air-line committed to coming here."

"Why would the county let you do that?"

"I've promised to bring in ongoing commercial service."

"It's like *Field of Dreams,* isn't it? You believe that if you build it, they will come."

He fixes me with a pragmatist's glare. "Yes, but this isn't a dream of foolish sentimentality. People want glamour and stars, and I'll give them that. The high rollers will fly into the cotton capital of the Old South on a Learjet and live *Gone With the Wind* for three days at a time. But that's all window dressing. What they really come for is the age-old dream of getting something for nothing. Of walking in pau-pers and walking out kings."

"That's an empty dream. Because the house always wins in the end."

Now his smile shows pure satisfaction. "You're right. And this time *we're* the house, my dear. But unlike that abomination floating under the bluff, which fleeces local citizens of their Social Security checks and sends the profits directly to Las Vegas, Maison DeSalle will keep its profits right here in Natchez. I'm going to rebuild the infrastructure of this town. A state-of-the-art industrial park will be first. Then—"

"What about the Indians?" I ask bluntly.

The cool blue eyes lock onto mine, silently chastising me. Grand-papa has grown unused to interruptions in my absence. "I thought you said they were Native Americans now."

"I thought you might answer my question."

"Those eleven Indians will become some of the richest people in Mississippi. Naturally, I'll receive fair compensation for spearhead-ing the venture and laying out the initial capital."

I see it now. My grandfather will be hailed as the savior of Natchez. Yet despite the stated nobility of his goal, I feel uneasy at the way he's going about it. "Can anything go wrong at this point?"

"Oh, something can always go wrong. Every old soldier knows that. But my Washington contacts tell me that federal certification of the Natchez Nation should come within seven days."

I walk away from the poker table, my eyes on a bottle of Absolut on the sideboard.

"Sure you don't want a drink?" he asks.

I close my eyes. I'd hoped to wean myself off the Valium today, but I'm going to need one for the drive to New Orleans. "Positive."

He takes a last look at his model, then carries it back to the gun safe. While his back is turned, I take a pill from my pocket and dry-swallow it. By the time my grandfather returns to his chair, the Valium is in my stomach.

"Tell me about the night my father died."

Grandpapa's eyelids seem to grow heavy. "I've told you that story at least a dozen times."

"Humor me. Tell me once more."

"You're thinking about that blood you found." He lifts his Scotch and takes another swallow. "It was late. I was reading here in the library. Your grandmother was upstairs with abdominal pain. Pearlie was with her. I heard a noise behind the house. A metallic sound. A prowler had knocked over a metal drum on the patio in the rose garden."

"Did you see that happen?"

"Of course not. I found the drum when I went outside."

"Were you armed?"

"Yes. I took a Smith and Wesson .38 out with me."

"What was in the drum?"

"Pesticide for the roses. It was a heavy drum, so I figured a deer had got spooked while eating the roses and knocked it down."

"Why didn't you call the police?"

He shrugs. "I thought I could deal with it myself. Your father was standing outside your house. I thought he'd left for the island, but he'd been down in the barn, working on one of his sculptures. He'd heard something, too. Luke was holding the old Remington rifle he brought back from Vietnam."

"The one that hung over our fireplace?"

"That's right. The 700."

"So he went into the slave quarters to get that?"

"Apparently so."

"And then?"

"We separated. I went to look behind Pearlie's house, while Luke circled around yours. I was on the far side of Pearlie's house when I heard the shot. I raced around to the garden and found Luke lying dead. Shot in the chest."

"Are you sure he was dead then? Did you check his pulse?"

"I spent a year in combat in the Pacific, Catherine. I know a gunshot death when I see it." His voice has the kind of edge that closes further questions in that line.

"Did you see the prowler?"

"You know I did."

"Please just tell me what you saw."

"A man running through the trees toward Brookwood."

"Did you chase him?"

"No. I ran into your house to make sure you and Gwen were all right."

I try to picture this scene. "Were we?"

"Your mother was asleep, but you weren't in your bed."

"What did you do?"

He closes his eyes in recollection. "The telephone rang. It was Pearlie, calling from the main house. She and your grandmother were in a panic. She asked if you were all right. I said you were, but at that point I didn't know."

"Did you tell her to call the police?"

"She'd already called them."

"What happened then?"

"I searched the house for you."

"And?"

"I didn't find you. I was worried, but I knew the man I saw running hadn't been carrying a child, so I wasn't panicked. I figured you were hiding somewhere."

"Did you wake Mom up?"

"No, I knew Gwen would panic. But she soon woke up on her own. She didn't believe Luke was dead, so I walked her out to look at his body."

"Did she ask where I was?"

"The truth? Not at first. She wasn't in very good shape. She'd taken a sedative. I think she assumed you were asleep in your bed."

How many mothers would assume that under those circumstances? "Was there a lot of blood around Daddy's body?"

Grandpapa tilts his head from side to side, as though filtering his memory of my father's corpse through decades of surgical experience. "Enough. The bullet clipped the pulmonary artery, and there was a good-sized exit wound."

"Enough for what?"

"For someone to track blood into your room, I suppose." My grandfather's face gives away nothing.

"When did I turn up?"

"Right after the police arrived. I was telling them what happened when you walked up out of the dark."

"From the direction of our house?"

"I didn't see where you came from. But I remember the eastern slave quarters behind you, so I guess so."

"Was I wearing shoes?"

"I have no idea. I wouldn't think so."

"Did I get close to Daddy's body?"

"You were practically on top of him before anyone noticed you."

I close my eyes, willing my memory of that image back into the dark where I keep it. "Was the prowler you saw running away white or black?"

"Black."

"You're sure?"

"Positive."

"What kind of shoes were you wearing that night?" I didn't mean to ask this aloud, but it's too late to take it back.

"I wore boots during the day back then, but that night . . . I don't recall."

"Did you go into my room after the murder?"

"I did. To help your mother calm you down."

"Was I upset?"

"Not that a stranger could tell. You didn't make a sound. But I could see it. Pearlie was the only one you'd let hold you. She had to rock you in the chair like she did when you were a baby. That's the only way we got you to sleep."

I remember that feeling, if not that specific night. Pearlie rocked me to sleep on many nights, and long after I was a baby.

"Well." He takes a conclusive breath. "Have I told you what you needed to know?"

I haven't begun to get the answers I want, but at this point I'm not sure what the right questions are. "Who do you think the prowler was, Grandpapa?"

"No idea."

"Pearlie thinks it might have been a friend of Daddy's, looking for drugs."

Grandpapa appears to debate with himself about whether to comment on this. Then he says, "That's a fair assumption. Luke took a lot of prescription drugs. And I caught him growing marijuana down on the island more than once."

"I never knew that."

"Of course you didn't. Anyway, I worried at times that he might be selling the stuff. When he was killed, I thought of telling the police to explore that avenue, but in the end I decided against it."

"Why?"

"What could it do but bring calumny on the family name?"

Of course. The family name matters more than anything, even justice. I want to ask him the final question I put to Pearlie. But Grandpapa always saw my father as weak, and if he'd believed that fatal rifle shot had been self-inflicted, he wouldn't have concealed from anyone this vindication of his instincts—not even to protect the family name. Because he didn't really see my father as part of the family. And yet . . . there could be factors I know nothing about. My mother, for example.

"Did you really see a prowler that night, Grandpapa?"

His eyes widen, and for a moment I'm certain my blind shot has struck home. Before he speaks, he reaches out and drains the last of his Scotch. "Exactly what are you asking me, Catherine?"

"Did Daddy shoot himself that night? Did he commit suicide?"

Grandpapa raises a hand to his chin and massages the flesh beneath it. His eyes are unreadable, but I see a shadow of conflict in them. "If you're asking me whether I think Luke was capable of suicide, my answer is yes. He was severely depressed a good deal of the time. But that night . . . everything happened just as I said. He died trying to protect his home and family. I'll give the boy that."

Only when I exhale do I realize how long I've been holding my breath. I feel such relief that it takes a supreme act of will not to get up and take a slug of vodka from the bottle on the sideboard. Instead, I stand and gather my fax pages from the table.

"You hardly draw anything from your trust fund nowadays," Grandpapa remarks. "You don't spend money anymore?"

I shrug. "I like earning my own."

"I wish the rest of the family would take a page from your book."

I take this for what it is, a thinly veiled insult to my mother and aunt, but most of all to my father. "You really didn't like him, did you? Daddy, I mean. Tell the truth."

Grandpapa's eyes don't waver. "I don't think I made a secret of that. Perhaps I should have, but I'm no hypocrite."

"Why didn't you like him? Was it just oil and water?"

"A lot of it was the war, Catherine. Luke's war. Vietnam. His mental problems, I guess."

"He was wounded, too, you know." I still recall the line of holes in Daddy's back, caused by shrapnel from a booby-trapped artillery round. I always got chills when he removed his shirt.

"Luke's physical wound wasn't his problem."

"You don't know what he went through over there!" I cry defensively, though I don't really know either.

"That's true," Grandpapa admits. "I don't."

"I heard some of the things you used to say to him. How Vietnam wasn't a real war. How it wasn't nearly as tough as Iwo or Guadalcanal."

He stares curiously at me, as though wondering how an eight-year-old child could remember something like that. "I did say those things, Catherine. And in the time since, I've realized I might have been wrong. To an extent, anyway. Vietnam was a different kind of war, and I didn't understand that then. But by God, I saw things in the Pacific that were about as bad as a man can see, and I didn't let it paralyze me. A few men did—good men, some of them—and I guess maybe Luke was like them. Shell shock, the doctors called it then. Or battle fatigue. I'm afraid we just called it, well—"

"Yellow!" I finish, trying to resist a rush of emotion. My cheeks are burning. "Why didn't you tell Daddy you'd seen good men react like the way he did? You called him yellow to his face. I heard you! I didn't know what you meant then, but I did later."

Grandpapa folds his still-powerful hands together and fixes me with an unrepentant gaze. "Listen to me, Catherine. Maybe I was too hard on your father. But at some point it doesn't matter *what* you've gone through. You have to pull up your bootstraps and get on with living. Because one thing's for sure, nobody else is going to do it for you. Your father's job was to provide for you and your mother, and at that job he failed miserably."

I'm almost speechless with fury. "Did you really want him to succeed?"

"What does that mean? I gave him three different jobs, and he couldn't handle any of them."

"How could he? You despised him! And didn't you just love being the big man, the one who paid for everybody's food and shelter? Who controlled us all?"

He settles deeper into his chair, his chiseled features hard as the face of a mountain. "You're distraught, my dear. We'll continue this at another time. If we must."

I start to argue, but what's the point? "I have to get back to New Orleans. Please don't go into my old bedroom before I get back. You can't see anything without special chemicals. And please don't let anyone else go in there. Mom's liable to try to scrub the place from top to bottom with 409."

"Don't worry, I'll keep the room secure. Test anything and everything you like."

I collect my papers and walk to the study door.

"You seeing anybody that looks like a potential husband?" Grandpapa asks.

A wave of heat shoots up my spine.

"I'm wondering if I'm ever going to see some children around here before I die."

If he knew I was pregnant now, he probably wouldn't even care that I'm not married. "I wouldn't worry about that," I say without turning. "You're going to live forever, aren't you?"

I open the door to find Grandpapa's driver staring at me, an open leer on his face.

"Hey," he says.

I brush past Billy Neal without a word, but as I walk away, I hear him mutter something that sounds like *Frigid bitch.*

On any other day I would turn back and bite his head off, but today . . . it's just not worth it.

Today I keep walking.

CHAPTER

12

I'm twenty miles south of Natchez when the Valium starts to soothe my frayed nerves. Sean has called twice, but I didn't answer. I needed a few minutes to decompress after meeting with my grandfather, and to prepare for questioning about Nathan Malik by the FBI. Whatever the reality of the night my father died, I have to put it aside for now and think about my two years in medical school. They will soon be the subject of intense scrutiny by the FBI.

The facts are simple enough. As Michael Wells heard through the grapevine, I had an affair with a married professor and it got out of hand. After four months, I tried to end it. He wouldn't let me. To emphasize my point, I slept with an ER doctor the professor knew. The professor promptly attempted suicide. He didn't end his life, but he did end his teaching career, and also my days in medical school. My grandfather could probably have used his influence to get me reinstated, but the truth was, I didn't want to go back. Certainly not like that.

The FBI will want to know all about Nathan Malik—or Jonathan Gentry, as I knew him then—but I don't remember much. I was drunk a lot of that time. What I do remember about those years begs a question. Why have I always involved myself with married men? Therapists tell me it's the impossibility of such relationships that draws me. Single guys always fall in love; they end up possessive and wanting me forever. I don't want permanence—I didn't back then, anyway—and married men are a pragmatic solution. They're romantic, sexually experienced, and committed elsewhere. I'm well aware of the Freudian implications of my lifestyle. I grew up mostly without a father, so I'm attracted to older men. What of it? The moral issue bothers me sometimes, but that's ultimately the man's problem. What's dismayed me more is learning firsthand just how little love there is in many marriages—even those of relatively short duration. Yet here I am now, wanting Sean for myself. For my baby. Forever. The irony is almost too much. And despite my dreams of a blissful future, I've always sensed a dark truth in my deepest being: there's no happily ever after for girls like me.

My cell phone is ringing again. This time I answer.

"Where are you?" Sean asks.

"Halfway to Baton Rouge, doing eighty-five in a forty-five zone. I've got my flashers on. If the Highway Patrol stops me, I'm telling them to call you."

"No problem. Look, the FBI got their court order. They'll have their odontologist at Dr. Shubb's office checking Malik's dental records long before you get here."

"Damn." I hate that it won't be me who makes the comparison, but the point of all this is to stop the killer, as I scolded Sean this morning. "Good. That's good. But X-rays may not be enough. He should take alginate impressions of Malik's actual teeth."

"That's specified in the court order. If he needs impressions to make the ID, he'll get them. They're also going to swab Malik's mouth for DNA."

My foot depresses the accelerator, and the Audi zips up to a hundred miles per hour. Even if it's not me making the comparison, I have to be involved in this. "Do they still want to talk to me?"

"Absolutely. John Kaiser wants to call you right now and ask you about Malik."

"I'm ready."

"Be totally honest with him, Cat. He's FBI, but he's a good guy. You can trust him. He was in Vietnam, like your dad."

This admonition angers me. "*Totally* honest, you said? So if he asks about you and me . . . ?"

"You know what I mean. I'll talk to you soon."

Sean cuts the connection. Less than a minute later, my phone rings. It's Kaiser. The FBI agent's voice is lower than Sean's, and more mea-

sured in cadence. He asks me to summarize my time in medical
school and my contact with Nathan Malik. I give him a concise
account, and he doesn't interrupt me.

"So you only met him a few times," Kaiser says when I finish.
"And never alone?"

"Right. I mean, we were alone in the sense of him cornering me in
the next room away from a dinner party. But that's it. All he did was
hit on me."

"What specifics do you remember about him?"

"He didn't drink."

"Why does that stick in your mind?"

"Because I did. A lot. We all did. But not Malik. He was the
observer type. Superior and aloof. Sat back and judged everybody,
you know? Sniped. It was when I was drunk that he came on to me.
Which surprised me, because until he did, I thought he was gay."

"Really?" There's a pause. I picture Kaiser making notes on a pad.
"And you've never seen him in New Orleans? Not in the supermar-
ket? The mall? Nothing like that?"

"No. And I'd remember."

"Do you have any idea why he changed his name?"

"No. Where did he get the name Malik?"

"It was his mother's maiden name."

"Huh. That's pretty common, I guess?"

"Not so much with men," Kaiser replies. "But it happens."

The FBI agent is silent for a brief period. "So basically, Nathan
Malik—then called Gentry—was a friend of this doctor you were
having an affair with. So it's the doctor I need to talk to."

"Definitely."

"Can you spell his name for me?"

"Christopher Omartian, MD. He's an EENT. I think he practices
in Alabama now. Mobile."

"How do you know that?"

"He sent me a letter a couple of years ago."

"Did you respond?"

"I threw it in the trash."

Kaiser thanks me for my time, says he might need to call back,
then starts to say good-bye.

"Agent Kaiser?"

"Yes?"

"What about the two female relatives of the victims? The ones you used to link Dr. Malik to the murders?"

"What about them?"

"Have you talked to them yet?"

"We've tried with one, but she's very suspicious. Bordering on paranoid. Won't tell us a thing about Malik. Look, I really need to run, Dr. Ferry. Thank you for your help."

Kaiser signs off.

I figure Sean will call back immediately, but my phone doesn't ring. Suppressing the urge to call him, I slow the Audi along the curving road to St. Francisville, where John James Audubon painted many of his famous birds.

The ANGOLA PENITENTIARY sign flashes past on my right, and my stomach does a little flip. Angola means many things to me. As a child I attended the prison rodeo and marveled at the cavalier way the convicts risked their lives with the bulls and broncos. But what Angola means most to me is the island. The prison road is the one we traveled to reach DeSalle Island from the eastern bank of the Mississippi. The old river channel that guards the island's eastern shore had to be crossed by boat for most of the year, but during the summer, an oil company maintained a low-water bridge to service its wells on the island. That bridge led to an exotic world of shadows and light, of joy and terror, of memory and forgetting. I made childhood friends on the island—black friends mostly—then lost them to the realities of a social order I didn't even know I was part of. I worked the ground only to see what I'd planted washed away by floods. I cared for animals only to see them slaughtered for food. I learned to hunt and to kill, and then to hate the killing.

Death and the island are inextricably bound in my mind. When I was ten years old, four hardened killers escaped from Angola by floating out into the river on a log. The prison chase team radioed my grandfather that the river's current might drive the escapees ashore on DeSalle Island. They sent men with dogs to comb the island for a solid day. They found nothing. The next night, Grandpapa, his white foreman, and two handpicked black men rode off on horseback with four prize hounds. At dawn the next day, two escapees were locked in the dog run behind the barn, their hands and feet bound with bailing wire. The other two lay dead on the barn floor, their bodies ravaged by dog bites and bullets.

Last year my grandmother drowned during a picnic on the sandbar. One minute she was laughing, the next she was gone. Sluffed into the current with thirty feet of sand, her body never found. I wasn't there that day, and it was probably best. I would have killed myself trying to save her. I know the Mississippi River in a way most people never will. Where most fear the great muddy tide, I respect it. When I was sixteen, I swam across it on a dare, to prove that I feared nothing. My reckless courage almost killed me that day. The island and the river have claimed many more lives than those convicts and my grandmother, but I don't want to dwell on that now. *Don't borrow trouble,* my grandmother used to say.

South of St. Francisville, the road broadens to four lanes. I open up the throttle and go flat out on the straightaway to Baton Rouge. I'm passing the main exit for LSU when Sean finally calls back.

"I'm in Baton Rouge now," I tell him. "One hour away."

"You can slow down, Cat."

My chest tightens. I can tell from his voice that the news is bad. "What happened?"

"Malik's teeth don't match the bite marks on the victims."

I blink in bewilderment. "Are you sure? Who did the comparison?"

"An FBI guy named Abrams. Says it wasn't even close."

"Shit. He knows his business."

"Looks like the Malik connection wasn't the break we thought it was."

I whip into the left lane and pass a rattling Winnebago. "Sean, there's no way Malik's connection to the victims could be coincidence. It's the key to the whole case. We just haven't figured out how it all fits together yet."

"You got any ideas?"

I think furiously. "Malik's DNA may still match the saliva in the bite marks."

"But his teeth don't match the marks."

"He might have used someone else's teeth."

"What?"

"It happened in that book, *Red Dragon*. The Tooth Fairy used his grandmother's false teeth to bite victims. With him it was part of the murder fantasy, but with Malik it could simply be staging."

"Where would Malik get false teeth?"

"Anywhere! He could have stolen an articulated model from Dr. Shubb's office. Just veer into the lab on his way out to the front desk, and boom, he'd have a working set of teeth."

"And the saliva could still be his? Like he licked the wounds or something?"

"Just like that. Or it could be someone else's. To throw us off."

"I'll check this, but it seems far out. The FBI has given the DNA test on Malik top priority, but you know what that means."

"Damn." I gun the Audi around a tractor-trailer. "Does Malik have alibis for the murder nights?"

"Two out of four. He was with patients, or so he says."

"Did they confirm?"

"Shit, he won't tell us who they are! He's stonewalling us."

"Can he get away with that?"

"Not for long. But he's one contrary son of a bitch, and so far he's hanging tough."

"Huh. Maybe he really is innocent."

"Why would an innocent man be so stubborn about hiding things? Especially with people's lives at stake?"

"You're thinking like a cop, Sean. We all have something to hide. You know that."

"Yeah, well, I am a cop. And I want to know what the son of a bitch is hiding."

"He may feel that his patients' privacy outweighs the risk to their lives. He may feel that even revealing their names could put them at greater risk."

"I think he's just an asshole."

I remember the cold fish I knew as Jonathan Gentry. "You could be right. Look, at this speed I'll be in New Orleans in forty minutes. Where should I go?"

"I don't know. Kaiser isn't sure how he wants to play it yet, and the task force is sort of paralyzed. You'd better just go to your place first."

"Where will you be?"

Static crackles through the silence. "I'd like to be there waiting for you."

I close my eyes. If we meet at my house, there will be no way to avoid the subject I've been keeping to myself for the past three days. Not without drinking, anyway. "God help me," I whisper.

"What?" asks Sean. "You're breaking up."

Something in my chest lets go. This morning's events at Malmaison combined with the anticipation of nailing Malik had blotted out almost everything else in my mind. But now reality is crashing in like a dark tide. I am pregnant by a married man. And no matter what kind of spin I try to put on it, the bottom line comes up the same: *I'm a fool. A whore. No, worse, a slut* . . .

"Cat? Are you there?"

"I don't know."

"What did you say?"

"I said I'll see you in an hour."

CHAPTER

13

I press my garage-door opener and anxiously watch the white panels rise. Sean's car is parked inside my garage. A dark green Saab turbo, ten years old.

I walk into my house with my purse in one hand and a paper sack in the other. The sack holds a bottle of Grey Goose, already half-empty. I pass through the kitchen and den like an exhausted soldier, then climb the stairs to the living room, which looks out over Lake Pontchartrain. Sean is waiting on the sofa, facing the lake. The picture window is covered with drops of condensation from the air conditioner, but I can still see sails on the horizon.

Sean isn't watching the sails. He's watching a golf tournament on ESPN. He points at the paper bag. "The news about Malik's teeth bum you out that bad?"

I set my purse on a glass-topped table in the corner. Then I take a highball glass from a shelf on the wall, pour two fingers of vodka into it, and take a bittersweet sip.

"I'm not thinking about Malik."

"Hey." Sean stands and comes to me. "You need a hug."

I do, but not the kind he wants to give me. As his arms close around me, I feel the temptation to yield to his embrace. He squeezes gently at first, working his fingers into the muscles of my lower back. A week ago I would have loved this. Now I feel a manic pressure building within me. As predictably as the evening tide, his erection presses into my abdomen. I feel only revulsion.

"Hey," he says as I pull away. "What's the matter?"

"I don't want that."

His green eyes soften. "It's okay. I can wait awhile."

"I don't want it later either."

Sean leans back to study me but keeps his arms around my waist. "What's the matter, babe? What's happening? Another depressive episode?"

His casual use of medical jargon irritates me. "I just don't want to, okay?"

"But you always want to."

"No, *you* always want to. I just never say no."

He stares at me in disbelief. "You mean you make love to me when you don't want to?"

"Sometimes."

"Sometimes? Like how many times?"

"I don't know. More than a few. I know how important it is to you."

His hands drop from my waist. "And you waited over a year to tell me this?"

"Looks like it."

The look of pain in his face is like the look of dumb hurt on an animal when it's been struck for no apparent reason. *God,* I think. *Is there anything on earth more fragile than male pride?*

Sean swallows hard and gazes out toward the lake. After a while, he looks back, his face composed. "You and I have been through some serious shit together. Your mood swings, some bad arguments. I've spent the night here and done nothing but hold you all night when you were suicidally depressed."

This is true, though on most of those nights he tried to make love with me.

"You *have* to tell me what's going on," he says.

I want to. Yet I can't. I take another sip from my glass.

"Why did you stop drinking? I mean it's great that you did, but what prompted it? Was it just another crazy tangent, like yoga? And why are you drinking again now?"

It would be so easy to tell him. But why do I have to? He's a detective, for God's sake. Why can't he figure out the situation and just tell me it's okay, without me having to say it? Is the answer that hard to see? Has anything else *ever* prompted me to stop drinking?

"Cat," he says softly. "Please."

"I'm pregnant," I blurt, and tears fill my eyes.

Sean blinks. "What?"

"You heard me."

"But . . . how? I mean, you're on the pill, right?"

"Yes. I was. But I took those antibiotics for my bladder infection, and that interfered with my pills."

He nods for a few moments, then stops. "Didn't you know that could happen?"

Here it comes. The accusation. "I only took three Cipros. I didn't think that would make a difference."

"But you're a doctor. I mean—"

My composure snaps like brittle glass, and suddenly I'm screaming. *"I didn't do it on purpose, okay? You gave me the goddamn infection! You're the one who wanted to have nonstop sex for three days!"*

Clearly unprepared for this level of anger, Sean takes two steps backward. "I know you didn't do it on purpose, Cat. It's just . . . a lot to get my mind around. How long have you known?"

"Three days, I think. Almost four now. I'm not sure anymore. My sense of time isn't working too well. I've been off my meds for three days. I know that for sure."

"Off your Lexapro?"

"And the Depakote. Depakote can cause spina bifida if you take it in the first twelve weeks."

"Okay, but shit, you have to get back on the Lex. You know what happens when you skip."

Yes, I go manic . . .

"You stopped drinking when you found out you were pregnant," Sean thinks aloud.

I can't think of anything to say.

"But you're drinking again now. Did you lose the baby?"

"No. I couldn't tell you I was pregnant without a drink. Isn't that pathetic? I've been taking Valium, too."

His eyes narrow in anger. "What the hell for?"

"To keep from getting the d.t.'s."

He tries to take the glass of vodka from my hand. When I resist, he grabs my wrist and jerks at the glass with his other hand. I let him take it, but then I get the bottle from the table. "Try to take this away and I'll brain you with it."

He starts toward me, then stops. "Jesus, Cat. Think about the baby, will you?"

My laughter rides an undercurrent of hysteria. "Is that what you're thinking about? Or are you thinking about the wife and kids you already have? And whether you can still keep me a secret through all of this?"

He rubs his forehead with both hands, drags his fingertips back through his hair. I see more gray when he does that. "Look, I just need some time to absorb this. To think about the implications."

"The implications," I echo. "Let's see . . . they're pretty straight-forward. A: I'm pregnant. B: I'm keeping the baby. C: a baby needs a father as well as a mother. D: this baby either has a father or it doesn't."

"It sounds simple," Sean agrees. "But it's not. You know that. Look, my honest answer right now is that I'm not sure what to do."

"Yeah, I got that."

He gives me a pleading look. "Did you think I'd know in the first five minutes?"

"I hoped you would."

He tries to come to me again, but I hold up my hands. "Just go, okay? Leave me alone." The next words spill out almost of their own accord. "And leave your key here when you go."

"What? Cat—"

"*You heard me!*"

Sean stares at me in silence for nearly a minute. In his eyes I see a long history of hurt and confusion. He looks away, then pulls his key from his pocket and lays it on the glass table. "I'm going to check on you tomorrow. Even if you don't want me to."

Then he goes downstairs.

When I hear his car start in the garage, I feel my chest caving in. But I have the antidote for that. Taking the Grey Goose bottle from the bag, I go down to my bedroom and lie on the duvet. With my free hand, I rub a little circle on my tummy.

"Just you and me now, kid," I say in a desolate voice. "Just you and me."

I sip from the bottle, savoring the anesthetic bite as it spreads across my tongue. I hate myself for doing it, but I swallow anyway. Self-hatred is a familiar emotion to me, and familiarity brings comfort. As the chemical warmth diffuses through my veins, I hear the sound of rain again. The rain from my waking dreams. Not the soft hiss of drops falling on my shingles, but the hard percussive patter of rain hitting a tin roof.

I hope oblivion comes soon.

I awaken to the hiss of rain, but this time the sound is real. My bedroom window stands open, and Sean Regan is leaning in through it, his hair and shoulders soaking wet. A corona of gray light shows behind him. I look at my alarm clock: 11:50 A.M. Sixteen hours have disappeared down a hole.

"You wouldn't answer your phone," Sean says.

"I'm sorry about last night," I reply, my throat dry and croaking. "That's not how I wanted to handle it."

"That's not why I'm here."

The bottle of Grey Goose spilled during the night, saturating my sheets. Self-loathing fills me like poison. "Why are you here?"

"Our boy hit again this morning."

"No way." I rub my eyes, not really believing it. "It's only been two days. Are you sure?"

"The victim was a fifty-six-year-old white male. Bite marks all over him. No forced entry, body found by the maid. We don't have a ballistics match yet, but we do have this."

Sean holds up a piece of paper and extends it toward the bed. It's a photograph. Even from this distance, I can see that it's of a window. On the glass above the sill, written in blood, are the words MY WORK IS NEVER DONE.

"Holy shit."

"We never released that to the media," he says. "So I'd say the ballistics match is pretty much a formality. Same for the bite marks."

I roll over and try to rise, but my whole body feels sore. Maybe after three days sober, the vodka was a shock to my system. Still, there was enough left to soak my sheets, so I didn't drink all of it. "Where was Nathan Malik last night?"

"Home all night. Under surveillance."

"Are you sure he was in his house the whole time?"

"We didn't have anybody sleeping with him. But he was there."

I wave Sean inside and push myself up to a sitting position. "What should I do? I want to do something. I want to help."

He climbs through the window and sits on the floor, his legs crossed Indian-style. The posture makes him look twenty years younger, but his drawn face betrays his age. From the shadowy circles under his eyes—eyes that carry twice the spiritual burden they did yesterday—I'd guess he's slept three consecutive hours since I last saw him.

"Do you want to talk about the baby?" he asks.

I close my eyes. "Not right now. Not like this."

"Then we'll do what we always do."

"What?" I ask suspiciously.

"Work the case. Right here."

I feel relief and a strange spark of excitement. "The kitchen table?"

"It's worked before." He picks the television remote off the floor, switches it on, and tunes the set to the local news. The screen shows Captain Carmen Piazza leaving a blue two-story house. Special Agent John Kaiser walks a step behind her.

"That's the scene," Sean says. "Old Metairie. The media's amping up. Story's going national. Some cops have started calling this guy the Vampire Lestat."

"Tell me you're kidding," I mutter, wishing I'd left a bottle of water by my bed.

Sean laughs darkly. "Hey, this is New Orleans. And it fits, if you think about it. No witnesses, no forced entry, affluent male victims, teeth marks everywhere."

I wonder what the killer will make of his new appellation. If my past experience with serials is a guide, he'll love it.

"Why don't you take a shower?" Sean says. "I'll give you the details when you get out."

I roll slowly off the bed and walk to the bathroom, unbuttoning my soiled blouse as I go.

"Hey, Cat?"

I turn back.

Sean's green eyes focus intently on mine. "When you're ready to talk about the baby, I am, too."

There's a hitch in my heartbeat. "Okay."

His eyes go back to the television.

CHAPTER

14

Sean and I sit on opposite sides of my kitchen table, case files and photographs spread out between us. We've enacted this ritual many times before, but in the past we sat on the same side of the table. Today this new arrangement seems more appropriate.

For the past fifteen months, it's been Sean's habit to build a private file on every major murder case assigned to him. He keeps these files in a locked cabinet at my house, selectively adding to them as new evidence comes in. He digitally photographs what he can't get me access to and dubs audiotapes of most witness interviews and interrogations. He's broken countless rules and probably some laws by doing this, but the result has been to jail more killers, so he doesn't struggle with the ethics too much.

Sean brewed coffee while I was in the shower, and by the time I emerged wearing scrub pants and a Pearl Jam sweatshirt, a cup was waiting by my chair. This kind of courtesy grew rare after the first few months of our relationship, but today it doesn't surprise me. The pregnancy is making him walk on eggshells.

Captain Piazza hasn't officially suspended Sean from the task force, but she did remove him as lead NOPD detective on the case. She only toured him through the crime scene this morning because his case clearance rate is so high. Piazza doesn't know that Sean uses a lot of help from me to accomplish this, but after the captain's little lecture at the LeGendre crime scene, I think she may suspect it.

In any case, Sean's information flow has not been cut off. His partner is shuttling between police headquarters and the task force headquarters at the FBI building, keeping Sean informed of all new developments by cell phone. Ironically, the fortresslike new FBI field office is situated just five minutes up the shore of Lake Pontchartrain from my house. Inside that building, at least fifty people are studying the same information we're looking at now.

"James Calhoun," I read, naming the fifth victim. "What makes him different than the others?"

"Nothing," says Sean, leaning his chair back on two legs. "He was alone in the house. No sign of forced entry. One paralyzing shot to the spine, then the bite marks, delivered antemortem like the others . . ."

Delivered is a pretty sterile word to describe the savage act of tearing human flesh with teeth. But that kind of semantic distance creeps into law enforcement work all the time, just as it does in medicine. When thinking about murder, I always try to keep the immediacy of the violence in the forefront of my mind.

". . . and a coup de grâce to the head," Sean finishes. "End of story."

"Trace evidence?"

"Aside from the note written in blood—the victim's blood—nothing new."

"This guy is too good," I say with frustration. "'My work is never done.' He must be wearing a space suit while he does this work of his."

"Then how is he biting them?"

"He left saliva in the bite marks again?"

"Yep."

"Huh. Is there any way Nathan Malik could have gotten out last night without his surveillance team knowing?"

"I don't think so." Sean leans forward, bringing the front legs of his chair back to the floor. "But there's always a way, I guess."

"No thermal-imaging camera to make sure a warm body was in the house?"

"No. They were going to start using one tonight. It's been about a week between each hit, like you said. I don't think the feeling of urgency was there last night."

"Famous last words. Time of death?"

"Probably about seven this morning."

I feel a peculiar shock of surprise. "So the crime happened in daylight. Lots of people moving around then. Getting their *Times-Picayune*, leaving for work."

He stares at me in an odd way, then shakes his head. "It's Sunday, Cat. Nobody's leaving for work."

"Church, then," I say quickly, my cheeks coloring with embarrassment.

Sean's gaze doesn't waver, and I sense that he's ruthlessly gauging my mental state. "No witnesses so far," he says at length. "We canvassed like crazy. We're still trying to locate a couple of neighbors, but so far, nobody saw anything."

"The killer could have entered the house during the night," I point out. "And only left during the day."

"Let's get off Calhoun for a minute," Sean says, tapping a pen on some papers in front of him. "The whole string—all five victims—what are you thinking? Just off the top of your head."

"I think it's Malik. And if he didn't do Calhoun this morning, somebody's helping him."

"That's who's leaving the bite marks? An accomplice?"

"Maybe, but not necessarily. That could still be Malik."

Sean squints as though he doesn't understand. "Yesterday you said something about the killer using fake teeth to make the marks. I didn't really catch all that. And when you got home . . ." He trails off, not wanting to mention the awful scene we played out while I was drunk.

"I said the killer could be using someone else's teeth."

"What did you mean? Like dentures?"

"Dentures would work."

"But how would he make the marks look real? Wear them over his own teeth?"

"He could do that. But he'd get his own saliva in the wound doing that. There's another way. When dentists make dentures, they're attached to a hinged metal device called an articulator. It simulates the opening and closing of the jaw. That's how we fine-tune the dentures for proper occlusion."

"Occlusion?"

"The way the teeth come together. The bite. Malik could make the marks with that."

Sean looks intrigued. "How easy would it be for him to get one of those?"

"He could order one off the Internet. Or as I said yesterday, he could have stolen one out of Dr. Shubb's office lab. You should check and see if Shubb has lost an articulator in the past couple of years. He might not even have noticed it missing."

Sean makes a note in a small wire-bound pad. "And the dentures?"

"Same thing. Malik could have stolen them. Or they might belong to a relative, like Francis Dolarhyde's grandmother."

Sean looks blank. "Who?"

"The killer in *Red Dragon*."

"Oh, yeah. You mentioned that. I saw the movie, but I don't remember anything about dentures."

"You should have read the book. It was a big deal psychologically, those teeth. But for us, the point is that Malik could be using dentures, and he could get them almost anywhere. A family member— living or dead—is one possibility. I want to go through everything you know about Malik's family."

"Just a minute. You couldn't tell the bite marks were made by dentures as opposed to real teeth?"

"No."

"What about the saliva in the wounds?"

"Again, that could still be Malik's. But it's more likely to belong to an accomplice, if there is one. Or the killer could even be swabbing in someone else's saliva."

"Where the hell would he get that?"

I shrug. "One of his patients? All we know from the saliva so far is that the DNA in it belongs to a Caucasian male."

Sean mulls this over. "I guess all Malik needs is some spit from a guy he knows we'd never check. I can see it." He takes a sip of coffee. "The paralyzing gunshot keeps coming back to me."

"It's not always paralyzing." I shuffle through the autopsy reports of previous victims. "Call it incapacitating."

"That's splitting hairs. The point is, excellent marksmanship."

"The fax you sent me said Malik served in Vietnam. As a medic, I think. Which means he probably saw action."

"That doesn't make him a good marksman. Especially with a handgun."

"Does Malik have any handguns registered in his name?"

"One. A .45 automatic."

The murders were committed with a .32-caliber pistol. "And they searched Malik's house already?"

"Top to bottom. No other weapon found."

"What *did* they find? A shrink's house . . . had to be some weird stuff in there."

Sean waves his hand as if he doesn't want to be distracted. He's always been more linear in his thinking than I have. "Let's stay with the gun for now. Funny weapon for this kind of crime, you ask me."

"More of a Saturday night special than an organized killer's weapon."

He nods. "Or maybe a cop's throwdown gun."

"Well, it obviously does the job." I point at a photo of Colonel Frank Moreland's naked corpse, a neat hole drilled through its forehead. "We should find out if Malik visits any shooting ranges around here. See if anyone knows how good a shot he is."

"The task force is already on that. We need to get outside the box, Cat. Think of things they'll miss. Like the dentures thing."

"Are you going to tell the task force my theory about that?"

"Sure," Sean says casually. "I'm talking to John Kaiser. He's a good guy, for a Fed."

"Are you going to tell him I came up with it?"

Sean freezes, his face uncertain. "Do you want me to?"

"What if I say yes?"

"If you say yes, I'll tell him."

I hold his gaze without blinking. "Yes."

"Okay, then. I'll tell him." Sean looks sincere, but I wonder if he'll follow through.

Colonel Moreland's photo brings another thought to mind. In some serial murder cases, close analysis of the first murder scene ultimately breaks open the case. The reason is simple. Serial killers, like any other hobbyist, get better with practice. They're frequently very anxious during their first murder—they may not even have meant to kill their first victim—and they make stupid mistakes. Mistakes they never repeat at later scenes. But the NOMURS killer is different.

"First-victim angle," I say, knowing Sean will understand my shorthand.

"Yeah?"

"It's led us nowhere."

"Right."

"Why?"

"The guy's a prodigy." Sean shakes his head with something like respect. "It's like he walked out of nowhere onto the pitcher's mound at Yankee Stadium and threw a no-hitter. And he's thrown nothing but no-hitters ever since."

"What does that tell you?"

"Either he's killed before, or . . ."

"Or he knows a lot about murder," I finish.

Sean nods. "Yeah."

"Who would know that?"

"A cop."

"Who else?"

"Crime-scene tech. Forensic tech. Pathologist. True-crime reader."

"Psychiatrist," I say softly.

Sean looks unimpressed. "Maybe. What's your point?"

"My point is that *every* killer makes mistakes the first time out. Maybe not a technical mistake. Maybe it's just his choice of victim. Why was Colonel Moreland killed first? Was he random? I don't think so. There's got to be a reason."

"Kaiser's all over that kind of thing, Cat. The task force is taking apart every victim's family."

"Just bear with me. Any likely suspects in Moreland's family? He's not from here, right? Just retired here."

"Yeah, but he's got a daughter living here and a son in Biloxi. Daughter is Stacey Lorio, a registered nurse." Sean shuffles through the pile of paper on the table and comes up with a five-by-seven photo. It shows a blonde woman in her midthirties with a hard-looking face. "Thirty-six years old, divorced. Works two jobs. A private clinic and nights at Touro Infirmary."

"Alibis for the murders?"

"Rock solid."

"The son?"

Sean comes up with another photo, this one a wallet-size shot of a good-looking man in a blue uniform. "Frank Moreland Junior. A major in the air force. Stationed at Keesler Air Force Base. Big family man. Medals out the yinyang. His alibis are bulletproof."

"Neither one has any connection to Malik?"

"Not that we can find."

"Shit." I shift in my chair and take a sip of coffee. "Okay, forget that for now. Let's talk about Malik's patients. Do you know yet if James Calhoun has any family members who've been treated by Malik?"

The hint of a smile plays across Sean's lips. "You're gonna love this."

"What?"

"Malik's still refusing to hand over that information."

"He hasn't given you the names of his patients yet?"

"Nope. He's arguing doctor-patient privilege."

"That won't hold up in a case like this, will it?"

Sean shakes his head. "No. We can show a judge a strong likelihood that the killer is choosing his victims from Malik's patient base. That creates a situation of imminent danger, which is a public safety issue. That should override the privilege."

Sean knows what he's talking about. Three years ago, he earned a law degree by going to night school. He didn't really want to, but after being wounded in the line of duty, he let his wife persuade him that a career change was in order. Hoping to improve his marital situation—not to mention his financial one—Sean attended night school while working full-time as a detective. He graduated seventh in his class, retired from the force, and went to work for a criminal defense firm. In less than six months he was going crazy. His wife pleaded with him to try working for the district attorney, but Sean despised the man. He told her he was going back to police work, and that she would have to deal with it. She did not deal with it well.

"Our UNSUB isn't actually killing Dr. Malik's patients," I point out, using the FBI's jargon for "unknown subject." "He's killed *relatives* of two patients. That's all you can prove. Maybe Malik is relying on that to shield his records from the police."

"Won't hold up," Sean says with certainty. "A judge will consider the privacy issue, but with our UNSUB killing so frequently, we'll get the names of Malik's patients, at the very least."

"But not the records?"

"We should get those, too. Everything but private notes Malik takes during sessions."

"Couldn't those be important?"

"Obviously. But we won't get them. Lots of precedent for that."

I stand and begin to pace my kitchen. "The real question is, why is Malik holding this stuff back?"

"He claims his patients' lives could be destroyed if things they've told him in confidence become public. He says some of them are at risk if it even becomes known they're in therapy."

Yesterday I suggested this rationale to Sean myself, but today—given the new victim—it seems a stretch. "At risk from whom?"

"He wouldn't say. I'm assuming from family members, since the two women we know about kept the fact that they were seeing Malik secret from their families. Maybe from boyfriends?"

"What if Malik's not the killer, but he's *shielding* the killer?" I suggest.

"Then he's an accessory to murder. If he has prior knowledge of a crime, he's bound by law to try to prevent it. That means telling the police."

I stop pacing. "What if he's only told about the crime after the fact? Is he like a priest hearing it in confession?"

"Same principle." Sean looks at the table, his lips pursed tightly. "Yes, I think that would fall under the privilege."

I sense that I'm onto something. "What if a patient comes in four weeks in a row, and says, 'I killed somebody a couple of days ago'?"

"Past conduct is protected under the privilege. If it weren't, nobody would ever disclose anything to their shrink. Or to their priest, or their lawyer. Exceptions to the privilege are based on the risk of imminent harm."

I take a banana from a bowl on the counter, start to peel it, then put it back. "Okay, so Malik could be shielding the killer. Legally. Why would he do that?"

"Because he's an arrogant asshole. An academic who can't even begin to imagine the reality of these murders."

"A combat medic probably has a pretty good idea about the reality of murder." As Sean concedes this with a sigh, I feel a sudden rush of excitement. "What if he's shielding the killer because he believes the murders are *justified*?"

"Like a twisted moral stand?"

"Maybe not so twisted. An abuse victim kills the man who's been raping her for years. In her mind, it's self-defense."

"And to Malik, justifiable homicide," Sean adds, an edge of enthusiasm in his voice. "The problem is, we have five victims. You think one of Malik's patients was abused by all five of these guys?"

"It's possible. If there was some kind of pedophile ring or something."

"You're saying the killings are revenge over something that happened a long time ago?"

"Malik specializes in repressed memories, right? Let's talk about sex for a minute."

Misunderstanding me, Sean gets a twinkle in his eye. He starts to make a joke, but the twinkle vanishes as he remembers our present situation.

"Does Malik treat both men and women?" I ask. "I think Dr. Shubb said he did."

"We know he's treated some men. We don't know how many. The task force is talking to every psychologist and psychiatrist in Louisiana and Mississippi, looking for anyone who's referred patients to Malik. They already found a psychologist who referred a guy to him last year."

"For sexual abuse?"

"The shrink wouldn't say without a court order."

"*Damn*. How long—realistically—before you can force Malik to turn over his patients' names?"

"Kaiser thinks he can get a judge to order it this afternoon. Maybe the records, too."

"And if Malik refuses?"

"He'll be in contempt of court."

"Immediate jail?"

"No, there'd have to be a hearing first. But he will go to jail."

"Do they set bail in cases like that?"

"No. Because on a contempt charge, the prisoner can walk out of jail any time he wants to. All he has to do is comply with the court's order."

"Do you think Malik will do jail time to protect his patients' names?"

Sean gives a knowing smile. "I think we'll have those names by tonight."

"Good. Hey, did you guys search Malik's office, too? For guns, I mean?"

"Yeah. Malik was present during the search, and he made sure no one looked at his records. The records were specifically excluded in the warrant. We didn't want to waste time arguing that with a judge."

"But were there records there? Did you see actual files in the cabinets?"

"I wasn't on the scene. I'll check, but I'm sure someone would have mentioned it if they were missing."

"Don't assume anything, Sean. I'll bet Malik's already moved those records off-site. Have you kept men at his office to pick up any patients who show up for appointments?"

"Hell, yeah. But nobody's shown up. We can't figure it out. How do they know not to come? We've tapped Malik's phones since we suspected him, and he hasn't called anyone to cancel. He doesn't *have* a fucking receptionist."

"And of course you've gone to the victims' families and asked point-blank if anyone is a patient of Malik's?"

"Yeah, but we're being cautious about that. Just in case Malik's right about his patients being in danger. It wouldn't look good if Malik warned us that his patients could be harmed, and then we got one of them killed in some kind of domestic dispute."

"Cautious how? Are they trying to get female family members off by themselves?"

"Yeah. But it's hard to know who they all are, what with marriages and divorces and all."

My mind drifts back to mid-July, after the second victim was killed. Andrus Riviere, the retired pharmacist. I went with Sean to interview the Riviere family, and there I saw a strange sight. A granddaughter of Mr. Riviere's was running joyously through the house as though preparing for a birthday party rather than mourning her grandfather. And it wasn't a momentary burst of energy. She continued to behave that way throughout our visit. About seven years old, she stuck in my mind because she didn't seem like an insensitive child. In fact, when I spoke to her, she seemed quite the opposite. The calm regard in her eyes made me feel as if I were talking to an adult.

"How do you feel about a woman committing these crimes?" I ask.

Sean stands and goes to the refrigerator, but instead of opening it, he looks back at me. "I like the revenge-for-abuse idea, but it's hard to see a woman doing what we've seen. There's almost no precedent in the literature. Female serial killers? Aileen Wuornos is about it."

"That's not strictly true. Almost five percent of serials are female."

Sean looks expectantly at me. He's an instinctive investigator, and while he is very good, most of his knowledge is based on his own experience or that of other detectives around the country—usually men with whom he has a personal relationship. I've made it a point to educate myself in the professional literature of serial homicide, and my knowledge is far broader. This often irritates Sean, but he's pragmatic enough to make use of what I know.

"Female serials operate for an average of eight years before being caught," I tell him. "That's twice as long as male offenders. And one of their hallmarks is a very clean crime scene."

"Okay," he allows, "but don't most of them have a male accomplice?"

"Eighty-six percent use an accomplice, but it's not always male. What works against a female here is the type of crime. Most female serials are so-called 'black widows,' who kill their husbands, or angels of death, who kill hospital patients. Often the victims are family members. The only female serial classified as committing sexual homicide against strangers and acting alone is Wuornos."

Sean looks almost smug.

"But I think she was wrongly classified," I go on. "Aileen Wuornos killed to punish men for sexually abusing her. One of Malik's patients could be doing the same thing."

"I'm not saying it's impossible," says Sean. "But the crime signature weighs against it. The marksmanship, the nudity, the torture—"

"Revenge," I argue. "You have very little cooling-off period in revenge killings, and that fits this case. And the bite marks are almost certainly made after the incapacitating gunshot. A woman would have to disable her victims before getting close enough to bite like that."

"Do you really see a woman ripping these guys up with her teeth?"

I've had some pretty violent urges myself. "A sexually abused woman probably carries around a lot of repressed rage, Sean."

"Yeah, but women turn rage inward. That's why they commit suicide, not homicide."

He's right about that. "What about Colonel Moreland's daughter? Stacey Lorio? Army brat, tough-looking woman. You said she had alibis for all the murders?"

"Yep, all corroborated. Couple of times with friends, couple of times with her ex-husband. Her ex doesn't even like her, but he confirmed. Talked to him myself. He said, 'To tell you the truth, I can't stand the bitch, but I still like to screw her now and again.'"

"Sounds like a great guy." Frustration is making me crave alcohol. "Okay then, a male patient of Malik's. Abused as a boy. A large percentage of convicted serial killers were abused as young boys."

"Now you're talking," Sean says, his tone warming. "The second we get that patient list, I'll start working that angle." He bends over and stretches his back, the vertebrae popping like Chinese firecrackers. "You want to take a break?"

My body tenses. Normally, when given an opportunity to be alone for an extended period like this, we would spend much of it in bed. But today the bedroom door is closed, and it's going to stay that way.

My eyes must have betrayed my thoughts, because Sean quickly says, "I was thinking of running over to R and O's, getting a couple of oyster po-boys."

I relax—a little. "That sounds good."

"I'll be back in twenty minutes."

"Look, you don't have to stay here all day. I want to read Malik's book."

Sean looks at me with calm sincerity. "I want to stay. If that's all right with you?"

I can't help but smile. "Okay. Why don't you get the food, then?"

He gets his keys and heads out to the garage. No kiss good-bye, just a light touch on my forearm.

I go into the bedroom and strip the vodka-soaked sheets, then carry them to the washing machine. The alcohol evaporating from the cotton is enough to ignite a craving that itches in every cell of my body. My mind goes to the Valium in my purse, but it's time to start weaning myself off that. A birth defect isn't the first gift I want to give the baby growing inside me.

To take my mind off my craving—as if anything could—I go back to the kitchen table and pick up Nathan Malik's book, which Sean borrowed from the Tulane Medical School library. Titled *The River Lethe: Repressed Memory and Soul Murder*, it's a thin volume, only 130 pages long. Its dark jacket shows an eerie, moonlit scene: an old, robed man standing in a boat in a river, and a frail young woman waiting to board. The image seems unlikely to inspire feelings of well-being in someone who's been sexually abused. But maybe it presses a button in such victims that prompts them to want to discover what's between the covers.

The book jacket has the opposite effect on me. Despite my desire to learn more about the inner workings of Nathan Malik's mind, the prospect of wading through 130 pages on child abuse is too much to handle right now. Maybe it's the pregnancy. Besides, Sean will be back soon. Better to start the book later, when I can read it in a single sitting.

While I wait for Sean to return, I scan a list of Malik's professional publications. His earliest articles focused on bipolar disorder, summarizing extensive work he did with manic-depressives. Then came a study analyzing post-traumatic stress disorder in Vietnam veterans. Judging by the abstracts of the articles, Malik's work on PTSD in veterans is what led him to study the same phenomenon in survivors of sexual abuse. This, in turn, led to groundbreaking research on multiple personality disorder.

"Oysters in the house!" Sean calls from the garage door.

He walks in carrying a brown bag spotted with grease. He's opening it on the kitchen table when his cell phone rings. Glancing at the screen, he says, "It's Joey." Detective Joey Guercio is his partner. "Joey? What you got?"

The smile vanishes from Sean's face. "No shit? Was Kaiser around when they found this? . . . Okay. I'll talk to him later. This could be big, though. . . . I appreciate it. . . . Yeah. They checking all the other vics for the same thing? . . . Okay. Call me with anything else they find." He hangs up and looks at me. "There's another connection between two of the victims. The first one and today's. Colonel Moreland and Calhoun."

"Through Malik?" I ask hopefully.

"No."

"What's the connection?"

"Vietnam."

I couldn't have been more surprised if Sean had said "Harvard." "What about Vietnam?"

"They both served there. Moreland and Calhoun."

"At the same time?"

"Their dates of service intersect. Colonel Moreland was career army. He served in-country from 1966 to 1969. James Calhoun was there in sixty-eight and sixty-nine."

"What branch of service?"

"None. Calhoun was a civilian engineer on contract to the Department of Defense."

I find it difficult to believe that this connection is relevant to our case. "Vietnam's a big country. There were five hundred thousand troops there. Is there any evidence that the two men knew each other?"

"Not yet. The task force just found this out. But it seems odd, don't you think?"

"Not really. Most of the victims are the right age for Vietnam."

"Yes, but most people that age didn't serve over there. A couple of my older brother's friends went, but that's all I knew. Now, out of five murder victims, we get two guys who did?"

I don't answer. I'm thinking about my father and his Vietnam service. How many of my schoolmates' fathers or uncles served there? None that I can recall. But I went to a prep school. Probably quite a few kids from the public school had fathers in that war.

"We're forgetting something else," Sean says. "Nathan Malik did a tour in Nam. Same time frame as Calhoun, which means he was there at the same time as Moreland, too. What do you think about that?"

"It is sounding less like a coincidence."

"We could be way off on motive, Cat. This directly links the victims themselves, not women who happen to be related to them."

"But you're using Malik as part of that linkage, and we got to Malik through those female relatives."

Sean nods. "You're right. And if these murders have to do with Vietnam, why are we seeing sexual homicides?"

"Maybe we're not. Maybe that's just staging. Think about it. There's been no sexual penetration of any of the victims. No semen recovered anywhere at the scenes, which means there's not even masturbation going on. Not unless it's into a condom, and I'm just not getting that feel from these scenes. To me, these killings look like punishment. Our UNSUB is punishing the victims for something in the past. The antemortem biting. . . . that could either be torture as punishment, or for humiliation. Like the nudity . . . humiliation."

"You're going too fast," Sean says.

"What about the gunshots? Why aren't neighbors hearing the gunshots?"

"We're assuming a silencer."

"For a Saturday night special?"

"Hell, you can get one for anything these days. Guys have machine silencers in their garage workshops now."

"Sounds like something a Vietnam vet might know how to do. Calhoun's body was found by his maid?"

"Right. Been working there seven years."

As I search in vain for some new angle on the facts, Sean's cell phone rings again. He looks at the screen, then up at me. "It's John Kaiser. Kaiser served in Nam himself. I wonder what he thinks about this." Sean answers, then listens for several moments. When he hangs up, his mouth is hanging slack.

"What is it? What's happened?"

He shakes his head as though in shock. The color has left his face. "Twenty minutes ago, Nathan Malik called the task force and said he wants to talk to you."

My blood pressure drops twenty points. "That's crazy."

Sean looks me hard in the eyes, and I know something bad is coming. "You haven't heard anything yet. Kaiser's outside right now."

"Outside where? *Here?* My house?"

"He knew I was here, Cat."

"Oh my God. Are they following you?"

"I have no idea. Maybe Joey told them I was here."

A hard knocking reverberates through the house. We both whirl toward the garage door as though expecting it to burst open, but nothing happens.

Sean looks at me in a dazed panic.

I shrug in resignation. "I guess you'd better let the man in."

CHAPTER

15

Special Agent John Kaiser is taller than Sean, and he fills the space in my kitchen in a different way. He seems denser somehow. And though clearly more reserved than Sean, he seems capable of sudden action if that becomes necessary. The friendly face from the LeGendre crime scene is gone, replaced by a piercing gaze that misses nothing.

"Dr. Ferry," he says, nodding curtly.

"Is this some kind of joke?" I ask. "Something you guys cooked up to scare Sean and me?"

"No joke. Nathan Malik has requested a personal interview with you." Kaiser's eyes tell me he's not lying. "Do you have any idea why he might do that?"

"No. Of course not."

"Did you tell me everything you remember about the period that you knew him when you were in med school in Jackson?"

"Absolutely."

Kaiser glances at Sean, then back at me. "Would you remember everything from that time?"

"What do you mean?"

"You told me that you drank quite a bit in those days."

The FBI man's attempt at tact does not lessen my sense of violation. I look at Sean, but he's staring blindly forward, his jaw set tight. "What the hell are you saying? What's going on here?"

Kaiser's eyes don't waver. "You know what I'm saying."

I take a step back, trying to tap my reserves of self-restraint. "Do I remember everything that happened at those dinner parties? Every word and gesture? Of course not. But everything big, I remember."

"You never blacked out in Nathan Malik's presence?"

"*Hell* no. Did he say I did?"

"Dr. Malik hasn't said anything, Dr. Ferry. I'm just trying to learn as much as I can."

"I never blacked out in his presence."

"Do you always remember when you black out?"

"How do you know I black out at all?" I ask, glaring at Sean. "Look, I met Malik under another name over ten years ago. He hit on me a couple of times. I rejected him. That's it."

Kaiser looks honestly perplexed. "Then why does he want to talk to you now? It seems a strange time for him to choose to renew a casual acquaintance, don't you think?"

"Ask him that!"

"He doesn't want to talk to us. He wants to talk to you."

Suddenly I know why Kaiser has come. "You want me to talk to him, don't you? To Malik."

The FBI man's face betrays nothing. "Do you want to talk to him?"

"I'm not answering that."

"Why not?"

I shake my head angrily. "Don't play games with me, Agent Kaiser. There's no right answer here. If I say I want to talk to Malik, you suspect I was involved with him. If I say I don't, you ask 'Why not?' like I'm hiding something. Do you want me to talk to the guy or not?"

Kaiser holds up his hands in apology. "I'm coming off like a jerk here. I'm sorry. Why don't we sit down for a minute?" He gestures at the kitchen table.

When I remain standing, he takes a chair and waits. I look at Sean, who shrugs and sits to Kaiser's right. After a moment, I sit opposite the FBI man.

"I know this situation is difficult," Kaiser says. "But it's nothing compared to what's about to come down on you outside that door. We've had two murders in three days. The media's in a frenzy. If they find out Malik asked to talk to you, that's bad enough. If they find out about"—Kaiser indicates Sean and me with a nod of his head—"you can pretty much kiss your careers good-bye."

"Why is that?" Sean asks, sounding defensive. "So we're having an affair. That doesn't have anything to do with our work."

Kaiser looks down at my table, which is covered with crime-scene photos and copies of police reports.

"Shit," mutters Sean. I can tell from his face that he can't quite believe this is happening. He's thinking of his wife and kids. His retirement. I feel more alone and isolated than I did last night.

"I'm more sympathetic to you guys' situation than you might think," Kaiser says. "I met the woman I'm with now during a high-profile murder case. I wasn't married at the time, but I have some insight into that problem, too. Okay? But right now, the thing for us to do is focus on this case. If we solve this case, a lot of shit gets resolved with it."

"How did you know about us?" Sean asks. "How did you know I was here?"

Kaiser throws him a look that says, *Give me some credit,* then turns to me. "You're right, Dr. Ferry. If you're amenable, I'd like you to talk to Malik. The judge is almost certainly going to order Malik's arrest today for contempt of court. He's flat-out refused to give up the names of any of his patients or their records. I'd prefer not to arrest him yet, but there's tremendous political pressure to force some kind of break in this case. We're already in an adversarial relationship with Malik. Before we jail him and make a bad situation worse, I'd like to learn everything we can from him. Because he's asked to speak to you, we have a unique opportunity to do that."

"But . . . ?"

"A meeting like that is risky, and in more than one way. Before we go ahead with it, I need to speak very frankly to you. No room for hurt feelings."

John Kaiser is only three or four years older than Sean, but he appears to possess a depth and honesty that make Sean seem a boy beside him. A weariness that has nothing to do with the simple passing of years. Yet Sean is no boy. He's a veteran homicide detective who's witnessed much human misery. What did this FBI man experience that aged him this way?

"I understand," I say, oddly excited by the prospect of speaking to Nathan Malik in person. "Ask away."

"Your father served in Vietnam, correct?"

"Yes."

"One tour? During 1969 and 1970?"

"Yes."

"He was later murdered in 1981?"

I resist the urge to shift in discomfort. "That's right. I was eight."

"I tried to get a copy of your father's autopsy record, but the State of Mississippi appears to have lost the original. Was there any aspect of your father's murder that could possibly relate to the murders happening here over the past month?"

"You mean bite marks? Like that?"

"Any similarity at all."

"Nothing. Are you suggesting that my father knew Nathan Malik in Vietnam?"

"It's possible. Maybe even before Vietnam. Nathan Malik and your father were both born in 1951, both in Mississippi. Different towns, it's true—separated by two hundred miles—but their paths might have crossed before Vietnam or after they were in-country."

Sean looks impatient. "What do their army records say? Was it possible?"

"If only it were that simple," says Kaiser. "I've seen Malik's file, but Luke Ferry's military record is sealed by the Department of Defense until 2015."

I feel a sudden dislocation from the world around me. "I can't believe that."

"What the hell are we dealing with here, John?" Sean asks.

"No way to know yet." Kaiser looks unhappy. "But it's safe to say this case is a lot more complicated than I first imagined it was." He turns to me. "I know it's upsetting to have your personal life pried open, Doctor. But if you can—"

"Ask what you need to," I tell him. "I know there's worse coming."

Kaiser looks as if he'd prefer not to venture down the path he's about to take. "After you and I spoke yesterday, I called Dr. Christopher Omartian. To find out what he remembered about Malik."

I close my eyes and steel myself. Chris Omartian tried to kill himself because of me. He probably had plenty to say, none of it good.

"Dr. Omartian said some unkind things about you," Kaiser confirms. "I sensed that he has some issues of his own, particularly as related to you. But I need to ask some questions based on what he said."

"Go ahead."

"He suggested that you might be manic-depressive."

"I'm not. But I have been diagnosed as cyclothymic."

Kaiser gives me a questioning look. "Cyclo-what?"

"Cyclothymia is a mild form of bipolar disorder. I have symptoms of mania that fall below the cutoff for true mania. They call it hypomania. The diagnosis depends on the frequency and severity of your manic episodes."

The FBI man clearly wants more specific information.

"Look, I suffer from depression. I also have occasional episodes of manic behavior. The periods alternate with varying frequency. Sean has suffered through these swings for almost two years. I can be suicidally depressed, then a week later, flying. I think I'm invulnerable, I take crazy risks. I do not-very-nice things sometimes. And *some-times*—not very often—I don't remember those things."

Kaiser glances at Sean, who surprises me by saying, "It's not as bad as she makes out. She's been doing really well."

"Dr. Ferry," Kaiser says carefully, "is there any possibility that you've ever seen Dr. Malik as a patient?"

"*What?*"

"I have to ask you that."

"Why? Do you think I have multiple personalties or something?"

"I'm just trying to put together a picture."

"Nathan Malik and I don't fit into the same picture! I don't know the guy."

"All right." Kaiser steeples his fingers, his eyes uncertain. "Do you feel that you're stable enough to handle a meeting like this?"

I start to answer, but he holds up a hand. "I'm thinking of your panic attacks at the murder scenes. There's no telling what kind of head games Malik might try to run on you."

"Where would this meeting happen?"

"Malik suggested his office. It's not far from here, actually. On Ridgelake. Just off Veterans' Boulevard. He wants to talk to you face-to-face and alone."

"You're kidding, right?" says Sean.

Kaiser shakes his head, but his eyes remain on me. "You'd be wearing a wire, of course. SWAT would be right outside, and you could trigger a rescue with a prearranged phrase if you became concerned for your safety."

"No way," snaps Sean. "Malik could shoot her before your guys even made the door. I've seen it happen, John. So have you."

Kaiser gives Sean a dark look. "Dr. Malik said Dr. Ferry could come to the interview armed if she wants to. He also told us we're welcome to tape the conversation." The FBI agent shifts his gaze back to me. "I think you know why I'm inclined to allow this meeting to happen at Malik's office."

"It's his territory. The more comfortable he feels, the more likely he is to say something that might be useful to you."

Kaiser smiles. "It's nice not to have to spoon-feed someone for a change." He gestures at the bloody crime-scene photos on the table. "Five murders in the past month, two in the last three days. I'd say our killer is decompensating rapidly. Anything we can do to stop him, I'm game for trying."

"This is bullshit," says Sean. "Pick a neutral location. A place you can control."

I lay a hand on his arm. "Let it go, Sean. When are we talking about doing this?"

Kaiser stands and looks down at me. "Malik's at his office now. I've got a wire team in the van outside. How soon can you get dressed?"

A thrill of anticipation shoots through me. For the first time in three days, my craving for alcohol has receded to the level of background noise. Five men have been murdered. Hundreds of law enforcement agents are working around the clock to find the killer, yet no one has come close. Now I'm going to walk into a room with the man most likely to have committed the crimes. A normal person ought to feel some fear. At least some anxiety. But I feel only exhilaration, the pure and distilled essence of being alive. The only feeling that comes close is the almost sexual rush of hyperawareness that signals the onset of a manic episode. And no normal person ever experiences that.

Kaiser and Sean are watching me with the wariness of doctors in a psych ward. I strangle the impulse to laugh.

"Give me ten minutes."

CHAPTER

16

I'm standing with John Kaiser at the bottom of a metal staircase that leads up to Nathan Malik's office building. The stucco structure has only one floor, but it's elevated on concrete columns so that patients can park beneath the building.

"Everything okay?" Kaiser asks from behind me. "Transmitter bothering you?"

"I'm good." An FBI technician taped the transmitter to my inner thigh, beneath my skirt. I almost came casual, but at the last minute I chose a pencil skirt and fitted top. If Malik was attracted to me during medical school, a subtle sensuality might serve me well in my quest for information today.

The transmitter on my thigh is the least of my worries. Two dozen cops are concealed in and around vehicles parked at the buildings adjacent to Malik's, eight of them members of a special weapons and tactics team. As soon as I'm inside Malik's office, that team will surreptitiously enter the building and cover me from one room away. Unless Malik plans to simply pull out a gun and shoot me as I enter—knowing that the police are outside—I should be safe. Yet now that I stand on the threshold of the meeting, reality has dampened my earlier excitement. I feel as though I'm about to enter the cage of a tamed tiger. The beast might be conditioned to show docility, but anyone who believes that savagery can be removed from a predator is kidding himself.

"Cat?" Kaiser says anxiously.

In the past half hour, it's become clear to me that John Kaiser is running the NOMURS task force. It may be a joint law enforcement operation in name, but in the primitive hierarchy that determines the true chain of command, Kaiser is the alpha male. I've tried to be very conscious about how I behave toward him in front of Sean. It's an old problem I have, a compulsion to make the dominant male in any situation want me.

"I'm all right," I assure Kaiser, silently repeating the safety phrase that he gave me a few minutes ago. *Do you follow Saints football?* This mundane sentence—in theory, at least—will trigger an explosive entry by the NOPD SWAT team.

"Whenever you're ready," Kaiser says. "It's your show now."

I climb the steps in a single steady effort, then open the door at the top before second thoughts can stop me. The FBI agent pats me on the back as I go in, and I'm thankful for the touch. It reminds me of my swimming coach wishing me luck before I took my place on the starting block.

Beyond the door is a hallway with doors running down either side. Threadbare green carpet on the floor, brown paneling on the walls. The place smells like a doctor's office, which surprises me. Most therapists' offices I've been to smelled like houses or apartments.

"Hello?" calls a male voice. "Is that you, Dr. Ferry?"

"Yes," I answer, embarrassed by the smallness of my voice in the dead air of the corridor.

"In here. End of the hall."

The door at the end of the hall is partly open. I walk to within two steps of it, then pause and flatten my skirt against my thighs. It crinkled during the drive over.

"Come in," says the voice. "Nothing to be afraid of."

Right, I say silently, and walk through the door.

Nathan Malik sits at a large table facing the doorway. Despite the summer heat, he's wearing black slacks and a black mock turtleneck, probably silk. There isn't a spare ounce of fat on his muscular frame, and his bald head seems posed upon his body like a carved bust on a shelf. His skin is fair, almost pale, a difficult feat to manage in the

New Orleans summer, but the paleness dramatically sets off his eyes, which have irises so brown they look black. His hands are small and appear delicate enough to be a woman's. I try to imagine those hands firing bullets into the spines of five men in the past month, then finishing them off with a shot to the head.

In a single fluid movement Malik stands and gestures at a sofa opposite his desk. Black leather squares in a tubular chrome frame—a Mies van der Rohe, or maybe a knockoff. As I sit, I glance quickly around the office, but the place is so sparsely decorated that I only register a few details. Soft white walls, teak shelves, a couple of long, vertical paintings that look Chinese. To my left hangs a samurai sword, its truncated blade gleaming with threatening purpose. To my right, on a sideboard, sits a stone Buddha that looks authentic enough to have been stolen from an Asian jungle somewhere.

"Everyone likes the Buddha," Malik says, taking his seat again.

"Where did you get it? I've never seen one like it."

"I brought it back from Cambodia. It's five hundred years old."

"When were you there?"

"Nineteen sixty-nine."

"As a soldier?"

A thin smile touches Malik's lips. "An invader. I regret taking it, but I'm glad I have it now. "

Behind the psychiatrist hangs a large painted mandala, a circular geometric design of brilliant colors woven into a mazelike pattern to stimulate contemplation in the viewer. Carl Jung was fascinated with mandalas.

"I'm curiously happy that you've come," Malik says.

"Are you?"

"Yes. I thought it would be you who showed up to take impressions of my teeth. I got a rather ugly little FBI dentist instead."

I'm confused. "Did he take impressions of your teeth?"

"No, oddly enough. I assume that's because my X-rays were sufficient to rule me out as a suspect. He did swab my mouth for DNA."

I'm sitting the way Lauren Bacall sits in old movies, knees together but showing beneath the hem of my skirt, sandaled feet tucked a little behind me. As Malik's eyes linger on my knees, it strikes me that I'm here to reverse the usual dynamic of the psychiatrist's office—to extract information from the doctor rather than the other way around. Since Malik is probably an expert at verbal games, I decide to be direct.

"How did you know I was involved with this case, Doctor?"

He waves a hand as if dismissing a triviality. "The FBI wanted a few strands of my hair as well, but alas . . ." He gestures at his bald pate and laughs.

Malik is testing me. "If the FBI came for hairs, they got them. One way or the other. Unless you're bald down low as well, which I haven't run across yet."

"My, my. You don't shy away from the earthy realities, do you?"

"Did you expect me to?"

He shrugs with obvious amusement. "I didn't know. I was curious to see how you turned out. I mean, I've followed you in the newspapers, but stories like that never offer any meaningful detail."

"Well? What do you think?"

"You're still quite striking. Beyond that, I don't yet know anything I didn't know before."

"Is that really why I'm here? You wanted to see how I turned out?"

"No. You're here because none of this is accidental."

"What?"

"Our juxtaposition in space and time. We knew each other years ago, seemingly in passing, and now we're brought together again. Synchronicity, Jung called it. A seemingly acausal linkage of events which have great meaning or effects in human terms."

"I call those coincidences. We didn't actually come together until you asked for this meeting."

"It would have happened sooner or later."

I have a sudden urge to ask Malik if he knew my father, but instinct takes me in another direction. "Do you have a thing for me, Dr. Malik?"

"A thing?" Feigned ignorance doesn't suit the psychiatrist well.

"Come on. An interest. A crush. A *jones*."

"Do many men react that way to you?"

"Enough."

He nods slightly. "I'll bet they do. You had them eating out of your hand at UMC. All those doctors in their forties salivating over you like a bitch in heat."

Malik uses the word *bitch* like a man who breeds dogs, as though referring to a species far down the evolutionary scale. "You were one of them, as I recall."

"I noticed you. I'll admit that."

"Why did you notice me?"

"You were out of the ordinary. Beautiful, highly sexual, you drank like a fish, and you could hold your own in conversation with people twenty years your senior. I was also bored."

"Are you bored now?"

A thin smile. "No. It's not often that I speak to someone with a live audience."

I slide up my skirt and part my knees enough for Malik to see the transmitter pack taped to my inner thigh.

"Hello, everyone," he says. "Voyeurs one and all."

"If we're done strolling down memory lane, I have some questions for you."

"Fire away. Only I hope they're *your* questions. I'd hate to think you volunteered to act as a mouthpiece for the FBI. That would be beneath you."

"The questions are mine."

"At your service, then."

"Do you treat only patients who have repressed memories?"

Malik seems to be debating whether to answer this question. "No," he says finally. "I specialize in the recovery of lost memories, but I also treat patients for bipolar disorder and for post-traumatic stress disorder."

"PTSD solely as it relates to sexual abuse?"

Another hesitation. "I also treat some combat veterans."

"Vietnam veterans?"

"I'd rather not get into specifics about patients."

I want to ask him about his service in Vietnam, but the time doesn't yet seem right. "I'm going to ask you this straight out. Why won't you reveal the names of your patients to the police?"

Whatever good humor was in the psychiatrist's face vanishes. "Because I owe them my loyalty and my protection. I would never betray my patients in that way."

"Would merely revealing their names constitute a betrayal?"

"Of course. Their lives would instantly be turned inside out by the police. Many of these patients are very fragile. They live in difficult family situations. For some, violence is a daily reality. For others, an ever-present possibility. I have no intention of putting them at risk to satisfy the whims of the state."

"The 'whims of the state'? The police are trying to stop a serial murderer who's probably choosing his victims from among your patients."

"None of my patients has died."

"Their relatives have. Two that we know about, and maybe more."

Malik looks at the ceiling in a way that's almost a roll of his eyes. "Perhaps."

Anger surges within me at his apparent smugness. "It's not *perhaps* for you, is it? You know who else is at risk, yet you refuse to tell the police."

Malik simply stares at me, his dark eyes flat and steady.

"How many of the murder victims were related to people you treat, Doctor?"

"Do you honestly think I'm going to answer that, Catherine?"

"Please call me Dr. Ferry."

A gleam of bemusement. "Ahh. Are you in fact a doctor?"

"Yes. I'm a forensic odontologist."

"To clarify—a dentist." Malik's eyes have taken on a sheen.

"With highly specialized expertise."

"Still . . . that's not *quite* a doctor, is it? Have you ever delivered a baby? Shoved your hand into the chest cavity of a gunshot victim to keep his heart in one piece?"

"You know I haven't."

"Oh, that's right. You left medical school in the second year. Before the clinical work really got started."

Malik is clearly enjoying himself. "Did you bring me here to insult me, Doctor?"

"No. I merely want us to be clear about who we are. I'd like you to call me Nathan, and I'd prefer to call you Catherine."

"How about I call you Jonathan? That's what you called yourself when I met you. Jonathan Gentry."

The psychiatrist's eyes go flat again. "That is no longer my name."

"It's the one you were born with, though, right?"

Malik makes a very European gesture of the head, the sophisticated version of a teenager's "whatever." "Call me what you like, Catherine. But before we go on, let's dispose of this issue of patient confidentiality. I tell you now, I'm quite prepared to spend a year in jail rather than betray my patients' privacy."

He sounds sincere, but I don't believe this refined professional man is willing to do actual jail time for a principle. "You're prepared to spend a year in the Orleans Parish Prison?"

"I realize that may be difficult for you to understand."

"Have you ever *seen* the parish prison?"

Malik turns up his palms on the desk, as though preparing to explain a complex concept to a child. "I spent six weeks as a prisoner of the Khmer Rouge. A year in an American jail can only be a vacation."

Some of my confidence evaporates. There's more to Nathan Malik than I've been led to believe. As I try to decide how to proceed, the psychiatrist puts his elbows on his desk, folds his hands together, and speaks in a voice that carries years of hard-won wisdom.

"Listen to me, Catherine. You walked in here from the world of light. The world of malls and restaurants and Fourth of July fireworks. You see shadows at the edges of all that. You know bad things happen, that evil exists. You've worked a few murder cases. But mostly it's abstract. The policemen to whom you lend your skills see more of the reality, but cops work very hard at denial. The ones who don't eat their service weapons, anyway."

Malik's pale cheeks color with passion. "But *here* there is no denial. In this office, I shut out nothing. Here the shadows come out and play. These walls have heard the most depraved acts of humanity recounted in all their sickening detail." He sits back in his chair and speaks quietly. "Here, Catherine, I deal with the worst thing in the world."

I fold my hands over my knees. "Don't you think you might be overdramatizing a bit?"

"You think so?" A humorless chuckle escapes Malik's lips. "What's the worst scourge of mankind? War?"

"I suppose so. War and the things that go with it."

"I've seen war." He gestures at the stone Buddha staring placidly from the sideboard. "Hand-to-hand savagery and anonymous slaughter. I've been shot. I've killed human beings. But what I've seen and heard inside this drab little office building is worse. *Far* worse."

The psychiatrist speaks with such conviction that I'm not sure what to say. "Why are you telling me all this?"

"To answer your question."

"Which question?"

"The same one all your friends are asking out there in the world. 'Why won't he give us the names of his patients? What's the big deal?'"

I let the silence stretch out, hoping to dissipate some of Malik's intensity. "I still think that the imminent danger to innocent people outweighs your patients' right to privacy."

"It's so easy to say that, Catherine. What if I told you that the majority of my patients are Holocaust survivors? Survivors of concentration camps that were never liberated, and that some of them still live with their Nazi guards?"

"That's not a fair analogy. It's not true."

"You're wrong." Malik's eyes flash. "Children suffering prolonged and repeated sexual abuse *are* living in concentration camps. They're under the power of despots on whom they depend for their very survival. They suffer terror and torture on a daily basis. Their own siblings, and often their mothers, betray them in the struggle for survival. Any identity these children have is systematically destroyed, and hope isn't even a memory. Make no mistake, Doctor, there's a holocaust going on all around us. Only most of us prefer not to see it."

Nathan Malik's preternatural calm has given way to a deep and abiding anger. He is nothing like the psychiatrists I've seen as a patient. At some level, I always craved this kind of passion in my therapists. But in truth, it's not their proper role. This kind of passion in a therapist is dangerous.

In a neutral voice, I say, "My memory from med school is that therapists should maintain objectivity at all costs. You sound more like a patient advocate than a dispassionate clinician."

"Should one be objective in the face of a holocaust? Just because one happens to be a physician? Do you know how many American women are believed to have suffered sexual abuse as children? One in three. *One in three.* That's tens of millions of women. That's women in your family, Catherine. For men, it's between one in four and one in seven."

I force myself to maintain my neutral tone. "Believed by whom?"

"That's hard data, not propaganda from some victims' group. The average duration of incestuous abuse is four years. Half of abused children are assaulted by multiple perpetrators. You want to know more, *Doctor*?"

"I'm a little confused," I say softly. "Are you treating children or adults?"

With an explosive movement Malik stands, as though the chair can no longer contain him. He's only about five-nine, but he radiates a power that seems to have its origin in his unearthly stillness. He projects a centeredness I've only seen in devotees of the martial arts.

"You're speaking in a chronological sense," he says, his voice almost too quiet for me to hear. "I can't afford to make such distinctions. A child's emotional development is typically frozen in whatever stage he or she was in at the time the abuse occurred. Sometimes I don't know whether I'm dealing with an adult or a child until the patient opens her mouth."

"So . . . what you're talking about now is repressed memories. Right?"

Malik hasn't moved toward me, but he suddenly seems much closer than he did before. And the SWAT team seems a lot farther away than it did a minute ago. My eyes go to the samurai sword on the wall to my left. Its placement opposite the Buddha on the right wall creates a disturbing impression of extremes: peace and war, serenity and violence.

"I think you know what I'm talking about," Malik says. *"Doctor."*

For the first time since entering the office, I am afraid. My scalp is tingling, and my palms are wet. The man before me isn't the man I knew in medical school. Physically, he is. But emotionally he has evolved into something else. The psychiatrist I knew was an observer, essentially impotent. This man is as far from impotent as I can imagine, and his agenda remains a mystery to me.

"I need to pee," I say lamely.

"Down the hall," Malik replies, his expression unchanging. "Last door on the right."

As I walk to the door, I feel as though his words emerged from the simplest cells in his brain, while the higher functions remained totally focused on his internal landscape—of which I am clearly a part.

Alone in the corridor, I exhale as though I've been holding in a single breath for fifteen minutes. I don't need to pee, but I walk down the hall anyway, certain that Malik would notice a lack of footsteps. As I pass an open door on my left, I see a man covered in black body armor kneeling in the doorway with a stubby submachine gun. His eyes track me as I pass, but he doesn't move.

When I pull open the bathroom door, I find John Kaiser standing inside. He quickly motions for me to enter the tiny cubicle.

"Do you really have to pee?" he asks.

"No. I just had to get out of there. He jumped up from his desk, and it scared me."

The FBI agent squeezes my upper arm, his hazel eyes reassuring. "Do you feel you're in danger?"

"I don't know. He didn't really threaten me. It just *felt* scary."

"You're doing great, Cat. Can you handle going back in?"

I turn the taps on the little sink and splash cold water on my neck. "Is it really doing any good?"

"Are you kidding? This conversation is the only window we have into this guy's head."

I lean back against the wall and dry my neck with a paper towel. "Okay."

"Do you feel confident enough to try to provoke him a little?"

"Jesus. How do you suggest I do that?"

Kaiser gives me a smile that tells me he knows me better than I thought. "I don't think you need any suggestions in that area. Do you?"

"I guess not."

"If you feel threatened, don't hesitate to pull the plug. We'll have him facedown on the floor in five seconds."

"Alive or dead?"

"That's his choice." Kaiser's eyes almost glitter in their hardness.

"Is it?"

The FBI agent reaches behind him and flushes the toilet. "You're right where you like to be, Cat. On the edge. Go nail this guy."

CHAPTER

17

Nathan Malik is standing at the sideboard, lighting a cone of incense on a burner before the Buddha. A tendril of gray smoke spirals upward, and the aroma of sandalwood reaches me. When he returns to his desk and takes his seat, the aura of threat that surrounded him before is gone. With his shaved head, spare frame, and black clothing, he looks almost like a choreographer from a Broadway show. But that's an illusion, I remind myself. This man has killed people in combat, if not in the city outside this office.

"Do you believe that traumatic memories can be lost, Catherine?"

In my mind I see the flashing blue lights on the night my father died, and feel the terrible blankness of the hours before that. "I don't reject the idea out of hand. I suppose I'm a little suspicious of it."

"Most people are. The word *repression* itself is freighted with all sorts of Freudian overtones. We should drop it altogether. Memories are lost by a sophisticated neurological trick called dissociation. Dissociation is a well-documented human defense mechanism. I'm sure you recall it from your med school days."

"Refresh my memory."

"Daydreaming is a common example of dissociation. You're sitting in a classroom, but your mind is a thousand miles away. Your body's in one place, your mind in another. When the professor calls your name, you might as well have been asleep. We've all experienced that."

"Sure."

"How about driving your car while totally focused on something inside it? The CD player. A child. Programming your cell phone. Your body and brain are performing the task of driving, of keeping the car on the road, while your conscious mind is entirely occupied elsewhere. I've actually driven quite a distance without consciously looking at the road."

"So have I. But I don't have amnesia for whatever I was doing at the time."

"You weren't in a traumatic situation." Malik gives me a paternal smile. "When used as a coping mechanism against trauma, dissociation has far more profound effects. When human beings are placed under such severe stress that fight or flight are the only sane responses, they must do one or the other. If they're in a position where neither response is possible, the brain—the mind, rather—will attempt to flee on its own. The body endures the trauma, but the mind, in effect, is not present. It may well watch the trauma occur, but it will not process it. Not conventionally, anyway." Malik has not moved a muscle apart from those that control his mouth and jaw. "Do you find this concept difficult to accept?"

"It makes sense. In theory."

"Then let's get down to cases. Imagine a three-year-old girl suffering repeated rape. Several nights a week—she never knows which—a man ten times her weight and strength slips into her room and does things to her body. Initially she may be flattered. She feels pleasure and participates. But eventually the secret nature of the activity comes home to her. She begs him to stop. He doesn't. Threats are made. Threats of violence, abandonment, murder. A tremendous amount of negative anticipation is set up inside her mind. She endures unimaginable levels of fear. Which night will he come? Does going to sleep make him come? But no matter what she does to prevent it, he still comes. This huge and terrifying man—usually a man who is supposed to love and protect her—climbs on top of her and begins to hurt her. Maybe she's four or five now, but she can't fight or run from him. So, what happens? Just as in combat situations, the brain attempts to cope with the unbearable as best it can. Massive defense mechanisms are set in motion. And dissociation is the most powerful of those mechanisms. The girl's mind simply vacates the premises, and only her body suffers the rape. In the most extreme cases, these kids develop DID."

"DID?"

"Dissociative identity disorder. What we used to call multiple personalty disorder. The mind becomes so adept at splitting off from reality that separate psyches come into being. Prolonged sexual abuse is the only known cause of multiple personality disorder."

"These traumatic memories," I say, trying to find my way back to the main thread of the conversation. "They remain intact? Even though the person isn't conscious of them? Intact and accessible at a later date? Years later?"

Malik nods. "The degree of recall varies, of course, but not the veracity. The actual memory is indelible. It's simply located in another part of the brain. This idea, of course, is at the root of the repressed memory debate."

"Well, how do you help patients access these lost memories?"

"In some ways, they're not really lost. If an adult woman finds herself in a situation similar to that in which the abuse took place—say normal sex with her husband, and he tries something new, like oral or rear-entry sex—she may suddenly experience panic, pain, heart palpitations, anything. A smell can trigger the same responses. A hair cream the abuser wore, say. Bathrooms can do it. This phenomenon is called body memory. The sensory part of the brain recalls the trauma, but the conscious mind does not."

"But how do you bring these memories to the conscious level? Talk therapy? Hypnosis? What?"

"Hypnosis has been largely discredited as a tool of memory recovery. Inexperienced clinicians have implanted too many false memories with it. Which is a pity. Throwing the baby out with the bathwater, I think."

"Do you use drugs?"

Malik looks impatient. "I use whatever approach I think best for a particular patient. Drugs, talk therapy, EMDR, hypnosis—I could run clinical jargon past you for hours, precise but pointless. I find it useful to use symbolism when discussing my work. Mythology, most of all. The Greeks knew a thing or two about psychology. Incest, especially."

Malik's gaze wanders to my legs again. I pull my skirt down over my knees. "I'm all ears."

"Are you familiar with the concept of the underworld? The River Styx? Charon, the ferryman? Cerberus, the three-headed dog?"

"I know the basics."

"If you want to understand my work, think of it this way. Victims of chronic sexual abuse aren't merely the walking wounded. They're the walking dead. The repeated trauma and dissociation I described to you has effectively killed their spirits. 'Soul murder' is how some clinicians describe this pathology. I see these patients' souls as trapped in the underworld. Call it the subconscious, whatever you will. The children that they once were are cut off from the world of light, wandering in eternal shadow. But though their souls have crossed the river to the land of the dead, their bodies remain behind. With us."

I remember the jacket of Malik's book, the old man in the boat waiting for the young woman to board. "What river do they cross? The Styx? Your book had *Lethe* in the title."

Malik smiles in surprise. "Five rivers bordered the underworld. Styx was merely the river the gods swore oaths by. My patients have crossed Lethe, the river of forgetfulness. And my job is to do what the living are not meant to do: journey to the land of the dead and bring back the souls of those poor children."

"Is that how you see yourself? A classic hero reversing the whims of fate?"

"No. But it's certainly a heroic undertaking. In myth, only Orpheus came close to accomplishing the task, and even he failed in the end. I actually see myself as Charon, the ferryman. I know the underworld the way most people know this one, and I guide travelers back and forth between the two."

I think about the metaphor for a while. "It's interesting that you identify with Charon. The main thing I remember about him is that he had to be paid to ferry the dead across the river."

"Your turn for insults?" Malik smiles in appreciation. "Yes, Charon had to be paid. With a coin in the mouth. But you misunderstand the metaphor. My fees don't pay the price of the patient's journey to the underworld. The patients have usually paid that price long before they see me."

"To whom?"

"To the darkness. The price is paid in tears and pain."

To avoid Malik's challenging gaze, I look over at the Buddha. "Repressed-memory work is pretty controversial. Aren't you afraid of lawsuits?"

"Lawyers are parasites, Catherine. I have no fear of them. I deal in truth. I journey to the land of the dead and come back with memories that terrify the most powerful of men. They haven't got the balls to sue me. They know that if they do, they'll be destroyed. Destroyed by eyewitnesses to their own depravity."

"What about your patients?"

"I've never been sued by a patient."

"Haven't you ever made a mistake? I mean, even if delayed-memory recall is a real phenomenon, there are many documented cases of such memories being proven false. Recantations by patients. Right?"

The psychiatrist waves his hand. "I'm not getting into that controversy with you. Recantations are a problem for therapists who are inexperienced, misguided, poorly trained, or downright gutless."

I understand why Harold Shubb warned me that the FBI had better have an ironclad case if they were going after Malik. The man has no fear, and he never questions his own judgment. But maybe that's his weakness. "I've been here for quite a while now, and you haven't asked me anything about the murders."

Malik looks surprised. "Did you expect me to?"

"I thought they would interest you from a psychiatric perspective."

"I'm afraid sexual homicide is depressingly predictable as a rule. I suppose trying to identify and apprehend particular offenders offers a certain lurid excitement—the thrill of the hunt, as it were—but I have no interest in that."

Malik's subtle cuts and backhanded insults remind me of my grandfather on a bad day. "You don't see sexual homicide as an extreme form of sexual abuse?"

He shrugs. "It's merely the dropping of the other shoe. The poisoned chicken coming home to roost. Childhood sexual abuse is almost universal in serial murderers. And they've frequently suffered the most systematic and violent forms of it. The rage they carry is unbearable. Their turning that violence back on the world is as inevitable as the setting of the sun."

I suddenly remember Kaiser and the others listening to the transmission from my "hidden" microphone. I have a unique opportunity to probe their most likely suspect, and I don't want to squander it. I close my eyes and try to let instinct guide me, but the voice that comes to me is not my own.

"Do you have nightmares, Catherine? Recurring nightmares?"

Before I can dissemble or deny, I see blue lights in the rain and my father lying dead, his eyes open to the sky. Hordes of faceless figures caper at the edges of the scene, the dark men who've tried to break into my house during countless dreams. Then the image vanishes, and I find myself riding slowly over a grassy pasture with my grandfather, in the round-nosed, old pickup truck that smells of mildew and hand-rolled cigarettes. We grind our way up a hill, toward the pond that lies on the other side. My grandfather is smiling, but the fear in my chest is like a wild animal trying to claw its way out of my body. I don't want to see what's on the other side of that hill. This dream began only two weeks ago. Yet each time it recurs, the truck moves farther toward the crest—

"Why do you ask that?"

Malik is watching me with compassion in his face. "I sense needs in certain people. I sense pain. It's an empathic ability I've always had. More a burden than a gift, really."

"I don't remember you as particularly empathetic. Or insightful, for that matter. Mostly I remember you as an arrogant smart-ass."

An understanding smile from the doctor. "You're still an alcoholic, aren't you? But you're not an annoying drunk. No . . . a secret drinker." His face wears the sad familiarity of a man for whom life holds no surprises. "Yes, that's you. Publicly an overachiever, privately a mess."

I want to pull the microphone from the transmitter on my thigh. John Kaiser and the FBI wire team are the only ones hearing this now, but God only knows how many people will listen to the tape later.

"I mentioned EMDR therapy earlier," Malik says. "Have you heard of it?"

I shake my head.

"It stands for 'eye movement desensitization and reprocessing.' It's a relatively new therapy that's worked wonders for PTSD patients. It allows you safely to reexperience your trauma without becoming too distraught to handle the information. You might derive great benefit from that."

I'm not sure I've heard correctly. "I beg your pardon?"

"You've obviously suffered severe trauma in your life, Catherine. You showed clear signs of PTSD when I knew you in Jackson. Similar to the Vietnam vets I was working with at the time. That's another reason I noticed you."

I don't want to let Malik know how close to the bone he's come, but he has gotten me curious. "What kind of trauma do you think I suffered?"

"The murder of your father, for a start. Beyond that, I have no idea. Merely living with him in the years prior to his death might have constituted severe stress."

I feel a rush of anxiety, as though my innermost thoughts have suddenly become visible to the man sitting in front of me. "What do you know about my father?"

"I know he was wounded in Vietnam, and that he suffered severe post-traumatic stress disorder."

"How do you know that? Did Chris Omartian tell you that?"

Another careworn smile. "Does it matter?"

"It matters to me."

Malik leans back and sighs. "Well . . . perhaps we can go into more detail at another time."

"Why not now?"

"We're not exactly alone here."

"I have nothing to hide," I say with bravado I don't feel.

"We all hide things, Catherine. Sometimes from ourselves."

His voice feels like a stiff finger probing the spongy tissue of my brain. "Look, if we're ever going to talk about this, now's the only chance we're going to get."

"I'm sorry to hear that. I thought you might consider coming to me as a patient."

My scalp is tingling again. "Are you kidding me?"

"I'm quite serious."

I cross my legs and try to keep my face impassive. "This is a joke, right? I don't even know what I'm doing here, except that you used to hit on me when I was a stupid kid dating a man twenty-five years older than I was."

"And married," Malik observes.

"And married. So?"

"You're over that now, are you? Dating married men?"

I don't want to lie, but Sean is already in enough trouble. "Yes, I'm over it."

"A peccadillo of your student days? All behind you now?"

"Go to hell. What is this?"

"A frank conversation. Exchanging confidences is the basis of trust, Catherine."

"Exchanging? You haven't told me a damn thing."

Malik gives me an expansive smile. "What would you like to know? We can trade stories. I'll show you mine, if you show me yours."

"Is that something you do commonly with patients? Trade horror stories?"

"I do whatever is required. I'm not afraid to experiment."

"Do you consider that ethical?"

"In the benighted times in which we live, I consider it essential."

"All right, then. Let's do some sharing. Your spiel about being the ferryman to the underworld sounded a little shopworn to me. The stuff about the holocaust was from the heart. You're not just a bystander to sexual abuse, are you?"

Malik looks more intrigued than angry. "What are you suggesting?"

"I think you have some personal experience."

"You're very perceptive."

"You were sexually abused as a child?"

"Yes."

I feel a strange quivering in my limbs, as though from a mild electric shock. This is the stuff Kaiser wants and needs. "By whom?"

"My father."

"I'm sorry. Did you repress the memory?"

"No. But it destroyed me anyway."

"Can you talk about it?"

Malik gives another dismissive wave of his hand. "The actual abuse . . . what's the point? It's not the crimes against us that make us unique, but our responses. When I was sixteen, I talked to my older sister about what had happened to me. Tried to, anyway. I was very drunk. She didn't believe me."

"Why not?"

"Sarah was married by then. She'd married at seventeen. To get out of the house, of course, the fastest way she could. I asked if our father had done anything like that to her. She was flabbergasted. Didn't know what I was talking about."

"Maybe she was just pretending she didn't."

"No. Her eyes were blank as a doll's. Two years later, I was drafted and sent to Vietnam. I did well there. I had a lot of rage inside, but also a desire to help people. A quite common paradox among abuse victims. They made me a medical corpsman, but I still managed to kill some Vietnamese."

"Vietcong?"

Malik raises one eyebrow. "Dead Vietnamese were by definition Vietcong. Surely you know that."

"Why would I know that?"

Another cryptic smile.

My sense of emotional nakedness has returned. "Look, if you have something to say about my father, why don't you get it out? You knew him, didn't you?"

"I know every man who served in Vietnam, more or less. We're brothers under the skin."

"You didn't answer my question."

Malik sighs. "I never knew your father."

"Are you speaking literally or figuratively?"

"Does it matter?"

"Jesus. You were the same age, from the same state, and you both went to Vietnam—"

"How much do you remember about the night your father died, Catherine?"

"That's none of your business."

"I'd like to make it my business. I think I could help you with it. If you would trust me—"

"I'm not here for therapy, Doctor."

"Are you sure? You look like you could use a drink. I have some Isojiman sake here. No vodka, I'm afraid."

How the hell does he know I drink vodka? Does he remember that from ten years ago? "Finish your story," I tell him, trying to steer the conversation onto safe ground.

"Did I not?"

"Your sister had been abused, too, right? But she blocked out the memory?"

Malik studies me for perhaps half a minute. Then he begins speaking softly. "During my tour in-country, I got a letter from Sarah. She'd been having nightmares for some time. But now she was having what she thought were hallucinations. While she was awake. Images of our father removing her clothes, touching her. Those were flashbacks, of course, not hallucinations. At the end of her letter, she told me she'd been thinking of harming herself. Of ending her life."

"What triggered all that? Your talking to her?"

"No. She had a daughter by then, and the daughter had just turned three—probably the age at which my father began abusing Sarah. That's a very common trigger for delayed memory recall in young adult women."

"What did you do?"

"I tried to get compassionate leave to go back to the States. The army wasn't having any. I wrote her letters every day, trying to keep up her spirits, pointing out all she had to live for. Some of it must have rung hollow, because I had my suicidal moments, too. I'd run to wounded men in the middle of firefights, when I was almost certain to catch a bullet. I ran through mortar fire, machine-gun fire, everything. They gave me a medal for my death wish. A Bronze Star. Anyway . . . my letters weren't enough. The flashbacks got worse, and Sarah came to realize that she was seeing something that had really happened to her. She couldn't bear that. She hanged herself while her husband and daughter were at the zoo."

Malik is no longer looking at me. His eyes have focused somewhere in the middle distance, and the glaze over them tells me his mind is far away. I don't even presume to express my sympathy.

"I want to know what I'm doing here," I say quietly.

The thinnest of smiles touches his lips, and then his eyes focus on mine at last. "So do I, Catherine."

It's time to end any semblance of a charade. "I'm here because I think you killed those five men."

Malik's eyes flicker above the smile. "Do you really?"

"If you didn't kill them, you know who did. And you're protecting them."

"Them?"

"Him, whatever. You get my point."

"Oh, Catherine. I expected so much more from you."

His condescension is finally too much for me to bear. "I think our murder victims are male relatives of your patients—sexual abusers—and that by killing them you see yourself as some kind of crusader against an evil you know only too well."

The psychiatrist watches me in silence. "What would you think of me if that were true? Pedophilia has the highest rate of recidivism of any crime. Abusers never stop, Catherine. They just move on to new victims. They cannot be rehabilitated."

"Are you saying that murdering them is justified?"

"I'm saying that death or infirmity are the only things that will stop them."

I pray that the transmitter is relaying all this to Kaiser and the others.

"Are you an expert shot, Doctor?"

"I can hit what I aim at."

"Do you practice martial arts?"

He glances at the samurai sword on the wall. "I could decapitate you with that before the SWAT team outside could get in here, if that's what you mean."

A shudder goes through me. I glance at the closed door behind me, praying there's a SWAT officer on the other side of it. I've forgotten the safety phrase. Something about football—

I almost jump out of my chair when Malik stands, but he only folds his arms across his chest and looks at me with something like pity. "When you leave, remember that we've barely scratched the surface of this subject. We haven't even discussed the guilty ones."

"The guilty ones?"

He nods. "How can a holocaust happen in our midst without the community rising up to stop it?"

"Well . . ."

"Think about that, Catherine. I have things to do now. You can tell me your thoughts at our next meeting."

"There won't be another meeting."

Malik smiles. "Of course there will. Much is going to come to you over the next few days. That's the way it works." He reaches back and takes something off a low table. Then he leans across the table that serves as his desk and holds it out.

It's a business card.

Out of curiosity, I stand and take it. On it is printed Malik's name, and beneath that two phone numbers.

"Call me," he says. "If they decide to jail me, don't worry. I'm quite capable of taking care of myself."

The meeting is over. I walk to the door, then turn back one last time. Malik looks odd standing there, clad in black from head to toe, so still that he could be carved in stone. I'm not sure he blinked once during the entire interview.

"Don't blame yourself," he says.

CHAPTER
18

I'm sitting in the backseat of an FBI Crown Victoria, leaning against Sean as the car roars down West Esplanade, skirting Lake Pontchartrain on its way to the FBI field office. John Kaiser sits up front with a Bureau driver, speaking on a large cellular phone that encrypts every word spoken over it.

"Find out everything you can about Malik's sister and her death," he orders someone at the field office. "Malik told Dr. Ferry she committed suicide. I want to know about his father, too, everything you can get. And get on the horn to the DOD. I want to know about Malik's captivity in Cambodia, if he's telling the truth about it. I didn't see that mentioned in his record. It's possible that he met one or more of the victims in a prison camp. . . ."

I tune out Kaiser's voice and sit up straight on the seat. Throughout the meeting with Malik, I held up fine, but once outside, I began to shake like a soldier after his first battle.

"You'll be okay soon," Sean assures me, squeezing my hand. "You did great."

"Did you hear it all?"

"Every word. I think Malik could be the guy. No shit."

I close my eyes and grip the door handle. Every nerve feels as though there's static electricity crackling along it. "I feel strange inside."

"Strange how?"

"Shaky. I don't really want to see anybody."

Sean grimaces. "They want to debrief you, babe. Can you handle that?"

"I don't know. Right now I feel like jumping out of this car."

He takes hold of my wrist, hard enough to restrain me if I try to jump. I've felt this compulsion before—during depressive episodes—and a couple of times I came close to doing it.

"I'll do anything you want, Cat. Just tell me."

Now Kaiser is talking to the chief of the NOPD. In about an hour, there's going to be a hearing before a district judge, where the FBI will argue that Malik should be compelled to give up the names of his patients. Malik apparently intends to forgo legal representation and argue his own case. Kaiser seems confident that the judge will rule in the Bureau's favor, but something tells me he may be underestimating his opponent. If not, I wonder if Malik will really go to jail rather than "betray" his patients.

"Everything okay, Dr. Ferry?" Kaiser has hung up and turned in the seat so he can look back at me.

"She can't go to the field office right now," Sean says.

Kaiser's eyes remain on me. "Why not?"

"She's too shaky. She's needs some time to regroup."

The FBI agent nods, but his eyes are all business. "Look, it's natural to lose it a little bit after something like that. We'll take some time in my office, decompress before we talk to the SAC or anyone else."

I want to explain myself to him, but for some reason I can't. Sean looks at me, then back at Kaiser. "You don't understand, John. If she says she can't go right now, she can't."

Kaiser's eyes probe me like a doctor's hands. Again I'm reminded of the swimming coach I had as a girl. Hard eyes gauging my capacity to continue after sustaining an injury. "Are you saying you can't do it?"

"I wish the answer were different. I'm sorry. Maybe later on."

"Your office is only five minutes up the lakeshore from her house," Sean says, as if Kaiser didn't just leave my house an hour ago. "I'll bring her over as soon as she's feeling better."

Kaiser studies me a little longer, then glances at the driver. "Take us back to Dr. Ferry's house."

I squeeze Sean's hand in gratitude.

"Do you mind answering a few questions for me now?" Kaiser asks, his eyes back on me.

"No. Go ahead."

"Was your father ever captured while overseas?"

"I don't think so. But I can't be sure. He wouldn't talk to us about what he went through. I mean, I was only eight when he died. But he never talked to my mother either. Or so she said."

"Maybe she was just trying to protect you from things she didn't think you could handle."

A week ago I would have argued this, but after finding the blood-stains in my bedroom, I'm not sure of anything. For all I know, my mother, my grandfather, and Pearlie have been insulating me for years from realities I never suspected. Starting with the truth about my father's death . . .

"Malik still makes the distinction we all made in Nam," Kaiser says to the agent driving the car. "You notice that?"

"What distinction?" asks Sean.

"Between where he is and the rest of the world. He says 'back in the World,' with a capital *W,* just like the grunts used to say it. Like he's in a war now. A free-fire zone. A place where the normal rules are suspended."

"He was so calm," I think aloud. "Most of the time, anyway. It was eerie."

"He wasn't like that when you knew him before?"

"I don't think so."

The driver turns right, and Lake Pontchartrain appears on our left, steely blue and rolling with whitecaps. Not many sails today.

"What's your gut feeling about him?" Kaiser asks. "You looked him in the eyes, I didn't. Did Malik kill those men?"

A gull drops low over the road and dives toward the surface of the lake. "If you're asking me whether I think he *could* do it, my answer is yes. I think he could kill without blinking an eye. But if you're ask-ing me whether he did—I can't say. He seems above these murders somehow. He wouldn't do it in anger. Not hot anger, anyway. If Malik is our killer, then everything we know about serials so far is going to be useless to us."

"I agree."

"What's *your* gut feeling?" I ask.

Kaiser looks thoughtful. "I used to be a profiler for the ISU at

Quantico. I had a knack for it, but I had to quit. Either of you know that?"

Sean glances at me, then nods slowly.

"Do you know why I had to quit?" Kaiser asks.

"I heard you burned out," Sean says.

"You could say that. I attacked a guy in prison. A child murderer. I was sitting there with the chief of my unit, calmly interviewing this con. Filling out a questionnaire, actually. And the killer was sitting there describing how he'd used his power tools on this little boy. I'll spare you the details. Anyway, I just snapped. Before I knew what was happening, I'd gone over the table and tried to punch a hole in his windpipe. Broke some bones, put out one of his eyes. My boss had to club me with a coffee mug to get me off the guy."

Kaiser's hazel eyes have a faraway look, like he's recalling a past life. "I got the same feeling when I was listening to Malik. Not relating him to that convict, but to myself. We all have a breaking point, you know? You sit there for years listening to this obscene stuff, being professional, maintaining distance. Then one day, before you even realize it, the veneer cracks. It's like you said in Malik's office, Dr. Ferry. If Malik is killing these guys, it's because he thinks he's right. It's a crusade. They're child molesters, and he's decided that taking them out is the only meaningful response to the situation."

"Do you think that's what's happening?"

"If it is, I hope the public never finds out."

"Why not?"

"Because a lot of people would probably agree with him." Kaiser sighs like a man wrestling with his own inner demons.

Before I can speak again, Kaiser's cell phone rings. He answers, then faces forward, his mind already back on logistical details.

We're close to my house now. I let go of Sean's hand and try to catch sight of it as we round the corner. I see the trees first, the weeping willow that shades the west side of the house, the stand of pines on the other. Though I have neighbors on both sides, the curve of the levee here gives the illusion of seclusion, and that's one of the main reasons I bought the place. That and the lake view from the second floor. I have to be near water.

The Crown Vic stops before my closed garage door, which has always shielded Sean's car from prying eyes. Not much point in hiding it anymore. Everyone in the department will know about our affair by tonight.

Sean reaches across me and opens my door. I wait to say good-bye to Kaiser, but his conversation shows no sign of ending, so I get out and start toward my front door. I'm nearly there when I hear a clatter of heels on the sidewalk.

"Dr. Ferry!" It's Kaiser, trotting after me.

I stop and wait. "You called me Cat back at Malik's office."

"That's how I think of you," he says. "But it's good to preserve some professional boundaries in these situations."

What situations are those? I wonder as Sean walks up behind Kaiser.

"I appreciate what you did today," Kaiser says. "I'd really like you to come over to the field office later, if you're feeling better."

I'm not really listening. "Agent Kaiser, do you think I'm involved with these murders in any way? Or with Nathan Malik?"

Kaiser's face changes about as much as a rock when the wind blows across it. He's probably a hell of a poker player. "I think you did everything you could today to help us solve this case," he says. "And I think the people who matter will see that."

"Why do you think Malik said 'Don't blame yourself' to me as I left?"

"I don't know. What do you think he meant?"

This is like talking to a shrink. "I have no idea."

Kaiser looks at the ground, then back at me. "We'll just have to try to figure that out together."

That's all I'm going to get. I offer him my hand, he shakes it, and then I walk inside my house without looking back.

CHAPTER

19

I'm standing at my picture window, gazing out at the lake. My meeting with Malik profoundly disturbed me, and I'm not sure why. His cryptic comments about my father stirred up a stew of fragmentary memories, but none has told me anything useful. I'm not even sure the images in my mind are real, and not things I've pieced together from old photographs and stories. A few things I'm sure of—salvaged from nights I sat in the loft of the barn my father used for his studio, watching him work into the small hours of the morning. The roar of the acetylene cutting torch, the hiss of steam as he dipped red-hot metal into the trough he used to cool it. The smell of acids he used for etching, the sound of the riveter as he linked various pieces of his sculpture into a whole that existed only in his mind. There were no sketches, no plans. Just raw metal and the vision in his head.

Now and then, he would remove his mask and look up into the loft at me. Sometimes he would smile. Other times he just stared, watching me with something like fear in his eyes. Even so young, I sensed that my father saw me as another of his creations, one too fragile to handle with confidence. He seemed afraid that, unlike the metal he shaped with such assurance, I might be damaged by a wrong word or move, and that the damage could never be undone.

I thought of the barn as my father's studio, but in truth he slept there for the last few years of his life. It was only a couple of hundred yards down the hill from the slave quarters where I slept with my mother, but the separation was absolute. No one was allowed into the barn when he was working. No one, except me. When I asked my mother for an explanation of these sleeping arrangements, she said it was because of the war. She wouldn't elaborate. My father told me that he had bad dreams at night, and that sometimes when he woke up, he didn't know where he was. At those times, he said, it was like the war had never ended, like he'd never made it home. When that happened, it was better for me and my mother if we weren't in the house with him. It was only later that I realized that, for our family, what my father believed during his flashbacks was true. The war *hadn't* ended for him. He had never quite made it home.

"What are you thinking?" Sean asks from behind me.

I don't turn. There aren't many boats out, but I need to watch them. A sail moving slowly across the horizon gives me something to focus on when my internal moorings start to come loose. Like now. The frantic feeling that awakened in me upon leaving Malik's office has not abated. "About my dad," I say softly.

"What about him?"

"Just stuff. Fragments. That's all I have, really."

Sean lays his hand on my shoulder and squeezes lightly. I jump at his touch, but I manage not to pull away.

"I need a drink," I murmur. "I really need it."

He waits a bit before answering. "What about the baby?"

"It's a drink or a Valium. At this point I'm not sure which is worse."

"Would one drink be that bad?"

"It's not just one drink. It's the first step off a cliff."

The grip tightens on my shoulder. "We need to get your mind off it. What can I do?"

"I don't know." The sail I was watching has vanished. The boat is tacking, fighting its way back toward shore. "Maybe we should make love."

Sean's other hand comes to rest on my other shoulder. "Are you sure?"

"No. I just need something to numb this thing inside me."

"What is it? Is it the manic feeling?"

"I don't think I've ever felt this before. I felt good before I went in to see Malik. And I was fine while I was with him. But now . . . it's like he flipped a switch in my head. All these feelings are flooding through me. Too many feelings."

Sean turns me around and steps close enough that our chests touch. I look into his eyes, trying to lose myself in them. I've done it before, lost myself in those green spheres like a little girl swimming in an emerald sea. Drifting and rolling—

I jerk backward. Sean has kissed me, and the touch stunned me like an electric shock.

"Hey," he says, worry in his face. "What's going on?"

"I don't know." I feel tears on my cheeks. "I don't *know*. I have this feeling that everything's connected, but I can't see how."

"What's connected, babe?"

"Everything! *All* of it. The murders, me, Malik. Kaiser thinks so, too. He just doesn't see any upside to telling me right now."

"Come on, Cat. How could everything be connected?"

"How could it *not*? A month ago, these murders begin. Then I start having panic attacks at the crime scenes, something that's never happened to me before. The only connection between the victims is a psychiatrist I happened to know ten years ago, a shrink who hit on me. Then you make another connection between the victims. Vietnam. Who went to Vietnam? My father, Nathan Malik, and two of the victims. Maybe more of them. And they were there in the *same year*. What are the odds of that, Sean?"

"I'm no mathematician, but it's not impossible. Coincidences like that happen all the time."

His attempt to minimize the significance of these facts infuriates me. "My father was murdered, Sean. And I don't know why." I reach backward and touch the picture window. The cool hardness of the glass reassures me somehow. "I don't remember anything about that night before seeing his body in the garden, but I found blood in my old bedroom. And I'm having nightmares. Recurring dreams and hallucinations. I've always had them, but now they're getting worse. The fucking rain . . . it won't stop. And what does Nathan Malik specialize in? Recovered memories."

Sean is looking at me strangely. "What rain are you talking about? And you found blood where?"

I forgot he knows nothing about my visit to Natchez. "In the bedroom I grew up in. Old blood. I think it dates from the night my father died."

"Cat . . . what the hell are you talking about? That was twenty years ago."

"Twenty-three. I only found the blood by accident. When I went home the other day—Jesus, that was yesterday—a little girl spilled some luminol in my room. I think they've been lying to me all this time. My mother, our maid, my grandfather. For a while I was afraid my father had killed himself, but I don't think that anymore. I think—"

Sean grips my shoulders tight enough to make me stop speaking. "You've got to calm down. I want to hear this, but you're starting to fly. Can't you feel it? You're going too fast. You told me to tell you when you sound like your thoughts are racing. Well, I'm telling you."

He's right. My thoughts *are* racing, and I don't want them to slow down. I've experienced amazing epiphanies during manic episodes. From that dizzying neurochemical height, the seemingly random details that confuse normal people form themselves into coherent patterns. I'm almost certain that if my brain kicks up to the next plateau, the connections among myself, Malik, his patients, and the dead men will leap into stark relief.

"I know what you're thinking," says Sean. "I can see it in your eyes. You're thinking riding the high is worth the low that'll follow the crash."

He knows me well. Thank God there's enough of my baseline identity left for me to hear him. In my present circumstances, the next crash could kill me.

"Tell me about Natchez," he says. "What happened there?"

"I think I may have seen my father murdered, Sean."

"Why do you think that?"

"The night he was killed, I stopped speaking."

"That sounds normal enough."

"For a year?"

His cheek twitches as though from the effort of trying to look calm. "Okay, maybe not so normal."

"And after talking to Malik today, I'm thinking maybe I was so traumatized by what I saw that night that I became dissociated. That the truth about his death is locked inside my head somewhere, but I can't reach it."

"What do you want to do?"

"I want to talk to Malik again."

Sean blinks in disbelief. "Jesus, Cat. The guy's going to be in jail soon."

"I don't care. I think he knows something about me."

"What could he know about you?"

"The reason my father died."

"You told me your dad was killed by a prowler. And your nightmares are consistent with that. Faceless men breaking in and hunting you through your house?"

"What if they're also consistent with something else?"

"Like what?"

"I don't know. Maybe his death had something to do with Vietnam. Our maid thinks one of my dad's friends came looking for drugs, and they argued. But what if it was about something else dating back to the war?"

"Like what? The Vietnam War ended thirty years ago."

"Yes, but it hadn't even been over for ten years when my dad was killed. And I really don't know what he did there."

Sean clearly wants to help me, but he has no idea what to do. We've been in similar situations before.

"Listen," I tell him, not at all sure I should confess this. "I didn't tell Kaiser this, but I have the feeling I've met Malik before."

Sean looks confused. "You *have* met him before. At University Medical Center."

"No, somewhere else. Or some other way."

"Shit. What way?"

"That's what I want to ask Malik."

"You're freaking me out, Cat. The guy did act like he knew things about you. Is Kaiser right? Could you have had more contact with Malik than you think, but blocked it out somehow?"

I turn up my palms in frustration.

"Cat?"

"I want to go to bed. Right now."

"To make love, you mean?"

"No. To sleep."

Sean closes his eyes, then opens them and gives me a long-suffering smile. "Okay. Let's get you tucked in."

After managing a smile of gratitude, I walk past him and down the stairs to my bedroom. I want to fall into bed, but my hygiene ritual is one of the things that holds me together. I manage to finish most of it, but my skin lotion will have to wait until tomorrow. As I climb under the covers, Sean comes in and sits on the edge of the bed in the least threatening position possible.

"Feel better?" he asks.

"No. What are we going to do?"

"About what we were just talking about?"

I shake my head. "About us."

He gives me what he must think is a brave smile. "I don't know, Cat. Now that Kaiser knows about us . . . there's no telling what kind of stories will spread."

"Can you leave them, Sean? Just tell me the truth. Can you leave your wife and children to be with me?"

He takes a deep breath and slowly blows it out. "I can. I can give up everything to be with you."

I see in his eyes that it's true. "But do you *want* to? Is it the best thing?"

"Best for who? For me? Yes. For the kids? I can't say that. It might be the worst thing that ever happens to them. It might ruin their lives."

I close my eyes. I don't want to ruin anyone's life. But I don't want to lose mine, either. "You've got three days to decide. After that, you're either all the way in my life, or all the way out."

Sean has witnessed terrible things in his life, but those quiet words seem to have put him into shock.

"I'm pregnant, Sean. I can't wait anymore. I have to live a real life."

He nods slowly. He gets it. "Can you sleep?"

"I'd sleep better if you were here."

"I can stay."

"How long?"

"It's still afternoon. Five or six hours, maybe. Unless the killer hits again. Then I'll have to go."

"If that happens, I want you to go. But I don't think it will."

Sean pats me on the shoulder, which I hate. "Go to sleep. I'll be out there watching TV."

"Wake me up if you have to leave. I don't want to wake up alone."

"I will."

He kisses my hair above the ear, which I like. As he leaves the bedroom, I prop one pillow so that it blocks the light from the window, then turn to the wall and let my eyes lose their focus. Malik's words are ricocheting through my head like bats in a cave. How did he get to me like this? What does he know about me that I don't? And how does he know it?

Ever since I was a child, I've had the feeling that the world makes sense, but according to a logic indecipherable to me. That the region of my mind that can decode life's symbols is inaccessible due to the chemical imbalances in my brain. Only in sleep do I travel to that place, and even then the faces I see are obscured, the words garbled as though spoken through water. As a teenager, I experimented with techniques that supposedly allow people to guide their dreams, but I had no luck. To this day, my subconscious remains off-limits to my conscious mind, like two hostile nations along a fiercely guarded border. When I do dream, terror and confusion are the primary emotions I experience. I'm a stranger in a strange land, trying to read signs printed in a foreign language, praying only to find my way back to the safety of the waking world. Nothing I've seen seems related to my father's death, though, at least not to the story I was always told. As sleep draws its curtain over my fevered mind, I ask myself again if the adults in my life long ago decided to protect me from a reality they deemed too devastating for me to endure.

Nathan Malik seems to think so.

Where wakefulness becomes sleep, I never know, because my dreams are as vivid as anything I experience while awake. This time I'm back on the island, in the ancient pickup truck, riding through the pasture with my grandfather at the wheel. He points out cows grazing by a fence, others standing with dumb satisfaction in a waterhole. The acrid scent of tobacco burns my nostrils. The truck's round hood is rusted orange and dented from a hundred impacts. The engine groans as Grandpapa forces the truck up the long slope toward the crest of the hill.

There's a pond on the other side of the hill. I've played in it many times, but today I'm afraid. Something terrible is waiting over there. Something I can't bear to see. I know it's there, but my grandfather doesn't. I can't warn him. My mouth is glued shut. I can only sit on the torn vinyl seat, eyes shut tight, praying God will spare us from the horror that awaits. . . .

Suddenly there's a crash of thunder, and then I wake to violence in the dark, battle erupting above and around me, thick arms flailing, fists cracking bone. I want to run, but I'm rooted to the bed. The combatants struggle over me in silent rage, their sole intent to kill. I've seen this battle before, but this time—unlike the other nights—I see the whites of two eyes flickering in the black mask of one face. As the face whips toward the bedroom window, I recognize my father.

And I scream.

CHAPTER

20

My eyes open in the dark. I know the nightmares are over, because the little teeth are gnawing at my veins again.

I need a drink.

My bedside clock reads 5:53 A.M. I've slept over twelve hours. Sean must be long gone. He promised to wake me if he had to leave, but it's morning, and here I lie alone. It doesn't surprise me much. Sean has broken promises before. I've broken a couple myself. Adultery isn't a fairy tale.

Sean is probably lying in bed with his wife right now. Soon he'll wake and drive to the FBI field office to work with Kaiser and the rest of them. Picking apart the tapes of my conversation with Malik, reexamining every scrap of evidence from the murders, waiting for me to decide I'm capable of handling "debriefing" by the FBI.

That's not going to happen today.

Lying in the dark, I know one thing with absolute certainty. I must return to Malmaison. Today. I may believe that one of the bloody tracks on my bedroom floor was put there by my foot twenty-three years ago, but until that's a proven fact, I can go no further with the information. I have the tools and the knowledge to prove it, and I won't feel any peace until I do. Because I keep my forensic equipment packed and ready at all times—even the stuff for tests that fall outside my discipline—I can be on the road in twenty minutes. I don't plan to take much longer than that. It's Monday, and I want to beat the traffic.

Walking down the hall to make coffee, I smell cigarette smoke. Then I hear a cough from the den. Sean quit smoking a year ago.

I creep to the end of the hall. The den is dark. As my eyes adjust to the gloom, I see a man sitting on the sofa.

I reach out and flip on the hall light.

Sean is wearing boxer shorts and his oxford shirt, unbuttoned all the way down. His face is as haggard as I've ever seen it. He looks like a man who has witnessed a terrible accident. An accident involving his own family.

"Sean? What are you doing?"

He doesn't look in my direction. "Thinking."

I pad over to the sofa and look down at him. A bottle of Bushmills stands on the coffee table, a saucer piled with crushed cigarette butts beside it. The bottle was new, but it's one-third empty now. An opened newspaper lies on the table as well, and the face of Nathan Malik stares up from it. Beside the close-up of the psychiatrist is a shot of Malik waving to the camera as he's led along Gravier Street by police—the so-called Hollywood Walk that leads from NOPD headquarters to the Central Lockup Unit.

"Are you all right?" I ask.

"No."

"Have you been here all night? In the house, I mean?"

"No." He still hasn't looked up at me.

"You told me you'd wake me if you had to leave."

"I tried. You wouldn't budge."

"Where did you go?"

At last he looks up. His eyes are glazed. "They know, Cat."

"Know what? Who knows?"

"Everybody."

"What's happened, Sean? What are you talking about?"

"Us. Everybody knows about us."

I take a step backward. "What do you mean?"

"Somebody talked." He shrugs as if he doesn't give a damn. "I doubt it was Kaiser. Maybe it was his driver, I don't know. But word got back to the task force. By suppertime rumors were flying through the department."

"You wouldn't be acting like this over rumors in the department."

He shakes his head. "Somebody called Karen. The wife of this detective I pissed off about a year ago. She called Karen and made it sound about as bad as she could."

I've been expecting something like this for months. Now that it's finally happened, I feel a strange numbness in my chest. "And?"

"Karen called my cell phone about eight last night. She told me not to come home."

"What did you do?"

"I tried to talk to her."

"In person? You went home?"

He nods. "She wouldn't let me in."

"You have a key."

Sean chuckles softly, the sound eerily devoid of humor. "She changed the locks."

Good for you, Karen, I say silently.

"She got a locksmith out there after hours and changed every damn lock on the house."

I look over at the picture window. A faint blue glow lightens the blackness on the left side of the lake. The sun is coming. I need to move.

"Look, I know this is a bad time . . . but I have to go."

He blinks in confusion. "Go?"

"Yes."

"You're ready to talk to the FBI?"

"No. I'm going back to Natchez."

He rubs his eyes like a man coming awake after a long sleep. "What are you talking about? You just came from there. Why would you want to go back?"

Trying to explain my reasons to Sean while he's drunk is more than I want to deal with. "Look, I don't need to be here right now. I need to go home."

He waves his arm broadly. "I thought this was home."

"I have to know what happened in that room. What happened the night my father died."

"Well, you can't just *leave.* Malik thinks he has some kind of connection with you. You're important to solving the case."

An image of the psychiatrist comes to me, a black-clad figure looking down a corridor like a concerned father. "Where's Malik now? What's that newspaper story about?"

"He's in the Orleans Parish Prison. He refused to obey the court order. The *Picayune* ran a story about his big moral stand against the Feds. Some people think Malik's a hero for protecting his patients' privacy, others think he's the killer, or that he's protecting the killer. All anybody agrees on is that he's the only goddamn lead in the case."

None of this surprises me. "Look, I did what Kaiser wanted. That's all I can do right now. I'm an expert on bite marks, but they've got somebody else doing that job. There's nothing I can do to alter events. I'm done. I'm going home."

Sean shakes his head as though trying to sober himself up. "Last night you asked me if I could give up everything for you. I told you I could."

I nod but say nothing.

"Well . . . we can be together now. Right now. No waiting."

I've dreamed of hearing him say this for more than a year, but now that he has, I feel only sadness. "You didn't make that choice freely, Sean. You got caught. That's a different thing."

He looks incredulous. "Are you serious?"

"On top of that, you're drunk. You don't know how you're going to feel when you sober up. For all I know, you'll be begging Karen's forgiveness and trying to sleep at home by tonight. I don't want to sound like a bitch, okay? I love you. But I have something important to do, and I can't put it off because you happened to get caught last night."

"You do sound like a bitch."

My laugh is a short, harsh bark that surprises even me. "Thanks for making it easier."

CHAPTER
21

At Malmaison, I find the wrought-iron gate standing open. Could the house be on tour? It's the wrong season for that. Carefully negotiating the blind curves of the high-banked lane that leads to the main driveway, I circle around to the rear drive and pull into the gravel lot behind the two slave quarters and the rose garden.

Mother's Maxima, Pearlie's blue Cadillac, and my grandfather's Town Car are in the lot. There's also an Acura I don't recognize. The Town Car is running. My grandfather's driver is sitting behind the wheel. Billy Neal gives no semblance of a greeting, but stares at me with a strange malevolence.

I'm about to walk over and ask him what his problem is when Grandpapa marches through the trellis at the rear of the rose garden. He wears a stylish suit cut by the Hong Kong tailor who travels through Natchez twice a year and takes measurements at a local motel. The dark fabric sets off his silver hair, and he wears a white silk handkerchief prominently in his pocket.

Billy Neal gets out of the Lincoln and opens its rear door, but by then my grandfather has seen me and turned in my direction. Neal leans against the trunk of the Town Car and lights a cigarette, his posture radiating insolence.

"Catherine?" Grandpapa calls. "Two visits in three days? What's going on?"

I'm not going to lie about my reason for being here, even though it might upset him. "I came back to finish the work in my bedroom."

He stops a couple of feet from me, his blue eyes twinkling with interest. "You mean the blood you found?"

"Yes. I want to check the rest of the room for blood and other trace evidence. Probably the rest of the slave quarters as well."

The twinkle goes dead. "What kind of evidence? Evidence of what?"

"Evidence of what, I'm not sure. But I'll find whatever is preserved after twenty-three years."

He glances at his watch. "You're going to do this yourself?"

"I don't think so. I wanted to. And my forensic equipment is packed in my trunk. But if something I discovered ultimately involved the courts, that could—"

"The courts?" He's giving me his full attention now. "What could possibly involve the courts?"

Why is he forcing me to say it? "Look, I know you told me that you and I probably tracked that blood into the bedroom from the garden that night, but . . ."

"But what?"

"It was raining that night, Grandpapa. Hard."

He nods as if only now remembering. "You're right."

"It's not that I don't believe you. But I can't stop thinking about that rain. How could anybody track enough blood over thirty yards of wet grass to make those footprints?"

He smiles. "You're as obsessive and tenacious as I am."

I can't help but smile back. "As far as me doing the work, the problem is objectivity. If any kind of legal proceeding involved me— and if I alone had discovered the evidence—that evidence would be suspect. I know people who work at the state crime lab in Baton Rouge. They do some moonlighting. Reconstructing crime scenes, testifying as experts in criminal trials—"

"Mississippi or Louisiana?"

"Louisiana."

Grandpapa gives a perfunctory nod, as though suddenly preoccupied with something else.

"They could work up my bedroom in half a day and videotape the whole thing. Any evidence they discovered would be beyond reproach. Honestly, I can't even pretend to be objective about this."

"I understand." He glances over at his driver, then back at me.

"Do you have any problem with me doing this, Grandpapa?"

He seems not to have heard me. The stroke he had a year ago wasn't supposed to have affected his conscious thought processes, but sometimes I'm not so sure.

"Whose car is that?" I ask, pointing at the Acura.

"Ann's," he replies, his eyes distant.

Aunt Ann rarely visits Malmaison. Her stormy personal life long ago alienated her from my grandparents. It's my mother who makes the effort to exert a positive influence in Ann's life, but her efforts mostly go in vain. Diagnosed as bipolar in her midtwenties, Ann— the beautiful and favored child of the family—became a cautionary tale in local society, an example of how great wealth doesn't necessarily confer happiness.

"Is she visiting Mom?" I ask.

"She's with Gwen now, but she actually drove up to see me."

"What about?"

Grandpapa sighs wearily. "What's it always about?"

Money. Mom told me that Aunt Ann long ago depleted the trust fund my grandfather set up for her. Yet she has no qualms about asking for money whenever she needs it. "Mom said Ann's new husband is beating her."

Grandpapa's face tightens, and I sense the slow-burning anger of a man who judges men by his own strict code. "If she asks me for help with that problem, I'll intervene."

I want to ask if he gave Ann the money she requested, but I don't. He probably wouldn't tell me.

He's looking at his watch again. "Catherine, I have a meeting with a member of the Mississippi Gaming Commission. It's about Maison DeSalle. I can't be late."

I suddenly remember the architectural model he showed me in his library, his plans for federal certification of a Natchez Indian Nation. "Oh, right. Good luck—I guess."

Across the parking lot, Billy Neal holds up his wrist and points at his watch. Grandpapa waves acknowledgment, then gazes deeply into my eyes, as though trying to communicate something important. Through his hypnotic blue eyes, he's brought the full weight of his considerable charisma to bear on me. His mental capacity hasn't diminished at all.

"Catherine," he says, his voice grave, "I'd like you to postpone your plans until I get back from this meeting. It won't take more than an hour or so."

"Why?"

He reaches out and takes hold of my hand. "It's a delicate matter. A personal matter. Personal for you."

"For me?" A strange buzzing has started in my brain. "Then tell me now. I was about to call the crime lab and get things moving."

"This isn't the proper place, dear. We should talk in my study."

"Let's go, then."

"I can't now. I have the meeting."

I shake my head in frustration. "I'm tired of being in the dark, Grandpapa. If you want me to hold off doing this, tell me whatever it is right now."

Anger flashes briefly in his eyes. But instead of chastising me, he walks slowly around the Audi and climbs into the passenger seat. His desire is clear. I get into the driver's seat beside him, but he's not looking at me. He's staring through the windshield with a faraway look in his eyes.

"Listen," I say, "ever since I found that blood—long before that, really—I've had the feeling you guys have been keeping something from me about that night. I'm sure you think you're protecting me, but I'm not a child anymore, okay? Not even close. So please tell me what this is about."

His eyes remain on the red sea of rosebushes in the garden. "The rain," he murmurs. "We were foolish to think we could lie to you and get away with it for long." His big chest falls with a deep sigh. "You always had finely honed instincts. Even as a child."

My extremities are tingling. "Please hurry."

Grandpapa suddenly faces me, his eyes solemn, the eyes of a doctor about to break bad news. "Darling, your father didn't die where we told you he did."

A strange numbness seeps outward from my heart. "Where did he die?"

"Luke died in your bedroom."

My bedroom . . . The numbness inside me turns cold, the numbness of frostbite. Internal frostbite. I look away, my eyes drawn to the roses I've hated for so long. "How did he die?"

"Look at me, Catherine. Look at me, and I'll tell you all I know."

I force myself to turn, to focus on the lined patrician face, and he begins to speak in a soft voice.

"I was downstairs reading. I heard a shot. It was muffled, but I knew what it was. It sounded the way our M1s did when we mopped up the Jap bunkers after the flamethrowers went in. When I heard the shot, I ran outside. I saw a man running away from the eastern slave quarters. Your house. I didn't chase him. I ran straight over to see whether anyone had been hurt."

"Was the running man black, like you told me before?"

"Yes. When I got inside, I found your mother asleep in her bed. Then I checked your room. Luke was lying on the floor, bleeding from the chest. His rifle was beside him on the floor."

"Where was I?"

"I don't know. I examined Luke's wound, and it was mortal."

"Did he say anything?"

Grandpapa shakes his head. "He couldn't speak."

"Why not?"

"Catherine—"

"*Why not?*"

"He was drowning in his own blood."

"From a wound to the side of his chest?"

"Darling, that rifle was loaded with hunting rounds designed to mushroom on impact. The internal damage was devastating."

I shut out the pain by focusing on details. "Did you touch the gun?"

"I picked it up and smelled the barrel to see if it had been discharged. It had."

"Did you call the police?"

"Pearlie did. She called down to check on you, just as I told you. The rest happened much the way I told you the other day. Your mother woke up, and you walked into the bedroom moments later."

"Where had I been? I mean . . . it happened in my bedroom."

He takes a moment to consider this. "Outside, I think."

"Who moved Daddy's body into the rose garden?"

"I did."

"Why?"

"To protect you, of course."

"What do you mean?"

Grandpapa shifts on the seat, but his eyes remain on me, deadly earnest and filled with certainty. "You were eight years old, Catherine. Your father had been shot by an intruder in your bedroom. If that story had been printed in the *Examiner,* there would have been no end to the morbid speculation. What happened to you before Luke arrived? Were you molested in some way? Raped? In this little town, that would have followed you for the rest of your life. I saw no reason to put you through that, and neither did your mother. Luke was dead. It made no difference where the police found his body."

"Mom knows?"

"Of course."

"And Pearlie?"

"It was Pearlie who helped me clean Luke's blood off the bedroom floor and walls before the police arrived. Not that it mattered. They never even checked the slave quarters."

"Why not?"

He looks at me as though the answer should be self-evident. "They believed what I told them. Luke was lying dead under the dogwood tree in the rose garden. I told them how it happened, and that was that."

Such a passive police response would be unimaginable in New Orleans, even back in 1981. But in the Natchez of twenty years ago? What local cop was going to question the word of Dr. William Kirkland, especially when his son-in-law had just been murdered?

"Did they do any forensic investigation at all? Did they search the grounds for blood or other evidence?"

"Yes, but as you pointed out, it was raining hard. They didn't put too much effort into it. It was a sad night, and everybody wanted it over."

I gaze across the rose garden to the slave quarters that was my home for sixteen years. Then I pan my eyes right, to the dogwood tree where for most of my life I've believed my father died. *Luke was dead . . . It made no difference where the police found his body.* But of course it does make a difference to me. It makes all the difference in the world.

"But Grandpapa . . . what if something *did* happen to me? Did you ever think about that?"

Before he can answer, his Town Car pulls alongside my Audi on the passenger side. Billy Neal gives my grandfather a pointed look.

"What's his fucking problem?" I snap.

Grandpapa frowns at the expletive, but he motions for Billy to pull away. After about ten seconds, the driver obeys.

"Of course I considered the possibility, dear. I examined you myself, after the police had gone."

"And?"

"I saw no evidence of assault."

"You checked me for sexual assault?"

He sighs again, obviously put out by the specifics of my question. "I did a thorough examination. Nothing happened to you. Nothing physical, I mean. The psychological shock was clearly devastating, though. You stopped speaking for a year."

"What do you think I saw?"

"I don't know. On the milder side, the prowler might have exposed himself to you. I suppose he might have fondled you or forced you to fondle him. But at the other end of the spectrum . . . you might have seen your father murdered before your eyes."

I want to hide my quivering hands—my grandfather despises weakness—but there's nowhere to put them. Then he closes one of his strong, age-spotted hands around both of mine, stilling my tremors with the force of his grip. "Do you have any memory of that night?"

"Not before I saw his body. I have nightmares, though. I've seen Daddy fighting with a faceless man . . . other things. But nothing that makes any sense."

He squeezes my hands harder. "Those aren't nightmares, dear. Those are memories. I've said some bad things about Luke, I know. And God help me, I've lied to you as well. Hopefully for a good reason. But one thing I told you, you can take as holy writ. Your father died fighting to save your life. He probably *did* save your life. No man could have done more."

I close my eyes, but the tears come anyway. I've always felt a certain amount of shame about my father's war-related problems. To hear now that he died a hero . . . it's almost too much. "Who did it, Grandpapa? Who killed him?"

"No one knows."

"Did the police really look?"

"You'd better believe it. I rode them hard. But they couldn't come up with anything."

"I can," I say quietly. "I can take apart that crime scene with tools that didn't even *exist* about back then."

Grandpapa is watching me with grief in his face. "I'm sure you can, Catherine. But to what end? What if you were to find DNA from an unknown person? There were never even any suspects. Are you going to take blood samples from every black man in the city of Natchez? That could be five thousand people. And the killer could easily be dead now. He could have left town years ago."

"Are you saying I shouldn't try to find out who murdered my father?"

Grandpapa closes his eyes. Just as I decide he has fallen asleep, he opens them again and turns them on me with startling intensity. "Catherine, you've spent your adult life focused on death. Now you're about to cross the line into full-blown obsession. I want my granddaughter to *live*. I want you to have a family, children . . ."

I'm shaking my head violently, not because I don't want those things, but because I simply can't think about them now. And because I already have a child on the way—

"That's what Luke would want," Grandpapa finishes. "Not some belated quest for justice with no chance for success."

"It's not just justice I want."

"What, then?"

"The man who killed my father is the only person in the world who knows what happened to me in that room."

At last my grandfather is silent.

"*Something* happened to me that night. Something bad. And I have to know what it was."

Grandpapa is saying something else, but I can't make out specific words. His voice seems to come from across a windy field. Pulling one hand loose, I yank open the door and try to climb out. He tries to hold me by my other hand, but I relax my fingers and the hand slips free. My feet hit the ground, and I start running toward the slave quarters.

Sensing something amiss, Billy Neal jumps out of the Lincoln and blocks my path.

"Get away from me, you shit!" I scream.

He grabs for my arms, but I pivot and reverse away from the buildings. Without looking back, I sprint down the hill toward the bayou, where the barn that served as my father's studio and sleeping quarters stands in the shadow of a wall of trees. I'll be safe there. Voices cry out behind me, one of them Pearlie's, but I run on, wind-milling my arms like a panicked little girl.

CHAPTER

22

I can't get into the barn. For the first time in my life, my father's sanctuary is closed to me. The main entrances are padlocked, and the secret ones I used for years have been nailed shut. If I could find a ladder, I'd try the loft door, but as I begin looking for one, I hear Pearlie shouting from the direction of the house.

She's running down the hill in her white uniform. That she's over seventy seems not to affect her speed at all. Her bony legs move in a herky-jerky motion, giving her the appearance of a marionette being controlled by invisible strings, but she moves fast. I wait by the barn, watching Pearlie come, wondering what she has to say that's so important. The air here smells of the bayou beyond the barn: decaying vegetation, dead fish, frogs, snakes, skunks. The mosquitoes have always been bad down here, too, but Daddy never seemed to mind them.

"What you doing here?" Pearlie calls.

"I want to look in the barn."

She slows to a stop, panting. "Why?"

Because I want to be close to my father. Because his grave does nothing for me. Because here, where his final sculptures are stored—unsold at my request—I feel a connection with him that has never died, or even faded . . .

"I just do," I snap. "Why is it locked?"

"All Mr. Luke's metalwork be in there."

"All? I thought there were only a couple of unsold pieces left."

"Used to be. But your granddaddy been buying up all the others. Whenever something comes on sale, he buys it. He got at least ten of them things in there. Big ones, too."

This seems impossible to me. "Why is he doing that? He never liked Daddy's work."

Pearlie shrugs. "Got to be money in it, some way. Them statues worth money, ain't they? Some of 'em he brought all the way from Atlanta."

"A few collectors think they're important. But they're not worth the kind of money that matters to Grandpapa."

Pearlie steps closer and looks me in the eye. "What happened in that car up there? Why'd you run away like that?"

I turn back to the barn door. "Grandpapa told me where Daddy really died."

She circles me so that she can maintain eye contact. I see fear in her eyes.

"What are you afraid of, Pearlie? What did you think he told me?"

"I ain't afraid of nothing! You tell me what he said."

"He told me Daddy didn't die under the tree. He was shot in my bedroom, saving me from the intruder."

Pearlie seems frozen in place. "What else did he say?"

"He told me that you cleaned Daddy's blood off the walls and the floor."

The old woman lowers her head.

"How could you do that? How could you lie to me all these years?"

Pearlie shakes her head, her eyes still downcast. "I got no regrets about cleaning that blood. Wasn't no good going to come from you knowing any different than what we told you."

"You don't know that! Isn't it always better to know the truth, no matter what?"

She looks up, her eyes brimming with emotion. "Maybe you ain't lived long enough to learn it yet, but some things it's better not to know. Specially if you're a woman."

"Why do you say that?"

"If everybody knew what everybody else was really thinking and doing all the time, there'd be a lot more people in the jailhouse. And there wouldn't hardly be one family left together. Hardly any left together now, come to that. Especially black ones."

"I want the truth, Pearlie. I don't want to be protected. I don't want to be lied to. I want the truth, however bad it is."

"You don't know what you're saying, girl. You think you do, but you don't."

I take hold of her arm. "You know everything that ever happened to this family. What else have you been keeping from me?"

"Nothing! What Dr. Kirkland done that night was right. Wasn't no use having everybody talking 'bout you being raped. All them old white ladies would have been whispering poison every time you walked into a room. You didn't need to carry that around with you. Not in this little town."

"I don't care what those people think! Not now, not then. You know that."

Pearlie nods. "You a strong girl, all right. Always was. But you didn't need that scandal hanging on you. Now, come back up to the house. Dr. Kirkland got the only key to this old barn. You gonna have to wait on him to get inside, and he gone to his meeting now."

I jump as my cell phone beeps out U2. It's Sean. My first instinct is to ignore the call, but something makes me answer.

"What is it?" I ask.

"Hold on to your socks," Sean says, his voice raspy from an obvious hangover. "At eight o'clock this morning, Nathan Malik gave up the names of his patients."

I can't believe it. There's no way a man who spent time as a prisoner of the Khmer Rouge was broken by one night in the parish prison. "Is he out of jail now?"

"Yep. And we were suspicious for the same reason you are. Why would Malik go to jail on principle, then suddenly crack? It's almost like he did it for the publicity, and once he got that, he caved. Well, Kaiser suddenly realized that without Malik's medical records, we had no way to know whether the patient list was complete. So he got a court order authorizing us to compare the list to Malik's computer records. Well, guess what? There *weren't* any. The hard drives at his office were wiped clean."

This I can believe. "The data can still be retrieved. You just—"

"You're not listening, Cat. The data's *gone*. All of it. The FBI technicians said it would take somebody who really knew computers to pull that off."

"Malik could do it."

"Hang on. . . . I gotta run, Cat. Things are popping down here. I miss you."

He clicks off, leaving me feeling utterly dislocated from my old life.

"Bad news?" Pearlie asks.

"Not good," I reply, wondering whether the list Malik gave the police has a single current patient's name on it.

I turn reluctantly from the barn and follow Pearlie up the hill.

As we reach the parking lot, my mother and Aunt Ann walk out of the rose garden. Each is rolling one-half of a matched pair of Louis Vuitton suitcases. From a distance they could be twins, but as we near them, Ann's age shows itself in her face. Only four years older than my mother, she's paid the price for years of alcoholism and hard living. A friend of mine from Natchez wrote a book about her troubled family. In it, she wrote, "Beautiful women are haunted houses." I always think of that line when I see Aunt Ann. Ann was the one that the boys always followed home. Her face had the classic proportions that transcended small-town prettiness, but beauty seemed to bring her more trouble than happiness, and by fifty it was mostly gone. Now her cheeks hang on the long-envied bone structure like ragged sails on the woodwork of a once-proud ship. Looking at the spider-work of veins in her face, I touch my own, knowing that one day my secret drinking will exact the same price from me.

"What have you two been doing down by the bayou?" my mother calls. "The mosquitoes will eat you alive down there."

"Looking at the barn," I answer. "I wanted to see some of Daddy's pieces."

The smile fades from Mom's face. "Well, they're all locked up now."

Ann props up her suitcase, walks over to me, and gives me a tight, sisterly hug, not one of the side hugs my mother favors. Then she draws back and looks into my eyes. Hers are as blue as my grandfather's, and almost as penetrating. "If I didn't know better, Cat, I'd think you've been crying."

I shake my head, wondering if Ann knows where Daddy really died.

"Good. That's my department. How are you holding up down in New Orleans?"

"Fine. I'm good."

She nods, though she obviously doesn't believe me. "You seeing anybody of the male persuasion down there?"

"I have a guy, yeah."

"Handsome?"

I force a laugh I don't feel. "Yes."

"Good for you. Every man's going to wear you down eventually, so you might as well pick one who's pretty to look at."

Ann gives me a conspiratorial wink, but I can't summon another laugh. There's a glitter in her eyes that makes me wonder if she's in a manic phase.

"Ann's headed back to the coast soon," says my mother. "But we're going to have brunch at the Castle first. Why don't you put on some decent clothes and join us?"

That's the last thing I want to do now. But looking for some of my father's sculptures won't qualify as a sufficient excuse in my mother's book. "I'd really like to. But I have some things to do."

Mom looks put out. "For example?"

I search for an excuse—any excuse—to skip lunch. "Dr. Wells asked me to come swimming over at his house."

Ann gives me another wink. "Sounds a lot better than lunch with us. You go on, Cat. We'll catch up with each other soon."

In the most casual voice I can muster, I say, "Mom, who in town has some of Dad's work on display?"

"Well, they still have that piece at the library. And there's the one at the Vietnam Veterans Building over at Duncan Park—the helicopter. Other than those and what's in the barn, everything's in private homes. Most of them are far from Natchez."

I give Ann another hug, then glance at Pearlie—who has watched this exchange like a silent sentinel—and set off through the trees toward Michael Wells's house.

My plan is to turn around as soon as Ann and my mother drive away, but they stand by the Acura talking to Pearlie as if they have all day. With little choice but to play out my charade, I walk deeper into the trees.

Something moves among the trunks to my right, and it startles me. Then I recognize Mose, the yardman. He's setting mole traps in the scraggly grass beneath the trees about thirty yards away. Looking at him bent over the ground, I recall Grandpapa's description of the prowler who ran away from the slave quarters on the night Daddy died. He was black. Could that have been Mose? He's lived on the property for decades. He always drank quite a bit, and it strikes me now that he might have had some dealings with my father over drugs.

I veer toward the old man and walk for several yards, but something makes me stop short of him. Mose had an open window into my life from infancy to age sixteen. Is it possible that he lusted after me? To the point that he came into my room and tried to molest me? Could he have done something before that night, even? On the grounds of Malmaison, maybe? Under the tin roof of the barn? Could that something have been so traumatic that I blocked it out? Before talking to Nathan Malik, I wouldn't have considered this. But now, thinking of the nightmares that have troubled me for years—faceless black figures breaking into my house—I wonder. The idea that a random prowler would walk all the way from the highway to Malmaison during a rainstorm has always bothered me. But if that "prowler" were Mose, he wouldn't have had to walk more than a hundred yards. Could he be the faceless black man in my dreams? The demon fighting my father in the dark?

I'll have to ask Pearlie that.

Mose hasn't seen me yet. Behind Malmaison, Ann and my mother are still talking by the car. I might be able to reach Michael's house without Mose seeing me, but Michael is bound to be at work. I could still use his pool, though. I think of the flat rock in his flower bed. Five or six minutes on the bottom of that pool might be just the thing to calm me down. I'm thinking of sprinting the rest of the way when the sound of a motor carries through the trees. Ann's Acura is backing up. I hear her shift gears, and then the car rolls slowly down the curving driveway toward the gate.

"Miss Catherine?" croaks a voice parched by thousands of hand-rolled cigarettes.

I whip my head around. Mose is standing erect, staring at me from behind his pile of mole traps.

"That you, Miss Catherine? My eyes ain't so good no more."

"It's me, Mose," I call, already walking back toward Malmaison. "Don't work too hard in this heat."

"Heat don't bother me none." He laughs. "I'll take it over the cold any day."

I give him a broad wave, then turn and race back toward the house.

CHAPTER

23

The Vietnam Veterans Building is closer to Malmaison than the public library, so I go there first. Situated in the city's main public park, the small, one-story building began its life as the pro shop of the public golf course. The Vietnam vets took it over when the golf course was expanded to eighteen holes and a new pro shop built in another part of the park. They used it for support group meetings, for parties, and for a place to hang out besides home.

The dilapidated building sits on a long slope below the oak-shaded public playground that Natchez kids have used for sixty years. Overlooking the playground is Auburn, an antebellum mansion that serves as headquarters for one of the local garden clubs. Across the lane from Auburn stands an old steam locomotive, a sort of living museum for children. In the distance I see the public swimming pool, the only decent pool where black children can swim en masse in the city. It's been closed for the past four years, due to lack of money for repairs. Down the long slope from the vets' building, red and green tennis courts bake in the sun, surrounded by the grassy, fenced triangles of Little League ball fields.

I expected to find my father's sculpture inside the veterans' building—where I last saw it—but as I pull into the parking lot, I see the shining rotor blades that crown the piece jutting over the roof. Have they mounted it on some kind of pedestal? I get out and walk around the corner.

A house-size structure stands on the lawn, built of wooden poles hung with parachutes and camouflage netting. Inside the netting is a grass hut, and in front of the hut an army tent forms the centerpiece of a simulated military campsite. A steel beam rises out of the center of this scene, and mounted atop it is my father's sculpture: a brushed-steel Huey helicopter with a wounded soldier suspended from its belly by a winch cable. It's one of the most realistic pieces my father ever did. Most of his work—especially the later stuff—was far more abstract, like the tall tree standing between the twin staircases at the public library. But the ascending helicopter pleased everyone. What it's doing in the middle of this thrown-together display puzzles me, though.

"Can I help you, miss?"

A heavyset man with a grizzled beard is walking toward me. He wears army fatigue pants, a black MIA T-shirt, and Harley-Davidson motorcycle boots. A gold earring decorates his left earlobe, and a braided, silver ponytail hangs over his right shoulder. He looks to be in his late fifties.

"I hope so. My dad sculpted that helicopter up there. I came by to see it."

A smile lights up the man's face. "You're Luke Ferry's kid?"

It feels good to be recognized as something besides William Kirkland's granddaughter. "That's right. Did you know him?"

"Sure. Not real well, of course, but he came to a few meetings here. Kept to himself quite a bit. But he did this helicopter for us. I tell you, for anybody who served in Nam, the Huey medevac is a thing of beauty. Like a guardian angel coming to pull you out of hell."

I nod, unsure what I've really come for. "I thought you kept it inside the building."

"We do, most of the year. But on July Fourth, the priest from St. Mary's does the blessing of the fleet out at Lake St. John. There's a boat parade out there, and contests for best float. We do one every year for the MIAs. To keep up awareness, you know? We've put your daddy's chopper on there four years running."

"It's been sitting out here for the past month?"

The bearded man looks embarrassed. "We had tarps on it till today. I'm actually here to break down the float. We brought it back from the lake on a flatbed, and this is as far as we got. Everybody was a little drunk. But, man, people love to see that Huey coming up the lake. Gives 'em a good feeling inside. Specially these last couple years, with all the boys overseas now."

I find myself smiling. "Daddy would have liked that."

The vet nods, then sticks out his hand. "Jim Burley, miss. Proud to know you."

"Cat Ferry."

Another smile. "Cat, huh?"

"Short for Catherine."

"Oh, I get it. Well, what can I do for you?"

Tell me my father was a good man. . . . "Well, I was only eight when my dad died, so he never really told me about the war. Do you know much about what he did over there?"

Burley thinks for a bit, then scratches his thick beard. "Why don't we sit down in the shade over here?"

I follow him to an olive-drab picnic table beneath an oak tree and sit opposite him. A bumper sticker stuck to the top of the table reads, FOR THOSE WHO FOUGHT FOR IT, FREEDOM HAS A FLAVOR THE PROTECTED WILL NEVER KNOW.

"Your dad was a quiet guy," Burley begins. "I guess you know that already. A few years younger than me, Luke was. Served his tour a couple years after mine. Lots of guys who come in here are quiet types, but they tend to open up after a while. Luke stayed quiet. He wasn't unfriendly or anything. Just needed a little more space than most people, you know? The war did that to some of us."

I nod, trying to picture my father inside the little building, or even sitting at this picnic table. He needed a *lot* more space than most people.

"All I really know," Burley says, "is that Luke didn't pull no run-of-the-mill tour. Way I heard it, he was a crack shot long before he got inducted. Hunted all his life out at Cranfield, probably. So when they took him into the Airborne, they made him a sniper."

"A sniper?" I've never heard this before.

Burley nods. "That's a tough job. One-on-one killing, you know? And not in the heat of battle, either. To do that job, you gotta be able to kill in cold blood. And unless you got a screw loose somewhere, that takes something out of you."

I can't believe no one in the family has told me this. But maybe they didn't know either. "Do you remember anything else?"

Burley takes a deep breath and sighs. "Couple of the guys wangled a few facts out of Luke. The picture we got was this. Your daddy was taken into some kind of special unit. Sort of a raiding unit. The kind they used to go into places we weren't supposed to be in."

"Like where?"

"Like Laos and Cambodia."

An inexplicable shudder goes through me. I close my eyes and see Nathan Malik sitting before me, telling me about his stone Buddha. *I brought it back from Cambodia. . . .*

"Do you know for sure that my father was in Cambodia?"

"I don't know nothing for sure, honey. But it was one of those places. Anyway, there was some trouble about this unit he was in. Accusations of atrocities, that kind of thing."

I shake my head, more from surprise than disbelief.

"The government got up an investigation for a bunch of courts-martial. Then they just dropped it all. Flushed the whole thing down the Pentagon toilet."

"When was this?"

"Some of it during the war, I think. Soon after it happened. Then again later on. I think Luke was dead by that time, though."

"Look, Mr. Burley, I want you to be straight with me. Do you think my dad was involved in war crimes?"

The vet thinks about this for a while. "I tell you, Cat, looking back on it now, a lot of what I done over there seems like crimes to me. But when I was *there*, I didn't think twice about it. It was part of the job. The rules of engagement didn't cover half the situations you ran into. It was survival. Hindsight's a luxury we didn't have. Now, a lot of Hollywood movies don't show nothing but grunts cutting off ears and killing women and kids. And some of that happened, I won't lie. That and worse. But most guys just served their tour and did the best they could to be honorable men."

"I'm sure that's true. But I'm not here about them. I want to know about my father."

Burley gives me a heavyhearted smile. "I'm telling you about him, though it may not sound like it. I'm telling you that whatever Luke did, you ain't gonna be able to understand by looking backward from the USA thirty-five years later. I'm not excusing atrocities or anything like that. I'm just saying . . . hell, I don't know what I'm saying."

A deep sense of frustration is building inside me. "Is there anybody I could talk to who might know more specific information? Somebody Daddy might have confided in?"

Burley shrugs. "There was a black guy Luke was pretty tight with for a while. Some of the brothers don't come around here as much as they could. We try to make 'em welcome—a vet's a vet, you know?—but it was the same in-country. Especially after sixty-eight, when Dr. King was assassinated."

"Do you remember this guy's name?"

"Jesse something. Can't quite recall his last name." Burley waves back toward the building. "Ought to have it inside, but I don't. Our records are for shit right now. Computer's busted. Jesse was in the Airborne, too, I remember that. Different unit from your daddy's. Same unit Jimi Hendrix served in. Jesse was real proud of that."

"Was Jesse from here?"

"No, Louisiana. Down the river a bit. St. Francisville, maybe."

"You can't remember his last name?"

Burley squints like man looking into bright sunlight. "I know it . . . I just can't *get* it. Old-timer's disease, you know? Wait a second. Billings? No. Billups? *Billups,* that's it! Like the gas stations we used to have around here. Jesse Billups, Spec 4, 101st Airborne."

I'd hoped I would recognize the name, but I don't. Glancing down the hill toward the tennis courts, I wipe sweat from my eyes. I played tennis down there a few times. In another life, it seems now. I look up at my car but feel no inclination to drive anywhere. "Do you need help taking down the float?"

Burley laughs. "I don't need it, but I'd sure love the company. I know you got better things to do than hang around here, though."

"I'm not sure I do."

"Hey!" He slaps the picnic table with a beefy palm. "You ought to be able to find Jesse real easy."

"Why's that?"

"You're Dr. Kirkland's granddaughter, right? Grew up over in that big house, where Luke lived in the barn?"

"Yes."

"Well, Jesse was related to the housekeeper over there. Second cousin, or nephew, something like that."

My scalp and palms are tingling. "To the housekeeper? You mean Pearlie?"

"*Pearlie.* That's it!" Burley laughs. "Jesse used to talk about her some, and not all of it good. His mama was related to Pearlie, some way."

I stand so suddenly that I feel light-headed. "I'm sorry, Mr. Burley, I need to go."

"Sure. No problem."

"Thank you so much." I'm already walking backward toward my car.

"Hey, listen," Burley calls. "Don't you worry about what your daddy done over there. He came back alive, that's the main thing, right there."

Is it? I wonder, trotting toward the Audi. *I wonder.*

"He made us this Huey," Burley says. "Anybody makes something that pretty and gives it away for free, he's gotta be all right down deep. You know?"

No, I don't, I think, climbing into the car. *I don't know anything anymore.*

CHAPTER

24

Pearlie Washington is sitting on her porch reading the newspaper when I drive into the lot behind the slave quarters. Aunt Ann's Acura hasn't returned—or else it's come and gone—but my grandfather's Lincoln is back. I see no sign of Billy Neal, though, and I'm glad for it.

"Where you been?" Pearlie asks, not looking up from her copy of the *Natchez Examiner*. She's wearing street clothes and a pair of reading glasses. They look expensive, unlike the Wal-Mart specials my mother wears.

"Driving."

"*Driving?* That sounds like what you used to tell me when you was a teenager out chasing boys."

"I never chased boys. They chased me." There are two rockers on Pearlie's porch. I sit in the empty one.

"Don't bother asking," she says. "I done told you all I know."

"About what?"

"Whatever it is you gonna ask me about."

I look over at the rows of blooming rosebushes. "Pearlie, I think you could talk from now until next week and not finish telling me everything you know about this family."

"I ain't paid to talk. I'm paid to clean." She licks her finger and turns a page. "Dr. Overton's wife died yesterday. She was a cranky old so-and-so."

"Tell me about Jesse Billups."

Pearlie goes still, like a deer sensing threat.

"Don't even try to pretend you don't know who he is."

She looks up from her newspaper at last. "Who you been talking to?"

"A guy who served in Vietnam. Jesse Billups knew Daddy, Pearlie. I want you to tell me who and where he is. You know I'll find out one way or the other. I can't believe you never told me about him before."

Pearlie closes her eyes as though in pain. "Jesse is my sister's child. Half sister, really. We had the same mama but different daddies."

"Your sister from DeSalle Island?"

Pearlie nods. "Ivy the only sister I got."

I see an image of a small, strong black woman with her hair pulled back in a bun. With this image comes the smell of alcohol and a memory of pain. Ivy gave me a painful tetanus injection once, after I stepped on a nail in the pond.

"Where is she now?"

"Ivy done passed, baby. Don't you remember? Been almost four years now."

I don't remember hearing that Ivy died, but I remember the woman well—not by name, but by occupation. She worked as my grandfather's assistant in the little building known on DeSalle Island as the clinic. Grandpapa maintains the clinic to treat the island's black population whenever he stays there, or when emergencies arise. At times, more than a hundred people have lived and worked on the island, many of them using chain saws and dangerous farm equipment daily. I saw Grandpapa stitch up so many lacerations there that by twelve I could do it myself if the need arose. He charged nothing for his services, so most islanders waited for his visits rather than seeking medical care on the "mainland" across the river. Ivy had no formal medical training, but she was smart, silent, and had deft hands. Grandpapa taught her enough to do a good deal of "doctoring" in his absence. Their most famous exploit was removing my aunt Ann's appendix by lantern light during a storm that cut off the island from the mainland in 1958.

"What about Jesse Billups?" I ask. "Is he still around?"

Pearlie sighs and rubs her forehead. "Baby, what you digging into all this old business for?"

I refuse to be sidetracked. "Is Jesse still alive?"

"Jesse's the foreman on the island now. Or caretaker, or overseer, whatever they call it now."

"Jesse Billups is caretaker on the island now? He runs the hunting camp, all of that?"

"Sho' do."

"How old is he?"

"Fiftysomething, I guess."

"If he was Ivy's son, why don't I remember him?"

Pearlie shrugs again. "He took his daddy's last name, for one thing, even though he was an outside child. Plus, he was gone a lot back in your day. Went off to the city with some big plan, but all he got was big trouble. Did him a hitch in Angola, right across from the island. Funny, when you think about it."

I've never seen much funny about Angola Penitentiary. "You don't sound like you care for him much."

"Jesse's all right, I reckon. I told you the other day. Some good boys went over to that war and came back different. Not their fault."

"What happened to him in the war?"

"Different things, I guess. Some inside, some out. He never talked about it. Same as Mr. Luke."

"Did you ever see Jesse talking to Daddy?"

"I seen 'em together some. Thick as thieves for a while. Mr. Luke spent a lot of time down on the island. Said he liked the quiet down there."

"What did they do together?"

"Smoked that dope, probably." Pearlie's voice is bitter. "That's about all Jesse done after he got back."

"And Daddy?"

"Mr. Luke did some of that, too. Not as bad as Jesse, though. Your daddy had a lot of pain from his wound . . . in his mind, too. I think he used that weed to help. No hard stuff, though."

"When was the last time you saw Jesse?"

"Been a long time, now. He stay on the island, and I don't go down there."

"Never?"

Pearlie shakes her head. "I don't like it. Don't like the peoples, and they don't like me."

"Why not? You were born on that island."

She snorts. "I'm a house nigger, girl."

"You're kidding me. That kind of stuff is ancient history."

She peers at me over the rims of her reading glasses. "Not on DeSalle Island it ain't. They never joined the modern world down there. Dr. Kirkland likes it that way, and I think the black peoples down there like it all right, too. Change is something they can't abide."

"Well, I'm going down there."

Pearlie's eyes widen. "When?"

"Today. I'm going to see Jesse."

"Child, don't you go messing round down there. Can't no good come of that."

"You think something bad will come of it?"

Pearlie folds her newspaper and lays it beside her chair. "You go poking a stick in a hole, you best be ready for a snake to crawl out of it."

I'm about to ask her what's she's afraid of when my cell phone beeps. The screen shows a text message waiting. I flip open the phone and hit a button. The message reads, *I'm going to call you in a second. Don't even think about not answering. It's about Malik. Sean.*

"Somebody trying to call you?" Pearlie asks. "I hate them phones."

"Someone's about to."

The phone rings on cue.

"Tell me," I answer.

"The shit's hit the fan," says Sean. "A little after eleven, we got an anonymous call telling us to check an apartment in Kenner. The caller said Malik rented it under an alias. We got a warrant and went there with some Jefferson Parish detectives. The landlord ID'd Malik from a photo, and we went in."

"What did you find?"

"A lot of video equipment, for one thing. Pro quality stuff, and a computer rigged for digital film production."

Video equipment? "What else?"

"We found the murder weapon, Cat."

My throat tightens. "What?"

"Thirty-two-caliber Charter Arms revolver. The handgun that killed our five victims. It had the serial number filed off. We're going to try to bring it out with acid, but we don't know anything yet."

"Did you arrest Malik for murder?"

"Yeah. Got him at his home."

"He resist?"

"No. Went like a lamb. And no Hollywood Walk this time. We booked him and took him to the CLU through the garage."

"Jesus. Who do you think the tipper was?"

"We don't know. Maybe one of Malik's patients? A girl he took to that apartment?"

"Or a guy," I suggest.

"The caller was female. Anyway, Malik was already so high profile because of the contempt story that we had to go ahead with his arraignment. The DA argued for no bail, but the judge set one anyway. A million bucks."

"Can he pay that?"

"Probably. He's got a house across the lake he could put up as surety. He was in Central Lockup, but they just moved him to the parish prison."

The anonymous tip about the location of the murder weapon bothers me. It was too easy. "Sean, do you really think Malik is the killer?"

"I'm a lot more convinced than I was yesterday. I just found out that ten days after Malik got back from Vietnam, his father was badly beaten. Spent two months in the hospital, and he never looked the same again."

"Did Malik's father ID his assailant?"

"Said he didn't see anything. It happened in his home, but nothing was stolen."

"Did Malik have an alibi?"

"Nobody even asked him for one. This was Columbus, Mississippi, not Berkeley, California. Malik was a hero, just home from the war. What did he have to be pissed about?"

As I consider this, Billy Neal walks into my field of vision, just below Pearlie's porch. "Dr. Kirkland wants to see you," he says, though I'm obviously using the phone. "He told me to bring you to the study."

"Tell him I'll see him later. I have somewhere to go first."

"What?" says Sean.

A strange smile distorts Billy Neal's mouth. "The island, you mean?"

"Sean, let me call you back." I put the phone in my pocket and address the driver. "Have you been eavesdropping here?"

Neal ignores the question. "He's waiting for you now. He doesn't like to wait."

I turn to Pearlie. "What's going on? What is it about the island that nobody wants me to know?"

Pearlie gets up from her rocker and gives me a hug. "It's not my place, baby. Go talk to your granddaddy. If you still want to go down to the island after that, maybe I'll go with you." She steps to the porch rail and gives Billy Neal a withering glare. "Get out of my sight, trash."

The driver laughs, a brittle sound that makes me think of a boy I once saw torturing a cat in a sandbox.

Pearlie turns and goes into her house without another word.

"Your grandfather's waiting," Neal says again.

"Tell him I'll be there in a minute."

"He said I should bring you."

"Listen, asshole, you keep standing there, you'll be waiting all day."

Billy Neal gives me his crooked smile. "I wouldn't mind that. You ain't half bad to look at."

The door behind me bangs open, and Pearlie walks out carrying a rifle. Her eyes are squinted nearly shut and her jaw is set tight. "Get away from here, trash," she says in a menacing voice.

"That's a pellet gun," says Neal, his smile broadening. "An air rifle."

"That's right." Pearlie raises the rifle until it's pointed at his midsection. "I use it to kill the possums that tear up the garbage. But if I shoot you in the balls with it, they gonna swell up like a watermelon, and you ain't gonna be bothering no womens for a long time." To emphasize her point, Pearlie puts her eye to the sight and aims the barrel at Neal's genitals.

The smile vanishes from the driver's face. "Your day's coming, nigger."

"If I tell Dr. Kirkland you bothering his grandbaby, your day's come and gone, cracker. Get out of here!"

Billy Neal laughs again, then walks slowly back toward Malmaison.

"Why did you do that?" I ask. "I can take care of myself."

"He's a bad apple. I don't know why Dr. Kirkland keeps him around here."

"He's a bodyguard, you said the other day."

Pearlie spits over the rail. "That boy got a law degree, too, from somewhere. You believe that?"

This revelation makes me think of Sean and his night-school law degree. He told me tales of con men and criminals taking the same courses and earning the same degree he did. "I believe it."

"I think he got something over Dr. Kirkland," Pearlie says softly.

"What do you mean? Something *on* him?"

She nods once, firmly.

"What could he have on Grandpapa?"

Pearlie shakes her head, her eyes still on the retreating figure. "His mama used to work for your granddaddy. Secretary or bookkeeper, something. She knew things."

"What could she know about? Something illegal?"

Pearlie turns to me, her eyes hard. "I don't know. Dr. Kirkland's careful with the family business. But it's got to be something. Your granddaddy wouldn't let that trash tie his shoes, otherwise."

Her comment reminds me that my grandfather—a man who places such value on integrity that he closes million-dollar deals with a handshake—has destroyed the careers of several men who crossed him, or who lied to him in business deals. "I wouldn't want to try to blackmail Grandpapa."

"Lord knows that's right. Be like climbing into a bear pit with the bear in it."

"You stay away from that driver, Pearlie."

She reaches out and squeezes my wrist. "You, too, baby. Things have changed around here."

"Have they?" I shake my head. "I don't think so. I think things were always this way. I was just too young to see it."

CHAPTER

25

Grandpapa is waiting for me in his study. He's sitting in the same leather executive chair he sat in two days ago, when he told me the same old lie about my father's death. What does he want to tell me now?

He doesn't speak when I enter. He sits erect in his chair, his left hand cradling a glass of Scotch, his blue eyes looking strangely wet. He's still wearing his suit and tie, and his tanned skin and silver hair give him the appearance of a veteran Hollywood actor awaiting a scene—not a character actor, but an aging leading man.

"Your driver said you want to talk to me."

"That's right," he says, his voice a commanding blend of baritone and bass. "I need to ask you a question, Catherine. Please sit down."

Something makes me want to take the initiative away from him. "Why do you keep that lowlife around?"

Grandpapa appears taken off guard. "Who? Billy?"

"Yes. He doesn't belong here, and you know it."

Grandpapa looks at the floor and purses his lips, as though reluctant to discuss this with me. Then he speaks in a tone of regret. "The casino business isn't like our other family businesses, Catherine. Las Vegas wears a corporate image nowadays, but the old unsavory practices are still around. The big Nevada boys don't like competition, and they have quite a stake in Mississippi. I need someone who knows that world inside and out. Billy worked in Las Vegas for twelve years, and he spent three working for an Indian casino in New Mexico. The exact nature of his experience is something into which I don't delve too deeply. I'm not proud of that, but sometimes to accomplish something good, you have to rub elbows with the devil. That's the nature of the gambling business."

"It surprises me to hear you talk that way."

He shrugs in the chair. "This town is desperate. We can't afford our high ideals any longer. Please take a seat, dear."

I sit in a club chair and face him across a Bokhara rug.

"Still off the alcohol?" he asks, motioning toward the sideboard.

"So far, so good."

"I wish I had your willpower. Must be the diving that gives you the discipline."

"You said you needed to ask me a question."

"Yes. This morning you mentioned hiring a professional forensic team to search your old bedroom. For blood and other evidence, you said."

I nod but say nothing.

"Have you shelved that plan, given what I told you this morning about Luke's death?"

"No."

Grandpapa doesn't react at first. Then he raises his glass and takes a long drink of Scotch, closing his eyes as he swallows. After a few moments, he opens them again and sets the glass on a table beside his chair.

"I can't let you do that," he says.

What do you mean? I ask silently. But aloud, I say, "Why not?"

"Because I killed your father, Catherine. I shot Luke."

The words don't really register at first. I mean, I *hear* them. I recognize the order in which they were spoken. But their actual significance doesn't really sink in.

"I know this is a shock to you," Grandpapa goes on. "I wish there were some other way to deal with this. That you'd never have to know. But you found that blood, and now there's no other way to put an end to this. I know you. You're just like me. You won't stop until you know the truth. So, I'm going to give it to you."

"I thought you gave it to me this morning."

He shifts in his chair. "I lied to you before, darling. We both know that, and you're probably wondering why you should believe me now. All I can tell you is this: when you hear what I'm about to tell you, you'll know it's true. You'll know it in your bones. And I wish to God it was a different truth."

"What are you talking about? What is this?"

Grandpapa rubs his tanned face with his right hand, squeezing his jaw. "Catherine, someday you will get old, and you'll hear from some doctor that you're going to die. But what you're about to hear will be worse than that. Part of you is going to die today. I want you to brace yourself."

My extremities are going cold. I felt a little like this when I saw my home pregnancy test turn pink. A temporary paralysis set in while my mind tried to adapt to the total transformation of my life. I feel that paralysis now, but with it comes a terrible foreboding. A fear that my whole world is about to be sucked inside out by something that's been kept from me my whole life. And the funny thing is, I'm not surprised at all. It's like I've known this moment was coming since I was a little girl. That one day I would find myself in this room, or a room like it, while someone gave me the terrible secret of why I am the way I am.

"There was no prowler here on the night Luke died," Grandpapa says. "You already suspect that. That's why you asked me if Luke committed suicide."

"Did he?" asks a faint voice that comes from my throat.

"No. I told you, I killed him."

"But why? Did you argue with him? Was it an accident?"

"No." Grandpapa squares his shoulders and looks me in the eye. "Two days ago you asked me why I didn't like Luke. I didn't tell you the complete truth. Yes, his reaction to his war service bothered me, and the fact that he couldn't provide for you and your mother didn't help matters. But from the very beginning, I had a bad feeling about that boy. Something wasn't right about him. Your mother didn't see it because she was in love. But I saw it. I couldn't put my finger on exactly what it was. I just sensed something, as a man, that made me recoil."

"I can't stand this. Please just tell me whatever it is."

"Do you remember that when Luke was having his bad periods— his spells, Pearlie called them—you were the only person he'd let near him? The only one he'd let into the barn while he worked?"

"Of course."

"He spent a lot of time with you, Catherine. You were his connection to the real world. You two had a very unusual relationship. And as time went on, I started to feel that it wasn't an appropriate relationship."

The numbness is spreading to my heart. "How do you mean?"

"That night Luke died, I wasn't reading downstairs. I had turned off all the lights downstairs and pretended to go up to bed, but I didn't. I'd done this several nights in a row. Luke was supposedly leaving for the island. That night, instead of watching from the window, I went out into the yard with a flashlight and sat on the grass." Another swig of Scotch. "After about an hour, I saw Luke coming up the hill from the barn. He wasn't walking like himself. In the dark I actually thought he was a different person. I thought he *was* a prowler. But it was Luke. He went through the door of your house without making a sound. I circled the house and went to your window. I saw a crack of light as he opened your door. I thought he might be checking on you . . . but he wasn't. The door opened and closed quickly, and I knew he'd gone into your room and stayed there."

I'm dreaming. If I can wake myself up, I won't have to hear this. But I can't wake up. I keep sitting motionless, and my grandfather keeps talking.

"I slipped inside the house. Gwen's door was open, but she was sound asleep. Then I opened your door and clicked on my flashlight."

"No," I whisper. "Don't."

"Luke was in the bed with you, Catherine. I hoped it was some kind of psychological dependency, something like that. That he needed to get into bed with you to be able to sleep. But it wasn't that. When I yanked back the covers—"

"Don't!"

"He wasn't wearing pants, Catherine. And your gown was pushed up to your chest."

I'm shaking my head like a child trying to reverse time: to bring back a dog that was run over by a car or a parent who was just lowered into the earth. But it does no good.

Grandpapa stands and looks at the French windows, his voice rising with emotion. "He was molesting you, Catherine. Before I could say anything, he jumped up and started trying to explain himself. That it wasn't what it looked like. But there was no denying the state he was in. I grabbed his arm and yanked him toward the door. He went crazy. He started hitting me." Grandpapa turns to me, his eyes bright. "Luke was so passive most of the time, it took me completely by surprise. But he could be savage when he wanted to be. He wouldn't have survived the war without that capacity for violence."

Grandpapa stops three feet away from me, looking down from what seems an enormous height. "I wanted to get you out of there, but he'd hit me several times and showed no sign of stopping. I remembered the rifle that hung over the fireplace in the den. I ran out and grabbed it, chambered a round, and went back in to get you.

"Luke was in the corner by the closet, down on his knees. Your bed was empty. I knew you must be terrified, and I figured you'd tried to escape through that closet. Back then it didn't have a back wall. It was like the old country places, where adjoining bedroom closets are actually the same space. Anyway, I told Luke to get away from you and stand up. When he didn't, I walked over with the rifle and told him to get the hell off my property and never come back."

Grandpapa shakes his head, his eyes cloudy with memory. "Maybe it was the sight of the gun that did it. Or maybe he couldn't deal with the idea that he was going to be exposed. But he attacked me again. He came up out of that corner like a wild animal. I pulled the trigger out of pure reflex." Grandpapa's hand actually jerks when he says this. "You know the rest. The round hit Luke in the chest, and he died quickly."

The silence in the study is absolute. Then, out of the vacuum that is me at this moment, a question rises. "Did I see it happen?"

"I don't know, baby. When I got to the closet, you weren't there. You must have crawled through to your mother's bedroom. I suspect you tried to wake her up but couldn't do it. Do you remember any of this?"

"Maybe that," I whisper. "Trying to wake Mom up. But maybe it wasn't that night, I don't know. I think that happened a lot back then."

"But you remember nothing of the abuse?"

I shake my head with robotic precision.

"I thought not. But you've never recovered from it, just the same. It's haunted you your whole life. I've watched you all these years, wishing I could do something for you. But I couldn't see *what*. I didn't see how telling you this about your father could help you.

They say the truth shall set you free, but I'm not so sure. If you hadn't found that blood in your room, I doubt I'd ever have told this thing."

He goes to the sideboard, pours a nearly full glass of vodka, and holds it out to me. The vodka might as well be water. I'm so anesthetized by shock that even my craving for alcohol is gone.

"Take it," he says. "Do you good."

No, it won't, I say silently. *It'll hurt me. It'll poison my baby.*

"What are you thinking, Catherine?"

I don't speak. I'm not sharing my only pure secret with anyone.

"I'm not sure what to do now," he says. "You've had problems with depression in the past, and I was damn little help to you. I was from the old school. If I couldn't palpate it, irradiate it, amputate it, or resect it, it wasn't a problem. I know different now. I worry that telling you this could trigger a major depressive episode. Are you still taking SSRIs for that?"

I don't reply. My silence must remind him of the wordless year that followed my father's death, because it spooks him.

"Catherine?" he says in an anxious voice. "Can you speak?"

I don't know. Am I speaking now?

"Surely you have some questions. You always do."

But I'm not me anymore.

"Well, after you've had time to absorb this, I think you'll see why I don't want you bringing outsiders here to search that room for more blood. No possible good can come from anybody learning what I just told you. None at all. But great harm could result."

"Who else knows?" I whisper.

"No one."

"Not Pearlie?"

A solemn shake of the head. "She might suspect, but she doesn't know."

"Mother?"

"No one, Catherine."

"Did you really examine me that night? After the police left?"

He nods sadly.

"What did you find?"

A deep sigh. "Vaginal and anal irritation. Old scarring. Your hymen wasn't intact. That's not conclusive in itself, but I knew what I'd seen. If I'd waited ten minutes to go into that room, I'd have found more evidence. And if a forensic team had tested your bedsheets back then—"

"Please stop."

"All right, darling. Just tell me what I can do."

"Nothing."

"I'm not sure that's true. Now that you know the truth about your past, it might be helpful to speak to someone. I can get you access to the top people in the country."

"I have to go."

"Where?"

"Anywhere."

"Why don't you stay here for a while? I'll have Pearlie fix a room upstairs. You don't ever have to go back into that slave quarters again. You'd have never lived there in the first place if it had been up to me. It was Luke who refused to move in here. I offered him a whole damn wing. I guess now you know why. Anyway, you take a few days and start trying to get your mind around this. It could take a long while to really deal with it."

I can't believe this is my grandfather talking. His philosophy was always unequivocal: *When life throws you a curveball, you knock that son of a bitch right down the pitcher's throat.* I actually heard him say that many times. Yet here he stands, talking like he's been watching *Dr. Phil* with my mother.

"I have to go now, Grandpapa."

I turn and walk quickly to the French doors that lead out onto the lawn. His footsteps follow me, then stop. In a moment I'm standing in bright sunlight on an endless plain of freshly mown grass.

And there the tears come. Great racking sobs that make my ribs hurt. I fall to my knees and bend over the grass the way I would if I were puking drunk. But I'm not drunk. I am desolate. What I want most is out of my skin. I want to take a knife, slash myself from my pubic bone to my neck, and crawl out of this disgusting body.

"Catherine?" calls a frantic female voice. "What's the matter? Did you hurt yourself?"

It's my mother. She's kneeling in the flower beds near the front entrance of Malmaison. The mere sight of her throws me into panic. When she gets to her feet, I stand and race for the far corner of the house.

Rounding the corner of Malmaison, I sprint along the back wall of our slave quarters. My bedroom window flashes at my left shoulder, and I shudder at the sight of it. There's my car. My connection to

New Orleans. My escape. Mom's cries fade as I slide behind the wheel and slam the door. The revving motor is the first thing that slows the spinning panic in my chest.

Throwing the Audi into gear, I roar out of the parking lot, spraying gravel against the wall of the slave quarters. Never have I wanted to leave a place so badly as I do Malmaison at this moment. Of course there is only one way to truly leave this place behind.

Die.

CHAPTER

26

DeSalle Island rises out of the Mississippi River like the back of a sleeping dog. The long, low line of trees stretches four miles north to south, three miles east to west. It's so big, you wouldn't know it was an island without crossing it.

The setting of my childhood summers, the island is as much a part of me as Natchez and New Orleans, yet it stands utterly apart from them. Apart from everything, really. Nominally part of Louisiana, it is in truth subject to no authority other than that of my family. It was created when the Mississippi River, having wound back upon itself like a writhing snake, finally cut off its own tortuous bend with a great rush of floodwater that shortened its course by more than five miles. Left in the wake of that cataclysm was a great island covered with timber, rich topsoil, wild game, and the shacks of a dozen black families that worked for my ancestors for 150 years—first as slaves, then as sharecroppers, and finally as wage earners. Floods eventually smothered the topsoil with sand and killed the oaks and pines, but the blacks worked on, raising cattle instead of cotton, managing a deer camp, and doing whatever else kept food in their children's bellies. The only whites who come here are members of my family, or business associates of my grandfather's invited here to hunt.

I'm parked where the narrowest part of the old river channel flows through a treacherous plain of mud. Here a dirt causeway stretches across the old channel to the island. Every spring it's washed away by overflow from the river, but every summer it's rebuilt, the cost being split between my grandfather and an oil company that operates several wells on the island. The river is high for this time of year, and the backwater laps against the edges of the causeway with maybe an inch to spare.

I've been parked at the end of the causeway for twenty minutes, trying to decide whether it's safe to cross. A line of thunderclouds has been blowing up from the south for the past hour. If they cut loose with enough rain, the causeway could disappear under the rising water. It's happened before.

I drove the seventy miles here in a state of near hypnosis, my only goal to reach this place where my father spent so much time, to somehow solve the tragic mysteries of his life and mine. I was conscious enough to call Sean twice, but he didn't answer. That means he's with his wife. If he were in a task force meeting or even at a fresh murder scene, he would have at least text-messaged me back. So . . . the father of my baby is almost certainly trying to save his marriage.

After failing to reach Sean, I felt an irresistible compulsion to speak to Nathan Malik. I called his cell phone, but it kicked me over to his voice mail. I wanted to leave a message, but I didn't. If the psychiatrist is still in jail, his cell phone is probably sitting on the desk of some FBI agent. It might even be in John Kaiser's pocket. Whoever has it has probably already put the Bureau's technical machinery in motion, trying to trace the number of the person who called their main suspect.

When I couldn't reach Malik, I started paging through my digital phone book. That's one thing you do when you're depressed. One thing I do, anyway. Go through my phone book calling friend after friend, praying for a sympathetic voice. I call people I haven't seen in months, and even years. But today . . . I didn't do that. As the rolling hills of southwest Mississippi swept me into the boot of Louisiana, I called directory assistance and got the number of Michael Wells's medical office. It took some convincing, but his receptionist finally put me through. I told Michael I'd really like to talk to him, if he had some time.

"I'm up to my ass in alligators right now," he said, laughing. "Sick two-year-olds, actually, but it amounts to the same thing. I'd love to see you later, though. Would you let me buy you dinner? We actually have a Thai restaurant in Natchez now."

I was silent for a moment—or maybe longer—because Michael said, "Cat? Is something wrong?"

"Umm . . . yeah. That's what I wanted to talk to you about. But we can do it some other time."

"Tell me what's wrong."

"Do you believe in repressed memories?"

"Related to what? That usually has to do with child abuse."

"Yeah. Like that."

He was silent for a bit. "Is this a hypothetical question?"

I wasn't sure how to answer. "Sort of."

"Forget about dinner. Come to my office right now. I'm on Jeff Davis Boulevard. You remember where that is?"

"Sure, but it's okay. Forget I called. I'm not even in town right now."

"Where are you? New Orleans?"

"No. Look . . . if I get back in time, I'll call you later, okay?"

"Cat—"

I hung up and put my ringer on silent. Why was I trying to involve a pediatrician who knew nothing about me and my problems? Because we'd known each other in school? Because he had a sympathetic face? Because he treated children, and right at that moment I felt about four years old?

Across the old river channel, a green johnboat is plying the shore in the shadow of some cypress trees. Squinting, I can make out the silhouette of a shirtless black teenager. He paddles a few feet, bends down, works at something, then straightens up and paddles on. When he hauls a fat, gray fish into the air, I realize what he's doing. Checking a trotline. The static line has dozens of hooks hanging from it, one every few feet, baited with something stinky to attract the catfish that abound in this old channel. It's been ten years since I visited the island, but life doesn't seem to have changed much.

As the boy works his way along the line, I pick up my cell phone and speed-dial Dr. Hannah Goldman. Hannah is my court of last resort. I don't call her often, but when I do, she answers immediately or gets back to me within an hour. You don't find commitment like that in too many therapists.

"Cat?" she says, apparently looking at a caller ID screen.

"Mm-hm," I say in a tiny voice.

"Where are you? We have a bad connection." Her statement is punctuated by a burst of static.

"Out of town. It doesn't matter."

"What's going on?"

"I just found out something."

"Do you want to tell me about it?"

"I don't know."

"Well, you called me. I think you want to tell me about it."

"Okay."

"Twenty words or less."

"My grandfather killed my father."

Not much throws Dr. Goldman, but this does. After several seconds, she says, "Please tell me some details. I thought your father was shot by an intruder."

"I thought so, too. But my grandfather just told me a different story. It's complicated. I found some blood in my old bedroom. A latent bloodstain, I wasn't even looking for it. But it got me thinking about that night. I started asking questions. I was going to bring in an outside forensic team, so he decided to tell me the truth."

"'He' being Dr. Kirkland?"

"Yes."

"Was the shooting an accident?"

"No. He caught my father abusing me. Sexually abusing me. And he killed him."

"I see," Dr. Goldman says in her most professional voice.

She says that to keep from saying *Dear God* or something similar. Hannah tries to be detached, but she's not. That's why she lets me call her this way. Hannah Goldman is the middle ground between professional detachment and the activist commitment of Nathan Malik.

"Do you believe what your grandfather told you?"

"He's never lied to me before. Except about this, I mean, by omission. He said he kept the truth from me to protect me. And I always felt like something was wrong with the story they'd told me as a child."

"Do you have any memory of the events he described?"

"No. But I've been thinking about repressed memories a lot lately."

"Why?"

"It has to do with a murder case I'm working on."

"The murders here in New Orleans?"

"Yes."

"I see."

"Do you believe in repressed memories, Hannah? I mean, do you believe that a person can totally block something from their conscious mind?"

"Yes, I do. It's a controversial subject. Very little is known about the neuromechanics of memory. But current evidence indicates that some trauma victims dissociate during their experiences and suffer amnesia for those events. The strange thing about your case is that it's happening backwards. You've been handed corroboration of abuse before you even started to remember it. Considering the issues we've been dealing with for so long, this information could be the greatest gift you ever receive. I know it's hard to see that now, but I think I'm right."

"Uh-huh."

"Listen to me, Cat. This is a very dangerous time. I want to see you as soon as you can get to my office."

"Like I said, I'm not in town now."

"Well, you need to get here. Are you drinking?"

"I haven't had a drink in . . . a long time. I'm pregnant."

"*What?*" This time Hannah can't mask her shock.

"I know I should have called you. But I'm doing okay."

"Listen to me. I think we should consider a hospital detox program. Then an inpatient abuse-recovery program somewhere. You can't do this alone. After what you've been told today, there's simply no telling what might happen. Flashbacks, body memories, suicidal impulses. Please tell me where you are."

"I'm all right, really. I just wanted to ask you something."

"What?"

"If my daddy was really doing that to me . . . how could my mother not know?"

Dr. Goldman takes her time before answering. "There are two or three scenarios in these situations that usually explain the mother's behavior. At *some* level she is aware of the abuse. But whether she's in denial or a silent coconspirator, I can't tell you without more information. In any case, the mother's primary goal is to keep her family together at all costs. Still . . . Gwen might have had no idea that this went on."

"Did *you* suspect it? Did you ever think I might have been sexually abused?"

"It's crossed my mind once or twice. But these days we don't bring up that idea unless the patient leads us there. And you never did. I thought the murder of your father was sufficient trauma to cause the problems we've seen. But now that this has surfaced, there's a lot of work we can do. That we need to do. I know some very good people in this area, Cat."

"Do you know Nathan Malik?"

"Why do you ask that?" Hannah's tone is suddenly guarded. "Do you know him?"

"I met him."

"Have you seen him as a patient?"

"No. Do you think he's good at what he does?"

"He's published some interesting articles. And he's had some surprising successes with recovered memories. But he uses radical techniques. They're unproven, and maybe even dangerous. I wouldn't want you under the care of someone like that. You're too fragile."

"I was just asking."

"Cat, are you in your car? I don't think you should be driving."

Dr. Goldman has received many calls from parking lots and from the shoulders of highways. "No. I'm just sitting here."

"Are you in a safe place?"

I look across at the island, ominous and even forbidding beneath the gray clouds. "Yeah."

"Where are you in your cycle? Up or down?"

"Neither. I'm numb."

A sharp intake of breath belies the calming words that follow. "Cat, my concern is that this new information will trigger a manic episode. You're in shock. You have no defenses left, other than mania. By going manic, you're brain convinces itself you're invulnerable. And if that happens, when you finally crash—" Static blots out Hannah's voice. "The main thing to keep in mind is that what happened between you and your father is *not your fault*. You were a child. You couldn't possibly make a free choice. You—" The static returns, this time like intermittent explosions in my ear.

"Thanks for answering," I say into the static. "Thanks for always—"

A blaring horn nearly knocks me out of my seat. I look in my rearview mirror and see a big white pickup truck parked behind me.

"Hannah?"

The connection is gone.

The truck honks again. It's waiting to use the causeway. The driver behind me may trust the muddy span, but I don't. I want to back up and get out of his way, but I can't seem to move. My hands lie on my lap like the hands of a quadriplegic. The horn blares again.

I can't move.

Half a minute passes. Then a black man who looks like he weighs three hundred pounds climbs out of the truck and walks toward my car. He's wearing a T-shirt stretched tightly over breasts much bigger than mine, and he doesn't look happy at being delayed. When he reaches my car, he knocks on the window.

Up close, the man has a kind face. He looks about fifty years old, and though it seems unlikely, I wonder if fate has put me in the path of Jesse Billups. With great effort I pull the switch that rolls down my window.

"You look like you in the wrong place, lady," he says in a deep and melodious voice.

"Are you Jesse Billups?"

The big man's mouth breaks into a broad smile. "*Hell* no. Jesse my cousin, though."

"Is he on the island today?"

"Jesse always on the island."

"I need to talk to him."

The man leans back and looks at my Audi, then laughs. "*You* got business with Jesse? That's kind of hard to believe."

"Is it? Well, I do."

"Wait a second. You with them *Sports Illustrated* people who shot that bikini spread here back in the spring?"

"No. I'm Catherine Ferry."

A blank look, then a faint spark of recognition in his eyes.

"Catherine *DeSalle* Ferry," I clarify.

The smile vanishes, and the man straightens up and starts to tuck in his T-shirt. "Sorry I didn't recognize you, ma'am. I'm Henry Washington. What can I do for you? You want me to lead you over the bridge and find Jesse?"

"Is it safe to cross?"

Washington cocks his round head to one side. "Well, that's a stretchy kind of word, *safe*. I been over this old thing many a time and it ain't caved in yet. But one of these days, it's bound to happen. Dr. Kirkland need to put a little more money in this old bridge. Make life a lot safer for everybody over here."

"I think you're right."

"Tell you what. Why don't you ride over with me? When you done talking to Jesse, he'll bring you back here to your car. And if he can't, I will."

"Sounds good to me."

Talking to another person—particularly a stranger—has forced me to reenter the world of time and motion. After backing the Audi under a pecan tree and locking it, I climb up into the cab of Henry's truck and perch on the passenger seat.

This truck is nothing like the pickup in my dream. It's high off the ground, with a fancy sound system, thick upholstery, and a roomy backseat. The truck in my dream is old and rusted, with round front fenders that make it look like a toy. A stick shift rises from the floor, and there's no upholstery at all, not even on the roof.

"You related to Dr. Kirkland?" Henry asks, putting the truck in gear and easing onto the soft dirt of the causeway.

"He's my grandfather."

"Huh. How come I ain't seen you down here before?"

"You probably have. It's been ten years since I visited, though. Longer than that since I spent any real time here."

"Well, it ain't changed much. We got electricity about five years back. Used to have to use generators when we wanted power."

"I remember. What about telephone service?"

Henry taps a cell phone on his belt. "These all we got, and they work about half the time. That's why we keep two-way radios in the trucks."

We hit a muddy patch, and the tail of the truck slides almost out from under us. I clench every muscle, but Henry just laughs as we straighten up again.

"You think you scared?" he booms. "My big ass goes into that water, it's all over but the crying."

"Why?"

"I can't swim."

Some people would laugh, but I can't. It makes me sad. As we near the shore of the island, a few raindrops splatter on the windshield.

"Will the rain cover the bridge?" I ask.

"Probably not," says Henry. "But I've seen it happen. Still, rain ain't gonna come down hard for another hour yet."

"How do you know?"

He looks at me and taps his nose. "The smell. They ought to put me on Channel Sixteen. I'm lots better than that weatherman they got."

"You have TV out here now?"

"Satellite. No cable, though."

Things have changed indeed. The last time I was here, DeSalle Island was as primitive as an Appalachian hollow. Two dozen shotgun shacks for the workers, my grandfather's clinic, some cabins near the lake for visiting hunters, and various utility buildings. Most of the shacks had outdoor plumbing. The only buildings with "modern" conveniences were my grandfather's hunting lodge—a plantation-style house built of cypress that overlooks the lake, designed by the noted Louisiana architect A. Hays Town—and the clinic.

"Almost there," Henry says, giving the pickup a little gas.

As the wall of trees gets nearer, I catch sight of a small shed near the water, and a chill runs through me. Like almost every other building on DeSalle Island, the shed has a tin roof. As the chill subsides, my heart suddenly pounds against my sternum.

Parked beside the shed is the round-nosed pickup truck from my dream.

CHAPTER

27

The moment Henry Washington's truck rolls onto the gravel road that follows the eastern shore of the island, a strange thrumming starts in my body. It's as though a mild current of electricity is sparking along my peripheral nerves, worsening the hand tremor that's bothered me for the past three days.

The island looks the same as it always did, the perimeter skirted with cypress trees growing out of the shallow water near the shore, the interior forested with willow brakes and giant cottonwoods. The cypresses are on my right now; we're driving north. I want to ask Henry about my grandfather's old truck, but a tightness in my chest stops me. As it falls farther behind, I try to remember the layout of the island.

From the air, DeSalle Island looks like a foreshortened version of South America. It's nearly bisected at the center by a horseshoe lake that was once a bend in the Mississippi River. Grandpapa's hunting lodge stands on the north shore of the lake, the shacks of the workers on the south. West of the lake lie five hundred acres of rice fields. The northern end of the island is pastureland dotted with cattle and oil wells, and south of the lake lie the woods we're passing now. Nestled among the trees at the lower edge of the woods are the cabins and utility buildings of the hunting camp, and below them—the Argentina of our island—

low-lying sand dunes and muddy slews tail down to the confluence of the old channel and the Mississippi River.

"Jesse's been on the north end chasing stray cows," Henry says, shaking his head as though such labor requires a certain level of insanity. "He said something about doing some plumbing work at the hunting camp after that."

In a few seconds the trees on my left will thin and reveal the lake and the cluster of shacks where the workers live.

"Didn't we already pass the road to the camp?"

Henry laughs. "The *closest* road, we did. But I don't take this truck into no slews. There's a gravel road goes into the camp from the north now."

I see the lake, dark green under the clouds, with small whitecaps whipped up by the wind. Henry turns left and follows a road that runs between the lake and the south edge of the woods. He waves broadly at a group of shotgun shacks by the lake. The sun has started to sink, and most of the porches have people on them, the old ones rocking slowly, the children scampering around in the dust with cats and dogs.

"Here we go," Henry says, turning right onto a narrow gravel road through the trees.

"What's Jesse like?" I ask.

"You don't know him?"

"No."

"Jesse's a mystery. He used to be the most laid-back cat on this island. Loved to smoke and talk. But now he's a hard-ass. I don't know why, exactly. But he is."

"Was it the war?"

Henry shrugs his big shoulders. "Who knows? Jesse don't talk too much. He mostly work, or watch other people work."

A minute passes in silence. The cabins of the hunting camp appear ahead. Unlike the shacks of the workers, many of which are made of tar paper or clapboard on brick stilts, the cabins are built of sturdy cypress, weathered gray and hard as steel. The roofs are corrugated tin that's rusted to dark orange.

"There Jesse," says Henry.

I don't see a man, but I do see a brown horse tied to the porch rail of one of the cabins. Henry pulls up in front of the cabin and honks his horn three times.

Nothing happens.

"He'll be here," Henry says.

Sure enough, a wiry black man wearing no shirt crawls from beneath the cabin, stands, and brushes himself off. At first he looks like a hundred other black workmen I've seen. Then he turns, and I see the right side of his face. Blotches of bright pink skin stand out like splatters of paint from his right shoulder to his right temple, and his cheek is a mound of deformed scar tissue.

"He got burned over in Vietnam," Henry says. "It looks bad, but we used to it now."

Henry leans out his window and shouts, "Yo, Jesse! Got a lady in here wants to talk to you!"

Jesse walks over to the truck—my side, not Henry's—and looks me in the eye. Henry uses his switch to roll down my window, which leaves only six inches of space between my face and Jesse Billups's scars.

"What you want with me?" he says in an insolent voice.

"I want to talk to you about my father."

"Who's your father?"

"Luke Ferry."

Jesse's eyes widen, and then he snorts like a horse. "Goddamn. All this time, and now you come back? I met you when you was a little girl. I knew your mama pretty well. How'd you get down here?"

Henry says, "Her car's parked on the other side of the bridge. I told her you'd take her back to it when she's ready. You got her okay?"

Jesse studies me for a bit. "Yeah, I'll take her back."

He opens my door and helps me down from the high cab. Jesse must have a half inch of calluses on his hand. As Henry drives away with a blast of his horn, Jesse leads me to the next cabin down from the one where his horse is tied.

"Hardass don't like strangers," he explains.

"You named your horse Hardass?"

"People call me hard-ass all the time behind my back, so I figured I'd let 'em know I know it."

He climbs onto the porch and sits against the wall of the cabin. I sit on the top step and brace my back against the rail. There's no doubt that Jesse Billups works hard for a living. He has to be fifty to have served in Vietnam, but his stomach is still as tight as a teenager's. His arms don't bulge, but the long muscles in them ripple with every movement. His face is another matter. It's hard to get an impression of his looks; I can't really see past the scars yet.

"Diesel fuel," he says in a ragged voice.

"What?"

"This face I got. I was cleaning toilets at a firebase when Mr. Charlie dropped a few mortar rounds on us for Christmas. We used to burn our shit with diesel fuel. I was standing next to five burning drums when the round went off. Covered me with shit and burning diesel. Would have been funny except for the infection I got from it."

"I'm sorry."

He gives me a cynical wink, then takes a pack of Kool menthols from his back pocket. Lighting one with a silver lighter, he inhales deeply, then blows blue smoke away from the porch. He seems to be settling in for a long talk. After another deep drag on his cigarette, he turns his dark eyes on me.

"You here to ask about your daddy?"

"I heard you knew him pretty well."

This seems to amuse Jesse. "I don't know about all that. But me and Lukie hung together some, yeah. A long time ago."

"I was hoping you could tell something about what happened to him in the war."

"You know anything already?"

"Somebody told me he was a sniper. I didn't know that. They also said he was part of a unit that was accused of war crimes. Do you know anything about that?"

Jesse snorts in derision. "*War crimes?* Shit. That the craziest expression I ever heard. War *is* a motherfucking crime, start to finish. It's only people who don't know that be talkin' 'bout shit like war crimes."

I'm not sure how to continue. "Well, there must have been some unusual events, at least, for the army to talk about prosecuting his unit."

"*Unusual?*" Jesse barks a humorless laugh. "Yeah. That's a good word."

"Can you tell me anything?"

"Luke told me a little about that. He was a country boy, see? That's what got him in trouble. He knew how to shoot. I'm a good shot, but that boy was something with a rifle. Like he was born holding one. Wouldn't kill nothing after the war, though, not even deer for food. Anyway, the army made him a sniper. And he did that job for a couple months. Then they took him into this special unit called the White Tigers. Supposed to be a all-volunteer thing, but I think the CO pretty much volunteered anybody he wanted into it. That's how old Lukie got stuck."

"The White Tigers? What was the purpose of the unit?"

"They was put together for one reason. What they call *incursion* into enemy territory. Only this incursion wasn't exactly legal. The Tigers went into Cambodia to try to hit the Cong where they hid from our bombers."

"Do you know what happened there?"

"Same shit that happened a lot of other places, only worse. The Tigers went from village to village looking for weapons, VC, or VC sympathizers. Thing was, they didn't operate like we did over in I Corps. In Cambodia, they didn't wait around to get shot at. They went in there to scare the shit out the people, keep 'em from helping Mr. Charlie. To *deny the enemy sanctuary and interdict lines of supply*, MACV would have said. Double-talking motherfuckers. Anyway, they had some bad boys in this Tiger outfit. Hard cases from other platoons. So naturally, they did some bad shit."

"What exactly falls into that category?"

Jesse stubs out his cigarette and immediately lights another. "Assassinated tribal chiefs and VC paymasters. Punished anybody known or suspected of helping the VC or the Khmer Rouge. Questioned people vigorously." He laughs bitterly. "That means torture."

"My father did some of this?"

He nods deliberately. "That was the job, you know? That shit happened down where I was, too. Especially shooting prisoners so you wouldn't have to drag them around with you. But if the wrong officer saw you, you could get in bad trouble. Luke's outfit was different. In the Tigers, it was the officers *instigating* the shit. Cutting off heads and leaving them on sticks to scare the Khmer Rouge. Taking girls from the villages and using them for recreation. Getting—"

"Wait a second," I cut in. "You mean they kidnapped girls and raped them?"

Jesse nods like it's no big deal. "Sure. That's how the CO rewarded his men. When his boys did good, they could pick a girl from a village and keep her for a couple days."

"What happened to the girl when they were done with her?"

Jesse raises his hand and makes a quick slicing motion across his throat. The deadness in his eyes makes me shiver. "I told you they done some bad shit."

"How did my dad feel about that?"

Jesse shrugs. "He blamed the government. Shit, that's who put him in the middle of it. He didn't ask for that. And what could he do about it? Way out in the bush . . . the whole operation off the books . . . CO had the only radio. So Luke did what he had to do and got the hell out."

"What about the war crimes investigation? Who started that?"

"Some rat in their unit, probably. Somebody looking to get his name in the papers."

This doesn't sound right to me. "Reporting that kind of thing seems like a good way to get dead. It must have been someone with a conscience who first went public."

Jesse shakes his head. "All I know is, when the government questioned Luke, he didn't tell 'em shit. The government dropped the investigation, end of story."

Jesse takes a drag from his cigarette, inhaling so deeply that he seems to draw sustenance from the smoke. As I watch him, it strikes me that his lean frame is not the result of good health. It's almost as if the fat that a normal human would accumulate is being consumed by a deep-banked anger.

"Well, do you think—"

"What you come down here for?" Jesse growls with sudden intensity. "You didn't come here to talk about no Vietnam."

"Yes, I did."

He barks another laugh. "Maybe you *think* you did. But there's something else behind these questions."

I look away, hoping to hide the guilt I feel over what my grandfather told me today. Because that's what I feel, I realize. Guilt. That's why I'm asking these questions. If my father really did those things to me, something must have pushed him to it. And if it wasn't the war, then what else could it have been but me? I've always craved attention, and I've always been very sexual—

"Hey," says Jesse. "You look like you about to cry on me."

I tilt back my head and blink away tears. "You're right. I don't know what I came here for exactly. I was hoping for . . . something. I don't know what."

"You looking for some kind of explanation for the way Luke was? Hoping I'd tell you he was a saint or something, behind that closed-up face of his? He was just a dude, like me. We all got good and bad deep down inside." He points a long-nailed finger at me. "But I ain't telling you nothing you don't already know. I can look in your eyes and see that. You Luke Ferry's kid, I know you got both inside of you."

Now the tears come, too many to blink away. "Why did my daddy spend so much time down here, Jesse? What was it that drew him?"

Jesse scowls and looks off into the trees.

"Was he growing dope down here?"

"He tried, but he wasn't no good at it."

"Did he ever deal? Drugs, I mean?"

The scarred head turns slowly left and right. "Shit, I had to get Luke's weed for him."

"What am I missing, then? How much time did he actually spend down here?"

"A lot. Specially in the winter. Summertime, your family was down here a lot. In deer season, Dr. Kirkland and his buddies would visit. But all the other times, Luke stayed down here."

"What the hell did he do, if he didn't hunt or fish?"

Jesse looks back at me, but the anger I sensed before seems to have leaked out of his pores. "He walked around a lot. Drew things in a notebook. Played a little music. Had him a guitar down here. I taught him some bottleneck stuff."

I faintly remember a guitar in my father's barn studio, but I don't remember him playing it. "Was he any good?"

"He was all right, for a white boy. He could bend a note. Had some blues in him."

"Well, did he—"

The ring of a cell phone stops me, but it's not mine. Jesse takes a Nokia from his pocket and answers. He listens for a bit, then says he'll get right on it and hangs up.

"I got to go," he says.

"Right now?"

"Yep. Gotta get some supplies from the mainland in case the water covers the bridge. S'posed to rain a couple of days straight, all along the river. We better get moving."

"But I have some more questions."

"We can talk on the way." He walks over to his horse, unties him, and leads him over to where I'm standing. Hardass flicks his tail at a buzzing horsefly. "I'm gonna get on, then pull you up behind me. You just stay clear of his hindquarters."

"I will."

Jesse puts a foot into the stirrup and expertly mounts the horse. Then he takes his foot out of the stirrup so I can get a foothold. When I do, he takes my left arm and pulls me effortlessly up behind his saddle. "You can talk, but hang on while you do." He puts the horse into a canter on the grassy shoulder of the gravel road. His broad shoulders are wet with sweat, and pink scar tissue dots the back of his neck.

"You work for my grandfather, right?" I ask.

"That's right."

"What do you think about him?"

"He's a tough old man."

"Do you like him?"

"Dr. Kirkland pays my wages. 'Like' got nothing to do with it."

I have a feeling the relationship between Jesse Billups and my grandfather isn't simple at all. "What are you not telling me, Jesse?"

I can almost feel him smile. "Dr. Kirkland beat me once when I was a boy. Beat me bad. But I'd have done the same thing in his place, so we're square enough on that, I guess."

I want to ask more about this, but before I can, I see a woman riding toward us on a bicycle. The gravel road makes her work difficult. She looks as if she might skid and fall at any moment.

"Mother*fucker*," mutters Jesse.

"Who's that?"

"Don't pay her no mind. She half-crazy."

The woman slows as she nears us, but Jesse spurs his horse as though he means to pass her without a word.

"Wait!" cries the woman.

"Stop," I tell Jesse.

He doesn't.

"*Goddamn you, Jesse Billups!*" shouts the woman. "*Don't you run from me!*"

I reach around Jesse and grab for the reins. "Stop this horse!"

He curses, then stops the horse on a dime. "You gonna wish we hadn't."

As agitated as the woman below me looks, I expect her to start shouting accusations of battery or paternity at Jesse Billups. But now that the horse has stopped, she acts as if Jesse doesn't exist. She has eyes only for me.

"Are you Catherine Ferry?" she asks.

"That's right."

"I'm Louise Butler. I want to talk to you."

"What about?"

"Your daddy."

"Did you know him?"

"I surely did."

Swinging my left leg over the horse's flanks, I drop to the gravel beside Louise Butler. She's about forty and very pretty, with the same milk-chocolate skin Pearlie has. She's watching me with what looks like suspicion in her large eyes.

"If you stay here and jaw," says Jesse, "you gonna have to get back to your car on your own. I gots to go."

"I know where my car is. I can get back to it."

Jesse kicks his horse and leaves us in a small cloud of dust.

I look at Louise and wait, expecting some explanation of her sudden appearance. But she only stares at the sky.

"Gonna rain soon," she comments. "I got a place by the lake. We'd better start back that way."

Without waiting for an answer, she turns her bike around and starts pushing it down the road. I watch her for a few seconds, noting her one-piece shift and Keds sneakers. Then I trot forward and fall in beside her, my feet scrunching the gravel as I walk.

"How did you know I was here?" I ask.

"Henry told me," she says, not looking over at me.

"So you knew my father."

Now she turns to me. "You might not like what I'm gonna say, Miss Catherine."

"Please call me Cat."

She laughs softly. "Kitty Cat."

A chill goes through me. My father called me Kitty Cat when I was very small. He was the only one who did. "You did know him. Please tell me anything you can."

"I don't want to make you feel bad, honey."

"You can't make me feel any worse than I already do today."

"Don't be so sure. Did Jesse tell you anything bad about Luke?"

"Not really. He might have, but you came along."

Louise wrinkles her nose. "You can't trust Jesse. Not about Luke."

"I thought they were friends."

"They was for a while."

"What happened?"

"Me."

"You?"

She looks at me out of the corner of her eye. "Darling, Luke was my man for seven years. From 1974 right up to the night he died. And a lot of people didn't like that."

I stop in my tracks. This woman can't be more than ten years older than I. And she's telling me she was my father's lover?

Louise walks on, then realizes I'm no longer beside her. She stops and turns back. "I don't want to hurt your feelings. I just wanted to talk to you about him, see if I could see him in you."

"Can you?"

She smiles sadly. "He's looking out of your eyes at me right now. Every line of your face got a shadow of him in it."

"Louise, what—"

Before I can finish my sentence, the clouds open up. Fat raindrops slap the cream-colored dust on the shoulder of the road, making dark circles of mud. The circles multiply too fast to follow, and then Louise and I are running down the road like little girls, she pushing her bike at first, then jumping onto it and riding beside me.

"You're in good shape!" she cries as the shacks of the little village come into sight. "My house ain't far, but it's past this bunch here."

We race past the gray shacks, their porches empty now, and turn down a muddy path that parallels the lake.

"There it is!" Louise shouts.

I hold my hand over my eyes to shield them from the rain. In the distance I see a shack that's not gray like the others, but bright blue, like a shack in the Caribbean. Now that I know where I'm going, I sprint ahead of the bike. My feet have better purchase in the mud than her bicycle, and I beat Louise to her porch.

Watching her ride the last few yards, I realize that I'm about to hear things about my father that he never meant for me to know. Does this beautiful stranger know things that might explain what Grandpapa told me today? Or at least confirm it?

"Go on in," she says, lifting her bike onto the narrow porch of the little house. "I'm right behind you."

I walk through the flimsy front door into a room that serves as a combination kitchen, den, and dining area. The moment I enter, two things strike me with startling intensity. First is the sound of the rain hitting the tin roof above me. It's my recurring dream made real, and the rattling almost takes my breath away. The second is the certainty that my father once lived here. On the mantel over a gas space heater is a sculpture of a woman. Though it's of African rather than Asian derivation—a blank oval face over a long neck and a trunk with graceful limbs—one glance tells me it's my father's work. The woman is lying on her side, with one knee raised and one hand on her hip, the way a woman might lie in bed watching her lover across the room. This sculpture is easily worth more than Louise's whole house.

The dining table, too, is my father's work. Brushed steel with inset glass plates, and flecks of mica fused to the steel. There's no bed in this room, but I'd bet anything that he built that, too.

"Luke wanted me to have my own place," Louise says from behind me.

Suddenly I'm wavering on my feet. The heat in the house is stifling, as though the place has been shut up for days, and the rattle of the rain seems to grow louder by the second. But that's only part of it. Today my father's life has turned from a patchwork of happy memories to a house of mirrors.

"What is it?" cries Louise.

"I don't know."

She rushes to an air conditioner mounted in a window and flips a switch. The rumbling roar of the old window unit does much to drown the sound of the rain, but it's too little too late.

"You're going to faint!"

As my knees go out from under me, Louise catches me under the arms and steers my falling body toward a sofa.

CHAPTER

28

"Drink this," says Louise, holding a glass of iced tea under my chin. "The heat got you, that's all. This place been shut up a couple of days, and it gets like an oven without the AC going."

"It's not the heat," I tell her, taking the glass and drinking a sip of syrupy sweet tea.

"Was it seeing Luke's things? I should have known that would upset you."

"That's not why I passed out."

She studies me with her deep brown eyes. "You look scared, more than anything."

I nod slowly. "It's the rain."

"The rain?"

"The sound of it. Rain hitting a tin roof."

Louise looks confused. "You don't like that?"

"It's not a matter of liking it or not. I just can't take it."

"Really? I love that sound. It makes me lonely, but I still love it. I used to lie in bed with Luke on rainy afternoons and listen for hours. It's like music."

I try to smile, but my lips won't do it.

"I'm sorry. You're upset, and I'm just thinking back on good times. Did something bad happen to you in the rain?"

"I wish I knew. Lately I've been hearing that sound in my dreams, and even while I'm awake."

"Sometimes that's the way of it," Louise says, walking to the sink. "I got a lot of things inside me I don't understand." She runs tap water into a carafe. "I got to make some coffee. It can be a hundred degrees outside, but I got to have my coffee. Addicted, I guess."

"Louise, what can you tell me about the orange pickup truck by the bridge?"

She switches on the Mr. Coffee, then comes and sits in a Naugahyde recliner on my left. "That old rusted wreck by the shed?"

"Yes."

"That was Dr. Kirkland's truck back in the old days."

"I know. But did my father ever drive it?"

She closes her eyes. "Yeah, Luke drove it some, when Dr. Kirkland wasn't around. Dr. Kirkland used to brag all the time about how long that junker had been running. He said it had never quit on him and never would. Finally did, though. Why?"

"I think I saw something when I was in that truck. I have this dream where I'm riding in it with Grandpapa. We're on the north end of the island, riding up a hill in the cow pasture, toward the pond."

Louise nods. "I know where that is."

"In the dream, we never get over the hill. We get closer and closer, but we never get over it. Lately, the closer we get, the more afraid I get."

"How long you been having this dream?"

"A couple of weeks, maybe longer. Do you know of anything that happened up there? Something bad I might have seen?"

She leans back in her chair and looks at the porch window. The storm clouds have brought a premature darkness, and the wind rattles the glass in its frame.

"Gonna get worse before it gets better," she predicts. "Lots of bad things happened on this old island over the years. But the pond . . . you think you saw somebody get beaten? Killed, maybe? Something like that?"

"I don't know." A different thought strikes me. "Did you and Daddy ever do anything at the pond? Sexually, I mean?"

A deep stillness comes over Louise. "We swam there sometimes. But not while you were on the island."

"Did you ever make love when I was on the island?"

She averts her eyes. "We tried not to. But sometimes we did. I'm sorry if that upsets you, but I don't want to lie."

"No, I want the truth. And I know how it is when you love somebody."

"Well . . . you could have seen us swimming naked in the pond.
But I don't think you did."

Sensing discomfort in Louise, I change the subject. "Did Daddy
ever talk to you about the war?"

"Not with words. But he let me see the pain in different ways."

"What do you think happened to him over there?"

Her large eyes fix on me, an earnest passion in them. "He got poisoned. That's what happened. Not in his body—in his soul."

"Louise . . . I've been told that his unit committed war crimes.
Atrocities. Do you understand what I'm saying?"

She nods solemnly.

"They tortured people. Kidnapped women and raped them. Do
you think Daddy could have done anything like that?" This is as
close as I can bear to come to asking Louise if she thinks my father
could have molested me.

She stands suddenly and goes to a drawer, then takes out a pack of
Salem cigarettes and lights one with a kitchen match. Despite the
passage of time, Louise still has a slim figure, with taut calves that a
lot of women would kill for. I can only imagine what she must have
looked like as a young woman.

"Luke had some problems, okay?" She exhales blue smoke.
"When he and I first got together, he couldn't make love."

"You mean physically?" A strange excitement awakens in my
chest. "He was impotent?"

She tilts her head as if unsure how to reply. "He was and he
wasn't."

"What do you mean, he was and he wasn't?"

Louise looks at me skeptically. "I don't see a ring on your finger.
You ever lived with a man?"

"A couple. Or they lived with me, rather. You don't have to pull
any punches with me, Louise. I know men."

She chuckles softly. "You know how when a man wakes up, lots of
times he's hard down there from having to go to the bathroom?"

I nod, my curiosity making me grip the arm of the sofa.

"Well, Luke would be like that in the morning. But if I tried to
make love with him, he couldn't stay that way."

"I see."

"I knew something in the war had done that to him. Not his wound. Something in his head. It took more than a year to get him where he could be with me. Where he could trust me. I think that's what it was, trust. But I'm no doctor. I don't know. He may have done or seen things over there that made sex something terrible to him."

Wild thoughts are spinning in my head. If my father was impotent, could he have abused me? *Of course he could have,* answers a bitter voice. *There are lots of sex acts besides intercourse.* I'm not even sure intercourse is the main form of child abuse. I should ask Dr. Goldman, or even Michael Wells.

A blast of wind makes the windows shudder, and the rain drives against the roof like hail. I focus on the drone of the air conditioner to block it out. "What did you say about you coming between Jesse and my father?"

Louise pours herself a cup of still-brewing coffee. "Jesse always wanted me. Watched me from the time I was a little girl. Always talking to me, bringing me presents. Following me around on his horse. But I didn't want him."

"Why not?"

"I just didn't feel right about it. I didn't know what I wanted, but it wasn't Jesse. Then I started seeing this white boy wandering around the island. He was a man, really—like Jesse—but he seemed more like a boy. Always off by himself, like me. Him and Jesse talked sometimes, but I think all they had in common was the war. Anyway, I'd figure out ways to get ahead of Luke on his walks, so he'd stumble on me, like it was an accident. I liked talking to him. I hadn't been nowhere but here and to school in West Feliciana Parish. And that was just an old country school for black people. Didn't learn nothing there. I'd just sit and listen while Luke talked. Which was funny, 'cause people who met him wondered if he could talk at all. But he could when he wanted to. He talked to me all the time."

"I did the same thing," I tell her. "I used to go into his studio every night to watch him work. He didn't talk much to me—because I was so young, probably—but he let me sit with him. I was the only one he'd let in."

Louise is smiling at me. We are sisters under the skin.

"How old were you when all this happened?" I ask.

Her cheeks darken in embarrassment. "I was fourteen when I

started following Luke around. But we was just talking, like I said. We didn't do nothing till I turned sixteen."

Sixteen . . . "I can see you were in love with him."

There's a faraway look in her eyes. "You want to know if he was in love with me, don't you?"

"Yes."

"He told me he was. I know that probably hurts you. But I'll tell you this, he wasn't ever gonna leave you to come to me. He hated that place, that Malmaison. Hated your grandfather, too."

"And my mother?"

Louise gives me an intense look. "He loved your mama, now. She just didn't understand him. But when I'd talk to him about leaving— and don't think I didn't. Lord, I begged him sometimes—he'd say, 'I can't leave my Kitty Cat, Louise. Can't leave my baby in that house with those people. So I can't come to you.' And he never did."

This confirmation of my father's love warms my heart, despite what I heard from my grandfather today. Yet as soon as I feel this emotion, something clenches in my chest. "Did he say anything else about my mother?"

She looks hesitant.

"Please tell me."

"He said your mama had problems with sex. Even before he went to the war."

"What kind of problems?"

"Well . . . she just couldn't do much. She did the one position, man on top, and she had to have the lights off to do that. Couldn't take her clothes off in front of him. Before they got married, he thought it was just shyness. But she never loosened up. Luke said he was patient, and I believe him. I think she'd just been taught that sex was something to be ashamed of. I know some women like that. And then, after he got back from the war, Luke had his own problems."

"Thank you for being so honest, Louise."

"I got no reason to lie, except to spare you pain. And you seem like you can handle it."

You'd be surprised at how much and how little I can handle some-times. "What did you do after Daddy died?"

She sighs deeply. "I left this damn place, for one thing."

"Where did you go?"

"St. Francisville. I fixed hair over there for a while."

"Why did you come back?"

"I got in some trouble over there. Got caught with some weed in my car. I didn't even like smoking that stuff, but it was better than drinking. Didn't make me fat. And it took away some of the pain of grieving. Luke taught me that."

"Were you arrested?"

Bitterness comes into her face. "Oh, yeah. They was gonna put me in jail. But Dr. Kirkland told me that if I'd come back to the island and get clean, he'd vouch for me. And that's what happened."

Of course, I think, with a strange feeling of resentment. *With a single phone call, the feudal baron restores order to his universe.* "When did you come back?"

"Nineteen eighty-three."

"You haven't left here since then?"

"Not to stay. This island's kind of like a prison, I think. People get out of Angola sometimes, and you'd think they'd be happy. But they're just lost. After all them years behind bars, they don't know what to do without 'em. So they do some crime to get put back inside again. This island's kind of like that. Lots of folks leave, but sooner or later, most of 'em come back."

Like me? Do all roads lead back here?

"You've got pretty hair," Louise says. "Even that reminds me of your daddy."

"Did Daddy talk to anybody else about the war besides Jesse?"

"I think he talked to Dr. Cage some, over in Natchez. That's who gave him his medication. Dr. Cage is a good man. I saw him a couple times. He likes to listen to people talk."

I remember Pearlie mentioning Dr. Cage.

"About the only thing I can think of that might help you is his diary."

My pulse quickens. "Diary?"

"It wasn't really a diary. It was a drawing pad. Luke used to carry it around, making sketches. Lots of times he would sit by the river and write in that pad. He talked about maybe writing a book one day. I think some of that writing was about the war."

My palms are tingling. "Do you have this sketch pad?"

"No. I wish I did."

"What did it look like?

"It was just a sketch pad, like they used to sell in the dime stores.

A thick one. He drew all kinds of pictures in it. He drew me once. I do have that picture."

She goes to a fiberboard cabinet, kneels, and brings out a photo album. Opening the large book, she brings out a piece of paper and holds it up for me to see. It's a charcoal sketch of a girl of no more than twenty, with stunning bone structure and shy eyes.

"You were beautiful."

"*Were?*" Louise snaps. Then she laughs with loud good humor. "Lord knows I've changed. But I was pretty then, and I'm glad. I brought some happiness into his life by being pretty." She shakes her head sadly. "Lord, I loved that boy. You know, he was only thirty when he died. You ever think about that?"

My father was a year younger than I am now when he died? "I don't usually. I guess I think about him the way I saw him as a little girl."

She nods knowingly. "God made a mistake on that day, taking Luke out of this world. Taking him, and leaving thousands of men who ain't worth spit."

My eyes have focused on one of the cabinet shelves. There's a line of books there. *Dispatches* by Michael Herr. Bernard Fall's book on Dien Bien Phu. Graham Greene. Tim O'Brien. *Koko* and *The Throat* by Peter Straub. *Siddhartha. The Bell Jar.* Four or five books on the My Lai massacre.

"It looks like Daddy put a lot into this house," I say, gesturing toward the dining table. I'm really trying to stall while my mind works out just what it wants to know from this woman, but Louise smiles with pride.

"This old house was falling down back then, but it sat apart from the others, and I liked that. So Luke fixed it up for me. He said he was fixing it up for himself, so Dr. Kirkland wouldn't pay no mind. But then I started using it when Luke was gone. After a while, we'd stay in here together. Everybody knew, but nobody said nothing, since Dr. Kirkland didn't. Some of these women round here called me a ho, but I didn't pay no mind. Narrow-minded and mean, most of them."

"My grandfather knew about the affair?"

"He'd have to have been blind not to. And that's one thing Dr. Kirkland *ain't.*"

"What do you think about my grandfather, Louise?"

She takes her time answering. "Dr. Kirkland's a hard man, in some ways. But soft in others. He's tough on dogs and horses. He's good at taking care of people, though. Saved a lot of lives out here over the years. Saved my uncle after a chain saw accident. Lost his arm at the shoulder and damn near bled to death, but Dr. Kirkland pulled him through. The doctor's got a temper, now. If he gets mad, there's hell to pay. Luke's the only man I ever saw defy him and get away with it."

"When was this?" I'm sure I never saw anything like that. In my experience, Grandpapa's word was always law.

"Dr. Kirkland and a cousin of mine was breaking some horses one spring. One of those broncs was stubborn, and Dr. Kirkland lost his head. He tied that horse to a fence and started beating it with a hoe. That animal was screaming something terrible. Dr. Kirkland was using the handle end at first, but the more he beat that horse, the madder he got. I think he was about to flip that hoe around and start chopping that poor creature to pieces when Luke grabbed his arm."

"No," I whisper, unable to imagine such a scene.

She nods once with an exaggerated motion. "Dr. Kirkland's a big man, you know that. And strong as an ox back then. But Luke knew things he never showed nobody. He caught ahold of Dr. Kirkland's arm some way that he couldn't move it. Dr. Kirkland was yelling he was gonna kill Luke when he got loose. He tried to beat Luke with his other hand, but Luke did something to that arm he was holding, and Dr. Kirkland turned white and dropped down to his knees."

"My God. What happened?"

"Luke kept squeezing until Dr. Kirkland let go of that hoe. Then Luke patted that horse, turned, and walked off into the woods."

"Did my grandfather do anything to get back at Luke?"

Louise shakes her head. "I reckon he did. He shot that horse five minutes later."

"Jesus."

"It don't pay to cross Dr. Kirkland. He don't play."

A strange current of emotion wells up from my soul. "Louise, what would you say if I told you Grandpapa killed Luke that night? Not a prowler?"

She stares at me for several moments, then begins shaking her head like a superstitious native confronted by a ghost. "Don't tell me nothing like that. I don't even want to *think* that."

"If it scares you that much," I say softly, "you must think it could be true."

She finally stops shaking her head. "What are you saying, Cat?"

"Nothing. Crazy thoughts." I want to tell her what I know, but something stops me. Is it my lack of proof of Grandpapa's motive or just common decency? Louise has precious memories of my father. What good could it do for me to smudge them with accusations of child molestation? "May I see your bedroom, Louise?"

A knowing expression comes into her face. "You want to see if Luke built the bed."

"Yes."

"Come look."

She leads me to a door set in the back wall and opens it. In the small bedroom beyond stands a bed that looks as if it belongs in a Manhattan loft. Four brushed-steel posts support an oval-shaped canopy frame, and within the headboard and footboard are ornate patterns rendered in different metals, some of them reminiscent of the mandala on Dr. Malik's office wall. It's one of the most detailed pieces my father ever did.

"My God," I whisper. "Do you know what that bed is worth?"

Louise laughs. "I got an idea. I guess this bed is what I've got instead of retirement."

"Please don't let anybody steal it. And if you ever want to sell it, give me a call."

"I may take you up on that one day."

She leads me back into the front room, and we stand in a suddenly awkward silence. The economic gulf between us could scarcely be greater than it is.

"How old are you, Louise?"

"Forty-six."

Older than I thought, but still only fifteen years older than I am. "What do you do for a living, if you don't mind me asking?"

She looks at the floor. "I got a man here takes care of me. I just keep up this house for . . . well, you know why."

This wasn't what I was hoping to hear. "Is the man Jesse Billups?"

Louise sighs, and for a moment I dread her answer. "Not Jesse," she says. "Henry. The man who drove you onto the island. He ain't pretty like Luke, but he's got a good heart."

"Are you married?"

"I ain't interested in getting married. I dreamed of it for a long time, but . . . the man I wanted to marry got killed. That was the end of that dream for me."

I reach out and take hold of her hand. I never met this woman before today, yet I feel more intimately bound to her than to people I've known my whole life. When I think about what Grandpapa told me about my father's death, it makes no sense. How could the man this woman loved so profoundly commit unspeakable acts with a child? With his *own* child. And yet . . . the professional in me knows that such things happen.

"Sounds like the rain's slacked up," Louise says.

"You're right. I should go now, while I can. Do you have a car?"

She shakes her head. "No, and Henry's gone to Lafayette to see his kids. They stay with his ex-wife."

"What about Jesse?"

She opens a kitchen drawer and takes out a cell phone. After dialing, she listens, then says, "Jesse, this is Louise. I still got Miss Ferry with me at my place. She needs to get back to Natchez. You carry your narrow ass back here and take her to her car. Call me back and tell me you're on your way."

She hangs up and looks at me helplessly.

"Does anybody else have a car we can borrow?" I ask.

"Lots of people here own cars, but they keep them on the mainland, by the ferry dock."

"What do they use for transportation here?"

"There's five pickups on the island, and Jesse got the keys to all of them. Use to be, lots of people had keys. But Dr. Kirkland started complaining about the gas they were using, so Jesse keeps all the keys now."

"What do you do in an emergency?"

"Make do. But Jesse'll call back in a minute. He's probably just checking that everything's tied down tight for the storm. The fishing boat on the south end, maybe."

"No, he left the island. He said he had to get some supplies on the mainland."

Louise looks bewildered. "That's funny. Jesse don't leave the island too often. And never at the same time Henry's gone."

"Somebody called his cell phone, and he said he had to leave right then."

"He say who it was?"

"No."

"That don't sound right." She shrugs, then goes to the front window and looks out. The sky is darker, if anything. "If Jesse doesn't call back, you can stay the night with me. I know it's not what you're used to, but I can sleep on the sofa. You can sleep in the bed your daddy made."

I stand motionless in the close air of the shack, listening to the rain drumming over the drone of the air conditioner. My skin is crawling. "There's no guarantee the bridge will be there tomorrow, is there?"

"Depends on the rain. But if it's flooded out, somebody can take you back to your car by boat."

"I appreciate it, but I think I'd rather get back to my car now, if you think I can make it."

She turns from the window and looks at me. "Oh, you can make it, if you don't mind getting wet. You can use my bike. Ain't much lightning out there. And if you cut through the woods, the rain won't be as bad, 'cause the trees make a tunnel over the road. Cut down through the hunting camp, then—when you hit the road to the boat ramp—turn back up along the shore till you come to the bridge."

"I can do that."

"Sure you can. It ain't even dark yet, really. Just cloudy. And I got a light on the front of my bike. I've ridden around this island in the middle of the night when I needed to. It's safe. Just watch you don't slide off the gravel into a ditch or something. Lots of snakes this year on the back side."

I shiver, recalling the hallucinatory snakes I saw in my apartment as the d.t.'s began. "How fast can the water rise? Could the bridge be covered up already?"

"I doubt it. If the river wasn't already so high, you wouldn't have nothing to worry about. But you'll be at the bridge in ten minutes. If you do have a problem, call my cell phone. Stay where you are, and I'll come get you."

"How will you come?"

"On my two feet." She takes my cell phone from me and programs her number into its memory. "If I need to, I can get there in no time. And if Jesse calls back, I'll send him after you. He can drive you across and bring my bike back both."

I move to the door, then turn back and hug Louise.

She squeezes me tightly. "You going through some tough times, girl. You come back and see me sometime."

I promise that I will, though I suspect I won't ever be here again. Then I walk onto the porch and carry her bicycle down to the path.

"Hey!" Louise calls through the rain. "Wait!"

I stand in the rain while she disappears inside for a minute. The air out here has a greenish tinge, like the look the sky gets before a tornado. The wind is blowing hard from the south, and the raindrops sting my face. I hope she's getting me a raincoat, but when she returns, she's carrying what looks like a Ziploc sandwich bag.

"For your cell phone!" she says over the wind.

Taking the Baggie, I slip my phone and car keys inside it, crush the bag to get the air out, then zip it shut and stuff it into the front pocket of my jeans. I start to pedal away, but Louise grabs my arm, her eyes desperate.

"I know you didn't tell me everything," she says. "I know you got something bad on your back. All I know is this: ain't no man all good or all bad. And if you find out something bad about Luke, I don't want to know. Okay?"

I wipe the rain from my eyes and nod.

"Time will heal you," Louise says. "Won't nothing else do any good at all."

I feel an eerie certainty that if I don't start for the bridge now, I won't make it to my car. Pushing down hard on the right pedal, I struggle toward the road that cuts through the woods toward the hunting camp.

The wind slaps the rain against my right cheek and ear, but soon I'm passing the shacks by the lake. The porches that were full of people an hour ago hold only dogs now. I'm alone again.

When I turn south on the camp road, the wind hits me full in the face, pushing against my body like a sail, trying to drive me back toward the lake. I lean low over the handlebars to cut my resistance and bear down hard on the pedals. The shoulder is so muddy in places that I almost take a spill, but the farther down the island I ride, the sandier the soil gets, and soon I'm making good time despite the weather.

Beneath the black storm clouds, the world has gone gray. Everything ahead looks as flat as a black-and-white photograph. The gray cabins of the hunting camp are almost invisible in the shadows beneath the trees. Even the grass has lost its color. Only a slight brightness low in the sky to the west lets me know the sun is there at all.

There should be a left turn soon. If not, I'll come to the southern tip of the island, a rolling, mosquito-infested hell of scrub-covered dunes and muddy slews that I always avoided when possible.

Out of the grayness ahead, the old channel of the river appears, and relief washes through me. A mile up the road that runs along this channel is the bridge that leads to my car. I'm about to turn onto it when two bright beams of light swing across me from behind. I look back over my shoulder.

Headlights.

They look high enough to belong to a truck like the one Henry was driving. Louise told me she would send Jesse after me if he called her back.

I stop the bike at the turn and wait.

To my right, a blue-white beam much larger than those cast by the headlights illuminates the far shore, then sweeps south again. For a moment this puzzles me. Then I realize it's the spotlight on a push boat. A quarter mile south of where I stand, the old channel runs back into the main channel of the Mississippi River. A push-boat captain driving a string of barges upstream is checking his course.

The driver of the pickup has spotted me. Forty yards away, he flicks his lights to high beam. The rain is blowing almost horizontally through their glare. I raise my hand to wave, then freeze.

The truck hasn't slowed at all.

As the hair on my neck stands up, something Sean told me before we were lovers sounds in my head: *That hair standing up on the back of your neck is two hundred million years of evolution telling you to get the hell out of wherever you are—*

The truck engine roars with acceleration in the same moment that I dive into the ditch on the left side of the road. I regain my feet as the truck crushes Louise's bicycle beneath its bumper and bounces after me across the ditch. My only hope is the trees, but I can't outsprint a truck, not even for thirty yards.

An unholy grinding of gears gives me hope. The bike must have been caught in the truck's linkage. As the driver tries to manhandle his vehicle off the twisted wreckage beneath it, I reach the first giant willow and dart behind it.

Looking back, I see headlights bouncing up and down. Then suddenly the truck's motor dies. The headlights remain on though, and the interior light flicks on behind them. There's a figure inside the cab—a man—but his face is obscured by distance and rain. He leans into the space between the door and the body of the truck. I'm squinting my eyes to try to see his face when a flash blooms in the dark and splinters pierce my left cheek. Only then does the super-sonic crack of the rifle bullet reach me.

I run.

CHAPTER

29

Panic drives me through the trees without direction. A single thought burns through the flood of endorphins in my brain: get away from the man in the truck. A second gunshot quickly follows the first, and one look over my shoulder tells me that the shooter has followed me into the woods. Now and then he flicks on a flashlight to find his way through the trees. From his careful progress, I know one thing: he's driving me southward, down an ever-narrowing strip of land. It's only a matter of time before he corners me on the tip of the island, a bare patch of sand with a mile of rushing water at my back.

I need to find a way to slip around him, but on this ground that's almost impossible. The island here is like tropical jungle. The willow and cottonwood brakes give good cover, but there's too much underbrush on the ground to move quietly, even in the rain. There's only one other chance.

The boat ramp is on the west side of the island, facing the main channel of the river. If the shooter were farther behind me, I might have time to launch the fishing boat before he reached me. But he's not. I've got to slow him down. But how? I have no weapons. As I fight my way through the underbrush, an image comes into my mind—*bull nettle*. Bull nettle is a twisting green vine about four feet high that bristles with thousands of hypodermic needles. Those needles inject a painful toxin into any animal that rubs against it. Horses will lie down in bull nettle to avoid brushing against more of it. In humans it causes painful itching and hives, and the effect is immediate. The southern tip of DeSalle Island is covered with bull nettle.

I veer south again. Tree branches whip my face, and peppervine claws at the legs of my jeans. Here the ground rises and falls in three-foot undulations, and I pray not to step on a cottonmouth as I splash through the dark slews. I've seen fifty moccasins together roiling the water in the drying pools.

The rain falls relentlessly, and the sound of my pursuer crashing through the brush grows nearer. Sweat pours from my skin, and my heart thumps against my breastbone. Free diving keeps me in good physical shape, but terror steals my breath, and alcohol withdrawal probably isn't helping matters.

As I slow to get my bearings, the rifle cracks again, driving willow splinters into my left arm. I duck down and scramble between two cottonwood trunks, then crab-crawl through the dark until my arms begin to itch like fire. *Bull nettle!* There's a thicket of the stuff all around me. I could never have imagined being glad to feel this pain, but at this moment I'm ecstatic.

Thirty yards into the thicket, I bear right, toward the boat ramp. Before I cover twenty yards, the sound of cursing floats through the trees. With a tight smile on my face, I rise and sprint for the west side of the island. A light beam cuts the air close by, but then a scream of male rage echoes through the trees. I can't make out his words, or even if there were any.

My heart lifts with hope as I hit a level patch of sand, cause for joy until I spy a string stretched across my path at thigh level. It's an old trotline strung with rusty fishhooks, and though I twist my body torturously in an effort to avoid it, nothing can stop my headlong flight. I swallow a scream as the hooks tear into my flesh. The line rips free from whatever held it as I fall, but the treble hooks are well and truly buried in my right thigh.

The rifle booms again, its echo rolling over sandy berms like cannon fire. My hunter heard my scream and got a new fix on my position. I pray he doesn't know about the boat ramp, but what are the odds of that? I'm almost certain that it's Jesse Billups behind me. Who else knew where I was?

At the top of a dune, I catch myself and stop. The main channel of the Mississippi has opened before me, its far shore a mile away, cloaked in rain and darkness. *Get down!* shouts a voice in my head. *You're silhouetted against the clouds!*

Sliding down the dune, I race south along the bank, skirting cypress knees and driftwood snags. There's the boat ramp, forty yards along the shore. Its concrete slab runs right down into the water at a steep angle. A glitter-coated bass boat sits on a trailer on the sand about five feet above the river. The problem is, it's totally exposed. To launch that boat quickly, I'll have to unsecure it from the trailer, lift the hitch end of the trailer, and heave both trailer and boat down the ramp into the water. If I can manage that, the boat should float free while the trailer sinks into the depths. I'll have to swim freestyle with the fast current to catch the boat and board it, but I can do that. I'd rather swim the damned river with one arm than fight this island on foot anymore.

The boat ramp looks deserted from here, but that means nothing. If I walk into that open space unprotected, a ten-year-old could pick me off with a rifle. I crouch near the river's edge, my senses primed for the slightest stimulus.

Something's not right. I don't hear my pursuer anymore. The wind is louder on the exposed bank, but I should hear *something*. The rain raking the water sounds like rain hitting a tin roof, only the pitch is higher—almost a hiss. The southerly wind blasting upcurrent is building whitecaps three feet high. Rough going for a bass boat.

I need a weapon. A tree branch? Not much good against a rifle. A rock? Same problem. What do I have with me . . . ?

Cell phone. If I can get close enough to my attacker to identify him before he shoots me, I can give his name to the police—and tell him I'm doing it. Killing me at that point would be the act of an idiot. *Or a lunatic,* counters the voice in my head.

Taking the Ziploc out of my pocket, I see silver metal but no electric light. Did the sealed bag somehow short it out? I squeeze the phone through the plastic, and the light of the screen clicks on. My joy is short-lived. The screen reads, *NO SERVICE.*

Shit! I need to move to higher ground. There's no true high ground on the island, but there are better spots than this.

A blue beam of light sweeps over me, nearly stopping my heart. It's the push boat again, driving its barges upriver. Any hope there? I could signal the crew by standing in the spotlight and waving my arms, but that would be suicide. I could try swimming out to the boat, but I would probably be sucked under its barges and into its massive propellers.

I'm thinking of sprinting north along the shore, away from the boat ramp, when a flashlight beam shines out of the woods behind me and moves steadily along the bank. In seconds it will pick out my hunched body on the sand.

Without even thinking I shove the Baggie into my front pocket, crawl to the river's edge, and slip into the current like a rat leaving a sinking ship. The water is cool but not cold, thank God, and it soothes the hives caused by the bull nettle. The waves are another matter. When I swam this river at sixteen, its surface was like glass. Now it batters me like breaking surf, and the rain lashes my face as I try to keep my head above the waves.

The flashlight sweeps over the spot I just left and lingers, but I'm no longer there. The current has me now. I'm moving along the shore at the speed of a jogging man, and a force like the hand of a giant is pulling me out into the river.

I feel no bottom below me because there are no shallows here. This part of the island forms the outside of a river bend, and so takes the full brunt of the current before deflecting it west. The cutting power of all that water is enormous. Wherever it hits a bank like this, the Mississippi gouges out a channel over a hundred feet deep. Compounding this effect, the river also narrows here, creating a sort of sluiceway that would knock down skyscrapers if they were placed in its path.

I've got to get my shoes off. My jeans, too. In this river, they're more lethal than Jesse's rifle. I'm reaching down to pull off my left shoe when the flashlight pins me to the crest of a wave. I don't feel or see the impact of the bullet, but the whipcrack by my ear knocks my heart into my throat. Whoever is firing that rifle knows what the hell he's doing. *I'm a good shot,* Jesse bragged, when telling me about my father.

I yank off the shoe and dive, exhaling to bleed off buoyancy, extending my limbs like sails to catch the current and drift more swiftly past the island.

When I surface again, the flashlight is gone.

Unsnapping my jeans, I try to peel myself out of them, but they're tight even when dry. I curse my vanity, sinking like a stone as I fight to get the soaked denim off my legs. My left leg comes loose, but the other won't. Kicking back to the surface, I see why. The fishhooks from the trotline have fastened the jeans to my thigh. Two prongs of the treble hook are buried deeply in my flesh. I'd like to rip the jeans to get them free, but even if I could manage to tear the wet denim, I can't afford to do it—not with what I have in mind.

I pull gently on the central stem of the hooks, and a trickle of blood runs toward my groin. Getting fishhooks out of flesh is a tricky business. I've seen my grandfather remove dozens. Sometimes he snips off the loop and pushes the barb out through unwounded skin; other times he widens the hole with a scalpel and frees the barb the way it came in. Both methods take tools I don't have.

It's really a question of pain.

My fingers can't grip the free hook firmly enough to rip out the other two, but my Tag Heuer watch has a steel band. Slipping the barb of the free hook into a crevice in the band, I turn my forearm so that I can jerk upward with maximum force. If I can stand the pain, this should rip the buried barbs out of my skin.

Taking a deep breath, I curl into a fetal position, then explode out of it, yanking my right arm up and my right leg down. The flesh of my thigh rises like a pup tent, and a scream bursts from my throat. Consciousness flickers, and my stomach starts to come up. My brain screams for me to stop, but in that moment I yank still harder, and something tears free.

Afraid it was only my watchband, I right myself in the water and look at my thigh. Where the hooks were embedded is now only a ragged hole streaming blood. It looks like a small, vicious animal took a hunk out of me. After retching in the water, I carefully remove the freed jeans leg, making sure I don't hook myself again. I'm tempted to let the jeans sink into the river, but that would be a fool's gesture. This pair of Banana Republics is going to save me.

Treading water with only my legs, I tie knots in both legs of the jeans. Then I put the jeans behind my head, take hold of each side of the waist, and whip them back over my head in a wide arc, trapping enough air in the makeshift life vest to keep me afloat for ten minutes. Then I lay my chin in the inverted crotch of the jeans, with the knotted legs sticking up like the arms of those inflatable figures you see at car dealerships. I learned how to do this on the swim team, and it works surprisingly well. Now I can devote some energy to trying to figure out where the hell I am in relation to the man who wants to kill me.

I'm fifty yards from the island now. All I can see is a narrow strip of beach, but then that, too, disappears. *Fifty yards. Only fifteen hundred left to swim. Maybe seventeen hundred . . .*

The safest thing to do would be to drift south along this bank for a mile or so, then climb ashore. The problem with that plan is that I'd be getting out of the river at a place called Iowa Point. This isn't a town or even a crossroads, but only a dot on the map. The nearest telephone lies across five miles of uninhabited swamp. Uninhabited by humans, anyway. There are plenty of alligators and snakes to keep you company. Very little chance of a cellular transmission tower. But if I *cross* the river, I'll come ashore less than a mile from Louisiana Highway 1, not far from the Morganza Spillway. There I can flag down a car—which shouldn't be difficult in my underwear—or easily walk to a place where I'll have cellular service.

Am I crazy to try it? Most people would say yes. But I swam this river fifteen years ago, and if I did it then, I can do it now. The fact that it almost killed me—under ideal conditions—is something best not dwelled upon. The trick, as I've told several people, is not to fight the current, or even to try to swim across the river. The trick is to float with the current and gradually vector out toward the *thalweg,* or deepest part of the channel. Once you reach that, the river will do its best to deposit you on the opposite shore of the next bend.

Under optimum conditions, that would happen about a half hour from now. But tonight there are complications. Darkness. Rain. Waves trying to beat me to death. A string of barges that I can't see and that could crush me like a tractor-trailer squashing a mosquito. Any normal person dropped into this situation would drown within ten minutes. But I'm not normal. And at least the madman with the rifle has been removed from the equation.

My makeshift life preserver is steadily losing air. I'll have to reinflate the jeans soon. Because of the pounding waves, I keep my right hand gripped over the jeans pocket that holds my bagged cell phone. Every time a wave carries me to its crest, I glance around to make sure I'm in no immediate danger. All kinds of debris gets swept into the river when it's high. The biggest threat is logs. Some float high and dry, but others ride half-submerged, like alligators, tearing the props off pleasure boats and staving in the sides of barges. From the bridge at Natchez, I've watched hundred-foot trees bobbing like twigs in the muddy flood below.

Ten minutes of steady kicking move me into the main body of the river, and in that time I probably drift half a mile downstream. Now it's barges that concern me. Though the last string has passed, others will come, and there's simply no way to see them with these waves. The front barge in a string carries only two lights: green on the starboard side, red on the port. The push boat itself might be a thousand feet behind those lights, its pilot ignorant of anything happening below the bow of his waterborne freight train. If I'm crushed by barges, no one will ever know, not even the man who killed me.

The sound of an engine penetrates the hissing rain, and it chills my blood. The pitch is too high for a push-boat engine; it's revving like a chain saw cutting its way across the surface of the river. If it were daylight, I might think it *was* a chain saw—sound travels amazing distances over water—but nobody's cutting trees at this hour.

That revving sound is an outboard motor. Probably the Evinrude on the old bass boat I decided to leave on the island.

Jesse has come looking for me.

CHAPTER
30

Kicking up onto a wave crest, I see a flashlight bobbing up and down about thirty yards away. It's hard to believe my pursuer could get this close by design, but maybe he heard my scream. If it is Jesse Billups, he probably knows the river well. I try to calm myself with logic: the odds of his sighting me in this maelstrom are low. As long as I keep my head down.

Pulling the deflating legs of my jeans beneath my arms, I lie flat on the surface and stop kicking. The whine of the motor gets louder, then dies, only to return again closer to me. Jesse must be as scared as I am. A submerged log could tear off his propeller, leaving him without power, or smash the side of his fiberglass boat and dump him into the river with me. His rifle wouldn't do him any good there. I wonder if he can swim. His cousin Henry admitted he couldn't. But Jesse was in the army. The 101st Airborne. They teach men to parachute in the Airborne. Do they teach them to swim? Maybe. It doesn't really matter, though. If I can get him into the water with me, I can kill him.

All I have to do is get close enough to tangle him up. Like a squid drowning a sperm whale. Even if he were choking me, I could drag him under and keep him there until his brain winked out like an old lightbulb. It's a strange thing to contemplate. The only person I've ever thought about killing before is myself.

The motor revs suddenly, not twenty yards from my right ear.

Sucking in a lungful of air, I duck my head and drop three feet under-water, clinging only to the jeans pocket that holds my cell phone. I hear the prop spinning, a high-pitched whine like a kitchen blender. The boat doesn't seem to be moving, though, only holding its posi-tion in the river. Did Jesse catch sight of me in the waves?

For two minutes I float like the fetus in my womb, listening to the spinning prop. He *must* have seen me. Why else would he remain in one place? Surfacing slowly, I raise my eyes above the water. This time a white shaft of light slices through the rain like the eye of God. For an instant I think it's a push boat, but the beam is too near the water. No . . . it's a Q-Beam spotlight mounted on a pivot on the bass boat's hull. Whoever is piloting that boat either just remembered that spotlight or just discovered it. Maybe the gunman *isn't* Jesse Billups. The foreman of the island would have switched on that spotlight as soon as he launched the boat.

The Q-Beam rakes over the waves like a searchlight in a prison movie. First this way, then that, occasionally returning to one spot or another in the frothing waves. Once, when the light lingers upstream, I see the massive root-ball of a tree moving in the glare. Half the twisted roots are above the water, and by the size of them, the tree itself must be eighty feet long.

The drone of the motor rises, and the searchlight moves closer to the tree. Its white beam probes the tangled root structure, its opera-tor obviously looking for a stowaway on this natural vessel. Without warning, the light whips back around toward me. Submerging again, I feel my jeans adding to my weight.

The air in them is gone.

I need to reinflate them, but whipping them over my head right now would be like waving a flag. Like most of my decisions, my next is made purely by instinct. Carefully removing the Ziploc containing my cell phone from my pocket, I let the jeans sink in the river. Then I kick toward the bass boat, using the spotlight as my guide. My goal isn't the boat itself—or the man in it—but the tree floating toward it.

After thirty seconds underwater, I surface to check my progress. The boat is fifteen feet in front of me, its pilot invisible behind the spotlight. Taking a gulp of air, I drop back under the waves and swim past the boat.

When I surface ten meters beyond it, the tree arrives like a sched-uled bus. With my right hand I reach out and catch a trailing root. It's like catching hold of a ski rope being towed by a speedboat. The root bloom is the bow of my adopted ship, the branches far behind me its stern. The trunk is easily four feet in diameter, which tells me it's probably a willow uprooted by high water. As the monster trunk drifts downstream, I climb from its submerged roots to the dry roots above the waterline. Suddenly the waves that were thrashing me around the river are merely scenery. I'm riding atop an eighty-foot willow like Cleopatra on her royal barge. The rifleman in the bass boat is already behind me, and though he could return to search this tree again, the tangle of roots and mud could easily conceal me.

I can see much more from this vantage point. The riverbank to my left—the eastern bank—is enveloped in darkness. But on my right, a haze of faint bluish light reflects off the clouds. That light is Louisiana Highway 1. That light is civilization. And the river, true to its course, is driving the tree beneath me straight toward the far bank of the bend beneath those lights. In about three minutes, I should be able to leap from these roots and swim no more than three hundred yards to shore.

Even the rain doesn't bother me here. The roots above my head shield me from most of it. Flipping over the Ziploc to check my cell phone, I see its screen glowing green in the darkness. It shows three bars under the antenna icon.

I have service again.

It's surreal. Riding down the Mississippi River in the root-ball of a floating willow tree, I can call any telephone in the world. Some people in this situation might call the Coast Guard, which maintains stations along the river. But my main concern is no longer reaching the opposite bank. It's catching a ride when I get there. Besides, the nearest Coast Guard station is probably thirty miles away, at New Roads. And what would I tell them to look for? A floating willow tree in a storm? A bass boat with its spotlight on? They'd never find the former, and the bass boat would go dark and disappear long before a Coast Guard vessel could catch it.

While deciding whom to call, I realize my screen shows four missed calls. Paging through screens, I see that one was from Sean, one from Dr. Goldman, one from Michael Wells, and one from Unknown Caller. I check the battery to make sure I have adequate power, then listen to the messages.

Sean: *Hey, it's me, I'm sorry about not answering before. I was with Karen. We're talking about the whole divorce thing, and about you. It's complicated. Look, there's something you need to know. Nathan Malik isn't in jail anymore. He made his bail. A million bucks. The FBI had him under surveillance, but Malik drove out to Lakeside Mall and pulled some kind of switch in the Dillard's store. They lost him. They should have let us tail him. Anyway, you need to watch your back. Malik hasn't been declared a fugitive, but if he leaves the state, he will be. He's already the target of a covert statewide manhunt here, and they'll be doing the same thing in Mississippi. His data's gone out nationally as a BOLO. You need to know, because the guy obviously has some kind of fixation on you. Don't come back to New Orleans, Cat. And even in Natchez you should—Shit, Karen's coming.*

There's a click, and the message ends.

So Malik is free again. Where is he now? I wonder. Could he be the man behind me in the bass boat? Sean's message was time-stamped 6:11 P.M. It's conceivable that Malik could have driven from New Orleans to DeSalle Island in that time, but how would he even know where it was? Or that I was coming here?

The next message is from Dr. Goldman. In her eerily calm voice, Hannah says, *Catherine, I'm very concerned about the things you told me in our earlier conversation. I want to see you as soon as possible. Call me any hour of the day or night. I consider this a crisis, and I want you under my direct care. The time for distance is over. This is the most dangerous and the most hopeful moment in your life. Please call me.*

The next message says, *Cat, this is Michael Wells. I got your cell number from your mother. I'm done with work now, and I'd really like to talk to you. You didn't sound good on the phone earlier. That stuff about repressed memories . . . all that. I'm not sure what you're dealing with, and you may be fine now. I just want you to know I'm here for you. As a friend, a doctor, whatever you need. My home number is four four five, eight six three. Call me, okay? No pressure.*

No pressure. God, how those words sound good to me.

The last message is only dead air, then static followed by a click. So much for Unknown Caller. For a brief moment I wonder if that could have been Dr. Malik, but the odds are against it. Probably just a wrong number.

No pressure, Michael said. The idea of calling Sean is nothing *but* pressure. And Dr. Goldman . . . maybe tomorrow. Right now I need a different kind of help. After checking my orientation to the river-bank—I have about a minute left before my swim—I dial Michael's number. He answers on the third ring.

"Dr. Wells," he says, sounding ready for anything from a toddler with a cold to an infant with spinal meningitis. Tears well in my eyes, and for some reason it hits me now that the chief difference between Michael and me is that he treats live patients, while I work with the dead.

"It's Cat Ferry, Michael."

"Cat! Are you all right?"

"Yes and no. I'm in trouble, actually."

"What kind of trouble?"

"I need a ride."

"A ride? Okay. I'll come get you. Where are you?"

I close my eyes in relief and worry. "I'm about forty miles south of Natchez by air, but more like seventy by road."

There's a pause. Then Michael says, "That's fine. Just tell me where to go."

God bless you . . . "I'm going to be beside Highway One on the west-bank side of the Mississippi River. Somewhere near the Morganza Spillway. Do you know where that is?"

"Yep. I've flown down the river several times to Baton Rouge and New Orleans."

"If you could just start in this direction, I can tell you exactly where I am when you get close."

"I'm leaving now. Are you safe, Cat? I mean, do we need police or anything?"

"Maybe a first-aid kit. I'm going to talk to the police myself. And there's no danger for you. I know this is a huge favor to ask, but—"

"Don't even think about it. I'm on my way."

I'm less than a quarter mile from the bank now, but the tree is starting to slide left beneath me. The current is sucking us back out toward the center of the river.

"I have to go, Michael. I'll call you soon. And thank you, thank you."

"I'm on my way," he repeats. "Don't worry about anything."

I hang up the phone, then replace it in the Ziploc. This time, when I seal the bag, I leave a small opening at one end. Through this hole I blow air into the bag until it's full, like a balloon. Then I seal it tight. If for some reason I drop it, at least it will stay afloat.

Clenching the Baggie in my teeth like a Saint Bernard, I climb down the ladder of roots until I'm half in the water. Then I push away and start swimming freestyle toward the bank. I do this for about thirty yards, just to get clear of the branches of the tree that saved me, then switch to the breaststroke. I could easily freestyle to the bank in calm water, but the waves are still bad. The breaststroke carries me up and down the waves in a more natural motion, and it's a good stroke for breathing.

Fifteen minutes of steady swimming bring me within twenty yards of the bank. My wind is still good, but my arms and legs are getting that leaden feeling I used to get during the longer solo races. The bank here is very steep. There's nothing I can grab to pull me up. In the end, I simply breaststroke along the river's edge and crawl snake-like onto the muddy slope, digging my fingernails into the earth for purchase.

I lie panting on the bank like a novice marathon runner, but it's not as bad as it could be. I've surfaced from free dives so fatigued that I had to be put on oxygen to maintain consciousness. The rain still lashes my face, but I hardly feel it now. The ground under me seems like the most solid thing in the world, and I don't want to get up.

My body tenses in fear.

Someone is whistling. The sound dies, then starts again. It's my cell phone, its ring muted by the Ziploc. Ripping open the bag, I press SEND.

"Hello?"

"Cat? It's Sean. Where are you?"

"You wouldn't believe me if I told you. Where are you? Home with Karen?"

Silence. Then: "Actually, I am. I'm calling because you need to know something. Did you get my message about Malik making bail and evading surveillance?"

"Yes." I'm still thinking about Sean being home with his wife.

"Have you heard anything from Malik?"

"No."

"The FBI knows you tried to call him."

"So?"

"So, are you out of your mind? It doesn't look good."

"I don't care."

"Do you care about staying alive?"

"Strangely enough, I do. I just found that out beyond any doubt."

"What do you mean?"

I'm laughing softly. "Somebody just tried to kill me."

"*What?*"

"It doesn't have anything to do with Malik."

"How do you know that?"

"It happened on the island. My family's island in the river. This is about something else. I'm not sure what, but it's not the murders in New Orleans."

"Where are you right now?"

"Lying on a riverbank with a hole in my leg and rain falling in my face. I don't have any clothes or shoes. And I feel a hell of a lot better than I did this morning."

"Cat . . . that sounds like your manic voice. Are you taking your meds?"

"I have to go, Sean. Don't worry about me."

"Cat, don't do this. The FBI wants to talk to you. Kaiser wants to talk to you."

"Tell Kaiser I'll call him tomorrow. And, Sean?"

"Yeah?"

"You know how we used to wonder about some of the things I wanted you to do to me? Sexually, I mean?"

His voice goes quiet. "Yeah."

"I just found out that my father abused me. So don't worry about any of that stuff. It had nothing to do with you. Same with the other stuff I did. The one-night things. I think all that stuff is from what happened to me when I was a kid."

"Cat, you don't sound good. Let me . . ."

"What? Can you leave home now? Can you come get me right now?"

"I may be able to, yeah."

"I'm an hour away from you. Maybe more."

Silence. "I can send somebody."

One more knife in the stomach. "Don't worry about it, Sean. Take care of your wife and kids. Good-bye."

"Cat—"

I hang up before he can finish. He can't help me now. He never really could.

Rolling onto my stomach, I lay my palms flat on the ground and push myself to my feet. The glow of the highway looks about a mile away.

I start walking.

CHAPTER

31

I'm sitting against the wall of an abandoned gas station on Highway 1, wearing only my underwear and waiting for Michael Wells to save me from the mosquitoes that are making a feast of my blood. The river coated my skin with a rank, oily film, but the mosquitoes here must be used to it. If I don't have West Nile virus by tomorrow, it will be a miracle. The narrow overhang above hardly protects me from the rain, but I don't mind the rain tonight. It's the only thing relieving the stifling heat. The dark is another matter. The only light comes from a diffuse glow behind the thunderclouds, and the occasional glare of headlights flying up the highway.

Michael told me to watch for a black Ford Expedition, but it's hard to get a look at the passing cars without exposing myself. Since I'm on the opposite side of the river from the man who was trying to kill me, I'm probably safe from him for a while. But if I stand on this highway wearing only my bra and panties, I'm asking to get raped. Besides, it's only been an hour or so since I called Michael. He couldn't be here yet unless he drove ninety or faster.

The moment I leaned against this cinder-block wall, a deep fatigue settled into my limbs. It wasn't exhaustion from swimming the river. I feel disconnected from everything, even from myself. There's a hollowness in my heart that must be the beginnings of grief. I've lost so much today. Sean—by my own choice if not by his. My father, who remained alive in my heart for all the years since his death, finally began to die this afternoon when Grandpapa told me what he'd done. My mother, who somehow could not protect me from my father's secret desires. Even Pearlie, who kept so much from me all these years. I'm not even sure I want to know what she knew and when.

And then there's me, the woman who despite alternating bouts of elation and depression managed to work her way to the top of her field. She isn't who I thought she was at all. Part of me was always a sham. The public persona—the superachiever who brooked no nonsense from anyone—was a professional doppelgänger who protected a little girl filled with self-doubt, who secretly drank vodka almost around the clock to numb a pain she didn't understand, and who needed a man to protect her from dangers that existed mostly in her head. Yet somehow that bundle of contradictions added up to someone who functioned efficiently in the world. Someone I liked reasonably well. But now the formless pain I always ran from has a face. And that face belongs to my father. Suddenly, the wild emotional gyrations of my past make sense. I am no longer a mystery. I'm an *Oprah* show.

My cell phone is ringing.

The screen reads, *UNKNOWN CALLER.*

I'm afraid to answer, as though by doing so I'll allow the caller to see where I am, like the Eye of Sauron seeing Frodo when he put on the One Ring. But that's crazy. After a quick breath, I press SEND.

"Is this Catherine Ferry?" asks a precise voice.

My body goes rigid. "Dr. Malik?"

"Yes. I didn't want you to think I was ignoring you. We can't speak for long, I'm afraid, but we should get together soon. I'm sure you've been going through some difficult times since our last conversation."

"I have," I admit, my hands already shaking.

"That's only to be expected, Catherine. Have you been having dreams? Flashbacks? Anything like that?"

"All of the above. I found out this morning that I was sexually abused as a child."

"I suspected that when you were a medical student. Dr. Omartian was twenty-five years your senior, after all. There were other signs, too. We can discuss all this, but I'm afraid it will have to be at a later date."

"My grandfather killed my father."

Silence. "Who told you that?"

"Grandpapa. He says he caught Daddy molesting me."

"Why would he tell you something like that after all these years?"

"I was on the verge of discovering it anyway."

A pause. "I see."

A pair of headlights flashes out of the dark and blows past the gas station. The glare doesn't touch me for more than a second, but being illuminated at all makes me shiver. "You know the task force is hunting you?"

"Yes."

"They think you killed the victims in New Orleans."

"Yesterday you thought that yourself."

He's right. I'm not sure what I think now. I only know that as I speak to this man whom the police and the FBI believe killed five men in brutal and premeditated fashion, I feel calmer than I have in days.

"Do you still believe that, Catherine?"

"I don't know. If the murders are true sexual homicides, I don't think you did it. But if they're something else . . . maybe you did."

"What else would they be?"

"Punishment."

A long pause. "You're a perceptive woman."

"That hasn't helped me much."

"It may yet."

"What was the video equipment for? The stuff the police found in your secret apartment?"

"Public education. I'll speak to you again soon, dear. I have to move now."

Separation anxiety pierces me like a blade. "Dr. Malik?"

"Yes?"

"Someone tried to kill me tonight."

Silence.

"Was it you?"

"No. Where did this happen?"

"In the middle of nowhere. An island in the Mississippi River."

More silence. "I can't help you with that."

"Do the murders in New Orleans have anything to do with me? With my life in Natchez?"

"Yes and no. I have to go now, dear. Be careful. Trust no one. Not even your family."

With one click he's gone.

I'm still holding the phone to my ear when a black Expedition wheels into the parking lot and blinks its headlights three times. I stay where I am until Michael Wells climbs out.

"Cat?" he yells. "It's Michael!"

"Over here." Keeping my back against the wall, I push myself erect with my legs and walk toward the Expedition.

CHAPTER
32

Michael looks worried as I approach the Expedition, but then he smiles. "Every time I see you, you're in your underwear."

"Seems that way, doesn't it?"

He reaches into the vehicle and hands me a T-shirt, a pair of warm-up pants, and some slippers about five sizes too large for my feet.

"Thanks. Do you have a towel or something? I don't want to ruin the pants. I've got a lot of blood on my leg."

He opens the passenger door and helps me up onto the seat. Then he bends over the ragged hole in my thigh. "Damn. I'll have to suture that when we get back. For now we'll just clean and cover it."

From a paper bag on the floor he takes a bottle of Betadine, soaks some gauze with it, and presses the soggy ball into my wound. After a few seconds, he removes the gauze and squirts half a tube of Neosporin into the hole, then covers it with a large Band-Aid.

"Most of my patients need a Tootsie Pop after this."

"Do you have one?"

He reaches into his glove box and, with a magician's flourish, whips out a chocolate Tootsie Pop. This actually brings a smile to my lips.

"How about we get the hell out of here now?" he says.

I nod gratefully.

Michael shuts me into the passenger seat and gets behind the wheel. As I pull the clothes over my underwear, he makes a three-point turn and skids back onto the highway, headed north.

"How did you get down here?" he asks.

"In my car. It's on the other side of the river."

"Do we need to get it?"

I would like to have my car back. But to get it, we'd have to cross the ferry at St. Francisville. That's the only way across the Mississippi River between Natchez and Baton Rouge—other than the ferry at Angola, which is used only for prison business—so it's an ideal ambush site for whoever was trying to kill me on the island. If the gunman waits for me near my parked Audi, he risks being caught if I bring the cops back with me. But the ferry is a choke point with plausible deniability. If I push my luck and try to cross there, he could get lucky.

"No. I'll get it tomorrow."

"Okay. Take it easy now. I'll have you back in Natchez in an hour."

I recline my seat and take a few deep breaths. With the air conditioner on, I feel like I'm resting in a suite at the Windsor Court.

"I don't want to pry into your business," Michael says, "but what the hell happened to you today? You sounded bad when you called my office this afternoon."

"I got some bad news."

"Okay."

He doesn't ask for details, but I don't see much point in holding back the rest of it. "Just before I called you, I found out that I was sexually abused as a child."

He nods slowly. "I thought it must be something like that, when you asked about repressed memories. I've been reading up on the subject today. You got me curious."

I've been in this vehicle less than five minutes, but already my head feels fuzzy. "We can talk about it," I murmur. "I just need to rest my eyes for a little bit."

"Cat? Wake up!"

I blink awake and look around. I'm sitting in a truck in a brightly lit garage

"Where are we?"

"My house," Michael says. "In Brookwood."

"Oh."

"I wasn't sure where you wanted to go. I tried to ask you, but you wouldn't wake up. I stopped by my office for some sutures, then brought you here. Let's get that cut stitched up. Then I'll take you to your grandfather's house."

Nathan Malik's words come back to me like a brand burned into my brain: *Trust no one. Not even your family.* "I don't want to go there."

"You don't have to. I'll take you wherever you want to go. Or you can stay here. I've got three extra bedrooms. It's up to you."

I nod thanks but say nothing. I don't know what I want to do. I definitely want my leg stitched up. It hurts like hell, and stitching means local anesthetic. At least I hope it does. "Did you bring some lidocaine?"

Michael shakes his head. "Nah. I figured anybody who can free dive to three hundred feet can handle a couple of stitches without breaking a sweat."

He looks serious, but after a few moments of eye contact, he reaches into his pocket and brings out a vial of clear liquid.

"The magic elixir," he says with a smile. "Let's do it."

Michael sutures my leg while I sit on the cold granite of his kitchen island. The gleaming room reminds me of Arthur LeGendre's kitchen, only there's no corpse lying on the floor. Michael's house was built in the 1970s, and until Mrs. Hemmeter sold it, the decor was original to the house. Avocado green appliances and heavy brown paneling like that in my old bedroom. Michael has totally redone the place, and with surprisingly good taste for a bachelor.

"This reminds me of my grandfather stitching me up on the island when I cut my knee," I tell him as he pulls the Ethicon through my skin with a curved needle.

"I guess he always carried his black bag with him?"

"Oh, he has a whole clinic down there. When my aunt Ann was ten years old, the family got trapped on the island in a storm. She had a hot appendix. Grandpapa removed it by lantern light with one of the island women assisting him. That's one of his hero stories, but it's pretty impressive."

Michael nods and continues stitching. "You'd be surprised what you can do when conditions demand it. I've been on a few medical mission trips to South America . . . saw some unbelievable things. OBs sterilizing women one after another in the open air. They stretch them out on benches, cut them open, clip their tubes with special plastic clips, and close them up again."

"Jesus."

He laughs. "I wouldn't recommend it to a suburban housewife, but it does the job."

Medical mission trips. I have a feeling there's a lot more to Michael Wells than most people know. "I like what you've done with this house."

"Do you? Your mom did most of it."

"You're kidding."

"No, when I first got to town, I was too busy to breathe, much less decorate a house. I stopped by Gwen's interior design store one afternoon and hired her to do the whole place."

"Now I'm not sure I like it."

He laughs. "You don't get along with your mother?"

"We do, as long as we don't see too much of each other."

He ties off the last stitch, then lays his forceps on the countertop. "You hungry?"

"Starving."

"Steak and eggs?"

"Are you ordering out?"

"No." He goes to the refrigerator and brings out a package of rib eyes. "Go sit on that sofa. You'll be digging into this in twenty minutes."

The sofa sits against the wall beyond a round table in the dining area. Too far away for conversation, or even to watch Michael cooking. Given my earlier experiences today, I don't really want to lie on the couch and let my mind wander.

Sliding off the counter, I sit on a barstool and watch Michael. It's strange to have a man cook for me, though Sean sometimes boils crawfish in my backyard.

"You want to talk about today?" Michael asks, meeting my gaze long enough to let me know he's genuinely concerned.

"It isn't just today. It's the past month. It's my whole life, really."

"Can you give me the gist in twenty minutes?"

I laugh. And then I start talking. I start with my panic attack at the Nolan crime scene, the one prior to Arthur LeGendre's house.

That leads me to LeGendre, then to Carmen Piazza removing me from the task force, and then to my trip back to Natchez and to finding the bloody footprints in my bedroom. I'm talking on autopilot, though, because what I'm really doing is watching Michael cook. He's good with his hands, and I can tell from the way he uses them that he's a good doctor. He asks questions during my pauses, and before long I'm telling him about the depression that began in high school, the mania that followed, and my serial monogamy with married men. He's a good listener, only I can't tell what he makes of all this. He looks as though he's hearing nothing out of the ordinary, but inside he may already regret rescuing this particular damsel in distress.

When the steaks and eggs are done, we move to the glass dining table, but I do as much talking as eating. I can't seem to stop. The funny thing is, he doesn't try to force me to eat, as most men would. He just keeps watching my eyes, as if they're telling him as much as my words. I tell him about my father, Grandpapa, Pearlie, my mother, Dr. Goldman, Nathan Malik—even the things Grandpapa told me earlier today. The only thing I don't tell Michael about is being pregnant. That I cannot bring myself to do.

When at last my stream of words slows to a trickle, he sighs deeply and says, "You want to watch a movie? I rented the new Adam Sandler."

I'm not sure whether I'm offended or relieved. "Are you kidding?"

He grins. "Yes. You want to know what I really think about all that?"

"I do."

"I think you're under more stress right now than most people could stand. I think your life is probably in danger from whoever is behind these murders, not to mention the risk of dealing with your disease without adequate therapy or medication."

I say nothing.

"Does it piss you off that I said that?"

"A little."

He holds up his hands, palms outward. "I know it's not my business. If you don't want to take your medication, fine. But I know a little bit about being bipolar. I had a good friend in medical school who was that way."

"I'm not bipolar. I'm cyclothymic."

"That's just semantics. Same symptoms, just a question of degree."
I concede this with a nod.

"What I learned from my friend was that a lot of bipolar people *tell* you they want to get better, but they really don't. They feel so good during their highs that they're willing to endure the lows as the price of that euphoria. Even if the lows are so bad that the person is suicidal when they crash."

"I can't argue with that. What happened to your friend?"

"He flunked out of med school."

"Just like me. Is that your point?"

"You didn't flunk out. They basically kicked you out for causing someone else to try to kill himself."

"Yep."

Michael's face is nonjudgmental. "I don't think any of that stuff was your fault, Cat. I don't know too much about the links between childhood sexual abuse and adult psychological problems, because I treat kids. That's why I knew so little about repressed memories. But I do know about child abuse. I've seen a lot of it, especially as a pediatric resident working ERs."

There's something in his eyes that reminds me of John Kaiser's eyes. Knowledge earned through pain. Wisdom never asked for.

"Those cases are the easy ones, though," Michael says. "The tough cases are the ones where you know something isn't right, but you're not looking at genital warts or something obvious like that. Dealing with those cases is how I learned the most surprising things about sexual abuse."

"Like?"

"Like it's not usually the physically painful, horrible thing that people imagine. It's not violent rape or even necessarily a terrible experience in itself. Not in the beginning. If it were, sexual abuse wouldn't be the invisible epidemic that it is. Sex is pleasurable, even to a child. Adult abusers know that. They seduce the child a little at a time, gradually raising the stakes. The family dynamics are altered in ways it would take Freud years to figure out. Complex power games are played between abuser and victim. You get young girls serving as surrogate wives in the home, sisters competing for the sexual attention of their father, fathers training sons to use women the same way they do. Of course, the reverse happens, too. You get older daughters trying to protect younger siblings by doing anything they can to keep the abusive father focused on them."

I close my eyes in horror. "I'll bet this isn't how you thought you'd be spending this evening."

Michael spears a piece of cold steak and chews it thoughtfully. "No, but I'm okay with it. I was always curious about you. Why you picked the guys you did in high school. And these repeated relationships with married guys. That's not hard to figure out now, is it?"

"My therapist tells me I pick unavailable guys so that I can't become too attached to a man. That way the loss I experienced with my father can't be repeated."

"Is it too late to get your money back?"

Michael's eyes silently apologize for joking about something so serious. But he's so honest about his opinions that it's difficult to get angry.

"I think it's the secrecy that's the root of your affairs," he says. "Secrecy was part of your sexual imprinting. I think you've been reenacting your abuse for most of your life. You thrive on a secretive relationship with a forbidden partner, a relationship that's very sexual in nature. Is that accurate?"

"Are you sure you didn't subspecialize in pediatric psychiatry?"

He shakes his head. "Once you know about the abuse, it's easy to see the connections. You may not feel comfortable telling me this, but do you have any quirks in your sex life that seem abnormal?"

I feel myself flush, and it surprises me. I'm usually quite candid with men about sexual matters, sometimes shockingly so. But tonight . . . "I'm not sure we know each other well enough to go there yet."

"You're right." He puts down his fork and lays his hands on the table. "Let me ask you another question."

"Okay."

"Did your mother have an illness that kept her bedridden for long periods?"

"After I was born, she had some kind of female problem. Pelvic inflammatory disease, maybe? I'm not sure. But she would stay in bed for weeks at a time. I was very young then, of course."

"What about later? Was she absent from the home a lot?"

"Yes." My main memories of my mother are of her leaving home or returning. And she always had something in her hands—something besides me. "Mom was completely obsessed with her interior design business. If you asked her whether I liked mayonnaise on my sandwiches or not, she couldn't have told you. But if you asked her how many shades of grass-cloth wallpaper were available in America, she could list them from memory."

Michael doesn't seem surprised. "Was alcohol a problem in your house? Or substance abuse?"

"Both. More drugs than alcohol. My dad used all kinds of drugs when he got back from Vietnam. Prescription, mostly. My mother didn't drink when I was growing up, so I thought she was clean. But apparently she was taking my father's prescription meds for years. Why are you asking these questions?"

"They're classic markers for an abusive situation."

His uncanny accuracy about my life makes me want to know more. But to learn more, I'll have to give more. Can I trust him with my secret self?

Michael reaches out and touches my hand. "You're shaking, Cat. You don't have to tell me any more."

"No, I want to," I say quickly.

He withdraws his hand and leans back in his chair. "All right, then. Tell me."

CHAPTER
33

"I've always needed certain things during sex," I say softly. "Pain, for example. Nothing masochistic really, but just . . . very physical penetration. With fingers, objects . . . I don't know. And choking. Sometimes I have this intense desire to be choked during sex."

Michael is still leaning back from the dinner table, but I sense a new alertness in him. "And?"

"I have a problem reaching orgasm. Even if I get those things I want, it just doesn't happen for me. On one hand I have this hyperactive sex drive, but on the other, I can't make it to the point of release. Not with a man, I mean. I can do it alone. But with men, it's this maddening spiral upward without ever being able to break through."

"But the men you're with think you're the best sexual partner they ever had, right?"

Now I'm really blushing. "They say so."

"All classic signs of past sexual abuse. Pain was part of your sexual imprinting, just like secrecy. Your father may have put his hands around your throat during sex. Or maybe you just felt you couldn't breathe during the acts. Maybe that's what you're trying to repeat with the choking. That makes me wonder about your free diving, too. Lying on pool bottoms for five minutes at a time to *relax*? That would put most people into a coma."

"I guess it is kind of a red flag."

"And your sexual performance? That's the easiest thing of all to understand. From childhood you were trained to please a man sexually. That was the only goal of the abuse, and your survival instinct made you learn it well. So, you're an expert at giving pleasure. You just can't feel it yourself."

"I guess."

"The good news is that now that you're aware of the abuse, this therapist you like—Dr. Goldman?—she should be able to make some real progress with you."

"Maybe. But right now I just want to pretend it never happened. Even if it's the answer to everything, I don't want to think about it."

"Who would? That's a normal response." Michael gets up and starts clearing the table. "I'm actually more concerned about this murder case you're working on. I mean, somebody tried to blow your brains out tonight."

I carry the glasses to the sink, and he starts rinsing the plates to put in the dishwasher. "I'm not sure that has to do with the murder case," I tell him.

"What, then? These revelations of abuse? Your father's been dead for twenty years."

"What about the Vietnam angle?"

"You think someone's trying to prevent thirty-year-old atrocities from coming to light? You said Jesse Billups served in a whole different theater of the war than your father. I don't think that's it, Cat."

"Then what?"

"I think the murders in New Orleans are somehow connected to your life here. To your past. Maybe even to your abuse, though I can't see how. But sexual abuse is the common factor in both situations."

It's oddly familiar, standing in a kitchen batting around theories about a murder case with a man. Only the man I'm doing it with is not familiar.

"Both Pearlie and Louise told you that Tom Cage was your father's doctor here in town. He's been practicing for more than forty years, and he's a great guy. You should talk to him about the Vietnam stuff. Do you know him?"

In my mind I see a tall man with a salt-and-pepper beard and twinkling eyes. "I know who he is. I don't think he likes my grandfather much."

"That wouldn't surprise me. Tom Cage is the opposite of your grandfather. He never gave a damn about making money. He just treats sick people. I'll be glad to call him for you, if you like. Set up a meeting."

"Maybe tomorrow."

Michael turns on the dishwasher, then takes a tub of Blue Bell ice cream from the freezer and starts scooping it into two bowls. "This is my reward for doing a good deed tonight," he says with a smile. "I didn't ask if you wanted any, because I knew you'd say no. I'll have to run an extra mile tomorrow morning."

"I think I already got my workout tonight."

"No doubt. Hey, who knew you were going to that island today?"

I think about it as we walk to the table. "Pearlie. My grandfather and his driver. Somebody probably told Mom after I was gone. I guess Mose, the yardman, could have found out."

Michael slowly stirs his ice cream. "Once you were on the island, word probably spread quickly that you were there. But I don't think it was anybody from that island who tried to kill you. I think somebody followed you there, or found out you went there and went after you."

"But I don't get it. What good does killing me do anybody?"

"*Good* is a relative term. What good did killing the other five victims do?"

"You're right. If I knew that, I could solve the case."

"I know you feel like this Dr. Malik isn't the killer. But you're not stable enough right now to make that kind of judgment."

"I know. When I'm off my meds, I feel much more alive and in the moment, but that comes at a price. My memory and logic definitely suffer. Maybe if I wean myself completely, they'll come back."

"Malik's at the center of this whole mess. He's the only known connection between you and the New Orleans murders. He's already demonstrated that he's fixated on you. I think you should consider him the prime suspect."

I hold some ice cream in my mouth, savoring the rich taste of vanilla. "Well . . . the FBI is already searching for him, and he couldn't have known I was on the island."

"You don't know that. You do know he's going to call you back, yet you haven't told the FBI that. Why?"

"How do you know I haven't?"

Michael's eyes say, *Give me a break.* "I think you want to talk to Dr. Malik without anyone listening in. You think he can figure out things about your life that other therapists never could."

"Like . . . ?"

"Like why this abuse happened to you. Proof that it *did* happen. That's one thing I read today about people with delayed memories of abuse. Even when they manage to find proof that their memories are real, they still doubt the truth of what comes back to them."

This gives me an unexpected chill. "Why?"

"Because accepting that the abuse really happened means accepting that the person who abused them never really loved them. To accept your abuse, Cat, the little girl inside of you is going to have to admit, *My daddy never loved me.* Do you think you can do that? I'm not sure I could."

I've never wanted ice cream less than I want it now.

"That's the core of this whole problem," Michael reflects. "Denial. Mothers deny it's happening to their children so they can keep their families together. The rest of us refuse to believe that our doctor or our minister or the nice mailman is having sex with his three-year-old child, because if we do, we admit that the whole veneer of civilization is bullshit. Worse, we'd have to admit the danger that our own kids are in. Because if we can't recognize the abusers we shake hands with every day, how can we protect our children?"

"This is a depressing conversation."

"You want to watch that movie now?"

"God, no. I want to sleep for thirty hours straight."

"Then that's what you should do." Michael shrugs as if we're on vacation together, deciding whether to go out to dinner or to eat in. "I don't blame you for not wanting to go home. Going back into the physical space where the abuse happened to you can't be a good idea."

"Do you really have a guest room I can stay in?"

He smiles. "I have three. You'll have total privacy. The whole second floor is yours. You won't know I'm here unless you come downstairs and find me."

I wait a moment before speaking. "I don't want to sound ungrateful, but guys have made me promises like that before. They never seem to live up to them."

"I'm not most guys."

"I believe you. But why aren't you?"

A self-deprecating smile. "Probably because my puberty years sucked so badly. I understand deferred gratification."

"Is that what you want from this relationship, though? In the end? Gratification?"

Michael suddenly looks very serious. "I'm not thinking that far ahead, okay? I don't even know if you're sane enough to handle a real relationship. I just like you. I always did. I also happen to think you're beautiful. But anyone can see that. The point is, you can stay here as long as you want, and you don't have to worry about sex being in the mix."

I don't know why, but I believe him. "Okay, deal. Show me the bedroom."

"You can find it. Upstairs is all you need to know. Take your pick."

The wide smile on my face surprises me. Before it can fade, I turn and walk to the foyer, where the stairs are. I remember the layout from when the Hemmeters owned the house. As I put my foot on the second step, I hear Michael's voice.

"I have to go to work in the morning," he says, walking into the foyer. "But I'm going to leave the Expedition for you."

"What will you drive?"

"I have a motorcycle."

"A motorcycle?"

"Does that surprise you?"

"Well . . ." A strange laugh escapes my lips. "You have a plane and a motorcycle. I guess I associate that with a certain kind of guy. And you don't seem like that kind of guy."

"It doesn't pay to stereotype people."

"Touché."

He takes a step back toward the kitchen. "I'll leave the keys on the counter."

I start to go up, but something has been nagging me since he said it. "Michael, what you said before . . . about why mothers keep quiet about abuse going on in their homes?"

"Yes?"

"You said they do it to keep their families together, right?"

"Right."

"I would think that's because the father in those situations is the primary breadwinner. The source of support for the whole family."

Michael nods. "Exactly. The abuser creates a situation in which everyone in the family is dependent upon him. By denying the abuse, the mother avoids her worst nightmares of abandonment and poverty."

"But that doesn't work in my case, see? For my family."

"Because your father wasn't the provider?"

"Right. My grandfather was."

"What about your father's sculpting?"

"He didn't make any real money from that until a couple of years before his death. Grandpapa paid for everything. I mean, we lived in his slave quarters, for God's sake. It sounds terrible, but if my dad had been hit by a bus, it wouldn't have affected our situation in the least."

"Materially speaking," Michael says. "But money isn't everything. Based on what you've told me tonight, I think your father's early death went a long way toward wrecking your life."

He's right, of course.

Michael steps back toward the staircase. "So why would your mother deny that your father was abusing you if she didn't have to fear losing him?"

I feel blood heat my cheeks. "Right."

"It may be that she didn't really know about it. But think . . . your father returned from Vietnam with severe post-traumatic stress disorder. He told you himself that you couldn't be around him at certain times. Now you've learned that he was part of a military unit that committed atrocities during the war. It would probably be difficult to overestimate your mother's fear of what that man might do to her— or to you—if she confronted him about abuse, or worse, tried to take you away from him."

Michael's logic leaves me in cold shock. Why is it so easy to see the essential nature of relationships in other people's families but not in our own? I've been angry at my mother for years, and I didn't know why. Today I thought I'd discovered the reason. But now . . . given an idea of what it must have been like to live with Daddy, not as a blindly loving daughter but as a wife, my mother seems a completely different person to me.

Michael lays his hand over mine, which is resting on the newel post. "Get some sleep, Cat. It's going to take a while for all this to sink in."

I've gotten similar advice countless times from the women in my life: *Go to sleep. Everything will look better in the morning.* But it doesn't sound the same coming from Michael. He has no illusions that things will be better tomorrow. "Thanks," I tell him. "I mean it."

"You're welcome." He withdraws his hand and walks back toward the kitchen.

I slowly climb the stairs and flick on the light in the first bedroom to my right. The walls are pale yellow, and the queen bed has a white comforter on it. Walking to the window, I see that it overlooks the glowing blue rectangle of the swimming pool.

I can sleep here.

The bathroom is stocked with towels and toiletries, even a new toothbrush. I strip off the warm-up pants and T-shirt Michael brought me, then lean into the shower to turn the faucet handles. Before I can, the opening notes of "Sunday, Bloody Sunday" fill the bathroom. I glance at the screen of my cell phone, and my pulse instantly accelerates. It's a New Orleans number that I don't recognize. Nathan Malik?

I press SEND and then hold the phone to my ear.

"Dr. Ferry?" says a man who sounds nothing like Dr. Malik.

"Yes?" I say cautiously.

"This is John Kaiser. I need to talk to you about Nathan Malik."

CHAPTER
34

"Is he alive?" I ask without any rational reason.

The silence that follows this question seems interminable. I sit on the lid of Michael Wells's commode and wait for Agent Kaiser to tip me off my precarious mental precipice.

"Why would you ask me that question?" he asks. "Didn't you speak to Dr. Malik earlier tonight?"

Sean's warning that Malik might be declared a fugitive from a murder charge comes back to me with all its implications. "Yes," I confess. "Briefly."

"You're aware Dr. Malik purposefully evaded surveillance and will be declared a fugitive if he leaves Louisiana?"

Two things hit me instantly: one, Kaiser is speaking for a tape recorder; two, Sean obviously told Kaiser about our conversation. "Yes. I think you know that."

"Did Malik give you any idea where he was when you were talking?"

"No, but you must have figured that out by now."

A brief pause. "He called you from a pay phone on the West Bank in New Orleans. By the time we got a car there, he was gone."

"Is that right?" I stall, trying to gather my wits. It's disorienting to deal with this call while naked in the guest bathroom of Michael Wells's house. I'd do better in my own house, or even in my car. But one thing I know: if Malik was on the West Bank when he called me, he could not have been shooting at me on the island.

"Dr. Ferry," Kaiser says in a softer voice. "You've asked me to call you Cat. May I do that?"

"Sure," I say, pulling the T-shirt back on.

"I need to cover several things with you quickly. I want you to tell me everything that pops into your head while we talk. Is there any reason you feel you won't be able to do that?"

"Such as?"

"Some sort of loyalty to Dr. Malik."

My cheeks burn. "I told you, I don't even know the guy! You heard every word of our meeting in his office."

"Yes, I did. But clearly the two of you feel some sort of rapport. An emotional connection. Perhaps it has to do with your similar medical histories."

I close my eyes, wondering how much Kaiser knows about my personal life. Did Sean tell him about my sexual abuse? "Please go ahead with your questions, Agent Kaiser."

"All right. Are you absolutely positive that Dr. Malik never treated you as a patient?"

"Yes."

"Did Sean Regan tell you that we finally found a patient of Malik's who would talk to us?"

"No."

"Like his other patients, she feels great loyalty to Malik, but she had to drop out of her therapy group with him. She found it too stressful."

This piques my interest, as Kaiser must have known it would. "Stressful how?"

"Apparently Malik does delayed-memory-recall work with several patients in the same room. That's highly unorthodox. The experience of hearing other women relive abusive experiences gave this patient acute anxiety attacks."

"And?"

"Well . . . that's what you've been having at our crime scenes."

"Give me a break. Anything can cause an anxiety attack."

"Nevertheless. Malik manages several different groups. His treatment protocols vary according to what he thinks each group can tolerate. Drugs with some, not with others. In this woman's group,

Malik encouraged aggressive confrontations with family members who had sexually abused the patients as children. Malik compared these confrontations to the solo flights of student pilots. The final step to freedom and independence. Anyway, this woman couldn't handle that, and she dropped out. We found her through the psychologist who initially referred her to Malik."

"That's all very interesting, but it has nothing to do with me."

Kaiser's sigh carries a lot of fatigue in it. "Cat, a lot of people on the task force are very angry with you. I'm not one of them, whether you believe me or not. I think you have some real insight into this case. Maybe insight you don't even realize you have. I also know that you gave Sean Regan a lot of help on one of the serial murder cases he got credit for solving."

"Who told you that?"

"Sean did."

"That's a shock."

"He really cares for you, Cat. Extramarital affairs are hard on everybody. But Sean thinks you're a genius."

Men always try flattery first to manipulate women. John Kaiser's no different. The threat will come later. "I'm no genius. I'm just obsessive."

"Whatever works. Sean told me somebody tried to kill you tonight."

"Yep."

"Do you know who it was?"

"Nope."

"Is this your Gary Cooper impression?"

I can't help but smile a little. "Nope."

"Do you think the attempt on your life was connected to the New Orleans murders in any way? Or to your work on those murders?"

"No."

"Why not?"

"I'm looking into a separate matter up here. A personal matter."

"A personal matter." Kaiser seems to mull this over. "Are you sure it's unrelated to your work in New Orleans?"

"You can't be a hundred percent sure of anything. But I'm pretty sure it's not."

"Did you tell Dr. Malik about the attempt on your life?"

"Yes."

"Did *he* suggest there might be a link between that and the New Orleans murders?"

I suddenly have the feeling that Kaiser has every word of my phone conversation with Malik on tape—that he's just testing my honesty with these questions. "I asked him that exact question. He said yes and no."

"Cat, I want you back in New Orleans. You're tied into these murders somehow. Surely you see that?"

There's an earnestness in Kaiser's voice that tells me he's really worried about me. "I concede that Malik has a fixation on me, okay? But if he called me from the West Bank of New Orleans this evening, he couldn't have shot at me on DeSalle Island thirty minutes before that. That's physically impossible."

"I'm not sure what we're dealing with here," Kaiser confesses. "But I know Nathan Malik is involved in the murders."

"He probably knows more than he's telling. But if you want to know what he knows, I have a lot better chance talking to him on my own than with you listening in."

"Do you plan to speak to him again?"

"If he calls me."

"Hm."

I get the feeling Kaiser would like to run this investigation one way, while his colleagues on the task force would prefer a stricter approach. "Are you listening in on my cell calls?"

"No. Not yet, anyway."

If Kaiser is telling the truth, it's only because he doesn't yet have a court order or the assets in place to bug my phone. But he soon will.

"Why did you go to DeSalle Island?" he asks. "This personal matter of yours?"

"I'm trying to find out something about my past."

"About your father?"

"How did you know that?"

"I'm extrapolating from your conversation with Malik in his office. Did you learn anything important?"

I'm not about to give Kaiser the sordid history of my childhood. "Nothing relating to your case."

"Well, the fact that Luke's military record was sealed bothered me, so I did some digging on my own."

My heart is tight in my chest. "What did you find out?"

"Luke Ferry was in a unit called the White Tigers. They made an illegal incursion into Cambodia in 1969. Details are tough to come by, but there's no doubt that the White Tigers committed war crimes during that period. Two major investigations were conducted by the JAG corps, but all charges were ultimately dropped. The whole thing was deemed too embarrassing for the government. However, I did learn that some veterans of the White Tigers were prosecuted for heroin trafficking after the war. Some as recently as the late 1980s. Your father was murdered in 1981, so I'm not ruling out anything."

I'm tempted to tell Kaiser that my father was shot by my grand-father, but something holds me back. "Have you found any connec-tion between Malik and drugs?"

"Yes. Malik tortured a Vietnamese prisoner with drugs in 1969. He was a medic then, remember? Apparently he did it on the order of his commanding officer. He was also arrested for selling army phar-maceuticals on the black market in Saigon. The charges were later dropped, and he was returned to his unit. No reason given."

"Was Malik a member of the White Tigers?"

"Not that I can prove. But a large-scale drug operation needs peo-ple all over the country. Again, I'm just not sure what we're dealing with here."

"For what it's worth, I don't think the murders in New Orleans or my father's death have anything to do with drugs. I just don't."

"Then what?"

Childhood sexual abuse, obviously . . . "I don't know, John. Is there anything else?"

"Be very careful if you speak to Malik. You could easily cross the line into aiding and abetting."

I don't even respond to this.

"I have to say this, Cat. I'd like you to accept round-the-clock FBI protection."

"No."

"You wouldn't even know we were there."

"Look, no women have died, okay? It's men who are at risk from this killer."

"Until you got shot at tonight, I might have agreed with you. We're very good at this, Cat. *No one* would know we were guarding you."

"Malik would know. I don't know how, but he would. And he wouldn't come near me."

A long silence. "Tell me why you want to talk to him."

"I don't know why, to tell you the truth. He just knows something I need to know. I sense that."

"Remember what curiosity did to the cat."

I groan. "Yeah, but cats have nine lives, remember?"

Kaiser delivers his retort like a valediction. "From what I understand, you've used up most of yours."

"I need to go, John. I'll let you know if I learn anything vital."

I click off before he can say more.

CHAPTER

35

The oily film that the river left on my skin has a sulfurous stink, and I want it off me. I turn the shower taps, and the water heats up fast. Stripping off the T-shirt again, I climb into the tub and stand under the steaming spray.

Except during my drive to the island—when I was pretty much in shock—I haven't had time to think about what Grandpapa told me this afternoon. Not critically, anyway. What I told Michael is true: when I stop taking my meds, my logical faculties go to hell. So does my short-term memory. But when Grandpapa told me he killed Daddy, it was as though the final piece of a jigsaw puzzle fell into place, completing a picture that had eluded me for most of my life. Only that story resonates emotionally with my past as I know it. According to Michael, accepting that my father abused me means accepting that he didn't love me. I suppose that's true, since abusing a child means using it purely for your own ends. But couldn't Daddy have loved me independently of that? Couldn't he have loved me, but simply been unable to resist the impulse to touch me? Or is that just wishful thinking?

For some reason, this thought makes me think of Michael. The guy drove out to the boondocks in the middle of the night to rescue me and asked for nothing in return. He even cooked supper for me. Then he gave me a room to sleep in. Using my past experiences with men as a guide, Michael should pull aside the shower curtain about now and climb in with me, saying he just couldn't resist. But he won't do that. I'm sure of it.

My ears pick out a strange harmonic from the water spraying from the nozzle. When it stops and begins again, I recognize the tones of my cell phone. Rinsing the soap off my face, I grab the phone, lean away from the spray, and look at the screen. *Det. Sean Regan.* I don't really want to answer, but I do want to know if Sean is sleeping at home with his wife or not. I press SEND and say, "Don't say anything until you tell me where you are."

"This isn't who you think it is," says a precise voice with a trace of humor in it.

My heart is pounding. "Dr. Malik?"

"None other. Are you alone, Catherine? I need to speak to you."

A current of fear shoots through my veins, not for me but for Sean. "How did you get Sean's cell phone?"

"I don't have his phone. I reprogrammed the phone I'm using to mimic Detective Regan's digital ID information. John Kaiser and the FBI won't pay so much attention to this call if the ESN belongs to your boyfriend."

How the hell does he know all that? "Go ahead, then."

"I'm calling you because I need to leave something with you."

I turn off the shower and wrap a towel around my chest. "What is it?"

"I'd rather not tell you on the phone. I just need to leave it with someone I can trust."

"You trust me?"

"Yes."

"Why?"

"Instinct."

"You shouldn't. I'm working with the FBI."

"Are you?" A hint of sarcasm. "I don't think so. It has to be you, Catherine. There's no one else."

"What about a friend?"

"I don't have friends. I have patients."

I feel exactly the same way. "I can relate to that. Patients and ex-lovers. That's about it."

Malik laughs softly. "I have only patients."

I have the distinct feeling that the psychiatrist is telling me his patients are his lovers. "If you're trying to give me your patient records, I can't accept them. The FBI named those in a search warrant. They'd prosecute me if I withheld them."

"It's not my records." Malik's indrawn breath stops suddenly. "It's a film."

"A film?"

"A film and the raw materials relating to it. Mini-DV tapes, DVD disks, audiotapes, like that. It's all in two boxes."

"What kind of film?"

"I'm making a documentary about sexual abuse and repressed memory."

This revelation comes as such a surprise that I'm not sure how to respond. Yet it makes perfect sense. Recalling Malik in his all-black getup, it's easy to see him as some sort of revolutionary film-maker.

"Nothing like it has ever been seen before," he says with gravity. "It's the most emotionally devastating thing ever committed to film. If it reaches the screen, it will shake this country to its foundations."

"What does it show? Actual sexual abuse?"

"In a way. It shows women reliving abuse in a group setting. Some of them obviously regress to a childhood state. Their experiences are shattering."

"I assume the women are patients of yours. Did they give their permission for you to record them?"

"Yes. They're part of a very special group. An experimental group. Women only. I formed it after years of watching conventional therapy approaches fail. I chose patients who were at the stage where the eruption of delayed memories was beginning to destroy their lives, and where multigenerational abuse seemed likely. They were highly motivated. I've spent seven months working with them, and we've done some groundbreaking things."

"Is that the extent of it? Women in group therapy?"

Malik makes a sound I can't interpret. "You shouldn't denigrate what you've never experienced, Catherine. Never fear, though. I've recorded certain other activities as well. I can't discuss those now. Let's just say they're highly controversial in nature. *Explosive* might be a better word."

Certain other activities? "Are you talking about the murders?"

"I can't discuss the specifics of the film with you now."

My heart rate is steadily accelerating. "Do you plan to show this film anywhere?"

"Yes, but right now I'm more concerned with keeping it safe."

"From whom?"

"A lot of people would like this film to disappear. My film and all my records. These people are terrified of the truths I know."

"If you're that worried, why not turn yourself in to the FBI?"

"The FBI wants to jail me for murder."

"If you're innocent, what does that matter?"

"There are degrees of innocence."

"I think you're talking about degrees of guilt, Doctor."

"That's a philosophical question we don't have time for. I'll turn myself in when the time is right. For now, I need your help. Will you keep my film safe for me?"

"Look, I couldn't do it even if I wanted to. The FBI is probably following me. They may even be listening to this call."

"By tomorrow maybe. We're safe for now. Do you have a pen?"

I glance around the bedroom, but there's nothing to write with. My purse is in my Audi, across the river from DeSalle Island. "No, but I have a good memory."

"Memorize this phone number. Five zero four, eight zero two, nine nine four one. Do you have it?"

I repeat the number aloud and commit it to memory.

"If you need to speak to me after this," Malik says, "leave a message at that number."

"I want to speak to you now, and not about your film."

"Hurry."

"Why did you tell me not to trust my family?"

"I'm trying to protect you."

"From what?"

Malik sighs as if unsure whether he can spare the time to talk to me. "Families like yours are made up of three types of people. Offenders, deniers, and victims. Every family member plays one of these roles. When a victim begins digging into her past and making assertions of abuse, the other family members become paranoid. Their interest is maintaining the status quo. You threaten that. The emotions that swirl around sexual abuse frequently spill over into family violence."

"That's shrink-speak, Doctor. I've heard enough of it to know. You have specific information about my family. About my father. Why are you keeping it from me?"

"I'm not your therapist, Catherine."

"I want you to be. I'll meet you somewhere for a session."

"You don't need to speak to me alone. You need a group. And my days as a practicing psychiatrist are clearly over."

"Why do I need a group?"

"Because your problem is sexual abuse. One of the main elements of the abusive relationship is secrecy. A one-on-one relationship with a therapist can mirror the primary abusive relationship. In group therapy, that cycle of secrecy is broken."

"Look, *you* chose *me*, okay? You started this secret relationship. I'm ready to talk to you now, and without the FBI listening in this time."

"You want a session? Keep my film for me. You'd be doing yourself a favor, too."

I'm tempted. I want to see what Malik really did behind the closed doors of his office. But the FBI could be listening to this call. "I'd like to see it, but I can't promise I'll keep it for you."

"Then we have no reason to meet."

"Why the hell would you meet me anyway? I could bring the FBI with me. Why would you risk that?"

"There's no risk. I do know things about your father, Catherine. I know why he was murdered. And if you bring the FBI with you, I'll never tell."

For once, I'm a step ahead of Malik. "I already know why my father was killed."

"You don't. You don't know anything."

My heart flutters like the wings of a panicked bird. "Why are you playing games with me? I just want the truth."

Malik's voice drops lower. "You already know the truth, Catherine. It's written indelibly in the convolutions of your brain. You just have to peel away everything that's laid over it."

"How do I do that?"

"You're already doing it. Just follow the memories where they lead. The truth will set you free."

"I can't wait for that! Someone's trying to kill me."

Malik sighs deeply. "Why were you having panic attacks at the crime scenes in New Orleans?"

"I don't know. Do you?"

"Come on, Catherine. You know how therapy works. I'm prodding you to find your own answers."

"You're fucking with me is what you're doing!"

"Who do you think tried to kill you today?"

"It might have been a black guy who knew my dad years ago. I don't know. Do you know?"

"No. But *you do*. If only you think about it in the right way."

"You said the New Orleans murders both are and aren't connected to my personal life. What did you mean by that?"

"What do you think I meant?"

I close my eyes and try not to scream. I feel like I'm in a Kafka novel. Every question is answered by another question; everyone around me knows the obvious truth about my life, but I can't see it. "What are you trying to tell me? Everyone keeps asking me if I was ever your patient. Have you given them that idea?"

"Do you think you might have been my patient at some point?"

"I'm hanging up this phone in five seconds."

"No, you're not. My experimental group is called Group X. Does that ring a bell anywhere?"

Group X? "No. Should it?"

"We don't have time for this," Malik says, his voice suddenly impatient. "Not now. But I do want to talk to you—preferably on film. Will you appear on camera?"

"*What?* No."

"Then—"

"I thought the FBI confiscated all your video equipment."

"I still have a camera with me. Quite a good one. Look, you can't understand it yet, but there's a symmetry to all this. An underlying symmetry that you'll ultimately appreciate. We need to find a safe place to meet, a place where we can speak privately. We should do it tomorrow. When we're finished, you take possession of my film. At that point, I'll turn myself over to the FBI."

"Why don't you just leave your film with your lawyer?"

"Because I despise lawyers. I intend to represent myself."

Of course.

"I don't wish to be ungracious," Malik says, "but if you don't come—or if you bring the FBI with you—you'll never know the answer to the mystery of your own life. Now, I've been in one place for too long. Do you remember the phone number I gave you?"

I spit the number back at him like a curse.

"Good. Call it tomorrow and leave a different number where I can reach you. Not your cell. And don't get too chummy with John Kaiser. He doesn't really care about either of us."

The phone goes dead in my hand.

CHAPTER
36

I feel like I'm going to puke.

I already know why my father was killed. . . .

You don't. You don't know anything. . . .

Fear is worse than death. Death is but the end of life, and I know it well. What I know, I can fight. What can be named, I can endure. But what lies in shadow, I can neither fight nor endure. My whole life seems a shadow now, a performance invented to fill the void of my true past. For every childhood memory I possess, a thousand have been lost. I've always known that. Back beyond a certain point in time, there's simply nothing. When other kids talked about this or that indelible moment from their time as toddlers, I reached backward and found only a blank wall. A child without a childhood—that's how I felt. And I never knew why.

This afternoon I thought I'd learned the answer. As terrible as it was, at least it put firm ground beneath my feet. But now that ground has shifted, a seismic change wrought by only a few words from a psychiatrist's mouth. *You don't know anything. . . .*

I don't want to think about the things Dr. Malik said.

I want the questions to stop.

I want a drink.

Failing that, I want a Valium. But I can't take one. And thinking of the reason why—the baby in my tummy—suddenly brings up my steak and eggs with a vengeance. I fall to my knees over the toilet, retching and shivering as I've done after my worst binges. Hugging the commode, I feel the substance of my body fading, as though I'm becoming transparent. I've felt this way before. I want to get up and check the mirror to make sure I'm wrong, but I can't bring myself to look. Instead, I turn on the hot water, climb under the scalding spray, and sit on the floor of the tub.

My skin blisters red as the water rises above my hips, then to the edge of the tub. I shut off the tap and lie back, submerging my head. Here Malik's words cannot hurt me. They'll vanish like words spoken in a vacuum, like a scream in outer space. It's not his words that matter anyway, but what was beneath them. A hidden key, waiting only for me to find it. Just as John Kaiser did, Malik asked if I thought I'd ever been his patient. That's not a question you ask a normal person. That's a question you ask someone with Alzheimer's disease. Or amnesia. Or . . .

Something's wrong. I'm bathing in zero gravity. The water won't lie in the tub . . . it breaks into millions of droplets and floats into the air. Clammy liquid bursts from my pores like overflowing panic. Under the scalding water it feels like sleet on my skin. *Do you think you might have been my patient at some point?* That's a question you ask a patient with dissociative identity disorder. *What we used to call multiple personality disorder. . . . Sometimes the dissociation during sexual abuse is so profound and repeated that the mind splits into separate parts in order to wall itself off from the pain. . . .*

"No," I say aloud, digging my fingernails into my palms. "Not possible."

I'm certain I never saw Nathan Malik as a patient. But then *I* is a problematic pronoun in a sentence spoken by someone with multiple personality disorder. "I" may not have seen Malik, but "someone else" within my brain may well have.

The disorientation I feel now is much like that I've felt after waking from an alcoholic blackout, or coming out of a hypomanic state. I know I've been somewhere—a party, an apartment, a house—but I'm not sure what I did there. How far things went. And yet despite this similarity, I've never felt so disconnected from myself that a whole separate *life* seemed possible.

"Take it easy," I say in a shaky voice. "What did Malik say before that?"

We were talking about group therapy . . . He said, *You shouldn't denigrate what you've never experienced.* Why would he say that if I had ever been part of his Group X? A sense of relief washes through me, then evaporates. Could I have seen Malik one-on-one in a dissociated state, then forgotten or repressed it? I have no memory of that, but neither do I have any memory of my childhood sexual abuse. That doesn't mean it didn't happen. Could Malik know so much about me because I told him *myself*?

I lurch up out of the tub and splash cool water on my face from the bathroom sink. As I peer at my bloodshot eyes in the mirror, a shudder goes through me, heralding a terrifying thought. At one point during the phone call, I had the feeling Malik was telling me his patients were his lovers. Or ex-lovers. Could he have consummated his old lust for me during a session of which I have no memory? I still recall the shock I felt when Malik's photo first scrolled out of my grandfather's fax machine. That was the first time I'd seen his face in ten years, I was sure of it. But what is the value of my certainty? Once you open the door to the idea that you don't remember parts of your past, anything is possible. And for someone who's dealt with blackouts and manic episodes, it's not a great leap to make.

Stop thinking, says a voice in my head—the voice of self-preservation. *Too much truth too fast can kill you. . . .*

Grabbing a large towel from the hanger on the door, I wrap it around me, then climb into bed and pull the comforter up to my neck. The light is still on, and I'm not about to turn it off. I set my phone to VIBRATE, close my eyes, and pray for sleep.

On any other night I'd need a drink or a Valium to shut off the thoughts racing through my head, but tonight exhaustion does the job for me. As consciousness blurs, Dr. Malik's face flashes before me, his eyes cold and penetrating. Then Michael Wells's face replaces it. Michael's eyes are warm, kind, and open. Something about him reminds me of my father, but I can't place what. It's not his eyes, or his build. It's just a *way*. A reluctance to judge, perhaps. Whatever it is, it draws me to him.

Why didn't I tell Michael I was pregnant? It was the only thing I held back. Was it because, deep down, *I'm* the one hoping for this relationship to progress? Am I afraid that when he learns I'm pregnant, he'll vanish like those men drawn by my body and my intensity would?

Stop! shouts the voice in my head. *Stop stop stop!*

I have a trick to deal with destructive thoughts. I put myself in a different place altogether, a place of peace. For me, it's the ocean. I'm free diving down a multicolored wall of coral, a steep wall that slopes down through Caribbean blue toward depths of India ink. There's no sound but the beating of my heart. My body knifes through warmth until warmth becomes cold, and my perception balloons out beyond the cage of my skull, taking in all that I see, and rapture comes over me, the rapture of the deep. I'm diving that wall now, down through the last glimmering stratum of wakefulness into sleep. I wish it were only darkness that awaited me below. But it's never just the dark. Dreams lie in wait, as they always have. The netherworld where I'm always a stranger, or a fugitive, or a soldier frozen in the midst of battle. Fear and confusion are my only companions there, and our journeys are always long ones.

When I was a teenager, I heard that dreams that seem to last hours actually happen in a span of six or seven seconds. I know now that this isn't true. Most dreams last ten or fifteen minutes, then fade into others in the deep reaches of REM sleep. Some dreams we remember, others we don't. Most of mine—though often more vivid than life—leave only fragmentary images behind, like tattered pages from a picture book.

Tonight will be different.

Tonight I'm back in the rusted orange truck. Back on the island. My grandfather is behind the wheel. We're rolling up the long sloping hill of the old pasture. On the other side lies the pond where the cows drink. Their patties dot the grass like dried mud pies. My grandfather's hair is black, not silver. The truck smells bad. Stale motor oil, chewing tobacco, mildew, other odors I can't identify.

It's going to rain. The sky is leaden, the air still. We roll steadily up the shallow slope, making for the crest. Terror has closed my throat, but Grandpapa's face is calm. He doesn't know what's on the other side of the hill. I don't either, but I know it's bad. I've dreamed this dream so often that I know I'm dreaming. Each time we make it a little closer to the crest, but we never top the hill. We're getting close now, though . . . I know I'll wake up soon.

Only this time I don't.

This time Grandpapa downshifts and steps on the gas pedal, and the old pickup trundles right over. The cows are waiting for us, staring with dumb indifference. Beyond them lies the pond, slate gray and smooth as glass.

I squeeze my hands so tightly into fists that my palms bleed.
There's something in the pond.

A man.

He's floating facedown in the water, his arms outspread like Jesus
on the cross. He has long hair like Jesus, too. I want to scream, but
Grandpapa doesn't seem to see the man. Mute with fear, I point with
my finger. Grandpapa squints and shakes his head. "Goddamn rain,"
he says. They can't work on the island when it rains.

As the truck rolls down toward the pond, Grandpapa points to
our right. His prize bull has mounted a cow and is bouncing above
her with violent jerks. As he stares at the rutting animals, I look back
toward the pond.

The man isn't floating anymore. He's getting to his feet. My palms
tingle with apprehension. The man isn't *in* the pond, but *on* it. He's
standing on its glassy surface as though on an ice rink. But it's almost
a hundred degrees outside. My heart pounds so loudly I can hear it
over the sound of the truck.

The man standing on the surface of the pond is my father.

I recognize his jeans and his work shirt. And behind the long hair,
his deep-set brown eyes. As I stare, he starts walking across the water,
holding out his arms to me. He wants to show me something. Grandpapa is mesmerized by the bull humping the cow. I pull at his shirtsleeve, but he won't look away. Daddy is walking on water like Jesus
in the Bible, but Grandpapa won't look!

"*Daddy!*" I shout.

Luke Ferry nods at me but says nothing. As he nears the edge of
the pond, he starts unbuttoning his shirt. I see dark hair on his
chest. He undoes four buttons, then pulls his shirt open. I want to
shut my eyes, but I can't. On the right side of his chest is a hole
where the bullet went in. There are other scars, too, the big sutured
Y-incision of an autopsy. As I stare in horror, Daddy puts two fingers into the bullet hole and starts to rip it open. He wants me to
watch, but I don't want to see. I cover my eyes with my hands, then
peer between my fingers. Something is pouring out of the wound
like blood, only it's not blood. It's *gray*. That's all I know, and all I
want to know.

"Look, Kitty Cat," he commands. "*I want you to look.*"

I can't look.

When he calls my name again, I shut my eyes and scream.

CHAPTER

37

"Wake up! It's Michael! You're dreaming!"

Michael Wells is shaking my shoulders, his eyes frantic.

"Cat! It's just a nightmare!"

I nod as though in understanding, but in my mind's eye I see my father pushing his fingers into the bullet wound in his chest, then pulling the skin apart—

"*Cat!*"

I blink myself back to reality and grab Michael's hands. He's wearing a UNC T-shirt and plaid pajama bottoms. "I'm okay. You're right . . . a nightmare."

He nods in relief, then stands and looks down at me. The overhead light is bright behind his head, but the bedroom window is dark. "Do you want to talk about it?"

I close my eyes.

"Is it one you've had before?"

"Yes. The truck, the island . . . my grandfather. Only this time we made it over the hill."

"What did you see?"

I shake my head. "It's too crazy. Did I scream out loud?"

He smiles. "You screamed, but I wasn't sleeping. I've been thinking about everything you told me."

"Have you?"

"I've come up with a couple of ideas, if you're interested."

I sit up and prop myself against the headboard. "Is it about the New Orleans murders, or my situation?"

"Your situation. I don't know anything about the murders."

"Don't feel left out. Neither does anyone else."

"Something you said stuck in my head. That thing about your dad not being the breadwinner for your family. I'd thought his sculpting earned a lot of money. But if it didn't, then your grandfather was that figure in your household."

"Absolutely."

"And from what you told me about your father, he wasn't a dominating man, or even a strong personality. He didn't try to control people. Is that right?"

"Yes. Daddy just wanted his own space. He hardly interacted with anyone except me. And of course Louise, the woman on the island."

"I don't know Dr. Kirkland well, but I would characterize him as a control freak."

"Oh, yeah. He's like a feudal lord."

Michael nods slowly. "Well, what I've been thinking is this. You grew up with one version of your father's death. You got that version from your grandfather. It's the same version he gave the police in 1981. Now, twenty-three years later, you discover some old blood in your childhood bedroom. You decide to investigate it, and you make no secret of the fact. What happens? Your grandfather instantly begins revising the story you grew up with, *his* original story. By his own admission, he told you the new version—supposedly the real truth—to stop you from investigating the scene further. As a result, you stop investigating the bedroom. But you *don't* stop probing the events of that night. And when you decide to bring in professionals to search the bedroom for more evidence, Dr. Kirkland changes his story yet *again,* this time to a 'truth' so horrifying that no one—not even you—would want to reveal it to anyone outside your family. In that version, he takes the blame for killing your father. But he also does something else, Cat. He lays the blame for your sexual abuse on your father."

I feel a strange buzzing in my head. With it comes an almost frantic desire for alcohol. "Go on."

"Are you sure you want me to? I think you know where I'm going."

"Just talk, Michael. Quickly."

"The only evidence you have that your father abused you is your grandfather's word. If you discount that, what evidence is there? Hearsay about your father's extramarital love life. Some possible brutality in Vietnam."

I swallow hard and wait for Michael to continue.

"You *do* have a long history of psychological symptoms and behavior consistent with patients who've suffered past sexual abuse. You *don't* have direct evidence as to who abused you. So . . . I'm just asking a question, Cat. Why should you believe that your grandfather's latest version of the 'truth' is any more true than his first story?"

"Because it feels right," I say softly. "I wish it didn't. But it does. It's like I can almost see it in my mind. The two men fighting over my bed in the dark. I'm afraid that I *did* see that."

"Maybe your grandfather did kill your father, as he said. But maybe not for the reason he gave you. I mean, why take his word for it that he caught your father abusing you? It could easily have been the other way around. Maybe your grandfather was the abuser."

There's something in my throat, a hot tightness that won't let any more words pass. "But . . ."

"I'm just using logic," Michael says. "You're so close to the situation, it's hard to see past the emotion. I don't think anyone could."

"I concede that, okay? I don't want to believe that my father abused me. I'm desperate to find hope that he didn't. But the idea of Grandpapa doing it just seems outrageous to me. He's like the model of propriety in this town. Famous for being faithful to his wife."

"You could be making my point for me. Kirkland didn't need affairs because he relieved his secret drives at home. And abusers often appear as paragons of virtue to the community. Especially in affluent families. I've seen that in practice."

"What put this in your head, Michael? Was it just the things I told you tonight?"

"Honestly, no. I've heard about your grandfather all my life. And I can't say I like what I've heard. All doctors want to make money, but they say Kirkland *lived* for the money. The general opinion around here is that he only married your grandmother for her money and social position."

"Gossips always say that when a poor boy marries into a rich family. And Grandpapa doubled the family holdings through shrewd management. Particularly of the oil."

Michael is filtering all this through some other knowledge, I can tell. In a neutral tone, he says, "The old docs around here say he did a lot of questionable procedures in his day."

"Questionable in what sense?" I can't keep the defensiveness out of my voice.

"As in *unnecessary.* You know, too many appendixes removed that turned out to be normal. Exploratory surgery for belly pain. They say he'd cut the gallbladder out of anybody who even looked like he had a stone. And a ton of hysterectomies for fibromyomas. He did one of those on my mother, in fact. Remember, this was the fifties and sixties. A surgeon could do just about anything he wanted to back then. But they still called your grandfather before a surgical review committee."

"Who told you all this?"

"I spoke to Tom Cage last night. He stopped referring patients to Kirkland for exactly that reason."

"Did Dr. Cage say anything about my father?"

"Yes. Apparently Luke told him a lot about his war experiences. Tom served in Korea, so your dad probably felt he was a more sympathetic listener than most."

"What did he tell him?"

"Tom wouldn't go into specifics with me. But he did say he thought your dad was a good soldier and a good man. That's really what got me thinking. If Tom Cage thought your dad was a good guy, it's hard for me to picture him as a child molester. I'm not saying he couldn't have been. Dr. Cage may have looked at your dad, seen a troubled veteran, and blinded himself to other flaws. But Tom wants you to come talk to him. I think you should hear what he has to say."

"I want to. God, I wish it were morning already. I'm not sleepy at all."

"You won't have to wait long." Michael reaches out and flicks off the room light. After a couple of seconds, the window changes from black to blue. "You've been asleep for six hours."

Dawn is breaking. I can't believe it.

"Cat, there's something else I think I should tell you."

"What?"

"Your grandfather could be telling the truth about your father abusing you, but lying about killing him."

"What do you mean?"

"There are other possibilities for the person who pulled the trigger."

For some reason, it takes me a moment to grasp what Michael is saying. But then I have it. "My mother?" I whisper.

He nods. "Easy to imagine. She denies the abuse for several years, but then one night she unexpectedly walks in on it. Maybe she's drunk or stoned on prescription meds. They argue, she grabs the gun from over the fireplace and kills him."

"With me in the room?"

"We don't know that you were in there. Afterward, your grandfather moves Luke's body to the rose garden and invents the story of the intruder to protect his daughter. If you ask me, in that scenario, your grandfather's a hero."

"Who else could have done it? Pearlie?"

"Sure. Same psychological process as your mother's, basically. Years of denial—or maybe even years of conscious knowledge—but then she finally snaps and kills him. Your grandfather might carry Luke's body out to the rose garden to protect a maid who'd worked for his family for fifty years. She was also your primary caregiver."

"You're right. God, I understand why everybody freaked out when I started talking about doing a forensic investigation of that bedroom. Who knows what kind of evidence a team would find in there?"

Michael watches me as though he has something else to say, but he's silent for some time. At length, he says, "I just think you should be aware of what you could find before you go tearing down this road after the truth. Like Pearlie told you . . . some things it's better not to know."

"No. I *have* to know."

"The truth shall make you free?"

"That's what Dr. Malik said last night."

Michael shakes his head. "I wouldn't use Malik as a guide for anything. And remember, those last possibilities only come into play if your father was your abuser. If your grandfather was molesting you, then your dad caught him in the act and Kirkland murdered him to keep him quiet. No other option."

I suddenly feel like I need ten more hours of sleep. "I have no idea what to do now."

"You need to find out who was actually molesting you. Forgive the crudeness, but my money is on your grandfather."

Something in the tone of Michael's voice pushes me to anger. "You've made your point, okay? But amateur detective work isn't going to cut it. You say my grandfather loved money and did unnecessary surgery to get it. That's unethical, but what does it have to do with child abuse? Louise Butler told me a story about Grandpapa beating a horse half to death. That makes me hate him, but does it make him a child molester? Hitler loved animals. My dad killed *people,* you know?"

"During wartime," Michael says softly.

"Yes, but his unit committed atrocities, including rape. And he had sex with a fifteen- or sixteen-year-old girl on the island. The point is, none of this is conclusive. I need *hard evidence.*"

"What about your bedroom? That's the source of all this."

"It can't tell me what I need to know. Say I find Grandpapa's blood, and Daddy's. It can't confirm one story or the other."

"What if there's something besides blood in there?"

This gives me pause. "Like semen?"

Michael nods. "Wouldn't semen be conclusive?"

"If we could get viable DNA after all this time, yes. But semen isn't as resilient as blood over so many years."

"But it's possible. Is the bed the same one you slept in as a child?"

A strange coldness comes over me as I recall my conversation with my mother after I first arrived in Natchez. "No. Mom had to get rid of the mattress because of urine stains. She said I wet the bed a lot as a child. But I don't remember that."

"Enuresis," Michael murmurs. "That's long been linked to sexual abuse. Sometimes it's a cry for help." He sits on the end of the bed. "You have no concrete memories of abuse?"

A hysterical laugh bursts from my throat. "What does it matter? Dr. Malik suggested I have dissociative identity disorder. I think Kaiser believes that, too. We're talking about multiple personalities, for God's sake. So what I *think* I know, I may not. And the real truth may be locked inside rooms in my head that I can't even get into—not as me."

Michael shakes his head. There's something like grief in his eyes. "Is that how you feel? That there are parts of your mind you can't reach?"

"Sometimes. But it's not really like other rooms, or a hidden personality. Yes, I have blackouts. Yes, there are blocks of time I can't account for. But I'm certain that's the drinking, not DID. It's more like *depth*, you know? I feel that the truth is buried in my mind, but it's too damned deep. It's like free diving. Four hundred feet is the holy grail for a woman. I want it *so* bad. But it might as well be the Mariana Trench. I just can't hold my breath that long, can't swim that far down. My true memories live at four hundred feet, and I'm not strong enough to get there."

"It's not a question of strength," Michael says. "When you first spoke to me about repressed memories, I didn't give much credence to the idea. But the more I've read on the Internet, the more I believe it. I was on Medline earlier. There's a lot of evidence that during severe trauma, information is encoded in an entirely different way than at other times. They've found physiological changes in the amygdalae of people with severe PTSD. Apparently, the neurotransmitters get all out of whack during that kind of trauma, and memories get pushed down into holes and blind alleys. They only make themselves known when that person finds himself—or herself—in a similar situation to the one in which the trauma occurred. Child abuse victims having sex as adults, say. Or combat veterans walking near a car that backfires, or under a news helicopter that flies too low. Those triggers bring back the emotions that were experienced during the trauma, but not necessarily the memories themselves. That's called body memory. It's fascinating, really."

"I've definitely experienced that. Especially during sex."

"What was tonight's nightmare about?"

I close my eyes and the vision is there, as though engraved on the backs of my eyelids. I relate the dream of the truck, the pond, and Daddy walking on water.

Michael shakes his head. "I'm no expert on dream interpretation, but walking on water is definitely a Christ image. Does Dr. Goldman interpret that kind of thing?"

"Sometimes. I'm sick of talking about all this, Michael. I want to *do* something."

"I know. Forgive my amateur detective work, but—"

"I'm sorry about that. I'm just really antsy. I'm getting a little crazy."

"Just a couple of questions."

"Hurry."

"What was your father's childhood like?"

"They were country people. He grew up out at Cranfield. His dad was a welder. He got killed on an oil rig in the Gulf of Mexico. I think Daddy was nine when it happened. He was raised by his mother for a while, but she died of lung cancer when he was eleven. One of his uncles took him in."

"Any other kids in that home?"

I see where he's going now. "I think so, yes."

"Siblings in the original home?"

"Two older brothers. They were split between a couple of uncles' homes. The brothers were never close later."

"What about your grandfather's childhood?"

I shake my head. "The stuff of legend. Both his parents were killed on the way to his baptism. Head-on collision with a truck. Grandpapa was thrown clear. He actually landed in a patch of clover. Not even a broken bone."

"You're kidding."

"He used to say that his mother saw what was going to happen and threw him out of the window before they hit the truck. But that's bullshit."

"Who raised him?"

"His grandfather. In east Texas."

"And grandmother?"

I shake my head. "The grandfather was a widower."

Michael nods thoughtfully. "Any other children in that home?"

"One girl, I think. She was my grandfather's aunt, but she wasn't much older than he was."

"How did she turn out?"

"I don't know. She died when I was young."

Michael folds his arms and sits silently for a while. "Did your mother ever remarry after your dad died?"

"No."

"Why not? She was what . . . thirty?"

"Twenty-nine. She dated some, but nobody was ever good enough."

"Whose opinion was that? Hers? Yours? Your grandfather's?"

"Probably Grandpapa's. Every man in town was intimidated by him."

"What about your aunt? You said she's bipolar?"

"Severely manic-depressive. The whole package. Alcoholic, shoplifting charges, promiscuity, three failed marriages. A great role model for me."

"All that could be a flag for sexual abuse in her past."

"It *could,*" I say in a taut voice. "But bipolarity has a genetic component. My grandfather's father was supposedly bipolar, the one killed in the car wreck. And I'm cyclothymic. So all that could just be our genes. Not abuse."

Michael is about to speak again when my cell phone begins vibrating on the nightstand. He picks up the phone and shows me the screen. It's the same New Orleans number that called last night. I press SEND.

"Agent Kaiser?"

"Yes. Hello, Cat. Sorry to bother you so early."

Why is he calling me? He probably found out that it was Malik I was talking to last night, and not Sean. "What is it now?"

"I have some information for you. It's probably going to be a shock, so—"

"Skip the Vaseline, okay? What happened?"

"A couple of things. First, we learned last night that Nathan Malik didn't pay all his own bail on the murder charge."

"I don't understand."

"A million-dollar bail meant that Malik had to come up with a hundred thousand in cash, and the rest in collateral. On paper he looked fairly wealthy, so when he put up his house across Lake Pontchartrain, we didn't look too closely at the cash. But your friend Sean had a talk with the bail bondsman last night—just rechecking details. Turns out that most of the hundred thousand was paid by someone else."

"Who?"

"Your aunt. Ann Hilgard."

CHAPTER

38

I feel like I'm in a falling elevator, the basement rushing up beneath my legs. The idea that my aunt would pay Nathan Malik's bail seems utterly beyond belief.

"You have to be wrong."

"No mistake," says Kaiser. "Ann Hilgard, née Kirkland. Resident of Biloxi, Mississippi. Two hours from New Orleans. She brought the bail bondsman a briefcase filled with cash."

My mouth is open, but I can't form words. The implications of Kaiser's revelation are too enormous to grasp. "Why didn't Sean call me about this?"

"That's probably something you should ask him."

No thanks.

"I only learned that she was your aunt a few minutes ago, Cat. Ann DeSalle Kirkland. Daughter of William Kirkland, sister of Gwendolyn DeSalle Kirkland Ferry. Maternal aunt of Catherine DeSalle Ferry, forensic odontologist. Is your aunt a patient of Dr. Malik's? Is that why you have a special relationship with him?"

"If she is, I hadn't a clue until ten seconds ago."

"She's definitely got the history for it. Confirmed bipolar disorder going back three decades. A string of bad marriages—"

"My God," I breathe. "No wonder Malik knows things about me. Jesus *Christ . . .*"

"We're trying to locate your aunt," Kaiser says, "but we're not having any luck. She's apparently involved in a bitter divorce. Her husband says she hasn't been living at home for the past couple of weeks."

"I saw her in Natchez yesterday. She was . . ." I trail off, remembering the manic gleam in Ann's eye.

"What?" Kaiser asks. "She was what?"

Borrowing money from my grandfather. Bail money, maybe? "Talking to my mother about her marital problems. You said you had a couple of things to tell me. What else?"

"We just found one of Nathan Malik's patients in a coma on the floor of her apartment in Metairie."

"Male or female?"

Kaiser answers softly. "Female. Her name was Margaret Lavigne. Twenty-seven years old. She lives about three minutes away from you."

"Was it the same crime signature? Two gunshots with bite marks?"

"No, this was a suicide attempt. We only found her because we'd got her name from the psychologist who referred her to Malik."

"You mean she wasn't on the patient list Malik gave you?"

"Exactly. He never really obeyed the court order."

Malik's voice sounds in my mind: *They're part of a very special group. An experimental group. Women only. I formed it after years of watching conventional therapy approaches fail. I chose patients who were at the stage where the eruption of delayed memories was beginning to destroy their lives. . . . My experimental group is called Group X.*

"What kind of suicide attempt?" I ask, trying to keep my voice even. "How did it happen?"

"We sent two agents over there to talk to her. They saw Lavigne through her bedroom window, lying in a pool of vomit. She'd given herself a massive dose of insulin."

A lot of suicides try insulin because it offers hope of a painless death. But usually all they manage to do is turn themselves into vegetables. I researched and discounted this method long ago. "Did she leave a note?"

"She did. You ready for this?"

"Come on, damn it."

"It reads, 'May God forgive me. An innocent man is dead. Please tell Dr. Malik to stop it. I couldn't reach him.' What do you make of that?"

Please tell Dr. Malik to stop it. "I'm trying to put it together."

"I had a head start on you. I think your friend Malik has been executing child molesters, Cat. I think he listened to his patients recount their horrors for one too many years. He finally snapped and decided to do something about it. I can't say I blame him. I snapped myself for almost the same reason. But we can't let Dr. Malik go around removing criminals from the planet without benefit of trial. Do you agree?"

"Of course. If you're right."

Kaiser says nothing for a few moments. "The trouble with vigilante justice is that eventually an innocent person gets lynched. Ms. Lavigne's note is telling us that's just what happened. I wonder what Malik will do when he hears that? Do you think he'll turn himself in?"

"I don't know. You're still speculating. Why did Lavigne's note say tell Malik to 'stop *it*' rather than simply 'stop'?"

"We'll probably never know."

"Was Margaret Lavigne related to any of our victims?"

"Not by blood. But I think you'll find this interesting. Ms. Lavigne's biological father was arrested just before her suicide attempt and charged with multiple counts of distributing child pornography. Interesting timing, no? He broke down under questioning and confessed to several incidents of sexually abusing children. Then his daughter tried to kill herself."

"I'm not sure I understand. Are you saying you think he's a potential target of our killer?"

Kaiser laughs drily. "He may be *now*. But remember victim number three? Tracy Nolan? The CPA?"

"I'll never forget him." I had my first panic attack at the Nolan crime scene.

"Tracy Nolan was Margaret Lavigne's stepfather."

"Holy God. Lavigne told someone her stepfather abused her, and that person murdered him?"

"Bingo," says Kaiser. "Then it turns out that her real father was the molester."

"Jesus."

"I think Ms. Lavigne was sexually abused as a child," Kaiser says. "She repressed her memories of these events. Dr. Malik tried to help her recall those events, and she did. Only she made a mistake about who the molester was. I mean, wouldn't most kids prefer to think their stepfather raped them rather than their father?"

All I can think about is Group X, and Malik's "groundbreaking" treatment protocols. What the hell did Malik do to those women? Or convince them to do?

"Cat? Are you there?"

"Yes."

"Have you talked to Dr. Malik since we last spoke?"

I want to tell Kaiser the truth—that I talked to Malik and that he denied committing the murders—but until I know exactly how Aunt Ann is involved with him, I'm not saying a word. If I knew the identity of anyone in Group X, I would. But I don't. "Look, I can't talk to you anymore right now. I've got to find my aunt. She could be in real danger."

"Help us find her, Cat. We'll protect her."

"If you need my help to find her, you can't protect her. She's bipolar, John. Do you have any idea what that means? She's tried to kill herself twice that I know about. Malik has obviously been manipulating her. Can you imagine what kind of stress she must be under? She could be *with* Malik now, for all we know."

"Yes, she could. So—"

"Listen to me. Those two patients of Malik's who were related to the victims . . . Riviere's daughter and LeGendre's niece?"

"What about them?"

"Ask them about something called Group X."

"Group X? What's that?"

"A therapy group. I think they might have been part of it. That's all I know that could help you right now. I have to go."

"Wait! How do you know that? Did Malik tell you about it?"

"I'm sorry, John."

I click END and almost leap out of bed, startling Michael to his feet.

CHAPTER

39

"What happened?" Michael asks. "You look like you're going to faint."

"My aunt Ann paid Nathan Malik's bail."

He shakes his head in disbelief.

"She must be a patient of Malik's. *That's* how Malik knows so much about me and my family."

Michael's eyes are bright with excitement. "If your aunt is a patient of Malik's, he's almost certainly treating her for sexual abuse. That means your grandfather is the one who molested you."

"Not necessarily. Malik also treats people for bipolar disorder."

"Exclusively? Or bipolar people who've also been sexually abused?"

"Exclusively, I think. Bipolarity, PTSD, and sexual abuse. Separate categories. May I use your phone?"

"Sure. Did your cell phone die?"

"No, but I don't want the FBI to hear this call."

Michael looks at me for several seconds in silence. "Are you calling Malik?"

"I'm going to leave him a message, yes. Are you okay with that?"

He goes out into the hall and brings back a cordless phone. "As long as you don't do anything to risk your life."

Even as I nod, I decide to tell Michael nothing about Margaret Lavigne's suicide attempt or her note. When I dial the number Malik gave me last night, an automated voice instructs me to leave a message at the tone.

"This is Catherine Ferry. I've just learned that my aunt paid your bail. I'm assuming she's a patient of yours. You've been dishonest with me, Doctor. I'd like to talk to you as soon as possible. You can reach me at—" I look up at Michael. "What's this number?"

Michael rattles off his number, and I repeat it into the machine. "If you don't return my call within an hour, I'm telling the FBI everything you've told me to date. Good-bye."

I hang up Michael's phone, pick up my cell, and scroll through the digital phone book. When I reach *Aunt Ann,* I press SEND.

A recording says, "We're sorry, but the Cingular customer you're trying to reach is unavailable or has traveled outside the service area. You may leave a voice mail at the tone."

When the beep comes, I say, "Ann, this is Cat. I'm sure a lot of people are trying to get hold of you right now. I'm not trying to bother you. Your life is your own. But I know about you and Dr. Malik. I've talked to him, and I know why you like him. I have no desire to hurt him, or to help anyone else hurt him. All I'm asking is for you to call me back. You don't have to tell me anything you don't want to. God knows, if anyone can relate to how you feel right now, it's me. Mood swings are my life. I promise I won't tell Mom or Grandpapa anything, and I won't talk to the FBI. In fact, I'd like to talk to you about Grandpapa. Also about Daddy. I'm trying to figure something out about my childhood, and I have a feeling you can help me. Thanks. Please, please call back."

Michael is staring at me like a doctor now, as though trying to decide whether I might be in a manic state myself. I'm tempted to call my mother and ask if she knows where Ann is, but I know better. All that would accomplish is to put my mother into a panic. If Ann wants to disappear, no one in the family will be able to find her. She's had too much practice.

"What can I do?" asks Michael.

"You already did it. You gave me a place to stay. Now I have to make some decisions."

"How stable is your aunt?"

"Two suicide attempts. One in college and one in her late thirties. If my mother called in the next five minutes and told me Ann was dead, I wouldn't be shocked."

"Jesus."

"Yeah. She was obsessed with having a baby, but she never could get pregnant. Outrageous mood swings. Her liver's pickled in gin."

"What was that other stuff this Kaiser told you? Did they find another murder victim?"

I hesitate. "I can't tell you about that. No offense, but the task force is obsessive about secrecy."

Michael looks suspicious. Last night I clearly broke every possible rule of confidentiality in my discussions with him, so why am I being—

"Cat?"

Before I can answer, Michael's phone rings. The ID reads *Unknown Caller.* I show it to him. "May I answer it?"

He nods.

"This is Dr. Ferry."

"Hello, Catherine."

I nod at Michael and silently mouth, *Malik.* "What kind of fucking game have you been playing with me, Doctor? You've been acting like you have ESP, diagnosing my problems and hinting things about my family. The truth is, you had the facts all along from Ann. Didn't you?"

He takes his time before answering, "Yes and no."

"Oh, for God's sake. Cut the shit, will you?"

"Such a potty mouth, Catherine. What does Dr. Goldman make of that?"

My heart stutters. Did I tell Ann the name of my therapist? "Where's my aunt, Doctor?"

"I have no idea."

"Is she with you?"

"No."

"Why did she pay your bail?"

"I asked her to. I was short of cash, and I knew she could get the money."

"You are one unethical son of a bitch. Were you treating Ann for problems related to sexual abuse or for bipolar disorder?"

"You know that's confidential."

"Bullshit! You break the rules when you want to and hide behind them when you don't!"

"We need to talk, Catherine. I don't have much time now. We need to meet face-to-face."

I close my eyes. "Tell me about Margaret Lavigne."

"Margaret . . . ? But . . . What about her?"

"She tried to kill herself with a massive dose of insulin last night. She's in a coma now, but she left a note implicating you in the murders."

The silence on the line is absolute. "You're lying."

"You know I'm not."

"What did the note say?"

"Something like, 'God forgive me, an innocent man is dead. Please tell Dr. Malik to stop it.'"

"Oh, my God." His voice is a ragged whisper.

"Margaret's biological father was arrested yesterday on child abuse charges. Stranger still, her stepfather was one of our five victims in New Orleans. Does any of this ring a bell?"

Malik's breathing fast and shallow.

"Do we still need to meet, Doctor? Or are you going to turn yourself in?"

"I can't . . . this is beyond belief. We absolutely must meet."

I could never have imagined Nathan Malik sounding this agitated. "Did you kill those men in New Orleans, Doctor?"

"No. I swear that to you."

"But you know who did."

"I can't tell you that."

"You have to tell someone."

"No, I don't."

"Was my aunt in Group X, Doctor?"

"I can't answer that."

"Is my grandfather's life in danger?"

"I can't talk to you about that. Not over the phone."

"You expect me to meet you in person when you could be the killer?"

"You have nothing to fear from me, Catherine. You know that."

For some reason, I believe him. But I'm not crazy. "Will you turn yourself in if I meet you?"

His breathing stops for several moments. I can picture him standing somewhere, utterly still. "If you promise to keep my film safe for me, I will."

"Where do you want to meet?"

"It has to be New Orleans, I'm afraid. Are you in Natchez?"

"Yes. Where in New Orleans?"

"I can't tell you this far ahead. Can you be here in four hours?"

"I could be."

"Call the number I gave you when you're five miles outside the city. I'll tell you where to go."

No matter what logic tells me, I can't refuse him. "All right."

"And, Cat?"

"Yes?"

"If you bring the FBI with you, you'll regret it. I don't want to threaten you, but I have to protect myself. I'm the only one who can tell you certain things about yourself, and if I don't, you'll never know the truth. Good-bye."

"Wait!"

"I know you're nervous about meeting me. But I'm not dangerous to you. Do you know why? Because I know the evil in myself. When we were talking about abuse the other day, I had to censor myself. The FBI was listening, after all. The main thing I left out was the pleasure of it."

A cold tingle races along my back. "The pleasure?"

"Yes." Malik's voice takes on a snakelike sibilance. "What we call sexual abuse is a very intense experience for both offender and victim. The offender experiences absolute power over another human being, while the victim experiences absolute surrender. Absolute submission. The partners occupy the extremes of control and helplessness. These experiences are imprinted for life, Catherine. And the *first* thing a sexualized child wants to do when it grows in strength is to reverse those roles. To experience control. You know what I'm talking about, don't you?"

I don't answer, but my mind has already filled with memories of my sexual past, things I wanted to do—sometimes did do—to men, and things I wanted done to me. So often my fantasies were about control, abandoning or possessing it. All my pleasure was tied up in that.

"Your silence is enough," Malik says, his voice hypnotic. "All my life I've had to fight that urge. It took years to master. But I know my enemy now. It's a poison that propagates through generations, like a bad gene. It lives within me, as it does in all the others who've survived those experiences. Eradicating that poison is my obsession now. My personal war. I've got to go now, Catherine. Call me when you're five miles outside New Orleans."

The phone clicks. He's gone.

"You're not meeting that guy alone," Michael says firmly.

Malik's words and tone are still spinning in my head. "You're not coming with me, Michael."

"If I'm not, someone else is. You should call the FBI right now and tell them everything. And I mean everything."

"That's not an option. Not yet. Malik knows things I have to know, and if I bring in the FBI now, I never will. I'll be this fucked-up for the rest of my life. Is that what you want?"

His eyes bore into mine with startling intensity. "I want you alive, not dead."

I nod slowly. "Sean Regan."

"Is that your married boyfriend?"

"Yes, but that has nothing to do with anything. Sean is trained for this kind of thing. He can protect me, and I can trust him to keep quiet about this."

Michael looks sad, but I can't take time to deal with his emotions now.

"Can I still use your Expedition?"

"Sure."

"Thanks. I need to go to Malmaison before I leave for New Orleans."

Michael reaches out and takes me by the shoulders. His grip is amazingly strong. "Do you promise to take Sean with you to meet Malik?"

Even as I make the promise, I know it's a lie. But I don't need Michael freaking out and calling the FBI about this meeting. He could give them the plate number of his Expedition, and I'd never even reach New Orleans.

"What's at Malmaison?" he asks.

"I need some clothes." Another lie. What I need from Malmaison is something that's always been there in abundance.

A gun.

CHAPTER

40

Dawn has only just broken, but the ground floor of Malmaison is lit up as though for a royal court party. I saw the yellow dome of light as I jogged through the trees from Michael's house in Brookwood, following the old trail I beat with my own feet so long ago. Pearlie's lights are on, too.

My Audi is parked beside Pearlie's Cadillac. Not far away stands a tall, white pickup truck like the ones used on the island—the kind that tried to run me over. Someone on the island must have found my car and brought it back. But if that's the case, why doesn't Grandpapa have the police scouring the countryside for me or my corpse? And why didn't someone call my cell phone?

After circling around to the yellow-flooded front lawn, I stop and check the phone. The call log shows three calls from my grandfather's number. With the phone set to vibrate only, I slept through them, and in my shock over the calls after I awakened, I failed to notice the misses. The last call probably came around the time I was having my nightmare. I press 1 and listen to the messages.

"Catherine, this is Grandpapa." His voice is resonant, even in the tinny cell-phone speaker. *"Henry found your car across the channel from the island. There was no sign of you. Louise Butler says you set out on a bike for the bridge, but no one knows whether you made it or not. Please call me if you get this. If you're hurt or in trouble, don't*

*worry. I've got the sheriff's departments on both sides of the river
combing the banks and roads for you, and Jesse's got a dozen men
searching the island. If you've had an accident, help is coming quick.
Call me, please."*

Hearing the concern in my grandfather's voice almost brings tears
to my eyes. His next message says, *"It's me again. If you're in any
other kind of trouble—that is, if there are other people involved—
then let them hear this message. This is Dr. William Kirkland speaking. If you're from anywhere around the part of the country where
you found my granddaughter, then you know my name. And you
know you've made a mistake. If you release her immediately, I'll look
no further into the matter. But if you hurt that girl . . . by God, you
won't live one day past the day I find you. And I will find you. You
ask around. You'd rather have the hounds of hell on your trail than
me, and that's a fact."*

My skin is crawling. The voice that spoke to my unknown abduc-
tors was that of an avenging angel, deathly cold and crackling with
violence, so certain of itself that nothing could stand against it. It's
the voice of the man who hunted down the escaped convicts on the
island all those years ago.

On his third call, my grandfather left no message at all.

Looking up at the floodlit face of Malmaison, I'm more sure than
ever that I don't want to see anyone inside. Not Grandpapa. Not
even Pearlie. That's why I came on foot. If I pulled up in Michael's
Expedition, I'd be seen and questioned by everyone at home. My
chances of discreetly getting a gun from my grandfather's safe would
be greatly reduced. But this way . . .

I trot to the far end of the mansion's east wing, where there's
hardly any light. Most of these rooms are closed except during
Spring Pilgrimage. I've known since the eighth grade that the lock on
one window here can be slipped with a credit card. I used to sneak in
this way to raid my grandfather's liquor cabinet. Today I have no
credit card—I left my purse in my car on the island—but Michael lent
me an expired driver's license to do the job. Judging by the picture on
it, he was about seventy pounds heavier when the license was issued.
I press the license steadily between the panels of the tall French windows. They part slightly, and the laminated license easily flips the
lock.

As I climb through the heavy draperies, I smell the scent of mothballs. Most of the furniture in this wing is covered with white slip-covers. I feel as though I'm walking through a deserted museum. In the hallway, I smell bacon frying. I move quickly to my grandfather's study, the room patterned after Napoléon's library. The door is standing open, and the desk lamp is on, but the room is empty.

The gun safe is quite large, big enough to hold the architectural model he showed me the other day, plus his collection of rifles, shot-guns, and pistols. The combination lock is easy to open—it's my birthday. Four clicks left, eight clicks right, seventy-three left, then turn the handle. I freeze once as I turn the dial, sure that I heard foot-steps in the hall, but no one appears.

When I turn the handle, the heavy steel door opens.

The casino model is gone, but the guns are there. Five rifles, three shotguns, and several handguns lying in holsters on the floor of the safe. The scent of gun oil is strong, but there's something else, too.

Burnt gunpowder.

One by one, I pull the rifles from their slots and sniff the barrels. The first two gleam in the light, their barrels clean. But the third has recently been fired. Holding the weapon in my hands, I turn it in the light. It's a bolt-action Remington 700, scarred from use but well maintained. As I stare, my pulse begins to race. I killed a deer with this rifle when I was a girl. But that's not why my heart is pounding.

I'm holding the rifle that killed my father.

As a child, I asked my grandfather several times to get rid of this gun, but he never did. He saw no reason to get rid of a "good gun" for "sentimental reasons." Knowing what I know now about what he did with this rifle—or at least the story he told me—it surprises me that he would keep it. Was it a trophy, like the Weatherby he used to bring down his bull elk in Alaska? But more important, who fired it in the last couple of days?

I don't have time to speculate.

Replacing the rifle, I grab an automatic pistol from the bottom of the safe. Nothing big or fancy, just a Walther PPK we used for target practice on the island. The black handgun looks wet and dangerous under the light. Ejecting the clip, I see that it's fully loaded. I'd like some extra ammunition, but I don't see any, and I don't have time to look. Besides, if six rounds isn't enough to get me out of whatever scrape I get into with Malik, another six probably wouldn't save me either.

Closing the door to the safe, it strikes me as odd that a man would leave so many guns accessible to a teenage girl who he knew suffered from depression. Grandpapa even used my birthday for the combination, for God's sake. What was he thinking? But then . . . Grandpapa never saw depression as an illness, only a weakness. Maybe he figured that if I wasn't strong enough to resist the temptation to kill myself, I didn't deserve to live.

Back in the hall, something stops me. Faint voices floating on the air. Grandpapa first. Then Pearlie. Maybe Billy Neal, though I'm not sure. Then a richer, warmer voice chimes in. It has a submissive tone, like the voice of a laborer in his employer's house. The warm voice belongs to Henry, the black man who drove me across the bridge to the island yesterday. He's talking about finding my Audi this morning, and how it threw him into a panic. He's worried that I fell into the river and drowned like my grandmother. Grandpapa says I might die a lot of ways, but drowning won't be one of them. Then he thanks Henry for bringing back the car and bids him good-bye. Heavy footsteps sound on the hardwood.

A screen door slams.

Someone speaks, and I recognize the careless voice of Billy Neal for sure. "Maybe she hitched a ride with somebody," he says.

"Why the hell would she do that?" Grandpapa snaps. "Her goddamn car was sitting right there with a spare set of keys in a magnetic case under the bumper. Who do you think put those keys there?"

"The Audi dealer, maybe?"

"Boy, have you got an ounce of brains in your head? Catherine put those keys there. That's the kind of girl she is."

"Maybe the car wouldn't start."

"It started right up for Henry this morning."

"Maybe she's still on the island, then. Maybe the bridge got covered over before she left."

"Get the hell out of here!" bellows my grandfather. "Don't come back till you start making some sense. That girl knows how to take care of herself. I want to know what happened down there. I've got enough to worry about with the casino project. Government questioning every goddamn thing on the applications, DNA tests on three-hundred-year-old teeth. Jesus. Get out of here!"

More footsteps, and the door slams again.

"What do you think, Pearlie?" asks Grandpapa.

I move closer to the door, close enough to hear Pearlie sigh.

"Am I paid to think?" she asks.

"I asked your opinion. Where is she? Where's my grandbaby?"

"I'm afraid somebody done hurt that girl, Dr. Kirkland. Like you said, she knows how to take care of herself. And she wouldn't leave that car behind without a good reason."

"She might if she went into one of her manic states. What you call her spells."

"Last time I saw her," says Pearlie, "she looked more down than up to me. No, if Louise put her on a bicycle, then somebody followed her. She never made it to that bridge."

"Who would do that?" asks Grandpapa.

"I'd ask that trash you got working for you where he was yesterday evening."

The silence stretches for some time. "You think Billy followed her down there?"

"Do you know where he was yesterday?"

"Doing some business for me in Baton Rouge. Picking up some things for me."

"Way I remember it, that island ain't far off the highway to Baton Rouge."

More silence. "What would Billy want with Catherine?"

"You'd know more about that than I would." Pearlie's voice carries a sharp rebuke. "What does any man want with any woman?"

Grandpapa makes a rumbling noise. "I'll talk to him."

The screen door bangs again.

I step into the kitchen.

Pearlie is standing at the sink, her back to me. She lifts an iron skillet and turns on the tap, then freezes. Slowly she turns, and her eyes go wide.

"Don't say anything," I whisper. "Not a word."

She nods silently.

"I'm leaving town, Pearlie. Are my extra keys in here?"

She glances at the counter. The spring-loaded Audi key is lying on top of some mail. I grab it and return to the doorway.

"Where you going, girl?" Pearlie asks.

"I have to meet someone. I want you to tell me something first, though."

"What?"

"Somebody did some bad things to me when I was a little girl. A man. It was either Daddy or Grandpapa. And I don't see how you could have taken care of me for so long—you did my mother's job, really—without knowing about that. I just don't."

Pearlie glances at the outside door, but her expression doesn't change.

"You won't tell me?" I ask.

Her face tightens in what looks like anger. "Listen to me, child. What you doing running down to the island stirring things up? What good you think you gonna do? Is any good gonna come from all this? For you? For your mama? For anybody?"

"I don't have any choice. I have to know how and why Daddy died. And I have to know why I'm the way I am. You don't understand that?"

She looks at the floor. "The Lord works in mysterious ways. That's what I understand. There's a lot of pain in this world—especially if you born a girl—but it ain't for us to question all that. We just got to deal with it as best we can."

"Do you really believe that, Pearlie?"

Her gaze returns to me, her eyes more intense than ever. "I got to believe it. That's the only thing got me this far."

"What do you mean 'this far'? To this house? This job? Working for my grandfather?"

Indignation comes into Pearlie's face. She speaks in a quavering voice. "I work for this family, not Dr. Kirkland. I came to work for old Mr. DeSalle in 1948, when I was seventeen years old. Your grandmama, your mama, you—you're all DeSalles. I worked for all of you. Dr. Kirkland just the man who signs my check."

"Is that all he is, Pearlie? Isn't he the man who says what goes? Hasn't he always been?"

She nods somberly. "There's always a man who says what goes. That's what people mean when they talk about the Man. And round here, Dr. Kirkland be the Man. Everybody knows that. Now, you gonna tell him you all right or not?"

"You can tell him after I'm gone." I'm about to turn and go when something Michael said comes back to me, accompanied by a fragmentary image from my dreams—the black figure fighting over my bed with my father.

"Did you pull the trigger that night, Pearlie?"

The whites of the old woman's eyes grow large. "Have you lost your mind, child? What you think you're saying?"

"Did you kill my father? That's what I'm asking you. Did you kill him to protect me from him?"

She shakes her head slowly. "Where you going in that car?"

"To find out the truth about this family."

"Where you gonna find that?"

"Don't worry about it. But when I find it, I'll let you know. And then you can pretend you didn't know all along."

Pearlie opens her mouth as if to speak, but no sound emerges.

I shake my head, then turn and run back up the hallway.

I expected to find Billy Neal and my grandfather talking behind the house, but there's no sign of them. Glancing around the parking lot, I move quickly to the Audi, flicking the electric unlock button as I go.

As I grab the door handle, Billy Neal rises from behind Pearlie's Cadillac. He's wearing black jeans, a green silk shirt, and snakeskin cowboy boots. His eyes are as dead as the snakes that adorn his boots, but they lock onto mine with mechanical precision.

"I'll be damned," he says. "A lot of people think you're dead."

"Is that what you thought?"

A faint smile plays across his lips. "I gave it even money."

"Why do you hate me, Billy? You don't even know me."

He walks up to the Audi and stares at me over the roof. "Oh, I know you. I've fucked girls just like you. Pampered princesses, trust fund waiting, never had to worry a day in their damn lives. And still you blow half your money going to shrinks."

"Why do you care?"

He lays his forearms on the roof and leans toward me. "'Cause you think your shit don't stink. You look in my direction and you don't even see me. In the daytime, anyway. But at night it's a different story, isn't it? At night, I'm just the guy you're looking for. I've heard about you, Miss Cat in the Hat. You like to party, don't you? People still remember you from high school. The rich girl who loved to have fun. They still remember your aunt, too. Same story, only worse."

"Exactly what do you do for my grandfather?"

"Things he's too old to do himself now. Things other people are squeamish about." Billy lights a cigarette and blows smoke across the roof at me. "I ain't squeamish."

I'll bet. "Have you fired the Remington 700 from the gun safe lately?"

A bemused smile. "You're a sneaky little piece, aren't you?"

Suddenly I've had all I can take from this grease-slick urban cowboy. "You know what? I'm tired of your act. I think we ought to bring my grandfather into this conversation."

Billy's smile only broadens, and I know I've made a mistake. "That's what I was thinking, too. You've been pissing him off quite a bit lately. He's moving heaven and earth to save this town with that casino, and you're busting your ass trying to smear the family name. He doesn't appreciate that at all. You could ruin the whole deal, in fact. So let's go talk to him."

I open the Audi's door. "I have to go somewhere first. I'll be back in twenty minutes."

Before I can hit the lock button, Billy yanks open the passenger door and puts a boot on the seat. "Not twenty minutes from now. *Now.*"

Without thinking about it, I reach behind my back, yank the Walther from the waistband of my pants, and aim it over the roof at his chest.

"This isn't a pellet gun, Billy. In case you were wondering."

His eyes focus on the barrel of the gun, and his smile begins to fade. Billy Neal probably carries a gun more often than not, but I don't think he expected to find himself in this situation before seven in the morning.

"Now," I say quietly, "take your fucking boot off my seat and back away from the car."

"You're one crazy bitch," he says, laughing softly. "I heard you were, but I didn't believe it until . . ."

"Now? Or last night on the island?"

The smile returns. "Don't know what you're talking about."

"Oh, I think you do."

"You and me are gonna have some fun one of these days, honey. Like I said, I know about you. Incest is best, right?"

The blood drains from my face. *What does he know about me?* I want to ask, but I know he'll only torture me any way he can.

"*Get away from my fucking car!*" I yell, brandishing the gun.

Billy doesn't move. "You haven't chambered a round."

"There's already one in the pipe."

I'm only quoting jargon I've heard from Sean, but it's enough to wipe the last of the smile from Billy's face. His boot slides back across the seat and down to the gravel.

"Shut the door," I order.

When he does, I reach down with my free hand and hit the lock button. Then I climb in, close the door, and start the engine.

Before I can pull away, Billy leans down to the passenger window. He makes a peace sign with his fingers, reverses it, then lays the V over his lips and flicks his tongue up and down between his fingers. My stomach does a slow roll. I'd love to shoot him, but I'd never make my meeting with Malik if I did. Instead, I put the car in gear and spray the asshole with gravel as I peel away from the slave quarters I once called home.

CHAPTER
41

My drive to New Orleans isn't filled with thoughts of Nathan Malik, but of my aunt Ann. Though I've never spent much time with her, she has left a deep impression. Ann is the beauty of the family—no small feat considering my mother's looks—and she was an overachiever until her second year of college. Head cheerleader and valedictorian in high school. Winner of the local Junior Miss pageant. Full music scholarship to Tulane. Named Queen of the Natchez Confederate Pageant in her sophomore year of college. Then she entered a profound depression and tried to kill herself with an overdose of pills. Grandpapa had her committed, and when she was released two months later, everyone—including Ann—acted as though she had miraculously been healed.

She wasn't.

But that breakdown happened before I was born. I knew Ann as the life of every family gathering—those she attended, anyway. Though four years older than my mother, Ann always seemed a decade younger. She knew clothes like nobody else. Her body was built for fashion; she could make off-the-rack stuff look like haute couture. In photos dating from the seventies—when she was just out of high school—she has the athletic body of a *Sports Illustrated* swimsuit model. But by the mideighties, she was cadaverously thin, and in snapshots from that period her eyes have the glaze I usually attribute to cocaine.

Whatever the source of her energy, Ann was something no one else in the DeSalle family ever quite managed to be—cool. She taught me how to dance, how to dress, how to wear makeup. She caught me smoking my first cigarette—stolen from her pack—and shared it with me. She gave me pointers on French kissing and told me how to get rid of guys whose attention I didn't want. She advised me always to have a guy waiting in the wings—even if I was married—because the guy you were with could and probably would betray you. Keeping another guy on a string wasn't cheating on your steady beau, she said, it was just looking out for yourself. And that, I figured, was the way cool girls worked it.

But coolness doesn't age well. As I got older, I overheard my mother getting calls at all hours of the night, and sometimes leaving to drive hundreds of miles to rescue Ann, who by this time—I later learned—had been diagnosed with bipolar disorder. Riding the highs of manic episodes, she would disappear for weeks at a time. Once the Mexican police found her working as a waitress in a Tijuana bar, thanks to an international search my grandfather had initiated. I've often wondered if *waitress* was a euphemism for what Ann was really doing when they found her in that bar.

But what I remember most about Ann was her obsession with having a baby. At times this fixation seemed the root of her mental illness. Because I left home for college at sixteen, I missed many of the travails of her quest for infertility treatment. All I know is that nothing ever panned out, and the fault lies with her, not her first two husbands. Only a teenager on speed could keep up with her during her manic periods, and no one—not even my mother—can stand to be with her when she's in the pit of depression. It's so unfair, really. I had no desire to become pregnant, yet I'm carrying a child in my womb. Ann was desperate to conceive, but it never happened.

What brought her to Nathan Malik's door? Was it bipolar disorder? Or emerging memories of sexual abuse? If Malik will stop playing games with me, I could have my answer in ninety minutes.

The sign for Angola Penitentiary flashes past on my right. I usually think of the island when I see that sign, think of it and then shut the memories away. But today the image that comes to me will not be banished. It's the one-room clinic where Grandpapa treats the black families who live on the island. The clinic where ten-year-old Ann had her emergency appendectomy. A legend in our family, the story is always the same, even in its details. A storm washes away the bridge and the boats . . . Ann suddenly develops a hot appendix . . . Grandpapa and Ivy work by the light of a Coleman lantern. Ann has a severe infection, but she survives, and the crowd of laborers standing watch outside cheers in jubilation.

Yet today, a new and terrible connection closes in my brain. What if Ann's problem *wasn't* her appendix? What if my grandfather had been molesting her? Could he have gotten her pregnant? Is it possible that the "emergency appendectomy" was actually an abortion? *My God.* If it was an abortion—and he somehow botched the procedure—could that have been what ruined Ann's chances for conception in later life? Before speculating any further, I dial Michael Wells's cell phone.

"Cat?" he says, the sound of a car radio in the background.

"Yes, can you hear me? I have a medical question for you."

"I hear you fine. Shoot."

"How young can a girl get pregnant?"

Michael turns down his radio. "That's a pretty broad question. Pregnancy in twelve-year-olds is relatively common in Mississippi."

"But what's the youngest a girl can conceive?"

"The youngest? Well, I'm not an OB. But pediatricians classify precocious puberty as secondary signs—that's breast tissue and pubic hair—appearing before age eight in African-American girls and nine in whites."

"You're kidding."

"No. But they can't conceive at those ages. I'm not saying it's never happened. Why do you ask?"

"I'm wondering if my aunt Ann could have gotten pregnant at age ten."

Michael says nothing for a few moments. "You're thinking your grandfather impregnated her?"

"Maybe. And I'm thinking that emergency appendectomy on the island might not have been an appendectomy at all."

"Wow. That would prove he's the one, all right." There's a pause, then Michael says, "When would this have happened?"

I do some quick math. "Like 1958."

"No way. No pregnancy at ten years old. The average age of onset of menses has been declining steadily for decades. Today? Maybe one in a million that young. In 1958, forget it. I see your line of reasoning, but I think you're into the Twilight Zone with this theory."

I don't know whether I feel relieved or not. "I'm sure you're right. My mind's just spinning with all this."

"Ann hasn't called you back yet?"

"No."

"How far are you from New Orleans?"

"Ninety miles."

"You're taking Sean with you to see Malik, right?"

"Right. Don't worry, Michael, really."

"I'm going to worry until you call me and tell me the meeting is over and you're okay."

His concern brings a smile to my face. "I'll definitely call you, okay?"

"Okay."

"Bye for now."

"Bye."

I take the Audi off cruise control and accelerate to eighty-five. Faces swirl endlessly through my mind like a Möbius strip—my grandfather, Ann, my mother and father, Billy Neal, Jesse and Louise—but speculation as to their true relationships is meaningless. In less than two hours, I'll be face-to-face with the man who can tell me the exact nature of his relationship with my troubled aunt, and probably the identity of the man who molested me.

At this point, that's all I care about.

Malik instructed me to telephone him when I was five miles outside New Orleans, but I didn't do it. Instead I pulled off I-10 at Williams Boulevard, one of the first exits at Kenner—the westernmost suburb of New Orleans—and drove to a liquor store.

I've been inside once, but I didn't buy anything. I stood staring at the bottles of Grey Goose, peering at the blue-and-white image of geese flying over the French Alps. I know that bottle like I know my own face. The French flag, the frosted glass, the blue cap. My right hand rose to a 750-milliliter bottle as though commanded by a hypnotist, but at the last moment I turned and hurried out of the store.

Now I'm sitting in my parked car in front of the store, my cell phone cradled in my shaking hands. The cashier probably thinks I'm casing the place for a robbery. Or maybe she's seen her share of recovering alcoholics fighting the same impulse.

It's not the physical withdrawal that's making me shake now.

It's Malik.

I promised Michael I would take Sean with me to the meeting, but I haven't called him. I won't be seeing Sean again. I don't think I need him for this anyway. The odds that Dr. Malik wants to hurt me are very low, and I am armed. What has me shaking is the possibility of finally learning the truth about myself. Whatever Malik knows, it will irrevocably change my perception of myself.

But that's what you came for, right? says a voice in my head.

With a soft curse, I get out, walk to the pay phone beside the liquor store, and punch in the number Malik told me to call. It rings four times, but just as I think it's going to click over to voice mail, he answers.

"Catherine?"

"Yes."

"Are you five miles out?"

"No, I'm parked in front of a liquor store on Williams Boulevard."

"Are you near the airport?"

"Yes."

"Good. I'm in a motel a mile away from it. The Thibodeaux. It's a dump with an orange sign, about a mile past the airport turn, on the right. Do you think you can find it?"

"I think I've seen it before."

"All the rooms are on the ground floor. I'm in room eighteen."

"Should I just pull up to the room?"

"Yes. I'll be watching for you."

I start to hang up, but I sense that he's waiting for something. "Dr. Malik?"

"Yes?"

"Do you know who abused me?"

"Yes and no."

Shit. "Still playing games with me?"

"You're the one who knows that answer, Catherine. Remember what I told you about trauma. The memory is repressed but intact. It's indelible. It's waiting for you to dredge it up. And I'm going to help you."

"Today?"

"Today. In a few minutes, I'm going to take you across the river Lethe. To the underworld. Then I'm going to lead you back to the world of light. When you return, you'll be whole again. You'll have your soul back. Your memory, too."

My palms are cold and coated with sweat. Malik's words have not lessened my anxiety but increased it.

"Don't be afraid, Catherine. Are you on your way?"

"Yeah."

"Are you drinking?"

"Stone fucking sober."

He chuckles softly. "I'll see you when you get here."

The phone goes dead.

I take a last look at the door of the liquor store—WE CARD EVERY-BODY—then get back in my car and start the engine. Before I back out of the lot, though, I open my purse, take out my bottle of Valium, and roll one yellow pill into my damp palm. With my left hand on my tummy, I whisper, "Forgive me, baby girl. Just one more," and dry-swallow the pill. Then I back out and join the stream of traffic headed toward the airport.

Malik was right. The Thibodeaux Motel is a dump. A low strip of rooms with a sagging roof and a row of bright orange doors. Three vehicles in the parking lot, all wrecks. I park four doors down from room eighteen and get out. The air stinks of aviation fuel and fast food. There's plenty of traffic on Williams, but if I hold the Walther along my right leg, it's almost invisible.

A 727 roars low overhead as I walk toward the door. Raising my left hand to knock, I hear the sound of rain sweeping toward me. It can rain without a moment's notice in New Orleans, but today the asphalt is baking in bright sunlight. It's my hallucination again . . . rain on a tin roof. The rattling sound is louder than the cars passing on the road thirty yards away.

Screw it. The end of that hallucination is on the other side of this door.

I chamber a round in the Walther, then knock hard on the orange door. It moves inward a few inches with the force of my blow.

"Dr. Malik?"

No reply.

Now I wish I'd called Sean. This is where pride gets you. Bringing my gun to chest level, I kick open the door and rush into the room, checking the corners for threats.

The room looks just as I imagined it: ratty green carpet, two double beds, a TV on a stand, a lavatory beneath a mirror on the far wall.

No Malik.

I cross the room and kick open the bathroom door, the Walther extended in front of me.

Malik is lying in the bathtub. He's fully clothed—all in black, of course—and the white tiles above his bald head are spattered with blood and brain matter.

My initial shock balloons into terror when I realize the blood is still running down the tile. Whoever killed Malik could still be close by. As I whirl back toward the room, the gun in Malik's right hand registers in my mind.

Suicide?

I can't believe that.

But then I see the skull in his lap. It's a human skull, entirely stripped of flesh, boiled clean like the skulls used to teach orthopedics. Malik is cradling it in his hands as he might an infant. Springs and screws hold the mandible to the maxilla, and the arteries and veins have been painted in red and blue across the white plates of bone. The skull wears the slightly ironic grin of all its kind, but this particular skull, I sense, is trying to tell me something. There's a reason it's here, and it wants me to know it.

I look at Malik's face for some clue, but he can't even help himself now. The psychiatrist's once piercing eyes are as dead as those in a stuffed deer head. As I stare, searching in vain for some explanation, Malik's chest heaves violently, and his head flies forward as if pulled on a string.

The Walther jerks in my hand.

The bathroom booms like a bomb-testing chamber.

Everything goes white.

CHAPTER

42

I'm snow-blind.

Lost in a sea of white, my head pounds incessantly from the cold. Far in the distance, someone calls my name.

"Dr. Ferry . . . ? Catherine!"

The voice is familiar, but I can't see anyone.

The wind stings my face.

A flash of darkness spears through the white, and then dirty-yellow light frames a blurry face. "Dr. Ferry? Can you hear me?"

Yes . . . over here.

"Cat? It's John Kaiser. Special Agent John Kaiser."

It is. It's John Kaiser. His hazel eyes hover only inches over mine.

"What happened?" I ask.

"I don't know. We're hoping you can tell us."

Blinking rapidly against the yellow light, I try to see who "we" is, and where I am. I seem to be propped against a bathtub, my hips beneath a commode, my legs splayed out in an open doorway. There's a paramedic behind Kaiser, and behind him I see the dark face of Carmen Piazza, commander of the NOPD Homicide Division. Piazza looks angry.

"Are you wounded?" Kaiser asks. "They can't find any injuries, but you were unconscious."

"My head hurts. How did you get here?"

"Don't worry about that. How did *you* get here?"

I turn to make sure Malik's corpse is still lying in the tub behind me. It is. "Dr. Malik wanted me to meet him here. I came."

"Jesus," mutters Captain Piazza. "Did you hear that? Did you fucking *hear that*?"

Kaiser shakes his head. "Did Malik try to kill you, Cat?"

No, I almost say aloud. But fortunately my common sense has survived whatever happened to me. "I want a lawyer."

Kaiser looks disappointed. "Do you need a lawyer?"

"I don't know. Can you promise not to arrest me?"

He glances back at Piazza, then looks at me again. "You know I can't do that."

"Then I want a lawyer."

He stands and tells the paramedic to check me out. While that happens, I hear someone clearing people from the murder scene. Then I hear Captain Piazza's voice, low and furious, while Kaiser tries to mollify her with a sonorous baritone.

"Can you walk?" asks Kaiser. He's standing in the door again.

"I think so."

"Then walk with me."

I get to my feet and, after a last look at Malik and the skull in his lap, follow Agent Kaiser into the parking lot. That skull is bothering me, but I don't have time to ponder it now. The parking lot that was empty before is nearly full, with NOPD squad cars, an ambulance, a coroner's wagon, and unmarked detectives' cars. Kaiser walks me about twenty yards along the row of rooms, far enough so that no one will hear us.

"Listen to me, Cat. I came to this scene directly from another one. Our UNSUB hit his sixth victim."

"Who was it?"

"You don't seem surprised."

"We haven't caught our killer yet. Why should he stop?"

"You didn't think Malik was the killer?"

"I wouldn't have come here if I did."

Kaiser studies me for some time. I glance back at the room and see Piazza talking to two detectives. She gestures at me, and the detectives both stare in my direction. They look like a pair of pit bulls awaiting a command from their master.

"Same crime signature on victim six?" I ask.

"Yes. Two gunshots, bite marks, the same message on the wall. 'My work is never done.' But while we were working the scene, task force headquarters got a call telling us Malik was hiding out here."

"Anonymous again?"

"Yes."

"Your caller is your killer, John."

Kaiser looks at me like a stern father. "Tell me about Group X."

"You didn't learn anything from the two patients you have?"

"We don't have them anymore. Both women disappeared this morning. Maybe last night, I don't know. What I don't get is how they knew to run. I checked their phone records; no one suspicious called them."

"Talk to *everyone* who called them," I say, realizing that Ann may now be the only person who can tell us who the members of Group X are—other than the women themselves. *Unless Malik's documentary can be found. Could he have had it in the motel room with him?*

"We're checking everybody," Kaiser says. "But you know more than you've told me."

"You keep me out of jail, we'll talk."

"That might not be possible."

"You need me to solve this case. Who's victim number six, John?"

He seems to debate whether to answer. Then he says, "A police officer. That's all I'm going to tell you right now, and I shouldn't have told you that."

"So why did you?"

"Because I need to know what you know about what happened here. If you lawyer up because you're paranoid, we're going to lose time we'll never get back. If you have nothing to hide—nothing relevant to this case, anyway—then you don't have anything to lose by talking to me."

I want to talk to him, but I know that an FBI agent, despite his best intentions, can't prevent the NOPD from arresting me for murder if they decide to do it. On the other hand, I can only benefit from Kaiser's support.

"What did you want from Malik?" he asks.

"I came to find out what my aunt's connection to Malik was. And also some things about my past."

"Did you talk to him?"

"He was dead when I got here."

"Why were you unconscious?"

"My head feels like somebody hit me."

"Your gun's been fired. The bullet went into Malik's chest."

An icy spark shoots through me. Could I have killed Malik by accident? No . . . His death spasm in the tub comes back to me in a sickening rush. "If that's true, he was already dead when I shot him. Or close to dead. The autopsy should prove that. He had a nerve spasm, and it scared the shit out of me. I fired by accident."

Kaiser watches Piazza over my shoulder for several seconds. Then he takes my arm and says, "Listen to me. Listen like you never listened in your life, and tell me the goddamned truth. Okay?"

"I'm listening."

"If you had killed Nathan Malik, would you know it?"

A gauzelike film drops over my eyes, a sense that I'm separated from Kaiser by a distortion of perception. His or mine, I'm not sure. "What do you mean?"

"I've been thinking a lot about you in the past few days. Your panic attacks at the crime scenes. Your psychiatric history—what I know of it, anyway. The crime signature, which primarily consists of bite marks that could be staged. Something you would know how to do better than anyone else. And the fact that you were sexually abused—"

"Who told you that?" I cut in, my voice quavering. "Did Sean tell you that?"

"Yes."

"Son of a bitch."

"I'm sorry, Cat. But I think your PTSD and past sexual abuse is what drew you to Malik and may have made you his patient, even without you knowing it."

"Holy God. Do you really believe I could be killing these men without *knowing* it?"

Kaiser shrugs. "I'm raising a possibility. One that others might raise. Carmen Piazza, for example. She doesn't know everything I know, but she doesn't like what she does. I've listened to the tapes of your meeting with Malik several times. He told you about dissociative identity disorder, and that's just multiple personality disorder under another name. Given the situation in which I just found you, it would be irresponsible of me not to suspect it."

Under the pressure of Piazza and her pit bulls staring at me, I can hardly summon the resources to defend myself. "John, I didn't kill Nathan Malik. Nor did I kill or help him kill any of the six victims in your case. Now, if I suffer from dissociative identity disorder, I grant you, I would not know I had done any of that. I'd believe I was innocent. But do you have any idea how rare that disorder is? Even among sexually abused people? It's one of those fascinating myths, like amnesia. There've been more cases of it in Hollywood movies in the past twenty years than in all of recorded human history."

Kaiser is watching me like a bomber pilot deciding whether to flatten a suspected enemy village. The slightest sign could tilt him either way.

"If you let them put me in jail," I tell him, "you'll be losing your best chance to solve this case."

"Why?"

"Dr. Malik told me I already know the truth about what happened to me, that I just have to find a way to pull it out of my head. I think the same is true about this case. They're connected, somehow."

"Maybe Malik was talking about some alternate identity inside you."

"Jesus, would you get real? You're talking to a woman who's pregnant by a married man. I'm trying to quit drinking, and I just found out I was sexually abused by someone in my family. I don't have *time* to run around killing people for fun or profit. Okay?"

There's a flash of something in Kaiser's eyes, humanity, maybe. Then he looks over my shoulder at Piazza again. Kaiser is my only hope of staying free.

"I talked to Malik on the phone," I admit. "He told me some things about the case. You arrest me, you'll never find out what they are."

"What things?" he asks, his eyes narrowed.

"Did you find a box inside that room?"

"No. What was in the box?"

I shake my head.

Kaiser grabs my wrist. "Come with me."

As he pulls me toward the Crown Victoria I rode in the other day, I glance over my shoulder. The two NOPD detectives are coming after me. Kaiser puts me in the backseat and climbs in after me. Closed into this small space with him, I feel again the personal magnetism I felt in my house that afternoon with Sean.

"What's about to happen?" I ask.

His face is taut. "I don't know, but it should be interesting."

One of the detectives knocks on the window.

"Don't get out of this car unless I tell you to," Kaiser says.

"I won't."

Kaiser gets out of the backseat and locks the door behind him. A heated discussion begins outside, but Kaiser moves the detectives steadily away from the car, so I only hear part of it. Words come to me out of an audio blur. *Arrest. Conspiracy. Aiding and abetting.* A woman's voice joins the fray. Captain Piazza is talking about jurisdictional control and federal interference. The word "psycho" reaches my ears. Kaiser must be speaking quietly, because I can't hear anything he's saying. Yet after a couple of minutes, it's Kaiser who returns to the car and gets inside with me.

"Are they going to arrest me?"

"They want to. Piazza thinks you've been lying to us from the start. That you've been feeding Malik information about the investigation. She's suspending Sean, and she wants your hide nailed to the barn wall. She wants to interrogate you herself."

"Great."

Kaiser's eyes bore into mine. "What was in the box you mentioned, Cat? At this point, that may be the only thing that could keep you out of jail."

"A film."

I see connections happening at light speed behind Kaiser's eyes. "The video production equipment," he says. "The stuff we found at Malik's secret apartment. That's what it was for?"

"Bravo."

"What kind of film is it?"

"Malik's making a documentary about sexual abuse. About an experimental therapy group he was working with. Group X."

"I'll be damned."

"Female patients only. He said it was radical stuff. It was his life's work. No way would Malik have killed himself before he finished that film. And he seemed to think a lot of people didn't want anyone to see it."

Kaiser takes some time to process this. "Did he tell you who any of the patients in Group X were?"

"No."

"Was your aunt one of them?"

"He didn't tell me, and I don't know."

"Have you spoken to your aunt?"

"No."

"*Shit.* With Malik dead, we may never find out who was in Group X. Not unless your aunt can tell us."

That's not all we'll never know, I think with desolation. *The secret of my life may have died with Malik. Unless Ann knows it. Knows it and will tell me . . .*

"But the film shows the women in Group X?"

"Yes. They supposedly relive their abuse in front of the camera."

"I guess Malik's killer took it."

I give Kaiser a thin smile. "I'd say so."

He glances back toward the NOPD detectives, who are staring angrily at the car. "Goddamn it. Tell me about that motel room, Cat."

"I didn't know where Malik was until five minutes before I got here. He gave me a phone number to call. When I arrived, the door was open. I went in and found him in the bathroom. The blood on the wall was fresh. Then I saw the gun in his hand."

"What if Malik was the killer, and he offed himself because his 'work' was done after all? After the sixth victim, I mean?"

I shake my head. "You know better, John. Malik's work was his film, not murder. Tell me about the sixth victim."

Kaiser looks back at the motel. Piazza is standing with her detectives again. "His name was Quentin Baptiste. He was an NOPD homicide detective."

"*What?* Shit."

"Yep. It was probably Baptiste who was feeding information to the killer, knowingly or not. That's one reason Piazza would like to pin that on you."

"How old was Baptiste?"

"Forty-one."

"The youngest victim yet. Is Sean at that crime scene?"

"He was on his way there when I left. He's probably heard about this by now. We need to get you out of here."

"What about female relatives?"

"What?

"Have you checked out Quentin Baptiste's female relatives? One of them could have been a patient of Malik's. One of them could be in Group X. If he was only forty-one, I'd check daughters, step-daughters, and nieces. Also brothers or fathers of those women."

"I was starting that when we got the tip to come here. Since Baptiste was a cop, it shouldn't be hard to—" Kaiser's face tightens. *"Shit."*

A dark green Saab screeches to a stop a few yards away from us. As Sean leaps out and races toward the motel, Kaiser lifts a walkie-talkie to his lips. "Richard, get out here *now*. Don't tell Detective Regan where Dr. Ferry is."

"Is Sean living at home again?" I ask.

Kaiser meets my eyes. "I think so, yeah. Trying to reconcile with his wife."

"Make sure he knows I'm not hurt."

"I will."

The front door of the Crown Vic opens, and a gray-suited FBI agent jumps behind the wheel. As he starts the engine, Sean bursts from room eighteen and scans the parking lot. Our eyes lock. He sprints toward the car, but Kaiser's driver screeches onto Williams Boulevard before Sean can reach us.

We're three blocks away from the motel when a revelation hits me like a body blow. "Turn around!"

"That would be a mistake," Kaiser says firmly. "For both of you."

"It's not Sean! It's the skull. I need to see that skull."

"Why?"

I try to rein in my excitement. "The teeth in that skull made the bite marks on the victims. I'd bet anything on it."

"Turn the car around," Kaiser orders.

Richard gets us back to the Thibodeaux in less than a minute. Sean's Saab is already gone. Captain Piazza must have made it clear to him that following us could be a catastrophic career move.

Summoned by Kaiser via radio, a female evidence technician walks out to our car carrying the skull in a large Ziploc bag. Kaiser reaches across me, rolls down my window, and takes the skull from the tech. Then he sets it in my lap.

The polished skull stares up at me with the ironic grin I saw in the motel bathtub. The bone has a slightly yellowish color, probably from aging of the varnish someone put on it.

"I need gloves."

"Give her your gloves," Kaiser orders the tech.

My heart pounds as I struggle to put on the technician's latex gloves, which turned inside out when she removed them. Even without opening the skull's mouth, I can see that its lateral incisors are slightly pegged, as were those that wounded the flesh of our victims. Once the gloves are on, I open the Ziploc and remove the skull.

I've held many of these during my career, some clinically spotless like this one, others dredged out of mass graves in Bosnia by a backhoe. The ones like this you see in dentists' and doctors' offices. They're good for patient education, and they lend a certain macabre severity to a medical office.

The jaw opens easily on the springs screwed to the interior surfaces of the zygoma and mandible. Doing bite-mark comparisons can be long, painstaking work, but sometimes it's a no-brainer. This is one of those times. The maxillary arch of the bite marks at the murder scenes is engraved upon my mind, and the one in this skull matches it tooth for tooth.

"Well?" says Kaiser.

"It's a perfect match."

CHAPTER

43

As we zoom along the shore of Lake Pontchartrain toward the FBI field office, Kaiser speaks on the phone to someone who obviously has a great deal of power. My head is still pounding, the pain focused behind my eyes. The skull is riding up front on the passenger seat, next to our driver.

At last Kaiser hangs up and turns to me. "The chief of police is going batshit because I wouldn't let Piazza arrest you. Now that I took you away from the scene, he's calling my boss. It's going to be a bureaucratic shitstorm."

"Am I going to be arrested?"

"The field office is task force headquarters. If you'll remain there a while without making a fuss, that's your best bet for staying out of jail."

"Look, my showing up at that motel was just lagniappe for the killer. It was the killer who tipped you where to find the murder weapon and the video equipment, and the same person gave you the motel and the skull. He's trying to frame Malik. My showing up was just a bonus. If you figured out the suicide was staged, I was right there to blame for staging it. And with my experience, I'd know just how to do it."

"It plays," says Kaiser, "but I can think of a scenario that plays equally well."

"Not your multiple personality fantasy."

"No. The women in Group X know Malik is killing abusers, and also that he killed an innocent man. One of them is having a crisis of conscience. Like the woman who tried to kill herself, Margaret Lavigne."

"Lavigne's still in a coma?"

"Yes. I was actually thinking our caller might be your aunt."

"Was the voice female again?"

"Yes."

I turn toward the lake and watch the gray waves in silence. I suppose Aunt Ann could be making the calls. But for some reason I doubt it. If Ann paid Malik's bail, what would so quickly turn her against him? Finding out that an innocent man had been murdered? Maybe. But I doubt that would sway her loyalty. "Were there bite marks on the face of the dead cop?"

"The worst yet."

"These are personal attacks, John. And the bite marks are created antemortem, like torture. But the victims have to be immobilized before they're bitten."

"So?"

"The killer's a woman. I've suspected it from the start. It's probably one of the women in Group X."

Kaiser blows out a stream of air. "That's a possibility, but a very remote one given the crime signature. There's no history of a woman ever committing sexual homicides like this. Not alone."

"Five minutes ago you practically accused me of doing it!"

"You're a special case. Your past, your forensic training. And I suggested you were assisting Malik. A male-female-team scenario."

"Why not two women? We don't know how many women there were in Group X."

"Go on."

"Once we connected Malik to those first two female patients, the killer knew we were getting close, even if *we* didn't know it. So she planted the gun at Malik's apartment and gave it to us. We kept getting closer, so she gave us Malik and the skull wrapped up in a neat package. Our girl is probably feeling pretty safe right now."

Kaiser is looking expectantly at me. Something is tugging at the back of my mind, but I can't quite make it out. "Did you get anything at all on Quentin Baptiste's female relatives?"

"Hang on." He calls Carmen Piazza. Their conversation is short and to the point. When he hangs up, he says, "Detective Baptiste had six female relatives by blood. A wife, three nieces, two daughters."

"How old are the daughters?"

"Piazza didn't have their ages, but one works as a teacher. The other is a day care worker. One of the nieces just graduated from the police academy."

"She'd know how to shoot," I think aloud. "So would the first victim's daughter, I'll bet. Moreland. An army brat? Daughter of a colonel?"

"We've been all over the Moreland daughter, because she was related to the first victim. She's clean, Cat. But I'll get the task force on Baptiste's relatives right away. Still . . . a female killer is very long odds based on precedent."

"There was no precedent for Aileen Wuornos either. Forget the past, John. Look at the evidence in front of you."

A tall white sail appears on the horizon. It soothes me to follow it with my eyes. As my eyelids grow heavy, I remember the Valium I popped before going to the motel.

"How's your head?" Kaiser asks.

"It hurts. I didn't sleep well last night, so I took a Valium before I went to the motel."

"You could have a concussion. Should we get you a CAT scan?"

"Just take me to the field office. I need to lie down."

"If you lie down, I'm putting a nurse in the room with you."

"Do whatever you want. I'm going to bed."

I lean against the window and close my eyes, but my cell phone starts playing "Sunday, Bloody Sunday." I reach into my pocket. It's empty.

"I've got it," says Kaiser, holding my screen where I can see it. "You know this number?"

"No, but that's a Gulf Coast area code. It might be Ann. I left a message for her to call me."

Kaiser thinks fast, then hands me the phone. "Whatever you do, don't tell her Malik is dead."

I nod and press SEND. "Hello?"

"Hey, Cat Woman!"

My heart thumps against my sternum. It's Ann. I nod quickly to Kaiser, and he tenses on the seat.

"How you doing, baby girl?" Ann's voice has the brittle quality

I've learned to associate with her manic episodes. *How do I play her?*

"Not so good right now, actually," I say in a tired voice.

"You sound like you need a drink."

"I wish. I'm on the wagon."

"Ouch. Your message said you knew something about Dr. Malik and me. What exactly do you know?"

"I know you paid his bail. The FBI knows, too."

"That's not against the law, is it?"

Ricochet-quick response. Definitely manic. "Dr. Malik is mixed up in some murders, Ann."

A pause. Then a craftier voice comes through the phone. "*Mixed up* is a pretty vague term, baby girl. Nathan couldn't do the things they think he did. I know men, honey. He doesn't have that in him."

Ann knows men like an arsonist knows fire. "I've been talking to him quite a bit lately," I tell her.

"Do you know where he is?" A hint of anxiety now.

"Yes." I close my eyes. "He's been arrested again."

"Arrested?" The alarm in that one word is shocking. "Where?"

"Here in New Orleans. I think you should drive over and see him. I'd like to talk to you, too. Are you in Biloxi?"

"No."

"Are you anywhere close?"

Another silence. "Sorry, baby girl. I don't feel like I can tell you everything at this point. You know how that is. You've always kept some secrets yourself."

"You're right. But sometimes I wish I hadn't. I wish all of us would have talked to each other more."

"Oh, honey . . . me, too. I wish you could do a group with Nathan. He's worked miracles for me."

"I wanted to," I reply, only half lying. "I just found out some things about my past that really messed me up. I'd like to ask you some questions. To see if some of the same things happened to you."

"Oh, baby girl," Ann says in a breathy voice, "I've worried about you so much. But you really should talk to Nathan about this, not me."

Is she telling me she was abused? Why else would she worry about me? "Why have you worried about me so much?"

"You're a lot like me, Cat. Gwen told me they diagnosed

cyclothymia, but that's just bipolarity under another name. We've got it in the blood. Nathan's the expert, though. I'm not in shape to give anyone advice."

Kaiser is mouthing words to me. It looks like he's saying, *Group X.*

"Dr. Malik told me about something called Group X. It sounded really cool. He told me about the film, everything. Were you part of that?"

Ann starts to reply, then catches herself. In the hiss of the open line, I can feel her listening to me. Listening with the concentration of the manic mind in its focused state. It makes my skin crawl. I know the feeling of hyperconcentration you experience when your mind is on that plateau. If you listen to the grass, you can hear it growing.

"Catherine?" she says, her voice so imperious that it could have come from my grandfather. "What are you not telling me?"

"What do you mean?"

"You know exactly what I mean."

Kaiser is watching me anxiously. "I don't. This is me you're talking to, Ann. And this is a dangerous situation we're in. Even Dr. Malik knew that."

"*Knew?*"

I grimace, and Kaiser curses silently.

"You just used the past tense, baby girl." The crafty voice again.

"Well, Dr. Malik's in jail now. And for murder this time."

"I hear your voice, Cat. You're afraid of something. Or someone. Or *for* someone."

"No. You're reading things into this."

"I want to talk to Nathan."

"Come to New Orleans. You can see him at the parish prison."

This time the silence drags forever. "I can't come there until you tell me the truth, Cat."

I grit my teeth and try to keep my voice even. "I've told you what I know. I'm worried that you don't trust—"

The hissing line takes on a deadness like a blanket dropped over my heart. "She hung up on me."

CHAPTER

44

The FBI field office is a four-story brick fortress on the southern shore of Lake Pontchartrain, between Lakefront Airport and the University of New Orleans. We stop at the heavy-iron gate topped with fleur-de-lis, so Kaiser can show an armed guard his credentials. Once inside, we park and hurry through an entrance adorned with flags, black marble, and the FBI motto: *Fidelity, Bravery, Integrity*.

There's red tape to be handled in the vestibule, where a woman waits behind bulletproof polycarbonate glass. Afterward, Kaiser ushers me through a metal detector, and we're on our way to the fourth floor, where the special agent in charge runs the field office and the 150 FBI agents spread across Louisiana.

When we get out of the elevator, Kaiser leads me down a hallway like those in every other corporate headquarters in America. Muted decor, more doors, more hallways. Kaiser knocks on a closed door, then enters and beckons me inside. Beyond the door is an empty office with four cots in it. Two are bare, but two are made up with sheets, blankets, and pillows.

"Best I can do, I'm afraid."

"It's better than a cell in the parish prison."

Kaiser gives me an obligatory chuckle. "I need to go straighten this mess out with the SAC. He may want to talk to you."

"I'm good. Whatever."

"Good or not, I'm going to send up a nurse. Her name is Sandy."

"I'll be asleep before she gets here."

He nods, then starts to leave.

"May I have my cell phone back?"

"Can't do that. Sorry."

"Nobody's read me my rights."

Kaiser's patience is straining at the seams. "Cat, you've obstructed justice and maybe acted as an accessory to multiple murder. If I let you interfere in this case anymore—which your cell phone would make it very easy for you to do—the SAC will throw you out the front gate and give you to the NOPD. And there won't be a damn thing I can do about it. Okay?"

"Fair enough. But you'll tell me if Ann calls?"

"Absolutely. I'll bring your phone in here and have you call her back."

He looks at me as if he's sure I have another question, but I don't. I do, however, have an idea. "I've been thinking about the skull, John."

"What about it?"

"From the very beginning, I figured the bite marks could be staged. Did Sean tell you my theory about the killer using dentures or an articulated model to make the marks?"

A smile touches Kaiser's lips. "Let's say he took partial credit for that."

"Par for the course. Well, my theory proved out. The killer was using the teeth from that skull to make the marks. Next question: Whose DNA have we been testing? Where does the saliva come from? We know it's not Malik's."

Kaiser nods. "Sure, but until we have a suspect, we have nothing to compare our samples to."

"Yeah, but I was thinking . . . saliva contains more than DNA, you know. We need to know everything we can about that saliva."

"Like what? What do you want to do?"

"Some basic nineteenth-century science. Everybody treats DNA analysis as the be-all and end-all of forensics. Fine, great. But the average mouth contains strep bacteria and all kinds of other bugs. Let's take the fresh saliva out of Quentin Baptiste's wounds, put it in a petri dish, and see what grows out. Maybe we'll get a strange germ that can tell us something. Sort of like the way we track where a corpse ate dinner by looking at its stomach contents. Impurities and things, you know?"

Kaiser looks skeptical. "What could we really learn?"

"I don't know. We might find our suspect suffers from a certain disease. We should give it a shot, right? Like Sean calling that bail bondsman back and figuring out that Ann paid Malik's bail."

"You're right. I'll tell the forensic team to do it."

"Tell them quick. Baptiste has the only viable saliva for this, and cultures take time."

"Done." He goes to the door, then turns back to me and speaks in an apologetic voice. "Hey. Are you really pregnant?"

I nod silently.

"Sean's?"

"Yes."

He closes his eyes for a moment, then looks at me again. "Are you going to have it?"

"Yes."

He doesn't blink. "Good for you."

I never saw or heard a nurse come into my room. The Valium carried me away from the waking world like a gentle river of Grey Goose. Maybe my alcohol withdrawal has made me hypersensitive to drugs. Whatever the reason, I slid down the bright coral wall into my dream ocean without interference, and the myriad images of my subconscious surrounded me like children penned up in a house all day.

Time flows forward and backward in my dreams. Not at my whim, of course. If intruders are chasing me and about to grab me from behind with clawed fingers, I can't reverse time and save myself. But events in my dreams don't always unroll in a forward sequence. Sometimes I'm getting younger as my dream life progresses—or *re*gresses, I suppose—turning from nine to eight at a birthday party, for example. I've never gone back beyond eight, though. The age I was when my father died is like an obsidian wall, an immutable fact of physics laid down by Newton or Einstein or even God. The sign on that wall doesn't read BEYOND THIS POINT LIE MONSTERS, like the legend on ancient maps. It reads BEYOND THIS POINT LIES NOTHING.

Nothing. Does such a thing exist? I've heard children ask this question: *Isn't even "nothing" something?* Space is something, isn't it? Time exists there. And gravity. Invisible things, perhaps, but they're real enough to kill you. I existed before I was eight, even though I don't remember it. I know that I existed then the way I know that doctors took out my tonsils while I was under anesthetic. *Something* happened, even if I wasn't mentally present.

I have the scars to prove it.

My scars aren't visible to the naked eye, but they're there. If a child stops speaking for a year, there's a reason. Something hurt me, even if it was only something I saw. What did I see? Eight years of lost images. Did they vanish down a well? Not all of them. I've always had fragments of that history. Images of animals, particularly, have stuck with me. A dog we had when I was very young. A red fox that Pearlie pointed out to me, running low and fast under the trees at Malmaison. Horses on the island, galloping across the sand as if they meant to swim the river to freedom.

And I remember my father. Those images I've hoarded, like gold smuggled out of a war-torn city. My father . . . Luke Ferry. Dancing to the sound of a car radio while he washed his beat-up white Volkswagen. Walking down the driveway of Malmaison with his head down and his hands stuck in his pockets, thinking hard about something. Screaming at my mother to stay out of the barn, even as he pulled me inside with one hand. Watching him from the loft of the barn while he sculpted with a cutting torch, bending the white-hot steel to his will. From where I sat, the fire from that torch looked brighter than the sun, and the roar of it filled my ears. The smell of hay closed around me in the loft, a smell no amount of cleaning could get out of that building. How many afternoons did I spend in that loft, watching him wrestle beauty out of a pile of bars on the floor?

More than he wanted me to.

Daddy didn't always know I was there. Sometimes I crawled up the ladder on the back side of the barn and slipped into the loft that way. It reminded me of black-and-white movies I'd seen about a little Arab boy in the bazaar, spying on people and having glorious adventures. Most times Daddy heard me—his eardrums must have been like butterfly wings—but other times he didn't. When he knew I was there, his head had a different tilt to it, as though he were making sure I could see what he was doing with the torch. I felt so privileged. He'd chosen *me* as his secret sharer, the only one allowed to see how the magician did his tricks. But some nights his head was hard down over his work, and I saw only the sweat running down his neck and back, soaking his white undershirt. On those nights he worked with a fervor I couldn't begin to understand. He worked like a man who hated the linear chunks of metal and was trying to destroy their essence by making them something abstract—something without function, yet meaningful.

I am back there now.

The loft.

With the hay smell and the wasp nests and the mosquitoes that buzzed in during the day to lie in wait for me at night. I don't slap them, because Daddy will hear me. I let them fasten to my skin and begin to fatten with blood, and then I slowly mash them into a paste of black and red.

When the cutting torch dies, the silence in the barn is absolute. In the silence, I hear the rain for the first time. I forgot it was raining. That's why he didn't hear me sneak in. The drops rattle against the tin roof like a barrage of hail, but the hypnotic roar of the torch was enough to drown them out.

Daddy is walking around on the floor, but I can't see him. Craning my neck, I find him squatting on the floor beneath the loft. He's beside one of the timbers that hold up the roof, working some kind of tool under a floorboard. After a moment, he looks around, then pulls the board up from the floor. Then another. And another. He pulls a bag from underneath the floor. It's dark green, like the jeeps I've seen parked behind the National Guard armory when I go to the flea market there.

I've never seen the bag before.

He takes something out of the bag, but I can't see what. A magazine maybe, or a big picture. Then he stands and walks to one of his worktables. His back is to me. He lays the object on the table and reaches down to his middle like he needs to undo his pants to pee. My face feels hot. He's not peeing, because there's no commode or even grass, just the table on the wooden floor.

His right shoulder is flexing the way it does when he's working on metal. Like it will never stop. The rain keeps hitting the roof close over my head, and the sweat keeps running down his back. Then his head goes back like he's staring at the ceiling, but somehow I know his eyes are closed.

I'm scared. I want to run, but my hands and feet are numb.

He turns sideways, and then I see what he's doing, and my heart swells into my throat. I can't breathe. His mouth is hanging slack, and the way it looks makes my stomach flip. When he groans and thrashes his head, something breaks the chains holding my limbs, and I'm suddenly running back to the ladder, running to save my life. My head slams into a board, and I lose my footing, and then I'm falling past the rungs of the ladder, throwing out my arms but catching only raindrops—

"Look, Cat," says Grandpapa, pointing at some trees. "Look at that fawn over there."

When I turn my head, I'm no longer falling out of the barn, but sitting in my grandfather's orange pickup as it rumbles up the low hill toward the pond. I'm back on the island. Fear is still stuffing my heart into my throat, but the smells have changed. The hay is gone, replaced by motor oil, mildew, chewing-tobacco juice, and smoke from a hand-rolled cigarette. It hasn't started to rain yet, but the sky is filled with leaden clouds as heavy as a pregnant cow's belly.

As we trundle over the crest of the hill, Grandpapa turns his head and watches his prize bull mount a cow. Pleasure lights his face. Why is he happy? Is he thinking of the money he'll make from the calf to be conceived? Or does he just like watching the bull thrusting and heaving over the cow? How many times must I watch this same movie?

Ahead, the cows by the pond watch us with dumb indifference. Beyond them the water lies smooth as glass, except where my father floats facedown in it, his arms outspread like Jesus on the cross. I squeeze my hands into fists. I want to close my eyes, but my eyelids don't work. Mute with fear, I point with my finger. Grandpapa squints at the clouds and shakes his head.

"Goddamn rain," he mutters.

As we roll down toward the pond, my father gets to his feet and starts walking across its surface. My heart pounds so loudly I can hear it above the sound of the truck. Daddy holds out his arms to me, then begins unbuttoning his shirt. There's dark hair on his chest. I pull at my grandfather's shirtsleeve, but he's mesmerized by the bull straining over the cow.

"Daddy, don't!" I shout.

He pulls his shirt open. In the middle of his chest is the big sutured Y-incision. To the right of that, the hole where the bullet went in. He puts two fingers into the bullet hole and pulls it open. Again I cover my eyes with my hands, then peer between my fingers. Something is pouring out of the wound like blood, only it's not blood.

It's gray.

"*Look, Kitty Cat,*" he commands. "*I want you to look.*"

This time I obey.

The gray stuff isn't liquid. It's a bunch of pellets, plastic pellets, a stream of them pouring out of my daddy's chest the way they poured out of my stuffed animals whenever I tore one open by accident. Louisiana Rice Creatures were really stuffed with rice in the beginning, but later they switched to plastic pellets. Cheaper, I guess. Or maybe the rice rotted after a while. The pellets pour endlessly out of my father's wound, a hissing river of them hitting the water.

When Daddy is sure I know what they are, he pulls his chest open still wider. Then he reaches into his wound and pulls out a Rice Creature, like a vet delivering a colt from a troubled mare. It's not just any Rice Creature, though. It's my favorite: Lena the Leopardess. The one I put in Daddy's coffin before he was buried, to keep him company in heaven.

I want to run to him and take Lena from his hands, but my door won't open. As I stare, Daddy holds Lena up so I can see her belly. It's messed up somehow. As he nears the edge of the pond, I see that Lena's belly has a stitched Y-incision in it, just like Daddy's chest. With his eyes on mine, he digs his fingers into the thread, rips it apart, then tears open Lena's stomach.

I scream.

Bright red blood pours out of Lena's chest, more blood than any doll could hold. Somehow I know it's my daddy's blood. He turns pale as I stare, then gray, and then his feet begin sinking. The water can't hold him up anymore.

"*Daddy!*" I shriek. "*Wait! I'm coming!*"

He keeps sinking, his face sadder than I've ever seen it.

"*I can save you, Daddy!*"

I jerk as hard as I can on the truck's door handle, but it won't open. I bang my fists on the window until my knuckles split, but it does no good. Then someone with soft hands takes me by the wrists.

"Catherine? Wake up, Cat. It's time to wake up."

I open my eyes.

Hannah Goldman is leaning over my cot, holding me by the wrists. Dr. Goldman has the kindest eyes in the world.

"It's Hannah," she says. "Can you hear me, Cat?"

"Yes." I smile for her, my best smile so she'll know I'm okay. It's easy to be okay with Hannah here, even if it is only a dream.

"I've come to speak to you about something important," she says. I nod understanding. "Of course. What is it?"

"Agent Kaiser asked me to come. I think that was wise of him."

"He's a wise man," I agree. "A very wise man."

Dr. Goldman looks almost as sad as my father. "Cat, you know I believe in honesty and frankness, but life always finds a way to test our beliefs. There's no easy way to tell you this."

I smile encouragement and pat her hand. "It's okay. I'm strong. You know I can take it."

"You are strong." She smiles back. "You may be my strongest patient. What I have to tell you is this. Your aunt Ann is dead."

My smile broadens. "No, she's not. I talked to her today."

"I know you did, dear. But that was yesterday afternoon. You've been sleeping for quite a while. And sometime last night, your aunt drove to DeSalle Island and killed herself by taking an overdose of morphine."

My smile freezes on my face. It's not Dr. Goldman's somber voice or sad eyes that convince me. It's the morphine. And the island.

CHAPTER

45

Hannah Goldman is about fifty, with graying streaks in her hair and deep lines at the corners of her eyes. Her eyes are kind, but the intelligence behind them is ruthless. Sitting under Hannah's gaze, you can feel like a child under the care of a loving mother or a lesser mammal being scrutinized by a scientist bent on dissection. Agent Kaiser was probably right to bring her here, but now that she's broken the news to me about Ann, I want Kaiser. Psychiatry isn't going to solve my current matrix of problems.

I sit up on my cot and set my stockinged feet on the carpeted floor. "Hannah, I appreciate you coming here to give me this news. But I need to ask Agent Kaiser some questions."

"I'll get him for you," she says. "But I want you to promise me two things."

"Okay."

"You'll let me sit in while you talk to him."

"Of course."

"And you'll talk to me alone afterward."

This I don't especially want to do, but it would be rude not to agree. "All right."

Left in the silence of the empty office, I enter a strange state where all the images in my mind spin wildly against each other. Foremost among them is my father bleeding plastic pellets from his chest, then

Lena the Leopardess pouring blood from her torn belly. I don't know what that dream meant, but I have to find out. And to do that, I need Lena in my hands again. Only she's buried in my father's coffin, in Natchez, two hundred miles away.

I have to get out of this building.

The sound of the door opening and John Kaiser's voice merge into one startling mix: *"Bam—Cat, what can I do for you?"*

I stand and face him squarely. "I want the details of my aunt's suicide."

Kaiser glances at Dr. Goldman.

Hannah says, "You don't have to treat her like she's not in the room with us. Cat's used to dealing with stress."

He looks skeptical. "What do you want to know?"

"Does my mother know about it yet?"

"Yes. She's enraged. She thinks Ann's husband murdered her."

"What?"

"Apparently your aunt was in the middle of a bad divorce. The husband wanted to keep her from getting any money. I talked to the guy. I don't think he even knew where DeSalle Island was until I told him. It feels like a suicide to me."

"Suicide," I echo. "In some ways Ann was already dead. She had been for a long time."

"What do you mean by that?" Kaiser asks, but Hannah is nodding.

"I'll tell you in a minute. I want to know exactly where Ann was found, who found her, how she did it, whether she left a note, everything. Forget I'm related to her, okay?"

Kaiser leans against the closed door. "A woman named Louise Butler found her in a one-room building on DeSalle Island. I guess you know all about that island?"

"More than I ever wanted to."

"Apparently Ms. Butler was looking for you. Your grandfather's search for you had been called off, but Louise was in the woods and never got the word. She found your aunt instead."

Despite the horror of this thought, the face of my father's mistress gives me a comforting feeling as it rises behind my eyes, brown and still beautiful at forty-six. I'm glad Louise found Ann, and not Jesse Billups. Thinking of my last afternoon on the island, a cold certainty comes to me.

"Did the building Ann was found in have a tin roof?"

Kaiser's eyes narrow. "How did you know that?"

My hands suddenly feel clammy. "Was she found in the building they call the clinic?"

He nods slowly, waiting for an explanation.

"Tell me how she looked when they found her."

Kaiser glances at Dr. Goldman but answers anyway. "She was naked, lying on the floor by an examining table."

A deep ache begins in my heart. A lot of suicides take off their clothes before killing themselves. But Ann's nakedness wasn't a matter of fastidiousness or infantile regression. "Did she leave a note?"

"No note."

Doing it in the clinic was her note. Kaiser sneaks another glance at Hannah, and I know he's holding something back.

"What is it?" I demand.

"She didn't leave a note, but she did leave something. Before she died, she drew two skulls and crossbones on her lower abdomen, about where her ovaries would be. There was a Sharpie marker lying beside her body."

For the first time, I feel the sting of tears.

"That means something to you?" Kaiser asks.

"Ann was obsessed with having a baby. She never could get pregnant."

"At fifty-six she was obsessed with having a baby?"

"No, but she never got over the failure. My grandfather performed an emergency appendectomy on her in that clinic when she was ten years old. He always said the infection she had then was what made her infertile. That it blocked her fallopian tubes. I think a dye test may have later proved that correct. Anyway, when she finally gave up on having a baby, she died inside."

Kaiser doesn't know what to make of this. I turn to Hannah. "I've been wondering if that appendectomy might really have been an abortion."

Hannah sits in silence, her mind clicking through what she knows of my family. "Ten is too young for pregnancy," she says finally. "I'm sure it's impossible."

"Sexual abuse again," says Kaiser. "That's why Ann was a patient of Malik's, right?"

"We don't know that for sure," I point out. "She could have been seeing him for her manic-depressive disorder."

"Well, we need to know which. I want an autopsy done on her as fast as we can get one. Would a botched abortion be detectable all these years later?"

"Possibly," Hannah says. "That depends on what kind of mistake was made. After forty years, scarring from infection would be difficult to attribute to therapeutic abortion based on pathological findings alone. There's also the complication of possible later abortions. But this is an academic question. If Ann was ten years old, she wasn't pregnant."

"You need to talk to my mother," I say softly. "When it comes to Ann, she's the only one who knows the private details."

Hannah looks puzzled by something. "*Why*," she says deliberately, "was there enough morphine to kill someone in a one-room clinic on a rural island?"

"I asked the same thing," says Kaiser.

"You ever see a chain saw accident?" I ask. "They're as bad as war wounds sometimes. A chain saw can take off an arm or a leg in two seconds."

This seems to satisfy Kaiser, who served in combat in Vietnam.

"What's your next move?" I ask him, wondering how I can get out of here.

"Rush your aunt's autopsy, if I can. Her body is already at the morgue in Jackson, Mississippi. I need to rule out murder. She was too close to Malik to discount that possibility."

"I want to see her autopsy report."

"I'm sure you'll be here when I get it. Carmen Piazza still wants you locked in a cell downtown."

This probably isn't the best time to ask if I can leave.

"I'll tell you what *I* want," Kaiser intones. "I want that film Malik was making. If we find that, we'll find our killer."

"Film?" Hannah asks. "Nathan Malik was making a film?"

"A documentary about sexual abuse and repressed memory," I answer. "It shows a group of female patients reliving sexual abuse, and some other things he wouldn't tell me about. He said it would galvanize the nation on the issue of sexual abuse."

"That's one film I'd like to see."

"Cat thinks the killer is a member of that group of women," says Kaiser. "Malik called them Group X. I think Ann Hilgard may have been part of it."

"Group X?" echoes Hannah. "Strange."

"With Ann and Dr. Malik dead, only that film or surviving members of Group X can tell us who the members are."

Hannah looks oddly at Kaiser. "I sense you have something to ask me."

"I do. Is there any possibility that Cat could have been a member of that group without being aware of it? Dr. Malik suggested that she might suffer from multiple personality disorder."

Hannah looks briefly at me, then back at Kaiser. "Ridiculous. Cat has certainly experienced dissociated states. But the idea that she suffers from full-blown dissociative identity disorder is preposterous. Put that nonsense out of your mind, Agent Kaiser. Nathan Malik had flashes of genius, but he was also a flake."

That's a fucking relief, I say silently.

Kaiser and Hannah are lost in their own musings, but something won't let me focus. It's not grief over Ann. I'm too numb to feel anything about that now. It's a sense of something missing.

"There's something you're not telling me, John."

He looks up and shakes his head. "Why do you think that?"

"I don't know. Have you told me everything about Ann's death? The scene? Did you leave anything out?"

His brows wrinkle. He looks like he's making an honest effort. "She injected the morphine into veins in both arms. That tell you anything?"

"Only that she was serious. What else? Do you have photos from the scene?"

He nods cautiously. "I had the West Feliciana Parish sheriff's department e-mail me their crime-scene stuff. That's how I knew the building had a tin roof. Are you sure you want to see them?"

"Yes."

He glances at Dr. Goldman again. Hannah studies me for a few moments, then says, "Cat's already in shock. If it will help solve the murders, I don't see any point in keeping them from her."

Kaiser promises to be right back with the photos, then leaves the room.

Hannah looks up at me from the cot where she's sitting. "I'm worried about your affect, Cat. You do know you're in shock?"

"I suppose so. I feel numb."

"And you're not drinking?"

"Not for days now."

Her eyes probe me like a metal instrument. "You're not taking your medication, are you?"

I hate to answer this. "No."

"How long?"

"I'm not sure. A week, maybe."

She shakes her head. "I dislike mechanical analogies, but today that's the only thing I can use. Watching you now is exactly like watching a machine. All the biology is working, but you're not present. You've described yourself as being that way when you have sex."

"I know, but this isn't that. I'm like this when I work."

"Always?"

"Yes."

Hannah looks over at the door, as though she hears Kaiser returning. "I was that way at times during medical school. But something about you seems different. And this isn't a normal case, no matter what you tell yourself. You can't pretend you weren't related to Ann. You were. You *are*. In the Faulknerian sense of the past never really being past. Faulkner said that if the past were truly past, there would be no grief or sorrow. Ann was your blood relation, Cat, and she took her own life. Something you've thought of doing yourself many times."

"I have to find the truth, Hannah. That's the only thing that will keep me sane now."

Her gaze doesn't waver. "Will it?"

"It's my only hope."

The door opens, and Kaiser walks in carrying some eight-by-ten photos. Before second thoughts can stop me, I take them from him and shuffle through the stack as I would photos from any crime scene.

Hannah was right. This is not just another case.

The mere sight of the clinic brings on a wave of nausea. A small, tin-roofed building sitting in a sun-scorched field of weeds. A lone fig tree beside it. I can feel splinters being pulled from my hands, tetanus shots being stuck into my shoulder.

The next photo makes me thankful I haven't eaten. It's not gross—no blood and brain matter covering a dinner table, no ejected shell casing lying in the blasted wreck of a human face. It's just my aunt, my once glamorous aunt lying naked on a bare wooden floor, her breasts and thighs sagging like pools of melted wax. Her mouth yaws open in the gape of sleep, eternal sleep this time, and—

"Cat?" Hannah says softly. "Are you all right?"

"Yeah."

It's a downward-angled shot. It shows the legs of the examining table, a pair of brown feet in sandals—probably Louise's—and the molding at the bottom of a cabinet. Just behind Ann's head, there's something rounded and dark, but I can't make out what it is. I slide the photo over and move it to the bottom of the pile.

And my heart stops.

In the next photo—shot from a different angle—a stuffed animal lies on the floor about three feet behind Ann's head. It's not just any animal. It's a turtle. And his name is Thomas. Thomas the Timid Turtle.

"Thomas," I breathe.

"What?" says Kaiser.

I point at the turtle.

Kaiser walks up to see. "Is that turtle important?"

"Thomas was Ann's favorite toy, ever since she was a child."

"I had no idea. Apparently there were several stuffed animals in the room. We figured they were there to let kids hold while they got injections or something."

"They were." Ivy always kept stuffed animals in the clinic. She would hand you one as you came in. But along with the feeling of comfort came a sense of betrayal, because you knew pain was coming soon. Still, you clung to the animal. The pain wasn't his fault. "Thomas didn't live at the clinic. Ann brought him there. I'm surprised she wasn't holding him when she died."

"She may have tried. There's some indication that she started out on the examining table, then fell to the floor after losing consciousness."

I don't know I'm crying until the tears fall onto the obscene photograph, one of hundreds I've studied in the past few years. I never want to see another one again.

"Cat?" says Kaiser.

I shake my head and try to get control, but the tears keep running down my face like they're never going to stop.

CHAPTER
46

Hannah gently takes the photographs from my hands and gives them back to Kaiser. "I think that's enough for now."

"No," I say. "We have to keep going."

"What does the turtle tell you?" asks Kaiser.

I quickly summarize my recurring dream about the pickup truck, the pond, and my father pulling Lena the Leopardess out of his gunshot wound. As I speak, Hannah's eyes focus on me with absolute concentration.

"Jesus," Kaiser says when I finish. "From the point of view of your life, I think that's probably very important. But it's hard to see how it impacts this murder case. It sounds to me like your aunt was molested as a child—just as you were—and this stuffed-animal angle is part of all that. The only relevance to our case is that the sexual abuse is probably what brought Ann into contact with Malik."

I take a step toward Kaiser. "I have to get out of here."

"Why?"

"I have things I need to do."

He glances at Hannah. "Such as?"

"I want to see the stuffed animal I buried with my father. It was my grandfather who suggested that I put Lena into his coffin. To keep him from being lonely, he said."

"You want to exhume your father's body to see a stuffed animal?"

"Yes. It's too much coincidence. Ann kills herself with her favorite stuffed animal. And my grandfather—after killing my father because he supposedly abused me—tells me to bury my favorite stuffed animal in the coffin? I want to get Lena and Thomas together and give them every test known to forensic science. And I want a new autopsy done on my father. You told me his original autopsy report was lost, right?"

"Yes," says Kaiser, watching me as he might a psychotic patient. "But I can't let you leave here. You know that."

"Because?"

"Cat, there are only two options for you. Stay here, or let the NOPD arrest you and put you in jail. You could raise bail, I'm sure, but it might be tomorrow before you got free."

An engine is spinning in my chest, building frantic energy that won't be discharged until I get out of this building and learn what I have to learn. "Can you order the exhumation of my father's body for a new autopsy?"

Kaiser glances at Hannah again, then looks pointedly at me. "I'm not sure what the law is in Mississippi."

"Don't patronize me, John. Is Mississippi law really the point? You're the FBI."

"Expediting your aunt's autopsy is one thing, Cat. She died under suspicious circumstances. She's a material witness to Malik's activities at the very least, and at worst an accessory to murder. Your father, on the other hand, was murdered twenty-three years ago. And though his death intrigues me, it has no clear tie to this case. His military record also happens to be sealed for the next fifteen years. If I tell the SAC that my next big idea is exhuming Luke Ferry to look at a stuffed animal, I'm not going to get a lot of traction."

I look to Hannah for help, but she's silent.

"If you want to analyze Lena the Leopardess, you're going to have to find a way to do it on your own. *After* you get out of here. Okay? The FBI isn't in the business of psychotherapy." Kaiser's tone sounds official, but something in his eyes is speaking to me in a different language.

"Right," I say. "Okay."

He moves to the door. "I only mentioned that Mississippi law thing because sometimes it's not that difficult to get a body exhumed.

By the family, I mean." He opens the door. "I've got a lot of balls in the air right now, one of which is keeping you out of jail. If I hear anything I think you need to know, I'll come tell you. And I'm having some food sent up from the cafeteria. You must be starving."

I'm not hungry, but I tell him thanks anyway.

And then he's gone.

Hannah takes my hand and pulls me down beside her on the cot. Then she puts an arm around me and hugs me like the sister I never had. "That was tough," she says. "You're a tough cookie."

"But?" I ask, dreading the inevitable.

"You want the truth?"

"Yes."

"I think you're very close to cracking."

I put my elbows on my knees. "It's the same old dilemma. Fall off the cliff into depression or start flying into mania. And I have no control over which it will be."

"That's not what I meant," Hannah says gravely. "This time, I'm afraid you'll do neither. This time you could really crack. I'm talking about total psychological collapse. A rubber room, Cat."

"Why? Why is this so different?"

"Because losing your aunt isn't merely an echo of losing your father. It's more like losing yourself. You've always been a sort of shadow of your aunt. Her illness was more extreme than yours, but in essence the same."

Hannah's right, but what am I supposed to do about it? "I haven't told you everything."

Her eyes tell me she knows this already. No patient ever reveals everything.

I recount the dream of seeing my father masturbating in the barn, and the rain hitting the tin roof over my head. She listens impassively until I fall silent.

"Seeing a father masturbating could be traumatic for a little girl," she says, "but that's a normal activity. Depending on what he was looking at while he did it, of course."

"I wonder why I couldn't see that in my dream?"

She shrugs. "Dreams always bring more questions than answers. So . . . you still have the same riddle. 'Who abused me? My father or someone else?'"

"I have to know, Hannah. I have to know whether my father was a hero who died trying to protect me, or a pervert who never really loved me. And the same for my grandfather. On the surface he was the war hero and my father the weirdo, but—"

"It might not be one or the other, you know."

"What do you mean?"

"It might have been both of them, dear."

A fresh layer of fear settles over the dread at the bottom of my soul. "Why do you say that?"

Hannah suddenly seems unsure whether to go on. "Many abuse survivors have been molested by multiple offenders, Cat. If your mother was abused by her father, she may well have married a sexually abusive man. It happens all the time."

"I don't think I could take that."

Hannah squeezes her arm tight around my shoulders. "I hope that's not the answer. But if you're going down this road, you should prepare for the worst."

To keep me from dwelling on this possibility, she changes the subject. "Do you think the green bag from your dream could still be hidden under the barn floor?"

"I don't see why not. I never saw it anywhere but in that dream. And the barn has apparently been locked up tight for some time."

"Why didn't you tell Kaiser about that dream?"

"I don't know. Maybe I want to see what's in that bag before he does." I take Hannah's hand and squeeze it. "Will you help me get out of here?"

She smiles. "You don't need my help. You're not under arrest. Even the FBI can't detain you without arresting you, unless it's on some trumped-up terrorism charge. Your problem is the NOPD."

"They're not a problem if they can't find me."

Hannah's smile vanishes. "You really want to go back to Mississippi?"

"I have to. And I got the feeling Kaiser wants me to exhume my father's body on my own. Did you sense that?"

"Actually, I did. He's very good at nonverbal communication."

"Yeah."

Hannah looks at me seriously for a moment, then giggles like a schoolgirl. "I'll bet he's good in bed."

"I knew you were thinking that."

"No, you didn't. But I think if you managed to slip out of here, Kaiser wouldn't look too hard for you."

"But I can't just walk out with you. There are cameras all over the place, especially around the entrance. You'll have to help me."

"How?"

"I need to use your cell phone."

She takes a silver Motorola from her pocket and hands it to me. Before she can change her mind, I dial Michael Wells's cell phone. For a few moments I think he's not going to answer, but then he does.

"It's Cat."

"Christ, it's about time. Are you all right?"

"Yes and no. My aunt is dead, and things are very crazy right now. I'm in New Orleans, and I need to get back to Natchez. The police aren't looking for me now, but they will be soon. Would it be completely shameless of me to ask you for help again?"

Michael takes a moment to process all this. "Where in New Orleans are you?"

"FBI headquarters."

"Where's that?"

"By the University of New Orleans."

"UNO is by Lakefront Airport."

"Yes. You can see the airport from the windows here." Not from the office I'm in, of course, but from the fourth floor.

"If you can get to Lakefront Airport, I can fly down and get you."

My pulse rate kicks up. "Are you serious?"

"Sure. I've flown in there a dozen times. Last time I watched the Dave Matthews Band at UNO."

"Michael . . . are you sure you can get away?"

"What will the police do if they find you?"

"Put me in jail."

"On what charge?"

"Murder."

"Did you kill anybody?"

"No."

"Then I can get away. I'll have to arrange for coverage, though. Call my cell phone in an hour. I should be airborne and on the way by then. We'll take it from there. If there's any problem with the phones, just get your ass to Lakefront and start watching the planes come in. I'll be in a blue and white Cessna 210. Registry number N324MD."

* * *

By the time I walk into the fourth-floor hallway, Hannah Goldman has been gone for ten minutes. She was to say her good-byes to Kaiser, then slowly make her way down to her car in the parking lot.

My job is to get to the FBI's motor pool without being seen by anyone who knows who I am. Occupying a large part of the building's basement level, the motor pool has huge garage doors that open into the parking lot. I've been down there a couple of times before, when I rolled out with the FBI forensic team on the serial case where I first met Sean.

The elevator is only thirty feet down the hall, and I'm nearly to it when I hear John Kaiser's voice.

"Cat? Where are you going?"

I turn and give him a little wave. He's standing by the office I just left, a tall figure who looks more than anything like a concerned father.

"I feel sick. I need to get to the bathroom."

"Down past the elevator, on the right." He starts walking toward me. "Did the food come? Did that make you sick?"

Someone did bring up a tray of sandwiches after Hannah left, but I didn't touch it. "No, I was about to eat it when I got a wave of nausea."

"That may be from the blow to your head. I was coming to show you this." Kaiser has almost reached me. He's holding something in his hand.

"What is it?"

"Early results on those cultures you asked for. The saliva from the bite marks on Quentin Baptiste."

The dead homicide detective . . . victim number six. "Oh, right. What does it show?"

He hands me the lab report. "You tell me."

I glance over the letters and numbers, trying to pretend that my nerves aren't shot and that my mind is on the piece of paper in my hand rather than on escaping this building. What I see is a microbiological snapshot of an average human mouth. Except for one thing.

"That's weird."

"What?" asks Kaiser.

"Maybe it's a mistake."

"What?"

"Well, twelve hours is early, but we ought to at least see some *Streptococcus mutans* growing. You have that particular strep in abundance in any mouth with teeth in it. *S. mutans* thrives on hard surfaces. It produces the acid that causes cavities."

"And you don't have it there?"

"No."

"Well, if it's not a mistake, what would that mean?"

"It could mean a couple of things. The saliva may have come from someone taking a course of antibiotics. That would disturb the normal flora of the mouth. I'd look for penicillin, or even more likely, penicillin with gentamicin." I try to concentrate on the lab report, but all I can keep in my mind is Hannah Goldman waiting for me downstairs.

"Cat?" prompts Kaiser.

"I'm sorry, I was thinking. This saliva could also have come from an edentulous person."

"What's that?"

I shrug, thinking the answer self-evident. "Someone without teeth."

"Somebody who wears dentures?"

"No. Somebody who owns dentures but doesn't wear them. Dentures have hard surfaces, with cracks and crevices that are ideal for bacterial colonization, just like real teeth. It might be someone who lives alone. Who doesn't feel the need to put in his teeth, because no one ever sees him."

Kaiser looks interested. "Would he necessarily have to be old?"

"God, no. Lots of people have teeth so bad they rot out by their thirties. You might look for somebody who needs dentures but can't afford them."

"A lot of convicts have their teeth pulled in prison," Kaiser reflects. "It makes positive identification harder in subsequent trials."

"Well, maybe this culture will get us somewhere, like I hoped. You can check all the male relatives of the victims for infections, prison records, or for teeth, period. Look, I really need to get to the bathroom."

"Oh, yeah. Sorry."

"May I keep this report?"

"Sure."

I stuff it into my back pocket. "Let's see what grows out after another six hours." *When I'll be long gone.* I pat Kaiser on the arm, then walk quickly up the hall to the bathroom. As I push open the door, I cut my eyes right.

He's no longer in the corridor. Backpedaling fast, I dart to the elevator. The fire stairs are tempting, but this is probably one building where if you open a fire door, all hell breaks loose.

Before the elevator door closes, a blonde woman wearing a blue skirt suit hurries in after me and smiles. I smile back and press the button for the basement. I sense her looking at my clothes. They look pretty rough. Definitely not the uniform of female FBI agents.

"Are you okay?" she asks.

"Oh, yes." I offer my hand. "Catherine Ferry. I've been working the NOMURS case as a consultant for John Kaiser. I'm a forensic odontologist."

She looks impressed and interested. "I heard they found another victim."

"Yes. A cop this time."

"Wow."

The elevator stops on the second floor.

"This is me," she says. "Good luck."

The door opens onto a cube farm with men and women walking purposefully between partitions. When the door closes, I breathe a sigh of relief and sag against the wall. In twenty seconds, the elevator opens to the concrete-floored motor pool.

About a dozen government sedans are parked diagonally against a wall on my left. To my right are two big black Suburbans, the SUVs used by the FBI forensic team. Thirty yards across the basement lot are the big overhead doors that can get me out of the building. I don't see anyone, but there's bound to be someone here.

Something clangs in the emptiness. The sound of a heavy tool being dropped on concrete. Praying that the careless mechanic is underneath a vehicle, I walk briskly across the lot toward the doors. As I near them, I see a large white button not unlike those beside the doors in ERs and surgical suites. I should have a story ready in case someone asks what I'm doing down here, but I don't. If someone challenges me, I'll just have to wing it.

I hit the big button, and an overhead chain drive lifts the big door in front of me with no more fuss than my garage door at home. When it's four feet off the ground, I duck under it and walk quickly up the ramp to the outdoor parking lot.

Hannah drives a white 5-series BMW, but I don't see it.

Bearing right, toward the main entrance of the field office, I watch the lines of parked cars. Sure enough, Hannah's white Beemer backs out of a space not far away, then pulls forward and stops beside me. Her window is open. Glancing over the roofs of the parked cars, I see the guard house at the main gate. I don't know whether the guard is watching me, but he's not going to let me ride out with Hannah without checking upstairs first.

"Did you open your trunk?" I ask her through the window.

"Yes, but I'm afraid you'll suffocate."

I walk to the back of her car and lift the trunk lid as though retrieving something. Then I take a deep breath, climb into the small space, fold myself almost double, and close the trunk lid over my head.

I have a few mental problems, but claustrophobia isn't one of them. I wouldn't be much of a free diver if I couldn't stand being closed into small spaces. People don't think of the ocean as a small space, but when you're three hundred feet beneath it, with cold water trying to crush you into jelly, you feel pretty closed in.

Hannah has stopped at the gate.

Shutting my eyes in the dark, I send my mind to its secret haven, the bright coral wall where I dive and dive until the blue turns black, and rapture blurs my sense of separation from the water until my mind takes in the whole of creation. If the guard discovers me in this trunk, it won't be because he sensed my presence.

I'm not even here.

The BMW jerks forward, pulling me out of my trance. After a couple of bumps, we're rolling along at a good clip. With each stop, I'm sure Hannah is going to get out and free me from the trunk, but she doesn't. For one irrational moment I'm terrified she's going to turn me over to the NOPD, but that's crazy. She's just finding a safe place to let me out.

At last the car stops and doesn't start again.

I hear her door open and close. Then the trunk lid pops open, and sunlight spears my retinas. A backlit silhouette takes my hand and helps me out of the trunk. The ligaments in my knees creak like horsehair ropes as I unfold them.

"You are really something," Hannah says. "I feel like Ingrid Bergman."

We're not at the airport. We're in the parking lot of a small, upscale shopping center. I've been here a few times, shopping for clothes.

Hannah notices my concern. "You'll attract a lot less attention here than at Lakefront Airport. That's not a busy place." She stuffs some paper into my hand. "That's eighty dollars. Call a cab at the last minute to take you to the airport. It's less than ten minutes away."

I hug her hard, then pull away. "Get out of here, Ingrid. You've done enough already."

Hannah takes my right hand in both of hers and squeezes tight. "You're close to finding out the truth, Cat. But don't expect a blinding flash of insight, or instant peace. In cases like yours, getting the true facts is only the beginning. Many sexual abuse survivors never get the kind of resolution they're looking for."

"I've been lost for a long time, Hannah. A beginning sounds pretty good to me."

She smiles sadly, then gets into her car and drives away. I look down at my watch and wonder if Michael is airborne yet.

I need to find a pay phone.

CHAPTER

47

I'm five thousand feet over the Mississippi River, flying north at two hundred miles per hour. Michael Wells is beside me, piloting his Cessna as if he'd rather be doing this than anything else in the world. Natchez is thirty minutes ahead.

The shocks of the past twenty-four hours have pushed me to the point that fl;ight in a small plane produces no airsickness at all.

"What are you going to do now?" he asks, his face somber.

"What I should have done in the beginning. Find out who killed my father. I'm going to exhume his body."

Michael looks at me like I've taken leave of my senses. "What will you learn from that?"

"For one thing, it will give me DNA to compare against any body fluids I find on my bedroom floor. I'm hoping I'll find preserved semen."

"Are you going to work the bedroom yourself?"

"No. I'm going to bring in a first-string team to do it, no matter what my grandfather says. I'm also going into the barn to see if my father's green bag is still under the floor. It's padlocked, but I shouldn't have much trouble breaking in."

"Do you think that green bag really exists?"

"Absolutely."

"Technically the barn is Kirkland's property, isn't it?"

"I'm not sure, actually. Some of the old DeSalle holdings are held in trust for me. I don't really know what Grandpapa owns and what he manages for my mother and me. It's very complicated. But if he tries to stop me, I'll go to the DA and make it an official murder investigation. It's not my father's body I really want, though. It's Lena."

Michael looks away from the Plexiglas windscreen long enough for me to see his confusion. "Your stuffed leopard?"

"Leopardess. I don't know what she'll tell me, but I know she's important. May I use your cell phone?"

He unclips it from his belt and hands it to me. My pride tells me not to do what I'm about to do, but I have no choice. I dial Sean Regan's cell number.

"Detective Sergeant Regan," he says.

"It's Cat."

"Jesus. They've got a statewide manhunt going for you, and you call my cell phone?"

"Sorry to be an inconvenience."

"Shit, it's not that. But Karen wants to see copies of my cell phone bill from now on. I'm sure Piazza will be reviewing it, too."

So, the women in Sean's life finally got wise to him. "Well, I'm sorry. This is a business call."

"Somehow I knew that."

"I need you to do me a favor, Sean, no questions asked."

"What favor?"

"That sounded like a question."

In the silence that follows, I sense him remembering what it's like to deal with me on a daily basis. "Okay, Cat. Whatever it is, I'll do it."

"Thanks. You know my aunt committed suicide last night?"

"I heard. I'm sorry."

"There's going to be an autopsy today in Jackson, Mississippi. Kaiser's expediting it. I need to see that report, or at least know what the findings are."

"Didn't Kaiser tell you I've been suspended from the department?"

"Yes, but I know you're still wired into the task force. Like knowing my aunt committed suicide. You're already angling for a way back into this case. And if you help me, I might be able to give you one."

More silence. "You need an actual copy of the autopsy report?"

"Whatever you can get. I'm particularly interested in anything the pathologist finds out about Ann's reproductive organs. Scarring, old operations, anything like that."

"Uh-huh." Sean sounds anything but excited.

"I need this as fast as you can get it. Like yesterday."

"I can't give you what I don't have yet."

"I know. I just want you to understand—"

"Cat?"

"*What?*" I snap, realizing I'm trying to avoid any personal conversation whatever.

"How are you doing? I mean with the baby and all."

Anger surges up from a well deep within me, darker and more intense than I could have imagined. "Fine," I say in a taut voice. "You don't need to worry about me. Us. Whatever. I'm not your problem anymore."

"You never were a problem."

Cut the cord, orders the voice in my head. "We both know that's a lie. Look . . . good luck piecing your life back together."

"Yeah. Hey, I'll get that report for you."

"Thanks."

"I miss you, Cat."

Not badly enough. "Hurry, Sean."

I hang up and punch in my mother's cell phone number. As it rings, I feel Sean touch my arm. Then I realize it's not Sean, but Michael Wells. For a moment I actually forgot I was sitting beside him in his plane.

"You're crying," Michael says. "Are you okay?"

"I don't think 'okay' is something to be aspired to at a time like this. I just have to keep moving forward."

He withdraws his hand and goes back to flying.

Just as I expect to be kicked over to voice mail, my mother answers in a sleepy voice that makes me think *sedatives.*

"Dr. Wells?" she says.

"No, it's Cat."

"Cat?" A brief pause. "I don't understand. Are you at Dr. Wells's house?"

"No. Mom, listen, I know about Ann."

"Well, I figured you must have heard by now."

"How are you doing?"

"Fine, I suppose. Considering. I'm at work, and it's a very busy time for me. Which is good, I guess."

At work? She sounds like she just woke up from surgery.

"I always knew this was a possibility with Ann," she says. "One of her doctors even told me to prepare for it. He said that if this ever happened, I should know ahead of time that there was nothing I could have done to prevent it."

"But is that how you really feel?"

She sighs heavily, and in the background I hear the Muzak she runs in her shop. "I don't know. Look, I told you, I'm really busy today. I have to get out to Dunlieth to show the owner some new drapery fabrics."

"Mom, I need to talk to you. Will you be at home this afternoon?"

"That depends on how long Dunlieth takes, doesn't it?"

"Please try to be home. This is no day to be worrying about work."

"Life goes on, Cat. I figured you of all people knew that."

"What about the funeral arrangements?"

"Your grandfather's taking care of all that."

Of course. Nothing but the best for one of my daughters . . .

"I don't mind talking to you," she says, "but I don't want you to start trying to tell me how to feel about this. I deal with my own feelings in my own way. You know that."

"Or you don't deal with them."

Chilly silence. "I may not wear my heart on my sleeve like some people, but I've managed just fine so far."

"Have you, Mom? Has life really been fine all these years?"

"I think I've done a pretty good job, considering the obstacles life put in my way."

God . . . "How is Pearlie taking it?"

"I don't know. She's gone to the island. Deserted me with barely a word."

This throws me. "The island? Pearlie hates the island."

"Well, that's where she went, right after she heard the news about Ann. I've got to go, Cat. If I don't see you later, make sure you're at that funeral. Ann would want you there."

Like I would miss my aunt's funeral? "Mom, why did I go riding in the orange truck with Grandpapa on the island?"

"What do you mean?"

"I've been having this dream about riding in that old truck with him, and it's always raining."

"Ohhh," she says, her voice suddenly musical. "Daddy always got so tense when it rained, because no work could be done. You were the only one who could calm him down. He'd ride around the island showing you the birds and cattle and deer, and when he got back, he'd be tolerable to live with again. I think children are the only thing that keep men from being altogether savage. I just—"

"Mom," I cut in, stopping what could become an endless flow. "Try to come home this afternoon, okay?"

"Bye-bye, darling."

I hang up and pass the phone back to Michael, more dazed than upset. John Kaiser described my mother as furious over Ann's death, and suspicious that she'd been murdered by her husband. Now Mom sounds like she's on Thorazine. She often sounded that way when I was a child. Distracted, bored, out of it. *Sedated.* For some reason, I sense my grandfather's hand in this. How easy it would be for him to give her a shot and remove the inconvenience of her emotions from his life.

"Cat?"

"I'm fine, Michael. Can you fly us over the island? Is it too far out of the way?"

"Well, the river's just over the horizon to our left. You said the island is opposite Angola prison?"

"Just south of it."

He banks the Cessna in a wide arc to the west, and almost immediately I see the silver line of the river ahead.

"Can you fly low?"

"Sure. We can buzz the treetops."

"No thanks. Just low enough to make out cars and people."

Michael laughs and begins descending.

Soon the river is a great silver serpent slithering across a vast green floor. On the near shore, endless ranks of trees march over the hills. On the far bank, flat fields of cotton and soybeans stretch as far as the eye can see. The river cuts through the land with implacable abandon, bisecting the continent almost as an afterthought.

"Can you believe we were right down there the night before last?" I ask. "Or all that's happened since then?"

Michael tilts the plane a little and looks down. "I can't believe you swam that river. I mean *shit*."

"Do you see an island?"

"I see a half dozen of them."

"This one's four miles long."

Michael whistles low. "I think I was looking right at it without knowing it. There's Angola prison. So that must be DeSalle Island."

I can't see it from my side, and Michael quickly realizes this. He banks and drops the nose, and suddenly we're boring in on the long, humped mass of the island like a fighter plane on a strafing run.

"How high are we?"

"I'm going to stay at four hundred feet. You can see all you need to from there."

In a matter of seconds, we're roaring over the island. I've seen it from the air before: once long ago from the cockpit of a crop duster, then later from the basket of a hot-air balloon. Today's view reminds me of that first trip, the landscape below flashing past at a hundred miles an hour. I see the hunting camp, the lake, the lodge, the pastures and the pond, and then we're banking left to avoid what might be restricted airspace over Angola.

"Can you make another pass?"

"Sure. What are you looking for?"

"A car. A blue Cadillac."

"I'll climb to a thousand feet. You'll have a better view between the trees."

Michael executes a 360-degree turn, climbing as he goes. This time the island looks more like a satellite photo, the chaos caused by proximity now softened into geometric patterns. I see the road that runs the perimeter of the island and the branch that cuts south of the hunting camp, widening into an open space near the cluster of cabins that house the workers. Four white pickups are parked by the cabins. To the left of them, a baby blue sedan stands gleaming in the sun.

Pearlie's Cadillac.

"Okay!" I tell Michael. "Let's go home."

"You saw the car?"

I nod and point northward, toward Natchez. I don't really feel like talking now. I just want to know what drove Pearlie Washington to travel to the island where she was born, a place where, according to her, she is no longer welcome. One more mystery among many. Yet something tells me that if I could read Pearlie's mind, all the other mysteries would be solved.

CHAPTER

48

The Natchez airport is a tiny facility, two runways and a brick administration building laid out near the origin of the Natchez Trace. Michael makes a perfect three-point landing, then transfers me to his Expedition, and within fifteen minutes we're approaching the driveway of Malmaison. The sight of the oak-bordered drive with its pink Pilgrimage tour sign gives me a strange feeling of foreboding.

"You want me to drive up to the house?" he asks.

I wave him past the opening in the trees. "Let's go to your house and walk through the woods to the barn. If Billy Neal and my grandfather are there, I'd rather have some privacy for this."

Michael pulls into Brookwood and drives to the back of the subdivision, where his house stands quietly under the trees.

"Do you have bolt cutters or anything?"

He shakes his head. "I may have a hacksaw."

"That could work. What about an ax?"

"Yeah. We going to tear the place down?"

"Be prepared. Weren't you a Boy Scout?"

Michael actually blushes when he says no.

Three minutes later, we're jogging through the trees toward Malmaison. I'm carrying the hacksaw, he the ax. When I sight the main house, I bear right, toward the low-lying land bordering the bayou at the back of the property. The city of Natchez is built on hills transected by bayous and deep gullies, a secret network of waterways known by the children but forgotten by adults. Most adults, anyway. I still know them all.

We approach the barn from the side, then circle around back, so as to be shielded from anyone glancing down from the parking lot behind the slave quarters. The wall boards are dry and weathered gray, but the door still resists a stout pull. I lay the hacksaw blade against the padlock and set to work. When the sweat begins pouring off my face, Michael takes over the saw. The cords and muscles in his forearms bulge as he works, and it strikes me that Michael is stronger than he looks—definitely not the fat boy I remembered from high school.

"There," he says, blowing metal shavings away from the cut. "Give me the ax."

I pass it to him. With the blunt side of the head, he bashes the lock off the heavy hasp. "Open sesame," he says.

Then he pulls open the door.

My indrawn breath remains locked in my chest.

Inside the barn are more Luke Ferry sculptures than I've ever seen gathered in one place. There must be twenty, most of them taller than my head, and some twenty feet high.

"Wow," Michael whispers. "It's like a museum. A private museum."

The sight of all that polished metal wrought into abstract yet beautiful forms by my father's hands is almost more than I can bear. When the smell hits me—the scent of hay that Daddy could never get out of the barn—my knees go weak. Even his tools are here, his cutting torch with its big gas cylinders, his metal saw . . .

"Cat? Are you okay?"

I clutch Michael's arm and take a step into the barn. "I didn't need to look at this stuff right now. It's too much, you know?"

"Yeah. It's powerful even for me, and I didn't know the guy. Did you know all this was here?"

"Not like this. My grandfather must have lost his mind. He never liked my father's work. Now, it's like he's cornering the market."

"Do you still want to look for the bag?"

"Hell, yes. That's why we're here."

I quickly thread my way through the sculptures to the foot of the timber post that my father walked to in my dream. It's uncanny how certain I feel that I'm standing in the right place. If that bag is beneath these boards, my dream was just as Nathan Malik described a repressed memory: buried deeply, but intact. And *true*.

"The ax?"

Michael passes me the ax like a nurse passing a retractor to a surgeon. With the head, I press down on one end of the first board I saw my father touch in my dream. When the other end of the board lifts a little, my heartbeat stutters. I catch that end of the board with my shoe, hold it in place, then reach down and pull the board out of the floor.

"Look at that," Michael whispers.

My hand tingles as I slip it into the darkness beneath the floor. Then it closes around dry, rubbery fabric. The bag. As I pull on the neck of the bag, two more floorboards come up with it, exposing an olive drab sack that looks as if it holds nothing more than old laundry.

"I think we just proved that repressed memories exist," I say.

Instead of poking blindly through the bag with my hand, I carefully shake out its contents on the floor. The first thing that falls out is a magazine. *Playboy*. It's dated 1970 and boasts the Playmate of the Year on its cover. Relief washes through me.

"This must be what he was looking at in my dream."

"What?" says Michael. "You didn't say anything about a *Playboy* magazine."

"It's nothing. This is a good thing."

"Why?"

"It's *normal*."

"Oh. I get it."

A miniature photo album for storing snapshots follows the magazine out, and my throat tightens a little. Then comes the sketchbook Louise told me about. Next, a small stack of envelopes held together with a yellow ribbon, followed by a sheaf of maps, some of them laminated. The top envelope in the stack of letters is addressed to Luke Ferry, and the return address is Malmaison. The canceled stamp is dated 1969. The bag feels empty now, but when I shake it hard, some rotten prunes strung together on a wire fall out on the floor. A shield-shaped patch falls beside them. The patch shows an eagle's head, and above that, a scoped rifle with the word SNIPER monogrammed in yellow thread above it.

"Hundred and First Airborne," says Michael.

"What?"

"That eagle. The Screaming Eagles, that's what they call the Hundred and First. I saw that eagle emblem all the time on that HBO miniseries *Band of Brothers*. Was your dad in the Airborne?"

"Yeah. I just found out the other day."

Michael flips through the *Playboy* as I go through the stack of letters. Most are from my mother to my father, some written from Natchez, but most from University, Mississippi, the post office of Ole Miss. My mother went to school there while my dad was in the army, but she didn't even manage a full year before he was wounded.

"Like what you see?" I ask Michael, who's still looking at the *Playboy*.

"It's funny. So dated. The cameras and the cars."

"Yeah, I'm sure that's what you're looking at."

"Well, Lola Falana doesn't look too bad here, I must admit."

"Lola Falana's black, right?"

"Mm-hm." He holds up the magazine. I see a short but well-shaped woman with an Afro riding a horse.

Tying the envelopes back together with the ribbon, I glance at the rotten prunes. Desiccated, wrinkled, and black, they look like something I might have brought home in my trick-or-treat bag in the days before Halloween candy was store-bought. The book of pictures seems the next logical choice, but I'm not ready for that yet. Passing over them, I rummage through the maps. The top one shows the Vietnamese-Cambodian border west of Saigon. The next shows something called the A Shau Valley. This map has handwritten names in English: Eagle's Nest; Berchtesgaden; Currahee; Hamburger Hill. There are elevations scrawled beside some of the names: OBJ Perry— 639; OBJ Hoptown—670; Eagle's Nest—1,487. Below the English names are typed words in another language: *Dong So; Ale Ninh; Rao Lao.* I have a feeling a lot of American boys died at those places, and that maybe they weren't supposed to be there. Sure enough, as I study the map some more, I realize I'm looking at the border area between Vietnam and Laos.

"My God," Michael exclaims, holding up the *Playboy*. "An interview with Tiny Tim. And a story by Nelson Algren. This is bizarre. Maybe your dad did buy this for the articles."

"You're a big help."

"Sorry. I didn't think you'd want me looking at that stuff until you'd checked it out."

"You're right. I'm sorry."

I'm down to the sketchbook and the photo album. I'm about to start working through the photos when Michael speaks again, this time in a voice I barely recognize.

"Cat?"

When I look up, his face is pale. "What is it?"

He shakes his head, then passes the magazine to me. Stuck between two pages are three photographs. Each one shows a different child. Two are boys, aged about six or seven. The third photo shows a dark-haired girl of about five.

All of the children are naked.

"Is that you?" Michael asks.

My eyes are swimming in tears. "No."

The boy in one photo looks oblivious to the camera, but the other boy looks scared. He's holding his little penis as though he's about to urinate, but I can almost see a man standing behind the camera, ordering him to touch himself.

My stomach is trying to come up. I want to stop it, but I can't. Dropping the magazine on the floor, I get to my feet, run to a corner, and puke my guts out. As I come up for air, spitting and dry-heaving, something touches my arm.

I whirl and lash out, striking Michael hard across the face.

He blinks in surprise but doesn't try to defend himself. I draw back my arm again and swing at his face with all my strength. Something clamps around my wrist and pins it in midair.

Michael's hand.

"Cat?" he says softly. "It's me. It's Michael."

A scream bursts from my throat with the force of an explosion. From deeper than my chest, really, deeper even than my diaphragm. The scream is what my fist would have been had it smashed into Michael's face. A bolt of rage and humiliation and other things I can't even name. When the scream finally dies, my hand still quivers an inch from his face.

"I think we should get out of here," he says. "We can talk about this stuff at my house."

I don't respond.

"I'll get the bag. We should take it with us."

He pushes my fist down to my waist, then lets it go and kneels on the floor. He puts everything back into the bag, then leads me by the wrist back through the sculptures, toward the barn door.

I stop in my tracks.

Hanging from a rafter above me is a sculpture I didn't see on my way in. It was shielded from view by the floor of the loft. But now I see it. It's a hanged man. Stylized, but a hanged man all the same. Life-size, and ugly as death. The face has the anonymous oval shape that the statue in Louise's house did, but the body is fuller. At first I think of suicide, but something about the sculpture has a more official look. As if the man was just hanged for some offense. The steel rope around his neck rises in a perfect line that terminates in a hook, which would allow it to be hung from almost anything.

"I've never seen that before. I thought I'd seen everything he ever did."

No, says a voice in my head. *You'd never seen the pieces in Louise's house either.*

"That's different," I say.

Is it? Apparently, your father did a lot of things you never knew about. Or never remembered . . .

"Cat?" says Michael. "Are you talking to me?"

"What?"

"Come on. That scream was loud."

He drags me toward the door, but my eyes remain locked on the hanged man.

CHAPTER
49

As Michael pulls me through the trees toward Brookwood, I keep thinking of my father walking on water in my dream. When I woke, I felt certain that he was trying to tell me something. To help me. To send me the secret truth of his life and mine. But maybe he wasn't. Maybe he was trying to apologize for something. Not literally, of course. I know he's not communicating to me from the dead or anything like that. It's my subconscious creating these images. And yet . . .

"I'm sorry I flipped out," I say. "You don't have to stay with me."

"Don't be ridiculous," says Michael. "You have no business being alone right now."

We're never going to reach Brookwood. My legs feel full of sand, and the humidity hanging in the air makes it difficult to extract oxygen from it. "I need to talk to my mother."

"Why?"

"She's my father's next of kin. I can't see getting any kind of exhumation permit without her support."

"Cat, you just looked at three Polaroids and a sculpture and you freaked out. Now you're talking about looking at your father's corpse? After it's been decomposing for over twenty years?"

I shudder. "That will be easier to look at than those pictures."

"Cat—"

"What else can I do, Michael? I have to keep digging until I uncover the truth. If I don't, I'll go mad."

He stares at me with eyes full of pity and compassion. "I think you should talk to Tom Cage before you do anything else."

"Dr. Cage?"

"Yes. Remember what he told me? Your dad confided in him quite a bit about the war. And Tom seemed to think a great deal of Luke. I think you need to hear what Tom has to say."

"Nobody's going to confess to their family doctor that they molested their own daughter."

"Don't be so sure. In the old days, the family doctor was like a priest. Especially in the South. He was the only person some people could legitimately unburden themselves to."

I stop walking and sag against the gray trunk of an oak tree.

"What's the matter?" Michael asks.

"Can you bring the car?"

He studies me for several moments. I see the doctor's brain behind his eyes, searching me for signs of . . . what?

"Do you promise to stay here until I get here?"

"Of course. What are you worried about?"

"I'm worried that all this stress will trigger a manic state. If it does, you won't know what you're doing. And I think you'll kill yourself one way or another."

I slide down the tree trunk and settle onto the soft ground. The pain of the bark scraping my back is strangely welcome. "Please, Michael."

"I'll be back in two minutes."

As soon as he disappears, I dump the contents of my father's bag on the ground in front of me. The *Playboy,* the maps, the letters, the prunes, the sniper patch, the sketchbook, the spiral album of snapshots. I hold my breath as I open the album, with its photos tucked into plastic sleeves for posterity. I've never been more afraid to look at something in my life. If I find more photographs of children, I'll simply keep holding my breath until I pass out. I've failed at that before, but today . . .

The first photograph shows a white-tailed deer in low light, a buck with ten antler points. Relief almost makes me exhale, but I don't. Every photo in this book is a potential horror.

The next picture shows a black bear cub. The one after, a cottonmouth moccasin coiled around a cypress tree.

My heart stutters in my chest.

The next photo shows a naked brown body. But it's not a child. Not a prepubescent one, anyway. It's Louise Butler, thirty years younger than when I talked to her in her little house on the island. She can't possibly be eighteen in this picture. She's standing on the edge of the river at sunset, facing the camera without a trace of shame. The grace and power of her nude body make Lola Falana on the pages of *Playboy* seem common.

I flip the page.

Louise again, at river's edge, this time sitting in profile against the sunset in what looks like the lotus position.

My mouth goes dry at the next image. In it, my father stands with one arm around Louise's waist. She's naked, but he's wearing an old pair of denim cutoffs and nothing else. Bronzed by the sun, he looks as fit and happy as I ever saw him in life. The image is slightly off-kilter, as though he had set the camera on a log and shot the photo with a timer. I never saw him look that happy when he was with my mother.

The next photo shows several black children playing in a dusty road, but they're all wearing clothes. As I flip through the little binder, the images blend into a montage of life on the island. Not the privileged life I knew as the granddaughter of Dr. and Mrs. Kirkland, but the daily life of the blacks who lived there year-round. One photo shows Daddy with a young black man—Jesse Billups with a 'fro?—sitting on a porch playing box guitars. Bottles of cheap wine stand on the porch rail, and a heavy black woman with pendulous breasts dances barefoot on the ground. Luke has a glass bottleneck on the third finger of his left hand. I can almost hear the cutting wail of the notes as he draws the slide quivering along the strings.

The last photograph is of me.

I'm sitting on the floor of the barn with my legs crossed, much like Louise in her lotus photo. My elbows are on my knees, my chin in my hands, and I'm staring into the lens with big round eyes that look exactly like my father's. I look more at peace in that picture than I've ever felt in my life.

I look about two years old.

What happened to me after that? What took away the peace in those eyes? *Who* took it away? The person who shot this picture?

With a long exhalation of relief, I drop the album. It falls beside the rotten prunes on the wire. There's something revolting about keeping food stuffed in a bag beneath a floor. The prunes have an especially nasty look, as though they were being saved for some reason beyond the ken of normal human beings. A necklace, maybe, like something a peasant would use to ward off vampires.

"Miss Catherine? That you over there?"

A black man in grease-stained khaki work clothes has appeared among the trees. It's Mose, the yardman. After so many years at Malmaison, he moves among these trees like a ghost. He and Daddy must have run into each other many times on their solitary forays under the canopy of oaks.

"It's me, Mose."

"You all right? You fall down or something?"

"I'm just resting."

He moves closer, but his advance is solicitous, the way Pearlie moves around houseguests who don't know her. Mose can't be much younger than my grandfather, and time has worn him down to a bent nub, like a tree that finally gives way to decades of wind and bugs and rain. The scleras of his eyes are yellow, and gray stubble grows high up his cheeks. It's hard to imagine that I once saw this man carry railroad ties across his shoulders.

"What you got there?" Mose asks. "You drawing pictures?"

He's noticed the sketchbook, the one artifact of the bag that I haven't yet examined. "I'm just looking at some old pictures my father took."

He nods agreeably, but then his eyes focus on something else. "What's that there?"

He's pointing at the prunes. "Some kind of rotten food. I think it's prunes."

Mose bends and picks up the string of blackened fruit. He studies one, pinches it between his fingers, then brings it to his nose and sniffs it.

"Mose, you're a braver man than I."

He laughs. "You ain't no man. You a girl."

I always wondered if Mose was simpleminded, but I've never known for sure.

"These ain't prunes." He places one of the blackened things between his front teeth and bites down, testing its texture. "This here be hide."

"Hide?"

"Skin. Some kind of animal skin. Chunks of something."

"Some kind of hunting trophy, maybe?"

Mose shrugs. "Something like that, I reckon."

As he hands me the necklace, the words of the grizzled vet from the Vietnam Veterans Building come back to me: *A lot of Hollywood movies don't show nothing* but *grunts cutting off ears and killing women and kids. And some of that happened, I won't lie. . . .*

I stuff the necklace quickly into the bag, nausea rolling through my stomach.

"Miss Catherine? You sure you all right?"

I nod and begin gathering the rest of my father's things. Far behind Mose, I see Michael's Expedition carefully negotiating its way through the trees.

"Do you know anything about DeSalle Island, Mose?"

His face wrinkles in thought. "Not no more, I don't."

"But you did?"

"Well, I was born down there, wasn't I?"

A current of excitement goes through me. "You were born on the island?"

"Sho was. I think everybody who ever worked up here for your family was born on the island. Dr. Kirkland always saying nobody knows how to work no more. He 'bout right, too. He say people from the island still do a day's work for a day's pay."

Poverty wages, probably. "Do you like my grandfather, Mose?"

"Oh, yes, ma'am. Dr. Kirkland been real good to me."

"I think you know what I mean."

Mose looks around as though someone might be eavesdropping. "You know your granddaddy, Miss Catherine. He a tough man, and he know how to squeeze a nickel till the buffalo shits—pardon my language."

I say nothing, leaving a vacuum that Mose feels compelled to fill.

"Dr. Kirkland be kind of like that story I heard a long time ago. The plantation owner gives a slave a pint of whiskey. Another slave asks how he liked it, and the first slave says, 'Well, if it'd been any better, he wouldn't have give it to me, and if it'd been any worse, I couldn't have drunk it."

Mose isn't simpleminded at all.

"Dr. Kirkland takes care of the people on the island, though," he adds quickly. "They better off than a lot of black folks here in town."

"What about my father, Mose?"

He looks confused for a minute. "Mr. Luke, you mean?"

"Yes."

He smiles broadly, revealing tobacco-stained teeth. "Mr. Luke always had a good word for me when he passed. Sometimes he gave me a smoke off whatever he was smoking, too. If you know what I mean."

"I do."

"I liked ol' Luke, but I had to be careful around him. Dr. Kirkland didn't like him none at all."

Michael's Expedition is close now, threading its way through the trees like a tank wary of land mines. "Did you like the island, Mose?"

He shrugs. "Didn't know nothing else back then. I wouldn't go back now, though. I like my TV in the evenings. And I don't like that river. Too many people done died in that water."

"Did you know somebody who drowned?"

"I had a cousin drown in it. Sho did."

"Girl or boy?"

"Boy. Name of Enos. But I believe a little girl drowned some years before that, too."

"Do you think the island is a bad place?"

Mose squints at me as though trying to make out something far away. "What you mean, Miss Catherine?"

"Is there something bad there? Something you might not be able to explain, but that you just feel? I used to feel something like that there."

The yardman closes his eyes. After a moment, a little shudder goes through him. Then he opens his eyes and looks at me like a little boy. "When I was young, the old folks used to say killers from the prison roamed the roads at night. From Angola, you know? Like they'd slip out of the prison at night, float over to the island, and walk the roads looking for children. All that seems like a fairy story now, something they used to scare us. But still, a lot of kids wouldn't get near them roads anytime round dark, and not even in the daytime by themselves."

"Why not?"

He shrugs again. "That's just how it was. You'd have to ask some-body else the why of it. But I'll tell you this . . . I got me a lot of kin down there, and I hardly been back there in forty years. And now that you ask me, I don't care if I never go back again."

As Michael's Expedition rumbles up beside Mose, the yardman gives me a wave and ambles off through the trees. By the time Michael rolls down his window, Mose has vanished. Like my father, he is another ghost of Malmaison.

I take up Luke Ferry's bag of secrets and climb into the SUV.

CHAPTER

50

Michael Wells and I are sitting on a leather couch in the private office of Dr. Tom Cage, a general practitioner in Natchez for more than forty years. Bookshelves line all four walls, some stuffed with medical treatises, others with histories of the Civil War. There's a stack of medical charts a foot high on Dr. Cage's desk, the bane of every physician. A half-painted lead soldier holding a musket stands in the shadow of the charts, a bottle of gray paint beside him. Like us, he seems to be waiting for the doctor to appear.

But what holds my attention now, what I've hardly been able to take my eyes off since arriving, is the polished white skull being used as a bookend in the shelf behind Dr. Cage's desk. The empty eye sockets stare at me with what looks like mockery, reminding me yet again that Nathan Malik is dead, that the murders in New Orleans remain unsolved, and that I am still a suspect.

Since finding the Polaroids of the naked children in my father's bag, I've been unable to think clearly. The voices that tormented me long ago have returned, a susurrant undercurrent of vicious commentary that I cannot silence. More disturbing, something deep within me seems to have cracked, leaving me broken in a way I cannot begin to mend. What is broken, I think, is my faith—my desperate hope that despite what Grandpapa told me, my father could not have done such terrible things to me.

But pictures don't lie.

Michael has done all he can to ease my anxiety. Though he believes it would be a mistake to exhume my father's body, he telephoned his attorney during the drive over and asked what was required to accomplish such a thing. There's no law in Mississippi governing the exhumation of bodies; in fact, not even a permit is required. What *is* required is the presence of a funeral director as a witness. However, when Michael phoned the funeral director, he was told that the funeral home would oversee no exhumation without a court order. Michael's lawyer believes such an order can be obtained from the chancery judge ex parte—without a hearing—but to do so will require an affidavit stating the reason for the exhumation from the decedent's next of kin.

My mother.

"Hi, Michael. Sorry to keep you two waiting." A tall man with white hair and a white beard marches into the room and pumps Michael's hand. Then he turns to me and smiles. "So, you're Catherine Ferry?"

I stand and offer Dr. Cage my hand. "Please call me Cat."

He takes it and squeezes softly with arthritic fingers. "And I'm Tom."

He moves behind his desk and takes a seat. A big cigar and several tongue depressors protrude from his white lab coat, and a red stethoscope hangs around his neck. It's clear that Tom Cage practices the kind of medicine my grandfather hasn't deigned to practice in many years.

Dr. Cage takes a Diet Coke from a minifridge behind his desk, pops it open, and takes a long pull from the can. After a long exhalation of satisfaction, he sets the can on the desk and fixes his eyes on me.

"Luke Ferry. What do you want to know?"

"I'm not sure. Everything you remember, I suppose."

"That's a lot. I treated Luke as a boy, treated his parents before they died, and I treated the uncle who raised him off and on. What are you most interested in?"

I look at the floor where my father's green bag rests between my feet. "Vietnam," I say softly. "The White Tigers."

Dr. Cage's eyes flicker. "You already know more than I thought you would. Cat . . . your father learned to shoot to put food on his family's table. He shot better as a boy than most men could after a lifetime of practice. But in the war they made him use that talent for another purpose. They made him a sniper. Luke had mixed feelings about that job. On one hand, he was proud of his professionalism." Dr. Cage gestures at his bookshelves. "As you can see, I'm a military history buff. I also served in Korea. Did you know that in Vietnam, the average number of rounds expended per dead enemy soldier was fifty thousand?"

"Fifty thousand!" Michael says beside me. "That can't be right."

"It is," says Dr. Cage. "That's one reason we lost that war. You want to guess how many rounds were expended by army and marine snipers during Vietnam per dead enemy soldier?"

Michael shakes his head. "One?"

"One point three nine. Those boys were very good at their job. But that kind of killing is much more difficult than returning fire at a man who's trying to kill you. It's done in cold blood, looking through a scope at a man ten times life-size. You watch him smoke a cigarette or take a piss, and then you blow his head into ragged chunks of gore and bone. Think of John Kennedy's head exploding in the Zapruder film. That's what you see every time you shoot. Once you have pictures like that in your head, they never go away."

Dr. Cage takes another sip of Diet Coke. "My point is, Luke was under great stress even before he was pressed into the White Tigers. And in that unit, things changed for the worse, and damn quick.

"The Tigers were essentially a terror unit, sent into Cambodia to harry and kill NVA forces hiding in a neutral country. These were covert operations carried out behind the lines, under the command of officers who had cast aside the rules of organized warfare. They took few prisoners. When they did, it was to torture them. Rape was used both as an intimidation tactic against the local populace, and also as a reward for the troops. They rarely distinguished between soldiers and noncombatants. Almost everyone they encountered was considered a target.

"When Luke protested against extreme acts of cruelty, he was ridiculed by his fellow soldiers and looked on with suspicion by his superiors. He soon learned that if he failed to go along with the prevailing authority, he'd wind up as dead as the rest of the people who came in contact with the White Tigers."

While Dr. Cage pauses to think, I rummage through the bag until I find the wire string of "rotten prunes." Fighting my revulsion, I hold the string out to the doctor.

"Do you know what this is?"

Dr. Cage takes the string from my hands and lays it on his desk. With a magnifying glass from his pocket, he examines one of the blackened chunks.

"Ears," he says.

"What?" asks Michael.

Dr. Cage looks up at us. "It's an ear necklace. Never seen one. Where did you get it?"

"Daddy kept it hidden in a bag with some other things."

"It's a war trophy. When some soldiers killed an enemy in Vietnam, they cut off one or both ears and strung them on a necklace, much like Indians taking scalps."

"I've heard of that," says Michael. "But I guess it never seems real until . . ."

Dr. Cage shrugs. "They did it with foreskins, too, but that's nothing new. They were taking foreskins as trophies back in the Crusades. War has always been barbaric. Only the tools have changed."

It's hard for me to visualize the father I knew living in the world Tom Cage is describing. "So, my father cut the ears off his victims?"

"*Victim* isn't the proper word during wartime," Dr. Cage says, "though it may be fitting in cases like this. But it's difficult for me to imagine Luke Ferry stooping to mutilation. There aren't more than twenty ears on this necklace, and Luke had thirty-six confirmed kills as a sniper alone. He probably killed many more without a spotter present to make it official. No, I'd be very surprised if this necklace belonged to Luke."

"Why?" asks Michael. "Given all that you've told us?"

"Because Luke risked his life to bring the men who'd done this kind of thing to justice. As soon as he got back to Vietnam from Cambodia, he went over the head of his CO and reported what he'd seen. Higher authority did exactly what they always do when someone ignores the chain of command. Within a week, Luke was back in action with the White Tigers. That's when he was wounded— according to Luke, by his fellow soldiers. It's a miracle he got aboard a medevac chopper alive. He said that if it hadn't been for one man, he'd have been left to bleed to death in a rice paddy."

"What happened to him after that?"

"He was never the same. The things he'd witnessed had pushed him beyond his limit. When he learned they were going to send him back to the Tigers again, he lost it. He started yelling about everything he'd seen, and the next thing you know, they were processing him out on some kind of special discharge. They didn't give him a section eight, but it amounted to the same thing. His post-traumatic stress disorder kicked in even before he made it back to the States. I could tell you about that, but something tells me that's not what you're really here for."

Michael was right: Tom Cage is a perceptive man.

"Go ahead," Michael says. "Tell him."

"What do you know about childhood sexual abuse?" I ask.

Dr. Cage looks surprised. "I've seen some in my time. I haven't treated children for years, but in the beginning I did. Treated anybody who walked through the front door." He takes a sip of Diet Coke and looks over at his bookshelves. "My fear is that I've seen a lot more sexual abuse than I realized at the time. That there were kids I could have helped if I'd only had more courage, or better eyes to see."

"Why more courage?" I ask.

"I think we see what we want to see. Or maybe what we can afford to see. When I started practice here, there was no such thing as Child Protective Services. Just the welfare department. And in those days, men had virtually absolute control over their families." Dr. Cage's eyes have focused somewhere in the middle distance. He might as well be alone in the room. I'm about to clear my throat when he snaps out of it and looks up at me. "I was thinking of some particular cases. Particular children. But that was a long time ago. I hope they turned out all right."

There's an uncomfortable silence that no one seems inclined to break. For some reason, I feel I can trust this man. Reaching into the bag, I remove the three Polaroid snapshots and pass them across the desk. "I found these in the bag with the other stuff that Daddy kept secret."

Dr. Cage takes a long look at each Polaroid, then looks up at me. "What's really going on here, Cat? What are you trying to figure out?"

"I think my father may have molested me."

"Do you have some reason other than these pictures to believe that?"

"Yes."

"I'm sorry." He glances at the snapshots again. "These pictures look like damning evidence, I know. But taken by themselves, they're like the ear necklace. Merely possessing them seems like evidence of perversion, but you don't know the circumstances by which Luke came to have them."

"Why would he hide them if he had nothing to be ashamed of?"

Dr. Cage shrugs. "We may never know that. Have you gone through everything in that bag?"

"Everything but this," I reply, holding up the sketchbook.

"Why did you pass over that?"

"I don't know." An image of Louise Butler comes into my mind. "Someone already told me what was in it. Sketches of DeSalle Island, stuff like that."

"Do you mind if I take a look?"

I pass the sketchbook across the desk, and he begins flipping through it.

"Looks like you're half right. There are some sketches of a black woman here . . . some poetry. A wildflower pressed between two pages. Wait . . . look at this."

"What?"

"It's a typed note. Oh yes, listen to this. 'Private Ferry, It's come to our attention that you've been talking about the time you spent west of the Mekong River. We thought you'd learned your lesson in sixty-nine. Since you didn't, here's a little reminder from your old friends who wore the tiger stripes. Keep talking and your ears will wind up on one of these. We might even have to run a night op on that little girl of yours. Remember those? You took an oath, soldier. Never forget it.'"

Dr. Cage sets the sketchbook on his desk. "Well, there's one answer for you. How Luke came by the necklace."

"They threatened his life," I say softly. "They really did."

"Luke was a stubborn boy," Dr. Cage says softly. "He tried a couple of times after the war to get an investigation started. He made some headway, but it never came to anything. It wouldn't surprise me to learn that the intruder who killed him at Malmaison was sent by the men who wrote this letter."

I wish he had been, I say silently.

Dr. Cage is watching me closely. "I can see there's more to this than what you've told me. Maybe a lot more. I just hope I've helped you a little."

Though there's really nothing else he can do to help, I want to tell him more. His opinion has become important to me. "If I asked you whether you think Luke could have sexually abused me or not, what would you say?"

A deep sadness fills Tom Cage's eyes. "I'd like to say no. I really would. But I'm too old a dog to be offering certainty on a subject like that. The human sex drive is a powerful thing. It dictates to us more than the other way around, often without our realizing it. Freud spent his life trying to understand it and fell far short. Luke was a good boy, but what he did in the dark of the night—or why he did it—I won't pretend to know. Whatever he did probably had more to do with what was done to him as a child than anything else. And that I don't know about."

"You said you treated his parents."

Dr. Cage turns up his hands. "They were good people, but they died young. I didn't much care for the uncle who took Luke in. He was a redneck loudmouth who spent most of his time trying to get Social Security disability benefits he didn't deserve. Of course, that doesn't make him a child molester. He's dead now. Lung cancer."

As I pack my father's things back into the bag, I say, "If I asked you the same question about my grandfather—whether you think he could have molested me—what would you say?"

Dr. Cage's eyes lock onto mine with a curious intensity. "I'd have to give you the same answer I gave you about Luke. None of us really knows anybody, and when it comes to sex, anything is possible."

When I don't speak, Dr. Cage adds, "You're looking down a deep, dark hole, Catherine. A lot darker hole than I thought when I walked in that door." He glances at Michael. "At least you've got a good man helping you do it."

He's about to speak again when the door beside the couch opens, and a nurse walks in. The doctor's face darkens. "I said I wasn't to be disturbed."

"I'm sorry," says the nurse. "But Dale Thompson just slid his motorcycle down a hundred yards of pavement. He's bleeding all over the waiting room."

"Why didn't he go to the emergency room?"

"He said you patched him up after his last wreck, and he wants you for this one. Looks like he needs about a hundred stitches, all told."

Dr. Cage shakes his head. "He needs some sense knocked into him. Put him in the surgery. I'll be right there."

The doctor comes around his desk and takes me by the hand. "I'm going to be honest with you, Cat. I never liked your grandfather. I respected his skill, and his work for the city, but that's about the only good thing I can say about Bill Kirkland. As for what you asked about, I can tell you this: the man's nearly eighty years old, and he takes as much Viagra as any patient I treat. I know that because he gets it free from one of the drug reps. And so far as I know, he doesn't see any women in town. But then I don't know half of what goes on anymore. So, that's not evidence of anything."

As I get to my feet, Dr. Cage says, "How's your aunt Ann? I used to treat her on and off for depression when she was mad at her shrinks."

"She's dead."

Dr. Cage is visibly shaken. "Dead how?"

"Suicide. Last night."

"Jesus Christ. I hate to hear that."

"Did Ann ever mention anything to you about sexual abuse?"

He shakes his head. "She was obsessed with having a child, that's what I remember most. And she had a real love-hate relationship with your grandfather. She depended on him for everything and hated herself for her dependence."

"Do you know anything about the appendectomy she had on the island?"

Dr. Cage laughs. "Hell, I've heard Bill tell that story a dozen times. He acts like he did a heart transplant with nothing but a pocketknife and some rubbing alcohol."

"Ann was ten when that happened. Do you think she could have been pregnant?"

Dr. Cage's eyes narrow, but after a while he shakes his head. "No. In over forty years of practicing medicine, I've seen one pregnant eleven-year-old. Maybe two. God almighty, you are walking through the abyss, aren't you?"

I nod. "It feels like it."

He looks at Michael. "You take care of this girl. She's tough, but she's not as tough as she thinks she is."

"I will."

Dr. Cage shakes Michael's hand, and then he's gone.

"You still want to exhume your father's body?" Michael asks.

"More than ever."

He sighs and leads me toward the waiting room. There's a trail of blood on the white tiles of the corridor, and a bloody footprint near the waiting room door. In an instant, I flash back to the bloody prints on my bedroom floor. The door ahead wavers in my vision, and my knees go weak. Michael braces my arm and leads me past the staring faces in the waiting room.

"I'm taking you to my office and running some tests," he says.

I blink against the bright sunlight, crazy images flashing in the glare. My father's tombstone . . . myself as a little girl putting Lena the Leopardess into his coffin . . .

"No. If I stop, I won't be able to start again. We keep going."

CHAPTER

51

The Natchez City Cemetery is one of the most beautiful in the world, but today it brings me no peace. I'm driving my mother's car down one of its narrow asphalt lanes, Mom in the seat beside me, looking as anxious as I've ever seen her. She has aged visibly since Ann's death. Her skin is drawn and pale, and her eyes look cloudy.

"I don't know why you want to come here," she says quietly. "We'll be here soon enough to bury Ann."

"I want to see Daddy's grave. I want our family to be together when I talk to you. The three of us."

"What has gotten into you?" Her eyes stare through the windshield. "You've got the FBI searching for you. You've got Daddy and Pearlie in an uproar. Daddy's got a very sensitive deal cooking to try and save the city, and he's terrified you're going to ruin it by causing all this trouble."

I continue down the lane through a tunnel of oaks, rolling between long wrought-iron fences and mausoleums hidden among the trees. Our family plot lies in the old section of the cemetery, where the gnarled limbs of giant oaks reach to the ground and Spanish moss drapes everything in shadow.

"Do you visit Daddy's grave very often?" I ask.

Mom doesn't answer.

If Michael hadn't stranded me at Mom's shop—as I requested—I would never have gotten her to the cemetery. But by offering to drive her home, I got control of the car and—for now at least—her.

"Mom, have you taken a sedative?"

She cuts her eyes at me. "You've got a lot of nerve. You've been drinking your sedative every day of your life."

"Yes, but I'm clean today. I have been for a week, believe it or not."

Mom says nothing.

"I only ask because I'm curious. Did you take it on your own, or did Grandpapa give it to you?"

A huff of anger. "Where else would I get it?"

I pull her Maxima onto the grass beside a low brick wall. The DeSalle family plot lies just beyond it. No mausoleums for us, just fine Alabama marble behind wrought iron that dates to 1840. You can't see the river from here—that view is reserved for the relatives of those buried on Jewish Hill—but the air smells of cedar and sweet olive, and the shade more than makes up for the panoramic view from the bluff.

A good portion of five generations of DeSalles lies behind this fence. Grandpapa would have preferred that Luke Ferry be interred elsewhere, but my mother—to her credit—insisted that he be buried here. It may be the only time that she stood up to her father and won. If I try to drag Mom through the gate, she'll resist me, so I simply walk through on my own and don't stop until I'm standing before my father's simple black headstone.

Before long, I hear the gate creak. Then a shadow falls across mine on the ground.

"Why are we really here?" my mother asks softly.

I reach out and find her hand with mine. "Mom . . . somehow I've reached the age of thirty-one without you and me sharing much more than small talk. I blame myself as much as you. I want us to do better in the future. But after today, you may never want to talk to me again."

"You're scaring me, honey."

"I won't say you shouldn't be. I want to exhume Daddy's body."

Her indrawn breath might as well have been an explosion. I know the turmoil inside her is almost more than she can bear. *How did I raise this crazy woman beside me?* she's wondering. Before she can scream or burst into tears, I push on.

"I need a sample of his DNA, but I also want another autopsy done. And I want Lena out of the coffin."

"That raggedy old stuffed animal?"

"Yes."

Her hand pulls out of mine. "Catherine? What's happened to you? Are you out of your mind?"

"No. I think I'm close to *not* being out of my mind for the first time in my life. I need your help to do this, Mom. I'm asking you to help me."

She's looking at the gravestone, not at me. "But why? What are you trying to do?"

"I'm not sure you want to know."

"If you're talking about digging up your father, I'd better know what you think you're up to."

I step onto Daddy's grave, then turn and face her. "Mom, I was sexually abused when I was a child."

She blinks several times quickly.

"Ann may have been molested, too. I don't know. And I won't know until I see Daddy's body and get Lena out of that coffin."

Mom has begun to shake. From her head to her toes, she's shivering as though stranded on an arctic glacier. Even her fitted linen suit is shivering, though the summer air is still as death. "Oh, dear Lord," she says, her voice almost a whimper. "Who put this nonsense in your head? Was it that psychiatrist Ann was seeing? The one who was murdered?"

"How do you know about him?"

"I spoke to the FBI, dear. An Agent Kaiser called me. He was very personable, and very concerned about you, too."

A sense of threat brings the hair on the back of my neck erect. "When was this?"

"Now, Cat, there's nothing to be afraid of."

"Did you tell Kaiser I'm in town?"

"I didn't tell anyone anything, baby. Daddy said our family business is none of their business."

Jesus . . . "Did Grandpapa talk to Kaiser?"

"I think so, yes."

"Mom, there's so much to tell and not enough time to tell it. My whole life I've had problems with sex. With men, with alcohol . . . lots of things."

She steps toward me, relief evident in her face. *Now I understand the problem,* she thinks. "That's not your fault, honey. Anybody who lost their father the way you did was bound to have some problems."

"No! It wasn't that. I always thought it was, but it wasn't."

"Baby, of *course* that's it. You suffered so much pain—"

"Mom, please! There's so much you don't know. Grandpapa tried to protect you the same way he tried to protect me. Only he didn't protect either of us."

The anxiety returns to her face. "What are you talking about?"

"I hoped I wouldn't have to tell you this, but there's no other way. Mom, the night Daddy was shot, there was no intruder at Malmaison."

"Of course there was. I told you—"

"No," I say firmly. "You never saw one, and there never was one. Grandpapa told me that himself. He made up that prowler to keep from having to tell you what really happened."

"What really happened?" she echoes, her eyes as wary as a timid dog's.

"Yes. Grandpapa said he caught Daddy molesting me in my bed that night. They fought, and Grandpapa shot him."

The blood has drained from my mother's face. She's so pale that I can't believe she hasn't fainted.

"I know that's a shock, Mom. But that's what he told me."

"I don't believe you."

I shrug. "I'm telling you the truth. Only I'm not sure anymore that Grandpapa was telling *me* the truth. There's a chance it could have happened the other way around—that Daddy caught Grandpapa abusing me. Only Daddy still got killed. And that's what I'm trying to find out. Not who killed whom, but who molested me. If it was Grandpapa, he probably did the same to Ann."

My mother has clapped her hands over her ears like a child, but I keep talking. "Ann killed herself in the clinic with Thomas the Turtle beside her. Did you know that? Did you know she had Thomas there?"

"She did that because of her infertility," Mom says almost defiantly. "She blamed it on the appendectomy she had there. Daddy said as much several times, as I recall. That the infection might have made her sterile."

"I'm not even sure that operation was an appendectomy, Mom. I'm afraid Ann might have been pregnant."

My mother's mouth is a cartoon O. "Ten-year-old girls don't get pregnant! My God, that alone should tell you how crazy this is!"

"Maybe she wasn't pregnant," I concede, recalling the unanimous opinions of Michael Wells, Hannah Goldman, and Tom Cage. "But something very bad happened to Ann in that clinic. And somewhere deep inside, you know that."

At last Mom realizes how foolish she must look, and she drops her hands to her sides. As she stares at me in silence, I cross the final, unspeakable line. "Mama . . . how could you not know? How could you not know that was happening to me? How could you let someone *do* that to me?"

Tears pool in the corners of her eyes, then slide down her face. "You need help, baby. We'll find somebody, somebody really good this time."

"No," I say, my voice breaking. "You can't pawn me off anymore. Nobody can help me through this except you. *You,* Mama. I know you've had problems with sex—just like I have—only they're different problems. I know there are things you can't do."

Her mouth begins to quiver.

"I spoke to Louise, Mom."

She flinches as though from a blow. "Take me home, Catherine. Don't say another word."

"I'm *begging* you, Mom. I'm standing here on Daddy's grave begging you to help me find the truth. I'm afraid if I don't, I may not live much longer."

"Don't do that to me," she snaps, angrily raising a forefinger. "Don't put that on me! Ann did it too many times already. Take me home, or I'm leaving you here."

"I have the keys," I whisper.

"Then I'll walk."

CHAPTER

52

When I pull into the parking lot behind Malmaison, I see my grandfather seated in a foldout lawn chair by the entrance to the rose garden. Billy Neal stands beside him, a brown beer bottle in his hand. Grandpapa leans forward to peer through the windshield of the Maxima. When he sees both me and my mother inside, he dismisses Billy with a wave of his hand.

"Give me your cell phone, Mom."

She refused to speak on the way home from the cemetery, but she passes me the phone. Then she gets out of the car, her purse over her shoulder, and waits for me. As I dial Sean's number in New Orleans, Billy Neal walks through the arbor and disappears into the rose garden without looking back.

"Detective Sergeant Regan."

"It's me, Sean. Do you have my autopsy report?"

"Not yet."

"Why not?"

"I'll be honest with you, Cat. I don't know if I'm going to be able to get it. The FBI has closed ranks on this thing. They're not giving the task force crap. It's like the old days when the Feds never shared anything."

Grandpapa is saying something to Mom, but she hasn't moved away from the car. I shut my eyes, trying to press down a sense of grim futility. "Sean, you get me that fucking report."

I hang up. I'd like to back out of the parking lot and drive straight to Michael Wells's house, but I can't let Mom face Grandpapa alone. Not after what I told her at the cemetery. As soon as I get out of the car, Grandpapa is up out of his chair and screaming at me. His face is red, his eyes blazing.

"What the *hell* do you think you're doing, Catherine?"

The sight of my grandfather angry still turns my insides to jelly, but today I stand my ground. "What are you talking about?"

"You want to dig up your father's goddamn corpse?"

I can't believe it. Either Michael lied to me when he said he didn't mention my name to his attorney, or someone in the chancery judge's office leaked word of my inquiries to my grandfather. That has to be it. I called the judge's chambers during the ride from Dr. Cage's office to my mother's shop, so that I'd have some idea of a time frame on exhumation when I discussed it with my mother. But Mom and I never got that far. And now what I had planned as a discreet little operation has, like everything else, become known to my grandfather.

"Well?" he roars. "What do you have to say for yourself?"

Remarkably, my mother interposes herself between Grandpapa and me. This may be a first. "Don't shout at her, Daddy," she pleads. "Cat's not herself right now."

"What do you mean?" he bellows.

"She's dealing with some problems."

He grits his teeth and nods angrily. "Oh, I know she's got problems. She's had problems her whole life, just like Ann. I've spent half my life cleaning up their problems, but today it stops. Today, I'm done. Today, I'm doing some bud-nipping, before this girl causes this whole town a problem it can't afford."

"What are you talking about?" I ask.

"The casino, goddamn it! I'm talking about the salvation of this city. We are one hairsbreadth from federal certification of the Natchez Indian Nation. And there's not a damn thing the state gaming commission can do to stop it. But *you*"—he jabs a thick forefinger in my direction—"you could blow the whole thing right out of the water with your questions and theories and getting tied up in the middle of mass murder. And now you want to dig up Luke Ferry's decomposed body for the whole town to read about in the newspaper? Well, I'm telling you right now, that's not going to happen.

Unless it's part of an official criminal investigation, you need your mother's approval to dig that body up."

Mom almost cowers when he glances in her direction, and I know that she's not about to give me what I need. But I will not cower. I'm done with that. I take a step toward my grandfather. "Then I guess I'm going to have to make this a criminal investigation. I didn't want to, but you're not leaving me any choice. I'll get the Natchez police out here, and I'll drag the FBI into it, too, before I'm done. I'll turn Malmaison into a three-ring circus, if that's what it takes to find out the truth."

"The *truth*?" Grandpapa echoes. "You think it's the truth you're after?"

"That's all I've ever been after! But all you've given me is lies. Every new story was just another lie to keep me from digging any deeper. What are you afraid of, Grandpapa? What can't you bear to have anyone find out about you?"

He glances at my mother again, then looks at the ground. When he finally raises his head, his eyes burn into mine. "It's not myself I've been trying to protect. It's you. The bottom of this damn mystery you're so keen to solve is something I prayed you'd never have to know, and I've done everything in my power to keep it from you. But you won't let this go. You'll tear down this house, this family, everything I've built to get what you want. You've proved that. So . . . you want the truth?"

A strange thrumming has started in the back of my head. But there's no turning back now. "I do."

"You want to know who killed your father?"

"Yes."

"You did."

The sound of rain is so vivid that I put up my hands to shield my face. My mother and grandfather suddenly waver in my vision, as though we're all standing underwater. I want to speak, but there's nothing left to say. With two simple words all my questions have been answered. Every piece in the chaotic puzzle of my life has finally fallen into place. The long black train that plowed silently over me in the gleaming kitchen of Arthur LeGendre has circled around again. The great black face of its engine roars out of nowhere, blotting out the scene before me: people, grass, trees, and sky. In the last instant before impact, searing images pass behind my eyes: the New Orleans murder victims, naked and mutilated; Nathan Malik lying dead in a motel bathtub, a human skull in his lap; Ann sprawled on the floor of the clinic with two skull-and-crossbones symbols drawn on her abdomen, her stuffed turtle beside her. But nowhere do I see my father's face. I try to summon it, but all that appears is a necklace of ears, a sculpture of a hanged man, photographs of naked children, and two black shadows fighting above me in the dark.

And then I see nothing at all.

CHAPTER

53

I'm running.

Harder and faster than I've ever run in my life. Tree trunks flash past the way they used to when I rode horses on the island, but it's only my legs hurling me forward, my feet flying from something too terrible to face.

You want to know who killed your father?

No! I want to turn back time. Push back the days to the point before I began asking questions—questions to which I thought I wanted answers.

Now I know better.

Some things it's better not know. Pearlie's voice.

Michael Wells's house appears between the distant trees. The sight of it brings a strange feeling of hope, the way a thief might feel sighting a church, his sole chance at sanctuary. I sprint harder, and soon the shining blue rectangle of the Hemmeters' swimming pool appears. But the Hemmeters' are gone now. The pool, like the house, belongs to Michael. Too many changes . . .

I stumble down to the concrete patio that surrounds the pool, my eyes plumbing its blue depths. Part of me wants only to slip beneath the surface, to lie on the bottom and hold my breath while my heartbeats get further and further apart, stretching into ever increasing increments of time, eventually reaching infinity.

But that's not the way it happens. Deprived of oxygen, the heart will eventually beat harder and faster, struggling to feed the starving tissues until at last it squirms frantically and uselessly in the chest. I would kick to the surface then. Not even a death wish can suppress instinct honed over millions of years. That takes coercion. Or a suicide method from which there is no turning back. Like intravenous morphine. That probably plunged Ann into blissful sleep so fast that any second thoughts quickly faded into oblivion. But I doubt she'd have turned back, even if she could.

In some people, the pain of living minute to minute simply grows so acute that they can finally stand to look into the face of death without blinking—even look at death as a friend—and cross that river Dr. Malik talked about without a backward glance. For me, even though I've crawled right up to the black rim of suicide, pain has always been preferable to the void.

Until now . . .

There's a light on in Michael's house. That alone draws me past the pool and up to the French doors at the back of the house. Suddenly I'm banging on the glass, banging hard, and the pain shooting up to my elbow doesn't stop me, but only reminds me that I'm alive. I see movement inside, and then Michael is hurrying to the door, his face all concern. Before he can speak, I throw my arms around his neck, stand on tiptoe, and hug him as tightly as I can.

"Hey, hey, what's the matter?" he asks. "What happened? Did you and your mother have an argument?"

I want to answer, but my chest is heaving against him in great racking sobs that make my whole body shudder. *I killed my father!* I scream, but nothing comes from my throat.

"Calm down," Michael says, stroking my hair. "Whatever it is, we can deal with it."

I shake my head violently, staring at him through a screen of tears.

"You've got to tell me what happened, Cat."

This time my mouth forms the words, but again no sound emerges. Then, like a distraught child, I manage to stammer out the truth. Michael's eyes go wide for an instant, but then he pulls me tight against him. "Your grandfather told you that?"

I nod into his chest.

"Did he give you any proof?"

I shake my head. "But I feel it . . . the minute he said it, I felt I'd finally heard the truth. Only . . ."

"What?" asks Michael.

"I was eight years old. Could I really have shot my father?"

Michael sighs with deep sadness. "When I moved back to Natchez, it was autumn. And one of the first things that struck me was all the pictures in the newspaper of seven- and eight-year-olds who'd shot their first deer."

I close my eyes in desolation.

"I thought about the possibility yesterday," he says. "I told you that if it was your father who had molested you, it could have been Pearlie or your mother who shot him. But, yes . . . it could have been you. Patricide is certainly the most convincing scenario for your retreat into silence."

What am I doing here? I wonder. *Standing in the house of a man I barely know, shaking like an epileptic?*

"If that is what happened," Michael says, "if you did shoot your father, it was a clear act of self-preservation. If an eight-year-old girl was driven to the point where she had to shoot her father, no one in the world would question the rightness of her actions."

I hear Michael's words but they have no effect. Words cannot penetrate the wounded region of my soul. He seems to sense this. Keeping one arm tight around me, he leads me to the master bedroom, pulls back the covers, and sits me on the edge of the bed. He kneels and removes my shoes, then stretches me out on the bed and pulls the covers up to my neck.

"Don't move from this spot. I'll be back in a minute."

He vanishes, leaving me in the cool, dry darkness of his air-conditioned bedroom. I feel strangely at home here. Mr. and Mrs. Hemmeter slept in this room for more than thirty years. They loved me like a daughter, and something of their spirits must remain.

Michael reappears beside the bed, a glass of water in his hand.

"This is a Lorcet Plus. It'll take the edge off."

I take the white pill from his hand and pop it into my mouth, but as the glass touches my lips, I realize I'm making a terrible mistake. I spit out the pill and put it on the bedside table.

"What's the matter?" Michael asks.

"I can't take this."

"Are you allergic to hydrocodone?"

I look up into his concerned eyes, wishing I didn't have to tell him the truth. Why has he done all this for me? He's disrupted his entire life to help me. There's got to be a reason for that. But I can't lie to him anymore. Not even by omission.

"I'm pregnant," I tell him, my eyes never leaving his.

He doesn't flinch the way my mother did when I mentioned my father's mistress, but something changes behind his eyes. The warmth slowly dissipates into a cool and wary look.

"Who's the father? The married detective?"

"Yes."

He stares silently at me for a few moments. "I'll make you some tea instead," he says awkwardly. "Decaf." He turns and walks quickly to the door.

"Michael, wait!"

He turns and looks back, his face pale, his eyes confused.

"I didn't want this," I tell him. "It wasn't planned or anything. But I'm not going to terminate it. I should have told you before now, I guess, but I was so embarrassed. I didn't want you to think badly of me. But now . . . with everything else you know, it's absurd to hold anything back." My next words take more courage than swimming into the middle of the Mississippi River. "If you want me to go, I'll understand."

He only stares at me, his eyes unreadable.

"I'll get the tea," he says finally.

I never got the tea. I never took the Lorcet either, but exhaustion gave me that most precious of gifts—dreamless sleep. When Michael woke me a few minutes ago, the clock beside the bed read 11:30 P.M. I felt neither rested nor tired.

I felt numb.

The room is all shadows now, cast by the spill from the bathroom light. Michael has pulled a chair up beside the bed. He's watching me as he might a patient in the ICU. At least he hasn't asked me how I feel.

"What do you want to do?" he says.

"I don't know. What do you think I should do?"

"Go back to sleep. See how you feel in the morning. I'll stay in one of the guest rooms upstairs. If you need me, you can call my cell phone."

"I don't want to be alone tonight."

He doesn't reply. He doesn't even blink.

"I'm not trying to make a pass or anything," I tell him. "I just don't think I should be by myself right now. You know?"

He cocks one eyebrow at me. "That's the first time a woman ever threatened to kill herself if I didn't sleep with her."

I'd like to laugh, but I can't. There's nothing left in me. I slide across the bed and pull back the comforter. Michael stares at the blank space in the bed, then gets up and walks into his closet. When he returns, he's wearing a pair of blue gym shorts and an Emory University T-shirt. He sits on the edge of the bed and sets the alarm clock, then slides under the covers and pulls them up to his chest.

It seems a weird parody of married life, both of us lying on our backs, staring at the ceiling as though we've been together twenty years and said all there was to say long ago. I expect him to talk, to probe me with questions. But he doesn't. What does he think of me? Does he regret the moment that he walked into his backyard and picked up the net to rescue me from the bottom of his swimming pool?

Tentatively, I slide my hand over the cool sheet and take his hand in mine. There's nothing sexual in the touch. I'm holding his hand the way I must have held my father's long ago—before he twisted our relationship into a perverted shadow of parental love. It takes a while, but Michael squeezes my hand in return. I may be mistaken, but it feels as though he's shaking. I'm sure he wouldn't want me to notice, so I say nothing.

After a time, another realization hits me. Michael is hard. I know this without feeling his erection against me. It's something about the way he's lying, a tension in his body. This knowledge does something to me. It always has. I feel not only desire, but a sense of compulsion, even obligation. In the same way a match exists to be struck or a loaded gun to be fired, the erect penis is a potential waiting to be released. I've seen a loaded rifle instantly transform a roomful of men from ennui to alertness. The moment a bullet enters the chamber, the inanimate weapon takes on an almost living presence, dangerous and impossible to ignore. For me, in this moment, Michael's penis is the same.

"I can help you with that," I say softly.

"What?"

I nudge his hip with mine. "That."

"How did you know?"

"I just do."

He keeps staring at the ceiling. "Why would you do that?"

"I don't know. Because you need it. You can kiss me if you want."

He's silent for a time. Then he says, "I don't want to kiss you right now. Not like this. I can't help the other. I've had a thing for you for a really long time, but I don't want to be what other men have been to you."

I squeeze his hand. "We don't have to make love. I can just use my hand. Or . . . whatever."

Michael pulls his hand out of mine, and I hear his breathing stop. Then he turns on his side and looks at me. I can barely make out his eyes in the dark. "I don't want that," he says. "Okay? That's not the way this is supposed to happen. You may not know that, but you need to learn. Now, go to sleep. I'll talk to you in the morning."

I guess I know how he looks at me now. I suppose I should be embarrassed, but I'm not. I should probably feel regret. But I don't. Here I lie, pregnant by a married man, sleeping next to the first nice guy I've come to know in a very long time.

And I feel nothing at all.

When you dream the same dream over and over, you begin to wonder whether, like a Hindu who has lived an immoral life, your punishment is to be reincarnated again and again in the same body, unable to rise up the chain of being until you learn the elusive lesson of your sin.

I'm back inside the rusted pickup truck, my grandfather behind the wheel. We're rolling up the sloping hill of the old pasture. I hate the stink inside the truck. Sometimes a river breeze blows it out of the cab, but today the air hangs dead and still over the island, as though trapped under the overturned bowl of steel-gray clouds. My grandfather grits his teeth as he drives. He hasn't spoken since we left the house. I might as well not be here. But I am. And soon we will crest the hill—crest it and sight the pond on the other side.

I don't want to see the pond. I don't want to see my father walk across the water like Jesus and pull open the bullet hole in his chest. I already know what he's trying to tell me. I already know that I killed him. Why won't he let me rest? If I could apologize to him, there might be some reason for this dream. But I can't. I can't speak at all.

"Goddamn rain," Grandpapa mutters.

He downshifts and steps on the gas, and we trundle over the hill. The cows are waiting for us as they always are, their eyes glassy with indifference. Beyond them lies the pond, a perfect silver mirror reflecting only sky. To my right, the prize bull mounts the cow and begins lunging forward.

Grandpapa smiles.

Dreading the sight of my father in the water, I cover my eyes with my hands. But sooner or later I will have to look. I peer between my fingers and brace myself against the horror I know is to come.

But it doesn't come. Today the pond is empty. My father isn't floating on its surface, his arms splayed out like those of a man on a cross. The perfect mirror remains undisturbed.

Grandpapa brakes as we roll toward the pond, then stops twenty yards from the water's edge. I smell decay, rotting plants and fish. Where is my father? What's happened to my dream? Even something terrible is more comforting than the unknown. I turn to Grandpapa to ask a question, but I don't know what the question is. I couldn't ask it anyway. Fear is clawing around in my chest like a trapped animal trying to get out.

A new smell cuts through the decay of the pond. Something manmade. It's the tonic Grandpapa uses on his hair. Lucky Tiger.

"Goddamn rain," he says again.

As I stare through the windshield, a curtain of rain sweeps across my field of vision like a great gray shadow, all the leaves trembling under its weight. In seconds the glassy surface of the pond is sizzling like water thrown into a hot skillet. Pearlie told me once that a person is like a raindrop, sent from heaven alone but destined to rejoin all the other drops at journey's end. I can't remember heaven, so I must have left it a long time ago . . . yet I still have such a long way to fall . . .

"All right, now," Grandpapa says.

He reaches across the seat, takes hold of my knees, and turns me sideways like a man shifting a sack of seeds. When he moves toward me, I beseech him with my eyes. He hesitates like a man who has forgotten his car keys. Then he reaches under the seat, pulls out Lena the Leopardess, and shoves her into my hands. As I shut my eyes and press her soft fur against my cheek, a feeling like warm water spreads through my body. The rain sweeps over the truck as Grandpapa pushes me back on the seat, and the hard, percussive patter of raindrops on a tin roof fills my ears. When his big hands unsnap my jeans, I don't feel them. When his leather belt creaks and jingles, I don't hear it. Lena and I are a million miles away, padding through the jungle, listening to the endless music of the rain.

And it begins.

When I wake to sunlight streaming through Michael's bedroom, I know.

Like Saul on the road to Damascus, the scales have been stripped from my eyes. My recurring dream was no dream at all, but a memory. A memory trying to come back to me any way it could. The business of my father walking on water was something grafted onto it, a different message from my subconscious, pointing me toward something I've yet to learn.

And today I will learn it.

Where Michael lay beside me in the bed, I find a note on the pillow with a house key lying on top of it. The note reads, *Gone to work. Tried to wake you, but you wouldn't budge. You're welcome to stay as long as you need to. Call me at the office when you wake up. Michael.*

I take Michael's phone off the bedside table and dial Sean's cell number.

"Detective Sergeant Regan."

"Tell me you got the autopsy report."

"Cat, I moved heaven and earth to get that fucking thing, but it's not to be had. John Kaiser's sitting on it like national security depends on it. If you want that report, you're going to have to ask Kaiser for it. I'm sorry, babe. I tried my best."

I hesitate only a moment. "Give me Kaiser's cell number."

"Shit. Are you sure? The Bureau's still looking for you."

"If Kaiser really wanted to find me, I'd be in jail now."

"Yeah. I guess you're right."

Sean reads out the number. I commit it to memory, then hang up and dial it.

Kaiser catches his breath when he hears my voice. "Do you have something for me?" he asks.

"No. I need something from you."

"That's not the answer I was looking for, Cat. The only reason you're not in jail is because I thought you could help me solve this case."

"I can. But it's a quid pro quo situation. You help me with my problem, I'll help you with yours."

"Christ. What do you want now?"

If I seem too anxious to get the autopsy report, Kaiser might not give it to me. "Tell me where you are with the murders first. What about the saliva cultures? Any *Streptococcus mutans* growth yet?"

"Not yet. The pathologist thinks it's still early, though, that we'll see it by the thirty-six-hour point."

"No, twenty-four hours is enough, if it's there. The saliva in those wounds is either coming from someone without teeth, or someone taking penicillin with gentamicin. You haven't found any victims' relatives who fit that description?"

"We've got a couple of male relatives with dentures. I'm going at them hard, but they look clean to me."

"Talk to their families. If they wear their dentures at all, they're not the source. What about the antibiotic angle?"

"That's tough to nail down," Kaiser complains. "Anybody could lie about that. We can't take blood levels on every male relative of six murder victims."

"Why not? The DNA evidence proves the source is male, and this is your only real lead. The British police did blood tests on thousands of people in one town to solve a murder case."

"This is America, Cat, not England."

"Okay, okay. Any sign of anaerobic spirochetes in the cultures? Bacteroides melaninogenicus? Anaerobic vibrios? Those are specific for teeth, and we could rule out edentulous people."

"Shit. I'm looking . . . I don't see anything like that."

"It's still early for those to show up, and they're difficult to culture anyway. I'll keep thinking about this angle. What about the skull in Malik's lap?"

"Nothing. The only fingerprints on it were Malik's."

"Naturally. What else?"

Kaiser blows out a stream of air in frustration. "We're checking all film-processing labs, in the hope that someone's done work for Malik. It was video equipment we found in his apartment, but I'm hoping for a break."

"What else?"

"I've got the technical services guys trying to resurrect data off the drives we took from Malik's office computers, but they've got nothing so far. I think his film really is our only chance. But if the killer got that when he killed Malik . . . we're fucked."

"I'm sorry I haven't been more help to you. I've had my hands full here."

"You just get me the names of the women in Group X. Do that, and I'll keep your ass out of jail."

"I'm trying, John. But I need your help, too."

"What do you need?" His voice is wary.

"The same thing I asked you for yesterday. The autopsy report on my aunt."

"What are you looking for? Cause of death, what?"

"You know what I'm looking for. Her reproductive organs. Anything out of the ordinary?"

Kaiser takes his time to answer. "I shouldn't give you this."

My throat tightens.

"Didn't you tell me that Ann was obsessed with having children?"

"Yes."

"Well, that makes no sense at all, Cat."

"Why not?"

"Because your aunt was sterile. She had been for decades. Probably from the time she was a teenager."

"What do you mean? Sterile how?"

"Her tubes were tied."

Something goes hollow inside me. "That's impossible. The pathologist must have made a mistake."

"You know better," Kaiser says wearily. "And the sterilization wasn't done by any normal procedure, either. That's how the pathologist knew it was done a long time ago."

"How was it done?"

"Apparently, in a tubal ligation the procedure is done fairly low down the fallopian tube. Your aunt's tubes were cut just below something called the fimbria, a flowerlike opening of the tube just below the ovary. They were tied off with silk sutures, and the silk was still inside the scarred tissue at autopsy. The pathologist said OBs haven't used silk for that procedure in decades."

A cloud of fog has descended in my mind.

"I know this is giving you some ideas about your personal situation, Cat. Please try to stay calm, okay? Maybe you should call Dr. Goldman."

"Did the pathologist say anything else?"

"He said that an OB wouldn't cut off the fimbria. That was something a general surgeon might do as a quick method of sterilizing somebody. He thought it was damned odd."

My hands are shaking, but not from fear this time. It's outrage. "I have to go, John."

"No!" he says quickly. "You can't just go. I've given you a lot of rope to play with, and I'm afraid you're going to hang us both. I've got superiors to answer to, like it or not. And every hour you're on the street comes out of my credibility. I'm looking for some help here."

Michael's clock reads 7:05 A.M. "Give me eight hours, John. In that time I'll have something to give you, or I'll come back to New Orleans and let you throw me to the wolves."

The silence seems interminable.

"What can you possibly learn in Natchez that can help me?" he asks.

Probably nothing, but I don't really give a shit. I just need you off my back.

"Eight hours," he says softly. "Cat, if I haven't heard from you by five o'clock today, I'll have the Natchez police pick you up on suspicion of murder."

If they can find me . . . "Thanks, John. Hey, could you fax me the autopsy report?"

Another pause.

"I'm a member of her family, for God's sake. Please."

"You're a pain in the ass is what you are. Do you want it sent to the same number where we sent you those files on Malik?"

"Perfect. I'll talk to you before five."

"Cat—"

I hang up, then get up and run for the bathroom. My father's body is coming out of the ground today, and nothing is going to stop that. If the judge needs an affidavit from my mother to issue a court order for exhumation, he'll get one. There will be no more denial for the women of the DeSalle family.

Denial is death.

CHAPTER

54

Mom is sitting at her kitchen table in a sweat-soaked housecoat, staring blankly into a mug of coffee. She doesn't even look up at the sound of the door. Only when I sit down opposite her do her eyes rise to take me in.

"Has Grandpapa been here?" I ask.

She shrugs.

I've already slipped into my grandfather's office and retrieved the autopsy report that Kaiser faxed there. I was lucky Grandpapa wasn't in his office when it arrived—though part of me wished he had been—but my luck ended when I tried to borrow another pistol from his gun safe. The combination had been changed.

"I have some things to tell you, Mom. They won't be easy to hear, but you don't have a choice anymore. You owe it to Ann."

Her eyes are shot with blood, and the skin of the orbits gleams blue-black. But her mind seems alert. Whatever drug she was on yesterday has been flushed from her system.

In a soft but deliberate voice, I tell her what the pathologist discovered during Ann's autopsy: that she was sterilized many years ago by an unorthodox procedure, probably during her "emergency appendectomy" on the island. Mom listens like someone being told that her child has been tortured to death. I have the sense that if I pricked her face with a needle, she wouldn't flinch.

"There's something else," I add. "I had a dream last night. It's the recurring one, about riding in the old pickup truck with Grandpapa. Last night I saw the end of it. He parked by the pond, and then . . . Mom, he started touching me."

Her eyes remain focused on the table.

"And right before he took my pants down, he pulled Lena from under the seat and stuck her in my arms."

A trembling has begun in my mother's hands.

"That's how they found Ann," I remind her. "With Timid Thomas beside her naked body."

"I had a dream last night, too," Mom says softly.

"You . . . you did?"

She lifts her coffee cup to her lips, takes a sip, then sets it rattling on the saucer. "Something happened on the island when I was young," she says in a voice I've never heard from her. There is no affect, no illusion, nothing added for the benefit of the listener. "I was fourteen. It was summer, and I'd gotten to be friends with a boy there. A Negro boy. He was a year older than I. It was innocent, mostly. But toward the end of the summer, we did some touching. He touched me, anyway."

She takes another sip of coffee, the tremor in her hand so pronounced that I fear she'll drop the cup. "We'd meet by an old shack near the river. Nobody ever went there. But one day a cousin of mine followed us. And he saw Jesse touching me."

"The boy's name was Jesse?" I flash back to a black man speaking through burn-scarred lips: *I knew your mama pretty well.*

"Yes."

"Jesse Billups?"

At last her eyes focus on mine. "Yes. He was in love with me."

"My God . . . Mom, I talked to him the other day."

"How did he look?"

"All right, I guess. He seemed to have a lot of anger in him."

"I'm sure he does, after what happened to him in the war. He used to be handsome, believe it or not. I did what I could for him. He has the best job on the island now."

Jesus. "That's not saying much, is it?"

She shrugs as if it hardly matters now. "The day my cousin saw us, he told his father. And *his* father told my father."

A chill goes through me. "What happened?"

"Daddy went down to Jesse's parents' house that night, dragged Jesse outside, and beat him within an inch of his life."

Jesse Billups's words come back to me with perfect clarity: *Dr. Kirkland beat me once when I was a boy. Beat me bad. But I'd have done the same thing in his place, so we're square enough on that . . .*

Tears are running down my mother's face. I grab a paper towel from the counter and hand it to her.

"Mom?"

She laughs strangely, a note of hysteria in her voice. "I thought Daddy did that because Jesse was black. You see? And I was miserable afterward. I was like you. I wouldn't talk. And Daddy got madder and madder at me. Finally he demanded to know why I wouldn't say anything."

"What did you tell him?"

"That he'd beaten Jesse like the boy had raped me or something, but the truth was that I'd *wanted* Jesse to touch me."

I try to imagine my grandfather hearing this from his daughter in 1966. "What happened?"

"Daddy's face went white. We were staying in a suite at the Peabody in Memphis. He yanked me up from my chair and dragged me back to their bedroom. He took off his belt and whipped me till I bled, and then he kept on whipping me."

"What was Grandmama doing?"

Mom shakes her head as if genuinely curious. "I don't know. She disappeared."

The way you disappeared when I was a girl and Grandpapa was angry. . . .

"The thing is," Mom goes on, "the thing I forgot and didn't remember until my dream last night was that he stripped me naked before he did it. He *stripped* me. My own father threw me on the bed and tore my clothes off. And while he hit me, he yelled things. Vile things. He called me a slut . . . a dirty whore. I didn't even know what those words *meant*. But the worst part was his face. His eyes."

"What about them?"

"It wasn't just anger I saw in them, Cat."

A rush of terrifying images flashes through my mind. Wild, unseeing eyes and a raging mouth. "What was it?"

Mom closes her eyes and shakes her head, like some primitive woman afraid to name a demon.

"Mama? What did you see in his eyes?"

Her answer is a fearful whisper. *"Jealousy."*

A shudder passes through my body, leaving fear in its wake. But somewhere beneath the fear is a feeling of elation. *She knows,* I realize. *More than that, she knows she knows. . . .*

"Do you have any memories of Grandpapa touching you?"

She shakes her head. "But you were right about what you said about my problems. There are things I can't do. I was such a disappointment to your father. He was very understanding. And I *wanted* to do the things he wanted . . . they were normal things. But I just couldn't. If Luke got behind me, my throat would close up, and I'd feel like I had to go to the bathroom right that second."

"Urinate, you mean?"

She blushes deep red. "No. And if he tried, I felt terrible pain. I don't want to talk about that, all right? I can't. I'm not sure what I'm actually remembering and what I might be making up. But one thing I do remember . . ." She crushes the paper towel into a wet ball and wipes her eyes, but it won't stop the fresh tears. "The way Ann looked at me. In the evenings, especially, when Mom was gone to play bridge. Ann would go into Daddy's study to keep him occupied. And I would stay in my room. I knew she hated going in there. I knew she was afraid of him. I was, too, down deep, though I wouldn't have admitted that to anyone. Not even to myself. How could I be afraid of my daddy? He loved me and took care of me. But whenever Ann left me to spend time with him, she looked at me the way you'd look at something you were trying to protect."

Mom's chin is quivering like a little girl's. I'm not sure she can endure much more of this. "And now," she says, "now I know that's exactly what she was doing. Protecting me from him. She was only four years older, but . . . dear God, I can't stand to think about it."

She crumples over the table, sobbing uncontrollably. I lean down over her and hug her as tight as I can. "I love you, Mom. I love you so much."

"I don't know how . . . at least Ann tried to protect me. But I didn't protect you . . . my own baby."

"You couldn't," I whisper. "You couldn't even protect yourself."

She sits up and grits her teeth, obviously furious at herself.

"Mom, you didn't even know what had happened to you. Not consciously. I don't think you knew until last night."

"But how is that possible?" Her eyes implore me for an answer. "*Ann* knew. Why didn't I?"

"I think we all shut it out, because to admit what he did to us would have been admitting that he didn't love us. That he wasn't taking care of us for us . . . but for him. To *use*."

Mom takes my hand in hers and squeezes it in a clawlike grip. "What are you going to do, Cat?"

"I'm going to make him admit what he did."

She shakes her head, her eyes filled with terror. "He'll never do that!"

"He'll have no choice. I'm going to prove that he did it. And then I'm going to see him punished for it."

"He'll kill you, Cat. He will."

I start to deny it, but Mom is right. Grandpapa sterilized his ten-year-old daughter so that he could continue to molest her after puberty without fear of pregnancy. He murdered her future children for a few brief years of pleasure. And in the end that drove her mad.

He murdered my father to protect himself.

He wouldn't hesitate to kill me for the same reason.

"Did he ever say anything like that to you?" I ask. "Did he threaten to harm you?"

"No," Mom says, her voice tiny. But suddenly her eyes jerk in their sockets. "*I'll kill your mother*," she hisses. "I'll send Mama down the river and she'll *never come back*. Just like the little niggers who disappeared."

Mom is speaking in the half whisper of a terrified child, and the sound leaves me cold. I hug her again in reassurance. "I know you're afraid of him. But I'm not. The best protection we have is the truth. And the truth is in Daddy's coffin."

Her eyes flicker. "Why do you think that? What can Luke's body tell you?"

"I'm not sure. It may be that Lena is the answer. In my dream, Daddy was trying to tell me something about Lena, and I have to find out what it is."

"Do you really believe that? That he was trying to reach you?"

"No. I think I saw something on the night Daddy died. Saw it and then blocked it out. But I won't know what it was until they open that coffin and I look inside. Maybe not even then. It might take a repeat autopsy. But, Mom . . . I can't do any of this without your help."

She looks down at the table, fear battling something else in her eyes. "Luke was a sweet boy," she murmurs. "Whatever he went through overseas hurt him badly, but it was our family that finished him off."

I wait for more, but she doesn't speak again. "Mom? Will you help me?"

When her eyes finally rise to meet mine, I see something I never saw in them as a child.

Courage.

"Tell me what to do," she says.

CHAPTER

55

The gravediggers have been at work for over two hours, their sweat-soaked backs bent over shovels and spades in heat that's already blistering at 11 A.M. There are six of them, elderly but muscular black men in khaki work suits. They dig slowly but steadily, like long-distance runners, their forearms rippling in the sun, and they take cigarette breaks every half hour. They retire behind a wall to do this, sharing their Kools with the backhoe operator, who sits on his yellow machine like an emperor, waiting to move the casket the last few yards to the funeral home's van. Because it lies in the oldest, most thickly wooded part of the cemetery, our family plot poses problems for the backhoe. But the gravediggers have got the coffin uncovered now. Its burnished lid gleams dully in the sun. They're widening the hole for their straps, and soon a hoist will bring up what was meant to lie here for eternity.

It took ninety minutes of dedicated effort to set this process in motion. First I drove my mother to the Wall Street office of Michael Wells's attorney, who'd left his breakfast to meet us to make out an affidavit. Then we walked across the street to the courthouse and filed the affidavit with the chancery judge, who signed an ex parte court order authorizing exhumation for a repeat autopsy on Luke Ferry. With the court order in hand, I dropped Mom by her shop and called the funeral director, the cemetery superintendent, and the medical examiner in Jackson. The medical examiner's office was so agreeable that I suspected they'd received a call from Special Agent Kaiser of the FBI.

As prescribed by custom in Mississippi, the funeral director is present as a witness. A kind and florid man of seventy, Mr. McDonough has monopolized the white burial trade in Natchez for fifty years. He stands in the shade in his shirtsleeves, his black suit jacket folded over a brick wall. He discouraged my intention to "view the remains," as he put it. I tried to allay Mr. McDonough's anxieties by telling him I have considerable experience with both death and autopsies, but he only sighed and said, "No matter how much experience you have, when it's your own folks, it's different."

I'll know in a few minutes.

My primary concern is the condition of my father's body. Mr. McDonough checked his records this morning and learned that Daddy's coffin wasn't placed in a vault before burial, which simplifies the exhumation process but also increases the chance that water has penetrated the casket. My grandfather—who handled the funeral arrangements—is apparently one of the few who knows the origin of the custom of using vaults in America. In the last century, to gain admission to medical school, applicants were required to provide one cadaver. This resulted in a great many thefts of corpses. The coffin vault was adopted as a deterrent to body snatching, because two or three strong men were required to lift the vault off a coffin. Most people today buy vaults believing that they'll prevent water from reaching their beloved, and this is partly true. But eternity is a very long time. Water carved the Grand Canyon, and it can penetrate anything made by man, given enough time. Grandpapa saw no reason to pay good money for a preventive measure that was only temporary.

He did, however, buy the finest bronze casket available, probably to impress his friends and to appease my distraught mother. That particular model had a gum-rubber burp seal, which allows gases from decomposition to escape the coffin but prevents the entry of moisture. So there's a decent chance that I won't have to endure a horror show when they open the lid.

I've passed the morning by watching the mound of dark earth slowly grow beside the grave I've visited as often as I could over the years. It's less dirt than you'd expect. Graves aren't six feet deep anymore. By law only twenty-four inches of earth are required above the casket lid, just enough to keep dogs from uncovering the dead after the mourners have gone.

One of the gravediggers in the hole shouts for something called a crow's foot. A man with a red bandanna on his head brings a five-foot-long bar with a flat toe on one end to the edge of the grave. I move closer to the hole and watch the first man insert the toe of the crow's foot under the end of my father's coffin.

"You got to break the vacuum, see?" says Mr. McDonough, who's now standing at my shoulder. "That coffin lies there all those years, it really settles into the dirt. But once you break that seal, you can pull her right on up."

The coffin comes loose with a sucking sound, like opening a Tupperware dish with something old inside. The gravediggers climb down into the hole and sling heavy straps under both ends of the coffin, then set up a block and tackle. With the combined efforts of man and machine, the long bronze box is soon resting on the grass beside the hole. Though covered with brown dirt, the casket still gleams like something brought up from a pharaoh's tomb in Egypt.

Mr. McDonough signals the backhoe operator to move as close as he can to the obstructing wall. As the driver cranks up the diesel engine, I tell McDonough to have him stand down.

"Something wrong, Miss Ferry?"

"I want to open it."

Mr. McDonough is obviously perturbed by my request. "Out here in the sun?"

"It's done routinely with exhumations for retrieving DNA samples."

The funeral director is well practiced at looking unflappable, but my aggressiveness with the dead is clearly not to his taste. "Well, I've never done one that way," he says finally.

"Nevertheless."

He shrugs in surrender. "The family owns the body. You can do what you want. I'll open her up for you."

"Thank you."

He takes a hexagonal key from his pocket, bends over the foot of the casket, and begins turning a recessed nut. The Tupperware sound returns, this time magnified tenfold, a long, slow release of pressure that carries with it the chemical odor of embalming fluid.

I tried to prepare myself before I came, by studying some old photographs of Daddy. But the dead never quite resemble our memory of

the living. The body changes quickly after death, mostly through loss
of water. Even if he's well preserved, the man I see when they open
the box might look like a stranger to me. He'll be wearing a suit,
which alone would make him a stranger in my eyes. I never saw my
father in a suit. Never saw him wear anything but faded Levi's and a
T-shirt. I thought they should have buried him in that, but the day
before the funeral, Aunt Ann showed up with an expensive black suit
that I suspected belonged to one of her ex-husbands.

Mr. McDonough straightens up from the casket and looks at me
with something like challenge in his eyes. "You want me to open it
now?"

"Please."

He turns and lifts the upper half of the coffin lid until the hinges
stop, then walks away without looking inside. The gravediggers have
moved away, though whether to escape the sight or the smell, I don't
know. It might be out of respect, but I doubt it. If I weren't here, they
would be horsing around like men on any job. I've seen it enough
times to know.

The open coffin lid blocks my view. I'll have to walk around the
casket to see inside. My palms are sweating. Contrary to what most
people believe, embalming is designed to provide a well-preserved
corpse for viewing at the funeral home, but not much longer. If the
embalmer does a poor job, the corpse can quickly become something like a prop in a horror movie, a ghoul floating in its own rotting fluids. Even if the embalmer does an excellent job, anaerobic
bacteria can survive in the body, waiting only for the slightest bit of
moisture to begin the process of decomposition.

Mr. McDonough looks pointedly at his watch.

As I take my first step, I force myself to recall my time in Bosnia
working with the War Crimes Commission. When the UN backhoes
uncovered the long trench, I saw three hundred men, women, and
children in various stages of decomposition. Mothers holding
infants. Toddlers riddled with machine-gun bullets. Little girls clinging to dolls, the last things they saw before their skulls were caved in
by rifle butts. Whatever is in this casket can't compare with that in
horror. And yet . . . the funeral director's voice whispers in my mind:
When it's your own folks, it's different.

I step around the casket and look down.

My first reaction is disbelief. Except for the black suit, my father looks much as he did in life. To a passerby, he would appear to be a young man napping quietly after Sunday dinner. A whiskery black beard covers his cheeks and chin, a beard he never wore in life. This beard is not made of hair—it's mold—but compared to the terrible changes I could have seen, a beard of mold is nothing.

"Would you look at that," says Mr. McDonough, a certain pride in his voice. "He looks as good as Medgar Evers."

Lena the Leopardess lies cradled in the crook of my father's arm. The sight of her orange-and-black-spotted fur is almost more than I can bear. I slept with Lena every night until my father was buried. And except for my dreams, I haven't seen her in twenty-three years.

"They exhumed old Medgar for James Earl Ray's trial a few years back," says Mr. McDonough, "and he looked like they'd just buried him. Your daddy's the same. Old Jimmy White was doing my prep work back then. You can't find help like that now."

"Could I have a few moments, please?"

"Oh. Yes, ma'am."

Mr. McDonough takes a few steps back.

I feel like a character in a Disney fairy tale. As though I've struggled on a long journey to get to this spot, and now, by simply bending over and kissing his cold lips, I can wake my sleeping prince and live happily ever after.

But I can't.

The longer I look at my father's face, the more certain that becomes. His cheeks have actually sunken in quite a bit—his eyes, too, despite the plastic eye caps they put beneath the lids to maintain the illusion of normalcy. With a quick motion like a bird pecking at something on the ground, I bend and pluck Lena from Daddy's arms.

"Close it up," I say.

Mr. McDonough closes the casket and signals his van to approach.

"You saw me remove this stuffed animal, correct?" I say.

"Yes, ma'am."

I know I should wait, but I can't. "Mr. McDonough, could you come with me to my car for a minute?"

He glances at his watch again. "I really should be getting back to the home. There's a service going on right now."

I meet his eyes and silently plead for chivalry, something that almost always works with Southern men.

"Well, just for a minute," he says.

"Could you bring your jacket?"

He retrieves his jacket from the wall, then follows me to my mother's Maxima, which is parked on the grass between two walled plots. I open the trunk and remove the box of forensic chemicals I brought from New Orleans to use in my bedroom. The sight of the luminol bottle makes me think of little Natriece and her saucer eyes on the day she spilled the fluid and found the bloody footprints. This job is too sensitive for luminol, which not only consumes the iron in hemoglobin as it reacts with it, but also damages the genetic markers in the blood it detects, making valid DNA testing impossible. Today I'm going to use orthotolidine, which will reveal any latent blood on Lena's coat, but also maintain the integrity of the genetic markers.

"Could you get inside with me?" I ask, climbing into the driver's seat.

After a brief hesitation, the funeral director gets into the passenger seat beside me. "What's in that bottle?"

"A chemical that detects hidden blood."

He purses his lips. "This some kind of criminal investigation?"

"Yes. Could you hold up your jacket so that it covers my hands and the leopard?"

"I guess so. You're not going to ruin it, are you?"

"No, sir."

As he unfolds his jacket, I carefully examine Lena. Parting the orange-and-black fur beneath her jaw, I can still see the stitching where Pearlie repaired her after the night my father died.

"Like this?" asks Mr. McDonough, making a tent of his jacket.

"Perfect." I hold Lena under the tent with my left hand and spray some orthotolidine on her coat with my right. Then I turn her in my hands and cover her other side with the chemical.

"What happens now?" asks Mr. McDonough.

"We wait."

Photographers once used suit jackets as portable darkrooms in the field. The advent of digital photography has probably made that practice a thing of the past, but on this day, the knowledge serves me well.

"Can you turn on some AC?" Mr. McDonough asks.

"No. We don't want this chemical blowing around the car."

"Is it toxic or something?"

"No," I lie.

"Huh. Well, what's supposed to happen?"

"If there's blood, it'll glow blue."

"How long does it take?"

"A minute or two."

Mr. McDonough looks interested. "Can I see?"

"Yes, if we get anything. I want you to witness it."

After two minutes pass, I raise the tail of the jacket and peer into the darkness. Lena's head is glowing as though painted with blue-dyed phosphorous.

My heart is pounding. Grandpapa never mentioned Lena in any version of the story he told me of the night my father died. But he definitely told me to put her into the coffin. And soon, I may know why.

"What do you see?" asks the funeral director.

"Blood."

"Can I look?" He sounds like an excited four-year-old.

"In a minute."

I carefully turn Lena in my hands and examine her head. Though smeared quite a bit—probably from cleaning by Pearlie—the blood appears to have been deposited in small gouts. There's also some fine spray that Pearlie apparently missed with her cleaning rag. Most of the blood seems to have been deposited on Lena's head, while very little touched her body. It's almost as though her head was stuffed into a wound to try to stanch severe bleeding. Did Daddy shove my favorite stuffed animal into his chest to try to save himself? It's certainly possible, though with the large exit wound in his back, that measure wouldn't have saved him.

You're looking right at the answer, says a voice in my head. *Looking but not seeing . . .*

The blue glow is stronger now. Slowly, I turn Lena's head and examine it from every angle. I study the stitches beneath her chin. Why was she torn there? If Daddy stuffed her head into a bullet wound, what could have torn her cloth covering? A smashed rib? Possibly. As I turn Lena's head to examine her nose, the answer hits me like ice water thrown in my face.

On top of Lena's snout is a perfect arch of glowing blue, almost exactly the size of the maxillary arch in an adult human being. There's not enough detail to make a comparison with individual teeth, but I know without checking that the arch on Lena's fur will perfectly match the arch of Daddy's upper teeth.

My father suffocated to death.

For the first time, the reality of that night plays out in my mind's eye exactly as it happened. Grandpapa shoved Lena into Daddy's mouth, possibly to muffle his screams of pain, but more probably to finish the job of murdering him. While Daddy lay bleeding on the floor like a gutshot deer, while Pearlie ran down from the big house to the slave quarters, my grandfather shoved my favorite companion down Daddy's throat and held his nose to finish him off. To silence him forever.

But my father will be silent no longer. Like the blood of Abel, Daddy's blood is crying out from the ground. And like Abel's murderer, my grandfather will soon be marked. Marked and punished.

"Can I look now?" asks Mr. McDonough.

I nod absently.

He lifts the jacket and stares into the darkness. "I'll be damned. Just like *CSI*."

"Just like that," I murmur. "I need to see the body again, sir."

He rolls down the window and cranes his neck to look around. "Van's already carried it back to the home."

"I need to see it before it goes to Jackson."

"You'd better get going, then. The van from the medical examiner's office could already be waiting there. They'll just transfer the coffin between vehicles without ever taking it into the prep room."

I crank the engine, back the car onto the asphalt lane, and accelerate toward the cemetery gate four hundred yards away.

"You got to drop me at my car, remember?" says Mr. McDonough.

"I can't take the time. I'll bring you right back."

He glares at me. "You stop this car right now, young lady."

"This is a murder investigation, sir. An FBI matter. Please sit back in your seat."

I don't know if Mr. McDonough believes me or not, but he sits back and shuts up. Thank God for small favors.

CHAPTER

56

Outside McDonough's Funeral Home, cars are parked along the street for two blocks in all directions. It's a Natchez tradition: you see the parked cars along here and you know someone has died. Someone white. Blacks have their own funeral homes. Their own cemeteries, too. Some things take a long time to change.

"Turn at the railroad tracks," says Mr. McDonough. "The prep room's just inside the garage door."

I turn left, then left again, and pull into a long vehicle bay. A tall black hearse stands gleaming in the sun, with several expensive sedans parked behind it. They probably belong to the family of the decedent having his service inside.

"This way," says McDonough.

He walks into an enclosed garage, past a Dodge Caravan fitted with rollers in the back. Beyond that stands the Econoline van that was at the cemetery. A teenager is washing mud out of it with a green garden hose.

"Man from Jackson come yet?" McDonough asks the boy.

"No, sir."

"Your lucky day," he says over his shoulder.

Past the garage door, a short corridor lined with upended caskets wrapped in plastic leads to a door marked with a biohazard symbol.

McDonough knocks, but no one answers. He pushes open the door.

My father's coffin lies on the floor of the prep room. The bronze has been wiped down, probably to keep mud out of the prep room rather than from any gesture of respect. This time I don't wait for McDonough. I go to the coffin and open the lid myself.

"Do you suture the gums shut?" I ask. "Or do you use the needle injector system?"

"You know your business," he says. "We've been using needle injectors since they come out."

Steeling myself against the emotions boiling in my chest, I don a pair of latex gloves from a box on the counter, then bend over my father and touch the line of his mouth. Gentle pressure does not part his lips.

"Sometimes we have to use Super Glue," says McDonough. "To keep them closed. Other times Vaseline does the trick."

Trying not to tear the desiccated skin, I pry a little harder.

The lips part.

The first thing I see is two lengths of silver wire twisted tightly together and folded back under the lips. This is what keeps the teeth together during the viewing of the body. Small screws are fired into the bones of the upper and lower gums by a spring-loaded injector. Each screw has a four-inch length of wire attached. Using forceps, a technician twists the two lengths together, tightening them until the corpse's teeth come together. Then the technician snips the leftover wire and tucks the twist out of sight.

"Wire cutters?" I ask.

McDonough goes to a drawer and rummages noisily through it. "Here you go."

Careful not to damage my father's teeth, I fit the blades around the twisted wires and snip them in half. The mandible sags immediately, mocking the mindless gape of sleep.

"You looking for something in his mouth?" asks the funeral director.

"Yes."

"What?"

"I'm not sure."

I tilt my father's head back a little, then open his mouth wide and insert Lena's head into it.

"What the hell?" mutters the funeral director.

"Turn off the lights, please."

He obeys.

A few moments after the lights go out, my pupils dilate sufficiently to see the glow produced by the orthotolidine reacting with the blood on Lena's fur. As I suspected, the glowing arch on her snout perfectly matches my father's maxillary arch.

"Lights please," I say, trying to keep my voice steady.

I can't begin to name the feelings swirling through me. It's a nauseating combination of excitement and dread. I've been hunting killers for a long time, but it strikes me in this moment that I've been hunting only one killer all my life.

The knock on the prep room door makes me jump. When McDonough opens the door, an elderly man stands there, looking inside with obvious curiosity.

"I'm from the medical examiner's office," he says.

McDonough looks at me. "You finished?"

"I need three minutes."

He closes the door. "Don't pay that fellow any mind. The ME's office pays retirees to drive for them. They pay by the mile. Drivers don't know crap about the business."

"Flashlight?"

McDonough passes me a yellow penlight from the drawer.

With my heart racing, I systematically probe my father's mouth with a finger. What am I hoping for? A tuft of fur? Some trace evidence of another person? As my finger slides between the upper gum and cheek, I feel something small and hard, like a kernel of corn. I remove it with my thumb and forefinger.

It's not corn. It's a plastic pellet—a gray one—exactly like the ones that were pouring out of my father's chest in my dream. *"My God,"* I breathe.

"What is it?" asks McDonough.

"A plastic pellet. It's from inside this stuffed animal. Originally they were stuffed with rice to make them soft, but after a while the company started using plastic."

"Is it important?"

"It's evidence of murder. Do you have a Ziploc bag?"

McDonough gets one, and I place the pellet inside. More probing reveals three more pellets: one behind the cheek, two in the throat.

"You saw me locate these," I say. "I'm replacing them exactly as I found them. Did you witness that?"

"Yes, ma'am."

"And you'll testify to that in court?"

"I hope it doesn't come to that. But I'll say what I saw."

As I pull off the gloves with a snap, a worrisome thought occurs to me. I should have searched my father's mouth before inserting Lena's head into it. The stress is getting to me. I pass Mr. McDonough the stuffed animal. "Please examine this and see if you can find any holes in her coat."

Surprisingly, he dons a pair of gloves and obliges me. "I don't see any."

I'd really like a few moments alone with my father, but if I'm alone with the body, that might cause legal problems later. In full view of the funeral director, I kneel beside the casket, lay my hand over my father's, and kiss him softly on the lips. A little mold isn't going to kill me.

"I love you, Daddy," I whisper. "I know you tried to save me."

My father says nothing.

"I'm going to save myself now. Mama, too, if I can."

For a moment I think Daddy is crying. Then I realize it's my own tears running down his face. The iron veneer of professionalism I've managed to maintain up to this point is cracking. It's no anonymous corpse lying in this box. It's my daddy. And I don't want to lose him again. I don't want him back in the ground. I want him to sit up and hold me and tell me that he loves me.

"Miss Ferry?" says McDonough. "You all right?"

"No, I'm not all right." I get to my feet and wipe my eyes. "But I'm going to be. For the first time in my life I'm going to be all right. But somebody else isn't going to be. Somebody else is going to *pay*."

McDonough looks embarrassed. "Is it okay to close the casket now?"

"Yes. Thank you for everything. I'll take you back to your car now."

"Don't worry about that. I've got people who can do that."

"Thank you."

My knees are barely steady enough to carry me out of the prep room, but they do. As I enter the coffin-lined corridor, however, a thought strikes me. I turn around.

"Mr. McDonough?"

"Yes, ma'am?"

"Have you spoken to my grandfather today?"

The funeral director looks quickly at the floor. And that is my answer.

"Mr. McDonough?"

"He called and asked me to let him know what you did at the cemetery."

I feel the grasp of my grandfather from miles away. "Sir, my grandfather is a powerful man. I know you know that. But you've just become involved in an FBI serial murder investigation. My grandfather is also part of that investigation, and not in a positive connection, if you get my meaning. If you interfere by communicating information on these matters to him, the FBI will be crawling up your ass with a two-foot-long halogen flashlight. They will have OSHA down here doing inspections on a daily basis. Do I make myself clear?"

Mr. McDonough looks as if he wishes he'd never set eyes on me. "Ain't none of this my business," he says. "I won't be talking to nobody about it."

"Good."

When I step into the sun outside the garage, I find myself facing several men wearing their Sunday best. They all have roses pinned to their lapels. They're pallbearers, I realize, and they've just carried the deceased to the waiting hearse. Soon the family will emerge from the side exit behind me.

I walk quickly down the side of the building, but I can't escape. A woman about my age rounds the corner with an infant in her arms. As I move aside, her mouth drops open.

"Cat?" she says. "Cat Ferry?"

"Yes?"

"It's Donna. Donna Reynolds."

I blink in confusion.

"Used to be Donna Dunaway," she says.

Recognition comes like a thrown switch. It's like the day I met Michael Wells. Only Donna hasn't lost weight in the intervening years like Michael. She's gained. But somewhere in her plump, rosy cheeks is the outline of a thin-faced girl I knew in junior high school.

"Is this your baby?" I ask.

She nods happily. "My third. Four months old."

My eyes fix on the baby's round face as I search for something appropriate to say. Nothing comes. My head is spinning from what I've just discovered in the prep room. The baby has huge eyes, a flat nose, and a laughing smile.

"What's his name, Donna?"

"Britney. She *is* wearing pink, you know."

"Oh, God, I'm sorry."

Donna isn't angry. She's smiling. "Are you here for the funeral? I didn't know you knew Uncle Joe."

"I don't. I mean . . ." As my words fade into silence, my gaze settles on the baby's toothless smile. A long string of drool drops from Britney's mouth, and the greatest epiphany of my life occurs. There's no blast of trumpets or bolt of lightning from the heavens—merely a sudden and revelatory flash of absolute certainty.

I know who killed the men in New Orleans.

CHAPTER

57

"Cat? What's going on?"

I gasp in relief. I'm almost to Malmaison, and I've been trying to reach Sean since I left the funeral home. "I know who the killer is, Sean."

"Whoa, whoa, which killer are you talking about? Your family stuff, or the New Orleans case?"

"New Orleans!"

"How the hell could you know who the killer is?"

"How do I ever know? Something clicked in my head."

"What clicked this time?"

I'm tempted to tell him, but if I do, there'll be no stopping the consequences. And right now I'm not at all sure I want the killer arrested. "I can't tell you that, Sean. Not yet."

"*Shit*. What are you up to, Cat?"

"I'm coming to New Orleans this afternoon. I want you to meet me at my house. Are you still suspended?"

"Yeah."

"Do you still have your badge and gun?"

"I've got a gun. And I have a badge that'll do in a pinch. What do you have in mind?"

"I want to talk to the killer before we do anything."

"Talk to him? About what?"

"It's not a him, Sean. It's a her."

I hear a quick rush of air. "Cat, don't do this to me."

"It's only a few hours. I know it's hard on you, but you'll understand when I get there." I turn into the drive of Malmaison and accelerate down the oak-shaded lane. The iron gate stands open. I drive through it and take the sweeping curve toward the main house.

"Why did you call me?" Sean asks in a strange voice. "Why not Kaiser?"

"Because I trust you." I'm lying. I picked Sean because—to a certain extent—I can control him.

"Okay. Call me thirty minutes before you get here."

"Be ready." As I swing into the parking lot behind the slave quarters, I'm shocked to find Pearlie's blue Cadillac parked beside Grandpapa's Lincoln. Shocked and glad. "I need one more favor, Sean."

"What is it?"

"I know who killed my father, too."

"Yeah? Who?"

"My grandfather. He's the one who molested me. Not my father. Daddy caught my grandfather abusing me, and Grandpapa killed him to keep him quiet."

"Fuck." In that one curse I hear two decades of homicide experience. "I'm sorry, Cat."

"I know. This isn't about that. Look, if I don't make it to New Orleans for some reason—if I'm dead, in other words—I want you to do something for me."

"What?"

"Kill him."

There's a long silence. "Your grandfather?"

"Yes."

"Are you serious? You mean take him out?"

"Yep. Remove him from the world."

The phone hisses and crackles. "That's asking a lot."

"If I'm dead, he'll never be convicted. And I think he's still doing it. You understand? If you love me, you'll do it. For me, Sean. And for your own kids. I have to go now."

"Wait! If something happens to you, how will I know who the killer down here is?"

I think for a minute. "I'll write it on a piece of paper and put it under the floor mat of my mother's car. Her name is Gwen Ferry. She drives a gold Nissan Maxima. Good enough?"

I hear him breathing. "I guess it'll have to be."

I hang up my mother's cell phone, then open the console and dig through it. About the only piece of paper big enough is a grocery ticket from Wal-Mart. On its long, narrow back, I scrawl the logical basis for my epiphany at the funeral home. As I lift the floor mat beneath my feet to conceal the note, I pray that Sean doesn't have to drive to Natchez to find it.

CHAPTER

58

Pearlie doesn't answer my knock. When I try to go in anyway, I find the door locked. This frightens me. Pearlie's door is never locked. At least it never was when I lived here. One more sign of how things have changed.

She's drawn her curtains, too. After trying the front windows on the ground floor, I go around back. One window there is barely latched. By jiggling the frame, I get the latch loose, then slide up the window.

Pearlie's bedroom is dark, her bed empty. A converted slave quarters like ours, her house has no hallways. I move quickly to the door and pass through to the kitchen.

Like my mother this morning, Pearlie is sitting at her kitchen table without lights, staring blankly ahead. Unlike my mother, she's smoking a cigarette. I haven't seen Pearlie smoke since I was a little girl. An ashtray full of butts is beside her, and a bottle of cheap whiskey stands beside her coffee cup.

"Pearlie?"

"I thought you was Billy Neal coming to get me," she rasps.

"Why would he come get you?"

"'Cause of what I know." Her voice has a frightening note of fatalism in it.

"What do you know?"

"Same thing you do, I reckon."

"What's that?"

A new alertness comes into her eyes. "Don't play games with me. Tell me what you come here for."

"I'm about to confront Grandpapa. I wanted to talk to you first."

She blinks once, slowly. "How come?"

"Because you know things I need to know. And I want you to know what I've learned about him."

"What you talking about?"

"Grandpapa murdered Daddy, Pearlie."

The orange eye of her cigarette glows bright. "You just think that? Or you can prove it?"

"I can prove it. What I want to know is, did you already know it?"

Pearlie exhales a long stream of smoke. "Not to prove, I didn't. I didn't see him do it, if that's what you mean."

"That's not what I mean, and you know it. Did you suspect it?"

"I had thoughts that night. Later on, too. But there wasn't nothing I could do about it."

I knew it. "You think Grandpapa's invulnerable, Pearlie. But he's not. I'm going to put him in jail. I've got evidence now. Remember Lena the Leopardess?"

A glint of memory passes behind her eyes. "The toy you buried with Mr. Luke?"

"That's right. Grandpapa suggested I put her in the coffin with him. Do you know why he did that?"

"I know there was blood on her. I know Dr. Kirkland told me to throw that toy away. When I told him it was your favorite, he told me I could wash it off and sew the rip back together."

"Do you know how Lena got torn?"

She shakes her head.

"Grandpapa stuffed her into Daddy's mouth so he would suffocate before you got downstairs. He wasn't dying quickly enough from the bullet."

Pearlie winces. "Lord Jesus. Don't tell me that."

"That's not the worst of it. You remember the story about Grandpapa cutting out Ann's appendix by lantern light on the island? How he was the big hero for saving her life?"

"Sure I do. Him and Ivy both."

"Well, he took out her appendix, all right. But he did a little something extra, too. He cut her fallopian tubes, so she couldn't get pregnant."

Pearlie bows her head and begins to pray softly.

"Why did you go to the island yesterday, Pearlie? You hate that place."

"Don't want to talk about that."

"You've got to start talking. You've been silent too long."

She sips whiskey from her coffee cup, then lights another cigarette and takes a deep drag. "I quit cigarettes twenty-three years ago," she says, smoke floating out of her mouth with each word. "I've missed 'em every day, like a pain that won't quit. But when I heard Miss Ann was dead, I had to have me one. I ain't stopped since."

I say nothing.

"I come to work here in 1948," she says, almost to herself. "I was seventeen. Miss Ann was born that year, but they was living in New Orleans then. Dr. Kirkland was still training to be a doctor. He and Mrs. Catherine didn't move to Natchez until 1956, and they didn't take over this place until sixty-four, when Mr. DeSalle died."

She looks at me as though making sure I understand. "That's why I missed it, you see? Miss Ann was sixteen when they moved in here. The damage was already done. But things still wasn't right. Not really. Any boy that come to call on Ann, Dr. Kirkland frightened away. Even the nice ones. Lots of daddies will do that a little, but Dr. Kirkland never gave an inch. He was jealous of that girl. Mrs. Catherine saw it, too, but she couldn't do nothing to change it."

"If they'd been living in Natchez since 1956," I reason, "surely you saw some other signs before they moved to Malmaison?"

The old woman chews her bottom lip. "I been thinking about that for two days now. There was times when they left the girls here, going on long trips and such. Sometimes Dr. Kirkland would leave me medicine for Ann. She didn't seem sick, 'cept she had to go to the bathroom too much, and it stung when she went. I'd give her the medicine, and she'd get all right. But looking back, she had too many of them problems. No other doctor ever saw it, though, you see? Her daddy was her doctor."

Oh, I see. "He was my doctor, too."

Pearlie lays her hand over mine, the skin papery over sinew and bone. "I know, baby. I knew something was wrong when Ann was just a toddler. I just didn't know *what*. She'd laugh at the right times, but the laugh never touched her eyes. Those eyes were like glass. Shiny, but empty at the same time. Lord, how the boys liked her, though. Ann was the most popular girl in town. They couldn't see the pain hidden in her heart."

"Or maybe they could," I say. "Maybe they sensed it, and that's what drew them."

"Maybe so," Pearlie murmurs, nodding sadly.

"What about Mom?"

She takes another sip of whiskey and grimaces as she swallows. "Gwen was twelve when they moved in here. She didn't have the same problems Ann did. She could smile and laugh, and she seemed like a normal child. But she married young as she could to get away from this house. But then she didn't get away after all. The war brought her back. And the older she got, the more problems she had. Looking back, I think Dr. Kirkland got to her, too. The damage got done when she was just a baby, same as with Ann. Just not as bad."

"I think Ann tried to protect her."

Pearlie nods slowly. "Ann tried to be everything to everybody. To save everybody. But she couldn't even save herself."

"Did Grandmama Catherine ever suspect anything?"

"She never said nothing to me. But Mrs. Catherine sure knew when to disappear. And she let Dr. Kirkland spend a lot of time with those girls alone. I saw it when they stayed up here during Christmas, when the girls was little. If Dr. Kirkland was gonna be around the house during the day, Mrs. Catherine would find somewhere else to be. It gave me a bad feeling, but what could I say about it? Times was different back then. A maid like me couldn't open her mouth about something like that. All I could do was be there for those girls when they got upset. Try to ease their pain a little bit."

"Did you ever see anything yourself?"

She shakes her head. "Looking back, I think Dr. Kirkland made sure I didn't."

"How did he do that?"

"He'd walk this property all hours of the night, just like your daddy. I think that's one reason he didn't like Mr. Luke. He couldn't prowl around without being seen anymore. The few times Dr. Kirkland caught me out after nine, he warned me to stay indoors. Said he might shoot me by accident, thinking I was a burglar. So I stayed right in this house unless I got called out by him or Mrs. Catherine."

In hindsight, it all seems so obvious. What's missing is the historical context. The idea that Dr. William Kirkland, respected surgeon and paragon of virtue, could be tiptoeing around his antebellum mansion molesting his daughters was virtually unthinkable forty years ago.

"What about the island?" I ask.

Pearlie shifts uncomfortably in her chair. "What about it?"

"Do you think he bothered any children there?"

"If he did, nobody would tell me about it."

"Why not?"

"'Cause I left there and never went back. I turned into a house nigger. They think I'm Dr. Kirkland's slave, bought and paid for."

"Why didn't you ever go back?"

She looks at me with something like scorn. "Why you think? There was a man there I had to stay away from."

"Who?"

"My uncle."

"Why did you have to stay away from him?"

She snorts. "Why you think, girl? Same kind of trouble as this."

"Sexual abuse?"

"They don't call it that on the island. They call it getting 'broke in.' The men do, leastways, and some of the women, too. I got broke in by my uncle when I wasn't but twelve. He wouldn't let me alone. If he hadn't had to go to jail for a while, I'd have wound up pregnant or worse. So when I got a chance to get off the island, I took it."

From somewhere in my mind, a new image rises. A small black girl walks along a gravel road. Out of the shimmering heat an orange pickup truck appears, and then the man who pays her father and mother offers her a ride . . .

"Ivy never told you any stories?" I ask. "Nothing that made you suspicious? Even I've heard things about the kids there being scared to walk the roads alone."

Pearlie folds her hand on the table. "Baby, a man with a taste for that kind of thing don't stop doing it. He takes what he needs whenever he can get it. I'll tell you something else. I think the women down there know about it. That's why they tell spook stories to keep their children off the roads. But they don't tell their husbands nothing, you can bank on that. They don't want them going to the death house at Angola for killing the boss man."

"Do you know that, Pearlie? Or just suspect it?"

She shrugs. "Does it make a difference?"

"In a court of law, it makes all the difference in the world."

She spits out air in a rush of scorn. "You ain't getting Dr. Kirkland in no courtroom. He too smart and too rich. Men like him don't go to jail. You got to know that by now, girl."

"Times have changed since you were young, Pearlie."

A parched laugh escapes her lips. "You believe that?"

"Yes."

"Then you ain't smart as I thought you was."

Pearlie's cynicism pisses me off. If all women were like this, we'd still be chattels and not citizens. On the other hand . . . I grew up in a much more privileged world than she did.

"You never answered my question, Pearlie. Why did you go to the island yesterday?"

The bow of her shoulders sags. "A couple of years ago, a family moved off the island real quick. I heard about it later. They had one child, a four-year-old girl. They just packed up and left without a word. I wanted to find out if that was because of Dr. Kirkland."

"Did you?"

She inhales from her cigarette as though drinking the nectar of the gods, then holds the smoke in her lungs for as long as possible before letting it out in a long blue stream. "No," she says finally. "Nobody would talk about it. They all scared."

"Was that the only reason you went down there?"

She turns her dark gaze onto me, and at last I feel the full power of her instinctive intelligence. All her life Pearlie has hidden her quick understanding; that's what she was raised to do. But the death of my aunt—one of "her babies"—has caused a tectonic shift in the old woman's soul, and Pearlie Washington is never going to be the same.

"I don't think Mrs. Catherine died by accident," she says in a whisper. "I never did."

This statement shocks me to the core. "Are you saying Grandmama Catherine was murdered? She couldn't have been. People saw her fall into the water."

"Did they?" Pearlie's eyes glint in the dark. "She was standing off by herself when she went in. But did she fall? Did that sandbar really cave in? Mrs. Catherine practically grew up on DeSalle Island. You think she'd stand on a weak sandbar like some city fool and not know it? No, child. No more than Mr. Luke would let somebody sneak up on him after he was in the war. I think Mrs. Catherine finally found out something so bad that she couldn't live with it. If she'd gone to the police, she'd have ruined her family name forever. Her children were already full grown . . . I think she just couldn't see what else to do but die. I think she drowned herself in that river, baby."

Suicide? A seventy-five-year-old woman? "What do you think she saw, Pearlie?"

The old woman's shoulders drop even lower. "A few years ago, when I was cleaning Dr. Kirkland's study, I found some pictures."

My breath catches in my throat. "What kind of pictures?"

"The kind you don't have to take to the drugstore to get developed."

"Polaroids?"

She nods.

"What were they of?"

"You and Miss Ann."

My face is burning. "Doing what?"

"Swimming in your birthday suits."

"Together?"

"No. They must have been took twenty-five years apart. Neither of you was more than three in the pictures, and nekkid as the day you was born. Both in a swimming pool somewhere. If those pictures had been mixed up with a bunch of others, I wouldn't have thought nothing of it." Pearlie holds up a bony finger, the nail painted with red polish. "But just those two . . . and took so far apart. It gave me a cold feeling. Like the devil walking over my grave."

"You think Grandmama found those pictures?"

"She found something. The month before she died, Mrs. Catherine wouldn't hardly say a word to nobody. Had a far-off look in her eyes. Hopeless."

"Pearlie, I found some pictures of naked children hidden in the barn—in Daddy's things."

She looks stunned. "Mr. Luke had pictures like that?"

"Yes. But knowing what I know now, I think he did exactly what *you* did. He found some of Grandpapa's pictures. But he kept them. I'll bet he was going to confront Grandpapa with them. They might even have been what made him suspicious enough to check my room on the night he died."

"I been looking for more pictures like that," Pearlie says, "but I ain't found none yet. Lord, the misery that man done caused. He's sick, that's what he is."

I get up and pull the curtains away from the kitchen window. Malmaison stands majestic and silent as a royal sepulchre. "He's not going to hurt any more children," I say softly. "That stops today."

"How you gonna stop him? Even the po-lice afraid of Dr. Kirkland. Lord, this place cost more than all the houses of every cop in this town put together. The mayor's house, too. Dr. Kirkland got friends all the way up to Washington, D.C."

"Don't worry about it. You just promise me that if you have to get up in front of a jury, you'll tell the truth about what you know."

"They make you swear on the Bible, don't they?"

"Yes."

"Well, I'm too old to lie with my right hand on a Bible. But you be careful. Dr. Kirkland ain't the only sick man around here. That Billy Neal be just as bad, and he's a lot younger and stronger."

"Younger, maybe. Not stronger. If you turned those two loose in the woods and only one could come out alive, Grandpapa would eat Billy's liver for supper."

Pearlie stands unsteadily and walks to me, then hugs me the way she used to when I was a little girl. The way my mother never quite could. "You remember when I told you I quit smoking?"

I think for a minute. "Twenty-three years ago, you said. That's when Daddy died."

She nods, her chin digging into my shoulder. "You know why I quit that year?"

"Why?"

"Because I knew cigarettes was poison. And after Mr. Luke died, I knew you was gonna need me around to look after you. I'm just sorry I didn't do more, baby. Sorry I couldn't save you from all the pain you been through." She pulls back and looks into my eyes. "You're the strongest of all my girls. I always said that. Dr. Kirkland think you got that strength from him, but I know better. Mr. Luke was a good man, and tough when he had to be. Old Mr. DeSalle, too. Maybe . . . oh, I don't know. I'm just gonna pray for you, whatever prayers is worth. Maybe with the Lord's help, you can come through all right."

I kiss her gently on the cheek, then unlock the door and walk out into the sunlight.

My grandfather's Lincoln is still parked beside Pearlie's Cadillac. As I stare at the two cars, I sense someone watching me. Turning to my right, I see Billy Neal staring down at me from the rear gallery of Malmaison.

He's smiling.

I turn toward him and start walking, my strides long and resolute. The closer I get, the more his smile fades. By the time I'm within speaking distance, he's scowling at me. He's also wearing a sport jacket in the dead of summer. Looking closer, I see the butt of an automatic pistol protruding from a shoulder holster beneath the jacket.

"What do you want?" he asks.

"You've hitched your wagon to a falling star," I say in a flat voice. "You should leave while you can."

He laughs. "What the fuck are you talking about?"

"Follow me and find out."

CHAPTER

59

Grandpapa is talking on the telephone at his rolltop desk, his broad back clothed in a custom-tailored shirt of French blue silk. His deep voice fills the room like a finely tuned bass viol.

"Hang up," I say sharply.

He rotates his leather chair, and his eyes fix upon me.

"I know what you did," I tell him.

"Just a minute," he says into the phone. He presses the mouthpiece against his shirt. "What is it, Catherine? I'm very busy right now."

"I know you murdered my father."

His only reaction is a slight narrowing of the eyes. Then he glances at Billy Neal, who's standing by the door. "I told you what happened that night, Catherine."

"You told me four different times. A different story every time. But I know the truth now. Evidence doesn't lie. You murdered him, and I can prove it."

Grandpapa raises the phone to his lips again. "I'll have to call you back."

"First you shot him. Then you shoved my favorite stuffed animal into his mouth to keep him quiet. Then I figure you held his nose shut with your fingers while he suffocated."

In the time it takes Grandpapa to hang up the telephone, his eyes change from the benign blue of a loving grandfather to the cold slits of a wolf sensing threat. The transformation chills my blood. I have never seen this face before, and yet I recognize it. This is his *real face*—the face of the man who put himself inside me when I was a baby.

"Are you wearing a microphone?" he asks.

I shake my head.

He doesn't believe me. For some reason, this sends a surge of anger through me. "You want me to strip for you?" I start to unbutton my top. "It's not like you haven't seen me naked before, is it?"

"Stop that," he snaps. Then he waves his hand at Billy Neal.

The driver takes something from one of the shelves and walks toward me. It's a black metal wand like the ones they use in airports to check for concealed weapons. He sweeps it up and down my body, lingering in the crotch area.

"She's clean," he says finally. He walks back to the door and stands beside it like a guard dog.

"Do you know anything about this?" Grandpapa asks, pointing at the far wall.

To my amazement, dozens of books lie strewn about the floor, as though someone ripped them off the shelves in a frantic search. Pearlie's words replay inside my head: *I been looking for more pictures like that . . . but I ain't found none yet.*

"Mice?" I say in a flat voice.

He starts to respond, then discards the whole subject as not worthy of his attention. "All right. I told you I was busy. Is there anything else?"

I can't believe his arrogance. "Didn't you hear me? I can prove that you murdered my father. I can also prove you sexually abused Aunt Ann. And worse."

He dismisses this with a wave of his hand. "That's ridiculous."

"I have evidence."

"Bloody footprints on a floor? I've already explained that."

"I have a lot more than that." I'd like to tell him about Pearlie, but I can't put her at risk. "And I'm remembering more every day. I know what you did to me."

Grandpapa's eyes narrow again. "*Remembered* evidence? It sounds to me like you've been taking your friend Dr. Malik a little too seriously."

What the hell is going on here? I had no idea that he even knew who Malik was.

"Catherine, so-called repressed memories count for exactly nothing in a court of law. I'm surprised you don't know that."

"Ann's body will count," I say evenly.

For the first time, I see a shadow of worry cross his face. "What are you talking about?"

"How could you do that to her, Grandpapa?"

"Do what?"

"*Sterilize* her! You cut her fallopian tubes when she was ten years old. *Jesus.* All your life you've acted like you're better than everyone else. The best surgeon, the best businessman, the best hunter, the best father. You're none of that! You're a fucking monster. A *freak*."

His steely eyes are riveted on my face. "Are you finished?"

"No. You're going to pay for everything you did. For Ann, for Mom, for me. For the children on the island, too."

The jaw muscles flex in his impassive face. I know more than he thought possible, and he doesn't like it.

"I'm not going to pay for anything," he says. "I have nothing to pay for."

"Do you deny what you did? That's what child molesters do. They scream they're innocent all the way to the pen. They're probably still screaming that when it finally gets done to them in the prison shower. Your kind doesn't fare too well in Parchman, Grandpapa."

William Kirkland has never been talked to this way in his adult life, but he only straightens in his chair and smiles coldly at me. "I'd fare well anywhere in the world, Catherine. You know that. But I'm not going to prison. Your so-called evidence is worthless. A stuffed animal taken from a coffin that's been in the ground for twenty years? You can't connect me to that."

"I can identify the maxillary arch of Daddy's teeth in the latent blood on Lena's coat."

He purses his lips in thought. "Luke must have grabbed Lena and bit down on her to fight against the pain after you shot him."

"Don't even try that," I snap, but I can see Grandpapa selling that story to a jury as smoothly as he's sold himself all his life.

"Ann's body *proves* that you sterilized her," I say softly. "You never dreamed she'd be autopsied, did you? Not back in 1958. You shouldn't have used silk sutures, Grandpapa."

He rises calmly from his chair and shoots his cuffs. "Catherine, you're obviously delusional. Ann was obsessed with becoming pregnant, everyone knows that. She went to all sorts of quacks for fertility treatments. She even went to Mexico. God knows what procedures she had done, or what butchers performed them. You'll never prove I did anything more than remove her appendix. Even if you did, what's the crime? Unnecessary surgery?" His eyes brim with confidence. "I've been accused of that before, and I came out smelling like a rose."

I hate the smell of roses. I have ever since I saw my father lying dead among them—

"Have you been taking your medication?" he asks in a condescending voice. "Maybe I should review your drug regimen with your psychiatrist. Are you still on the Depakote?"

I was prepared for extreme reactions when I entered this room—rage, denial, rationalization, even begging—but supreme confidence wasn't one of them. He hasn't even denied the abuse. He's just shooting down my accusations as though he were playing games with a poorly prepared lawyer. I want to shake that confidence. I want to see the worm of fear work its way through his gut and up into that megalomaniacal mind.

"I'm not the one you have to worry about," I tell him. "It's Dr. Malik who's going to nail you."

Grandpapa glances at Billy Neal again. "That would be quite a trick. Since the good doctor happens to be dead."

A dry chuckle from Billy. I'm starting to wonder if it was Billy Neal who faked Malik's suicide in the Thibodeaux Motel.

"Dead or alive doesn't matter," I say with confidence I don't quite feel. "He's going to speak from the grave. You're going to be revealed for what you are on TV screens from coast to coast."

Neither Billy nor my grandfather is laughing now, and I thank God for it. If they were, I'd be pretty sure that Dr. Malik's film had already been destroyed. But it hasn't—not by them anyway. They don't even know about it.

"I see you don't know about Dr. Malik's documentary on sexual abuse."

In seconds, the threatened wolf is back. I hear a creak to my left. When I look that way, Billy Neal is gone. Did Grandpapa signal him to leave? Whether he did or not, he takes Billy's exit as a cue to advance toward me, six feet six inches of rage, with blazing eyes and a voice like Moses' down from the mountaintop.

"Do you have any idea how much trouble you've caused me? I'm sweating blood trying to save this town, and you're working around the clock to sabotage everything I've achieved!"

What the hell? I accuse him of sexual abuse, and he's screaming at me about a business deal?

"Federal certification of the Natchez Nation could come any day!" he roars. "The state gaming commission would *love* an excuse for a federal injunction to stop that. I am *deep* into this deal, Catherine. I have money on the table. Not other people's money. *Mine.* Your inheritance, if you give a goddamn—which you probably don't."

"You're right," I say quietly. "I don't. All I care about is what you did to this family. That's all you should care about, too. But that was the problem all along, wasn't it? You didn't care. We didn't exist, except to pleasure you when the mood struck you."

He takes another step toward me, but I don't back up. "I remember what you did. It's taken almost thirty years, but it's coming back. The pond . . . the island . . . the orange pickup . . . the rain."

Something flickers in his eyes, an emotion I can't read. The fury he displayed only moments ago seems to have been discharged. "Do you remember?" he asks, his voice suddenly much softer. "Do you remember how you felt? You loved being my special girl. My little angel. You loved being better than your mother. You gave me what the others couldn't, Catherine."

He's very close to me now. The moment has an obscene intimacy that makes my bowels turn to water. "You do remember. They all liked it . . . but not like you. No one else responded the way you did. You're just like me."

"No," I moan. "Shut up."

Grandpapa squares his broad shoulders and looks down at me. "Has anyone made you feel the way I did? I've watched you go from man to man . . . always searching . . . None of them are man enough to handle you, are they?"

I was right not to give Sean the identity of the killer in New Orleans. She and I are sisters. If I had a gun in my hand, I would open fire and keep firing until the gun was empty.

Grandpapa folds his arms and looks down at me the way he used to look at his patients. "I'm going to speak frankly to you, Catherine. What's the point of going through life with illusions? Mine were taken away when I was a little boy, and

I'm glad for it. It made me strong. It saved me a lot of heartache later on."

"What are you talking about?"

"Everything you've said today is true. I had relations with Ann. Gwen, too."

I want to interrupt, but my voice won't come.

"Great men have great appetites, darling. It's that simple. More hunger than one woman can satisfy. Your grandmother knew that. She didn't like it, but she understood."

"Liar!" I shout, finding strength in my grief and outrage. "How do you convince yourself of this shit? Grandmama didn't *understand*. She suspected you for years, but she did everything she could not to validate her fears. Just like the rest of us. Because to believe it, we'd have to admit that you never loved us. That you only kept us around to *fuck* us!"

"You're wrong about your grandmother."

"No. Somewhere beneath all the lies you tell yourself, you know the truth. When she finally figured out what a monster she'd married, she drowned herself, so she wouldn't have to live with what she'd let happen to us."

Grandpapa's composure comes apart slowly, like mud cracking in the sun.

"You say she wasn't enough for you. Why didn't you divorce her, then?"

He walks away from me and stops before a painting of the Battle of Chancellorsville. "It was my destiny to manage the DeSalle fortune. The fact that I've quadrupled it in size proves that."

"Take a mistress then. Why come to *us*? Your own children?"

He shakes his head. "A mistress makes you vulnerable."

"And having sex with your own children doesn't?"

"Exactly." When he looks back at me, he reminds me of a math teacher puzzled by kids who can't grasp the simplest concept. "Your grandmother didn't suspect what I was doing, Catherine. She *knew*. How could she not? She knew I needed more than she could give me, and she preferred that I get it at home rather than embarrass her in society."

A coldness unlike any I've ever known envelops me. Could he be right? Could Pearlie be wrong? "I don't believe you."

He shrugs. "Cling to your illusions if they make you feel better."

"You're saying you had sex with us for utilitarian reasons? And Grandmama knew that?"

Exasperation tightens his features. "Damn it, girl, you act like I'm the first man who ever did this. The same thing happened to me when I was a boy. My grandfather was a widower. He used me for sex. I'm not whining about it. But the fact is, that kind of sex does something to you. It gives you a taste for something that nothing else can satisfy. It's like war. You get a taste for killing, and you have to keep doing it. Only this craving is stronger. I know you've felt it, too. That's the way it works."

I shake my head in denial, but I'm not so sure he's wrong.

He holds up his big hand and stabs a forefinger at me. "I'm going to tell you a hard fact of life, Catherine. A woman is a life-support system for a pussy. Period."

I blink in disbelief.

"You know I'm right. You're a scientist. But heredity has given you a chance to rise above that primitive function. You've got brains, and you've got will. But you'll never transcend your sex if you blind yourself to the realities of life."

"You're insane."

"Am I?" He goes to a shelf and pulls out a large black volume, then tosses it at my feet with a bang. It's a King James Bible. "Take a look at the book of Leviticus. There you'll find all the biblical proscriptions against incest. All the rules laid down for everyone to see. A man is forbidden by God to have sex with his mother, his wife's mother, his sister, his aunt, with an animal, with another man, or with a woman having her period. It even mentions the daughter-in-law. But one relationship is specifically *not* mentioned."

I feel like I'm standing on the ledge of a skyscraper in a high wind. "Which is that?"

"Father and daughter. Old Leviticus skimmed right over that one. Because he knew the reality of life."

"Which is?"

My grandfather's eyes shine with the conviction of a zealot. "You came from my loins, Catherine. Your mother and Ann, too. You are the issue of *my blood*. You were *mine*. To do with as I saw fit."

He walks to the gun safe, quickly spins the dial, and opens the heavy door. From it he takes a rifle, which he calmly loads with a cartridge from a box on the shelf. As he walks toward me, I recognize the Remington 700 that killed my father.

"It's still true," he says, his eyes locked on mine. "You're *still* mine."

He works the bolt and chambers the round. "What if this gun were to go off?" He brings the barrel within a foot of my face. "What if it blew your brains all over the wall? What do you think would happen?"

"You'd be convicted of murder."

He smiles. "Would I? I think not. A woman with your psychiatric history? Documented bipolar disorder, unstable past, threats of suicide? No. If I really considered you a threat, you wouldn't leave this room. But you're not a threat. Are you, Catherine?"

I should back down. Show submission. Live to fight another day. But I can't. I've done it all my life for him, and I won't do it anymore. "Oh, I'm a threat. I'm going to make sure you die in prison. And you should know this: if you kill me now—or before I get back to New Orleans—someone's going to do the same to you."

He looks more interested than afraid. "You mean Detective Regan?"

I feel the blood drain from my face.

There's a hint of humor in his eyes. "Catherine, do you honestly believe I don't know who you see down there? I *own* Sean Regan. Do you think he would kill me in revenge when that would result in photographs of the two of you rutting like animals being sent to his wife and children?"

No . . . he wouldn't.

"If this Malik film you spoke of really exists, you'd do well to get it for me or destroy it. I'd hate to give you something to really be depressed about."

"What are you talking about?"

"Life's little tragedies." He smiles again. "You hate me for being this way, but one day you'll thank God that you have my blood flowing through your veins. My genes determining your fate."

When my voice finally emerges, it's utterly devoid of emotion. "You're wrong. I wish I'd never been born. You don't know this . . . but I'm pregnant. And for the first time since I found out, I'm wondering whether I should bring that child into this world. I feel contaminated. Like I can never wash your poison out of me."

He lowers the rifle and steps closer, his eyes glowing. "You're pregnant?"

"Yes."

"Boy or girl?"

"I have no idea."

He reaches for my arm. I jerk backward.

"Take it easy, girl. Who's the father?"

"You'll never know."

"Don't be that way. You'll come around. You've got more of me in you than you think."

"What do you mean?"

A knowing smile now. A man hoarding a secret. "I could be your father, Catherine. Do you realize that?"

With these words, what's left of my composure crumbles. My very being is unraveling into nothingness. My grandfather's face is red, the way it gets when he's stalking game on the island.

"Luke spent all his time on the island," he says, "chasing that nigger girl, Louise. And your mother just lay sleeping in her room here, half-looped on Luke's medicine." He nods slowly. "You see now?"

The triumph in his face is absolute. It's the triumph of the hunter standing over his dying prey. He's shoved the steel into my heart and broken off the handle. He revels in the pain in my face, just as he must have all those years ago. The savage joy in his eyes brings me back to the world, and in returning, I feel a horror I never thought imaginable.

"Is that true?" I ask in a small voice.

He shrugs. "It's certainly something to think about while you're making plans to talk to the district attorney."

I'm backing away from him, reaching blindly for the doorknob.

"And if you're thinking of Pearlie testifying to anything, forget it. She'll never do it."

My hand closes around the brass knob. "Why not?"

"Because she knows the order of things. You might get her stirred up with a lot of nonsense, but in the end she won't say a word against me. Pearlie knows her place, Cat. Same as the niggers on the island. Your ancestors taught them well, and I've reinforced the lesson." He goes to the sideboard and pours some Scotch into a glass. "You know your place, too, honey. Deep down, you do."

I drop my shaking hand from the knob, then raise it and point a quivering finger at him. "No. You were too strong for me when I was a baby. But not anymore."

With a bemused look on his face, he drinks off the Scotch and wipes his mouth on his cuff.

I pull open the door, stumble through it, then run down the hallway toward the kitchen. I don't know where I'm going, only that I have to get away from this house. Sean expects me in New Orleans, but it's hard to imagine functioning in any normal capacity. Simple linear thought seems beyond me now.

I crash through the kitchen door and race through the rose garden, toward the parking lot behind the slave quarters. Mom's Maxima is parked where I left it, a few yards away from the Lincoln and the Cadillac. As I near the cars, I hear a muted banging. Then the passenger door of Pearlie's Cadillac opens, and Billy Neal climbs out. There's a pistol in his hand. He aims the barrel at a spot between my breasts.

"I've been waiting a long time for this," he says. "Let's take a ride."

"What's that noise?"

With a gleeful smile, he opens the trunk of the Cadillac. "Come see."

I walk to the back of the car.

Pearlie lies bound in the trunk, her hands and face covered with blood. Her wig is gone. A grayish white fuzz covers her narrow skull, which is wedged against the spare tire. I've never seen her eyes so filled with terror. As I reach down to help her, Billy's gun pokes the ribs under my left arm. He slams the trunk shut, then shoves me toward the driver's seat.

"You're driving," he says, pushing me behind the wheel.

"Did you shoot her?"

"Don't worry about that old bitch. Worry about the driving."

"Where are we going?"

"Where do you think?" He grins so broadly that it makes my cheeks hurt. "The island."

CHAPTER
60

My last ride to the island is both dream and nightmare.

Highway 61.

A narrow, winding strip of asphalt following the Mississippi River.
Mythical American highway.

Escape route for northbound refugees, most of them black, fleeing a place that held no hope but where their hearts remained nonetheless, yearning for the body's return. I tried to use this highway as an escape route, too, only I never got away. For thirty-one years I've driven up and down this road between two lovely, sleepy cities, but always the island lay between them, a dreamworld shrouded in fog and memory, waiting like an empty stage for my life's final act.

Today it will be played out.

The messenger of my fate is Billy Neal.

It seems wrong, somehow. I never really knew this man. This black-haired, pale-skinned, dime-store-handsome Vegas punk with snakeskin boots and a night-school law degree. What the hell is he doing in my life? Obligingly, he answers me without being asked.

"You still don't know who I am, do you?"

I grip the wheel harder and keep my eyes on the road.

"*Man,* I've been waiting for this," he says, his gaze moving over me like a wet tongue. "You've had this coming a long time. The nigger, too."

If Pearlie weren't tied in the trunk, I'd take my chances and ram the Cadillac into a tree, just to kill this bastard. That's probably why he put her in there.

"You don't know shit, do you?" he says.

"Guess not."

"Look at me."

"I'm driving."

He reaches out with his gun and pulls my face around. He looks as angry as he does triumphant. *Why?* I wonder, my eyes lingering on his pistol. It's an automatic, ugly and clean as a fresh scalpel. It'll do its job.

"Did my grandfather send you to do this?"

Billy smiles strangely. "A smart officer doesn't give orders like this. But a good soldier knows what to do when trouble comes. A good soldier doesn't have to be told."

"Soldier? I know what kind of soldier you are. The kind my father got stuck with in Cambodia."

His eyes narrow. "What?"

"Nothing. You wouldn't understand."

Billy kicks a snakeskin boot up onto the dash of the Cadillac. "You think you're pretty smart, don't you?"

I don't answer.

"You smart enough to know what's about to happen to you?"

"You're going to kill us."

He laughs. "You get the prize, sweet thing. But that was the easy part. The question is, *why?*"

I know better than to take this bait. The more interest I express, the less he'll tell me. That's his nature. He's never had much power, so he takes it however he can get it.

"Well?" he presses. "Do you?"

Pearlie bangs twice on the trunk lid. It makes my heart hurt, but at least she's still alive.

"Because you're in my way," Billy says in a reflective voice. "That's why."

"What do you mean?"

"If you stay alive, you'll inherit my money."

This wasn't the answer I expected. "Your money? What are you talking about?"

He laughs again, this time almost a cackle. "Kirkland's my father, you dumb cunt. You haven't figured that out yet?"

After all I've heard today, this revelation doesn't have much effect.

After all I've heard today, this revelation doesn't have much effect.

"My mother worked for one of those DeSalle companies. Book-keeping. She did a lot of work at home. Dr. Kirkland would go by her house to check up on the figures. I guess the main figure he was interested in was hers. Anyway, he nailed her. And I was the result."

"You sound proud of it."

Billy shrugs. "Nothing to be ashamed of. He paid her hush money nice and regular. Sent me to school, got me out of a couple of scrapes. That's how I wound up in the army."

"The army or jail, was it?"

"Something like that. He paid for law school, too, when I got out. Anyway, that makes me your uncle—or that's what I thought until today. After hearing what he told you in the study, it sounds like I may be your half brother, too." Billy laughs again.

"That's bullshit."

"You wish it was." He checks the safety on his pistol, then flicks it on and off a couple of times. "The thing is, I already got a piece of the gross of the Indian casino. I did a lot of work prepping that deal for him. Wet work, you know what I'm saying? But the thing is, there's more money to be had. A lot more. My mama's got records of it. There's money you probably don't even know about. Cayman Islands, Liechtenstein, all over. And now that your pretty little aunt offed herself, you and your mother are the only living heirs in the will. You believe that?"

I believe it. Grandpapa may have wanted sons, but nothing would cause him to bequeath one dollar outside the legitimate family, not even to charity. Not unless he got something in return.

"He's been relying on me more and more lately," Billy says. "He's seen what I can do. While *you've* been doing nothing but fucking up. You're a pure liability to him now, that's a fact. When you disappear, he'll breathe a sigh of relief."

"You're probably right."

Billy looks at me in surprise, but then he nods with satisfaction, glad to have his intuition confirmed.

Highway 61 unrolls steadily ahead of us, curving through the hardwood forest, leading us ever southward. A gray mass of clouds is gathering to the southeast. If we went on toward Baton Rouge, we'd probably miss it, but the bulk of the storm seems to be piling up over the river, right about where the island faces Angola Prison.

Only fitting, I suppose, that my last bit of thread should play out in the rain.

We're ten miles down the Angola road when the rain sweeps over us. The sound of drops hitting the roof sends me halfway into the trance I learned to enter before I could even think for myself. Billy Neal seems to think the rain a good omen. Smiling with contentment, he tunes the radio to a country station.

"You like the rain?" I ask.

"Today I do."

"Why today?"

He turns to me and purses his lips, as though debating whether to confide something. "Because you're going to drown today, Sis."

This strikes me as so absurd that I almost laugh out loud. "How's that?"

"You're gonna drive off the bridge to DeSalle Island."

I say nothing, but in my mind I see Brer Rabbit crying, *Please don't throw me in that briar patch!* Is this the best that Billy can come up with? If he drives me into the old river channel in this car, I can get myself and Pearlie to shore without even breaking a sweat.

"I see you thinking," he says. "Don't worry, I know all about your free diving. You're gonna be down at the bottom *way* too long to save yourself."

"If you tie me up, it won't look like an accident."

He smiles his secret smile again. "You're not the only one who can swim. After you've been down there twenty minutes or so, I'm going to go down and take the ropes off. No muss, no fuss. A drunk manic-depressive runs herself and her nigger maid into the river in a storm. Open-and-shut case."

"I'm not drunk."

"You will be." He opens the glove compartment and takes out a pint of Taaka vodka. "Found this in the slave quarters. Guess your mama likes vodka, too." He uncaps the bottle and shoves it at me. "Drink."

"No, thanks."

"Not up to your standard?" He presses the barrel of his gun against my temple. "Drink."

"I can't. I'm pregnant."

"Pregnant!" He laughs from deep in his belly. "Shit, you're going to be dead in an hour!"

"So you say."

The blow from the gun is so sudden and sharp that everything goes black for a moment. I feel the car swerve, but I manage to right it.

"You fucking drink this," he commands.

"No."

He's tensing to hit me again when I see the turn for the island. "Look!"

"Go on," he says. "Take it."

Just ahead, a narrow dirt track leaves the road and heads into the deep woods. How many times did I take this turn as a little girl, terrified it would rain when I reached the island, yet powerless to stop the journey? Thirty years later, I've come full circle.

Billy Neal takes a swig from the vodka bottle, then screws the cap back on and throws the bottle into the seat behind us.

"You'll drink it," he says. "Or I'll beat that nigger to death right in front of you."

CHAPTER

61

Billy watches me with visceral hatred as I navigate the Cadillac down a road that is mostly mud. The tail of the car keeps trying to come around on me, forcing me to drive slowly. Still, the road seems all too short. When I sight the low-water bridge leading to the island, Billy points into the trees on the right.

"Pull in there. Ground's hard enough. There's a little clearing up ahead."

"How do you know that?" I ask, driving over the ground where I parked the Audi on my last visit.

Billy gives me a tight smile. "That's where I parked when I followed you out here the other day."

"You chased me into the river?"

"Who the fuck else do you think it was? Jesse Billups? That spade wouldn't get out on the river in a storm if his life depended on it."

"Did my grandfather send you to kill me that night?"

Billy stops smiling. "What does it matter? Pull up there and stop."

A clearing has opened ahead. There's plenty of room for the Cadillac between the tree trunks, but the forest canopy protects us from the brunt of the rain. Billy reaches over and switches off the motor. Soon there is only the ticking of the engine and the soft drip of water on the hood and roof.

"Nice, huh?" Billy says.

"I thought you were going to kill us on the bridge."

"You in a hurry?" He points the gun at me. "Turn and face the window. Put your hands behind you."

"Why?"

He jams the gun barrel under my jawbone. "Do it now."

"You can't shoot me. You want it to look like an accident."

"You're right, I'd rather not. But I don't mind popping a cap in your smart-ass maid one bit. Nobody's going to make a fuss over that dried-up old jig."

Will he shoot Pearlie? Yes. But if I let him tie my hands, what chance will I have to save us? Some . . . But if he ties them to the steering wheel, I'm in trouble. Can he do that now? He still has to get the car onto the bridge. . . .

It may be the most foolish act of my life, but I turn on the seat and face the window. I'm expecting rope, which I saw on Pearlie in the trunk, but there's a soft tinkle of metal, then steel bands close tight around my wrists.

Shit! If I go into the water with handcuffs on, I'm in trouble.

Billy gets out of the car. For a moment I think he's going to get Pearlie out of the trunk, but then he starts unbuttoning his jeans. I turn away, expecting to hear him urinate, but what I hear instead is a swish of cloth against flesh. Then he leans back into the open door.

"Hey," he says. "Look here."

I turn. He's wearing black bikini briefs, and his eyes are shining.

"What are you doing?" I ask.

"What do you think?" A lurid smile. "I want a taste of what the boss man had."

He pulls off his underwear and climbs back into the car, pulling at himself as he sits beside me. The gun is still in his other hand. "You got an ass on you, that's for sure. And you won't have no more use for it after today. Might as well take it for one last spin, right? Nobody'll know. We'll keep it all in the family."

My heart flutters like a panicked bird beating its wings to pieces. With a pair of handcuffs, Billy Neal has turned me into the helpless little girl I was when my grandfather raped me.

"Straighten your legs out on the seat," he says. "Let's get those jeans off."

I shake my head.

The glaze in his eyes brightens. "I'm gonna get out and pump four bullets into that trunk."

"You're going to kill her anyway."

"True enough. But later's better than sooner, right?"

I don't know what to do. My synapses don't seem to be firing properly.

"It's human nature, plain and simple," Billy says, stroking himself to erection. "People will do anything they think will keep 'em alive for five more minutes. The Nazis knew that. Used it all the time to control people. Right up to the moment they slammed the door to the gas chambers."

"You a big fan of the Nazis?"

He laughs. "Straighten out your fucking legs."

Billy's right. I want to live every second I can. Every second of life is another chance at escape. The irony is exquisite. All my life I've flirted with suicide, yet here I sit, desperately wanting a few more moments of air and sunlight. I'm only alive now because this man wants to have sex with me. And if I become too much trouble, he'll shoot me.

Billy's smile has a manic edge. "There's another option you may not have thought about. I can shoot you first and fuck you after. You'll still be plenty warm."

My mouth goes dry.

"I'd prefer it the other way around, but it's your choice."

At least if he shoots me first, I won't know I'm being raped. I won't feel it. But suddenly it hits me: *I don't have to feel it anyway.* That's the one magic trick I learned as a child—dissociation. Billy Neal can do what he likes to me, and I can watch it all from the balcony, a disembodied observer.

"Guess you made your choice," he says, getting out of the car. "The nigger pays for your pride."

"Wait!" I cry, extending my legs down the length of the front seat.

He leans back into the car, reaches out with one hand, and unsnaps my jeans. Then he unzips them, digs his fingers into the open fly, and yanks brutally until most of my legs are bare.

"Kick 'em off," he says, breathing hard from the effort.

As if his voice controls my limbs, I obey.

He throws my jeans into the backseat, then points his pistol at my face and tears off my panties.

It's eerie how quickly I dissociate from what's happening. I'm already watching myself the way I watch characters in a movie—

fascinated but at a critical remove. I've actually asked lovers to act out this scenario with me: rape as pleasure. A lot of normal women have probably done the same. I've asked men to tie me and choke me and slap me around. And now that the real thing is happening, it's not much different from the playacting. It should be, I know. It *would* be for a normal woman.

But it's not for me.

Would most women endure rape to live a little longer? Or would they fight to the last breath to keep their so-called honor? Fighting isn't going to stop Billy Neal. It's just going to make him hurt me more. Besides, what is it for me to be raped once more? It's happened so many times already that one more violation has no meaning. I see now that I was raped even as an adult. Even when I was saying yes, something beyond my understanding was driving me to repeat the only kind of sexual union I knew.

"I know about girls like you," Billy says, pulling me across the seat until I'm facing forward like a passenger on a Sunday drive. "Girl's who got broke in young. They know how to please a man better than a Thai hooker."

He kneels on the floor in front of me and transfers his gun to his left hand. With his right hand he pumps his penis, causing it to swell and grow red. The sight is bizarre yet familiar: a man I barely know is about to insert himself into me. It's happened more times than I let myself remember.

"You wet?" he asks, reaching out and checking me like a mechanic checking the oil in an engine. "Shit." He spits in his palm, then slathers his organ with saliva. Then he spits again and puts his fingers inside me. "There you go," he murmurs. "Now you're getting there."

Numbness spreads through me like a narcotic, masking everything but the sudden fullness of penetration. It's nothing to me, though. Only a reenactment, a ritual, a role I learned to play before I learned almost anything else.

Only this time it's different. This man doesn't want merely to use me. He wants to kill me. Like the men of my father's unit, the White Tigers, who kidnapped village girls as a reward, then raped them all night and killed them to keep them quiet.

Those girls are my dead sisters.

Something metallic bangs behind me, and for a moment I'm

dragged back into the present, my heart aching for the old woman lying terrified in the trunk. But Pearlie Washington must bear her own burden now. In some ways she's the lucky one.

"Yeah," Billy grunts, thrusting his hips with the fury of an angry carpenter driving nails. "It's good . . . yeah."

Good? This is good? I've heard this word before. But it doesn't make sense. How can this be good? But he tells me it's good . . . that I'm good . . . and more important, that I'm special. That's good. I want to be special. . . .

"You're too far back," he gasps, lunging harder. "Scoot up to the edge of the seat."

I obey.

Pearlie keeps banging on the trunk lid, a pitiful sound diminishing in strength, like the struggles of someone freezing to death. I imagine she's praying, though why I don't know. When I last left her, she told me that with God's help I might just make it through. But God isn't going to help me. That's one thing I've always known.

Water is falling on my face. At first I think it's rain leaking into the car, but it's not. It's Billy Neal's sweat. He pushes up my shirt and yanks down my bra, exposing my breasts. "Yeah," he says in a ragged voice, kneading them roughly. "Fuck, yeah."

His mouth is fixed in a grimace, as though this act causes him physical pain. His breath is bad enough to penetrate my trance. I see the cause of it, too. His mouth is in bad shape. He thrashes his hips wildly, banging me against the seat back, his neck muscles straining like he's lifting weights, his external jugulars distended like two pipes ready to burst. I'm not sure whether it's the sight of those veins or the proximity of his teeth that awakens me, but it's one of the two. Because in the midst of this savage assault, my mind begins to work very fast and with clinical precision.

The masseter muscle of the jaw is the strongest in the human body. It can generate two hundred pounds per square inch of biting force.

Nine pounds of force will tear off a human ear. I learned that while working in the ER when I was in medical school.

What could two hundred pounds per square inch of force driving a mouthful of sharp teeth do to a human neck? It's a matter of some interest to me now, because Billy's neck is exposed directly above me, his veins bulging from the exertion of violent intercourse. A caveman could tell me the answer. Teeth and nails were the first edged weapons *Homo sapiens* ever possessed. I tell that to homicide detectives when I brief them on my forensic speciality. I could bite straight through to Billy's jugulars, no problem. Clamp down and whip my head back and forth like a pit bull until he's spewing blood. That would scare the hell out of him—and hurt like blazes—but it wouldn't kill him. It might not even disable him badly enough to keep him from shooting me in the head.

A torn carotid would, though. A torn carotid artery would kill him. It would also send him into instant panic. Not many people can watch their blood spurt three feet into the air and remain calm. But the carotids are protected by many layers of tissue.

The jugular veins lie just beneath the skin.

Billy has stopped thrashing. He's settled into a steady rhythm now, working over me like most men I've had sex with, grunting and heaving, eyes blank, breath coming in quick, ragged gasps.

His breath . . .

The trachea is a hollow tube of cartilaginous rings, held together by the muscle and fibrous tissue that fills the spaces between the rings. Car accident victims frequently die when their tracheas are crushed by steering wheels. Would two hundred pounds of pressure crush a trachea? My instinct and training tell me yes.

Besides, two hundred pounds per square inch is a round number. Eskimos—who feed on a much more robust diet than the rest of us—commonly generate twice that amount of biting force. A woman trying to save her life ought to be able to match that.

Already my gaze has moved from Billy's bulging jugulars to the exposed semicircle of his windpipe. To get a firm purchase, I'd have to turn my head sideways, so that my bite was perpendicular to the tube. That's the way a leopard takes down an antelope, by biting the throat with its long canines. And that takes a sideways grip.

Not like a leopard, I think. *Like a leopardess. Like Lena . . .*

There's a mole at the base of Billy's neck. Dark brown, with black hairs sprouting from it. His neck muscles are flexed so hard that his Adam's apple is invisible. But I know it's there. My target is just above it, the smallest and softest stretch of the trachea—

"Unhh," he grunts. *"Oh, yeah . . . getting close."*

The gun is in his left hand—not his dominant one. He could still shoot me with it, though, no question. But I don't have time to wait for a miracle. Tilting my head as far to the side as possible, I open my mouth and begin sucking his neck.

"*Fuck, yeah,*" he gasps. "*Oh, yeah . . .*"

I open my mouth wider, exploring the soft geography of his neck with my tongue. There's the left external jugular . . . the ridge of the sternothyroid muscle, the buried larynx . . .

As Billy approaches the pinnacle of his labors, he throws back his head, as some men are wont to do. I open my jaws as wide as they will go and clamp my teeth down on his windpipe with every ounce of strength I can bring to bear.

Cartilage crunches loudly between my teeth.

I feel like I've bitten through a chicken breast, bones and all. Billy's body goes rigid as blood fills my mouth in a hot rush. All I can see in my mind is the gun coming up to my head, blowing my brains all over the car.

But it doesn't happen.

Billy flails his arms and legs like a man caught in a threshing machine, but the harder he tries to pull away from me, the more room I have to yank back my head with all my strength. For a few moments we're locked in savage combat, and then my teeth tear free. His hands fly to his throat, and hope surges through me like a bolus of adrenaline.

He's not holding the gun!

Frothy blood pours from a ragged wound in his throat, but it's not the blood that shocks me. It's the wheeze of air escaping from the hole with every respiration. That wheeze is the sound of impending death.

And Billy Neal knows it.

CHAPTER

62

I've never seen panic like that in Billy Neal's eyes, but I'm not waiting around to enjoy it. With a wild lunge, I throw my body most of the way out of the car. He makes a halfhearted grab for my feet, but by kicking hard, I manage to get clear.

Scrambling to my feet, I fight the urge to look back as I stagger into the trees. One moment of hesitation might be all he needs to pick up the gun and kill me. I'm still stumbling through the trees when I hear the engine start.

Terrified for Pearlie, I turn and race back toward the car. It's hard to run with your hands cuffed behind you. I fall several times, and by the time I get back to the clearing, the Cadillac is gone. I hear its motor accelerating up the dirt road.

Naked from the waist down, I struggle down to the old river channel and work my way along it toward the bridge. It's muddy by the water, but there's a lot of sand in the soil, so the going isn't too bad. Soon I am trotting herky-jerky across the bridge to the island like some armless woman running for charity.

On the far side of the bridge I see my grandfather's orange pickup rusting in the weeds. This time it doesn't faze me, because a hundred yards to the right of it, a white pickup is rolling down the perimeter road, heading for the bridge.

I can't wave my arms, but I can scream.

With tears streaming down my face, I shout for help again and again, sucking in great lungfuls of air that Billy Neal only wishes he could inhale right now. I don't know if it's my screaming or my nakedness that draws the driver's attention, but the truck turns onto the bridge and comes straight toward me. For a moment I think he means to run me over, but then the brakes squeal and the truck shudders to a stop. A black man jumps down out of the cab, his eyes wide. His face is a mass of scar tissue.

"Sweet Jesus!" cries Jesse Billups. "What happened to you?"

"Get back in the truck! I'll tell you on the way!"

"Where are we going?"

"Pearlie Washington's hurt! She's locked in the trunk of a car, and the driver's going to kill her."

"My aunt Pearlie?"

"Yes!"

Jesse isn't sure what's going on, but he gets behind the wheel and throws the truck into gear. When I climb up into the cab beside him, he reaches behind the seat, grabs a dirty Windbreaker, and ties it around my waist.

"Go for the Angola road!" I shout. "I hurt him bad. He's got to be trying to get to a hospital."

Jesse steps on the gas and heads for the shore. "Who you talking about? Who did you hurt bad?"

"Billy Neal."

Jesse wrinkles his lips. "That's a no-count motherfucker, right there."

"You know him?"

"Oh, I know him. He the one called me away from the island the night you disappeared. You remember? We was talking at the cabin, and I got that call."

"I remember."

"He told me he needed to talk to me down in Baton Rouge. Said it was real important, and for me not to tell you about it. I drove down there to the hotel he said he was at, but he was gone. He never showed."

"He tried to kill me that night."

Jesse shakes his scarred head. "Why ain't you got no pants on?"

"Billy tried to rape me."

The foreman gives me a quick once-over. "Tried?"

"He was raping me, okay? He was going to kill me. Pearlie, too."

"How'd you hurt him?"

"You'll see, if you catch him. Get this damn thing moving!"

When we reach the dirt road, Jesse pushes the truck as fast as it will go in the mud, which is bound to be faster than Pearlie's Cadillac. I remember the Caddy sliding back and forth on the curves like a heavy boat navigating a bayou.

"Damn," Jesse mutters. "Ain't that Aunt Pearlie's car there?"

Fifty yards ahead of us, a baby blue Cadillac is sitting nose-first against a pecan tree, steam rising from its hood. The driver's door is open, and a man's torso and head are lying out of it. The man's face is covered with bright red blood.

"Hurry!" I shout. "Pearlie's in the trunk!"

Jesse skids to stop a few yards from the car. Billy Neal isn't moving, but that doesn't mean he's dead. The blood on his face could be from nothing more serious than a broken nose.

"Do you have a gun?" I ask.

Jesse reaches behind the seat and brings up a bolt-action deer rifle.

"Cover Billy while I get the trunk key."

"How you gonna get the key out the ignition with them handcuffs on?"

"You're right. You do both."

Jesse gets out of the truck and chambers a bullet with a reassuring snick of metal. I jump down awkwardly from the cab and walk close behind him as he approaches Billy Neal.

"That fucker moves, I'm wasting him," Jesse says.

"Fine by me."

He edges up to the Cadillac with the rifle barrel extended toward Billy, the way he might approach a wounded rattlesnake. As he gets closer, I sense the tension in his body easing. And then I see why.

Both of Billy's hands are empty, and the graying fingers are covered in blood. In the red flag of blood that is his face, two eyes stare skyward, the life in them all but gone. When I get close enough to touch him, I hear a faint whistle. Tiny red bubbles are frothing from the hole in his throat.

"How the fuck did he do that in a car wreck?" Jesse asks.

"He didn't. I did it."

"With what?"

"My teeth."

Jesse leans down closer. "Mother*fucker*."

"Get the keys, Jesse."

"Yes, ma'am."

While Jesse retrieves the key from the ignition, I kneel beside Billy. His eyes widen in fear, and then freeze that way.

The whistling has stopped.

I've killed a man. I've killed a man, and all I can think is that I'm glad I got my father's teeth. DeSalle teeth are small and round. Kirkland teeth are large and square but prone to decay. Ferry teeth are hard as stones, the incisors square, the canines sharp. I remember my daddy popping the caps off Coke bottles with his bottom teeth when I was little. He said he learned it from his father. As this memory passes through my mind, an intoxicating current of elation flows through me. *I could not have Ferry teeth if Luke Ferry weren't my father.* It's not as conclusive as a DNA test, but I know teeth like I know nothing else.

Luke Ferry was my father.

"Look at *this* shit!" Jesse cries. "Get up out of there, Aunt Pearlie!"

I jump up and go to the back of the Cadillac. Having laid his rifle on the ground, Jesse is now lifting his aunt carefully out of the trunk. Pearlie's face and hands are still bloody, but compared with Billy Neal's, her eyes are full of life.

"Are you all right, Pearlie?" I ask.

She points at my naked legs beneath the Windbreaker. "Are *you*?"

"Yes."

She closes her eyes and shakes her head. "I told you . . . with the Lord's help, you'd come through."

I don't even try to argue. "Yes, you did."

Jesse sets her gently on her feet and holds her erect while she tests her legs. Then he leaves us alone. Without her wig, Pearlie looks a hundred years old. But she's not. She has a lot of life left in her.

"What you gonna do now?" she asks, looking down at Billy Neal's corpse. "What Dr. Kirkland gonna do?"

"I don't know. I can't worry about that now. I have to get to New Orleans."

She looks shocked. "Now?"

"Right now."

"How come?"

Because I have a killer to talk to, and I need to beat everyone else to her. "If I don't, the FBI is going to arrest me."

Pearlie shakes her head. "Well, you do what you have to do, then. Jesse can take me to the island."

"You need a hospital, Pearlie."

She makes a scornful face. "A drink of whiskey is what I need."

Jesse returns with a small silver key in his hand. "You want those handcuffs off?"

I turn my back to him, and he removes the cuffs. Rubbing my wrists to get the blood flowing, I go to the car and retrieve my jeans from the backseat.

"Aunt Pearlie said you need to get to New Orleans," Jesse says, walking up to me.

"That's right."

"How you plan to get there?"

"I'm going to take one of the island trucks."

He looks uncomfortable. "Dr. Kirkland know about that?"

"No, he don't," Pearlie snaps from behind him. "And he ain't *gonna* know."

Jesse turns toward his aunt. She's standing with her hands on her hips, arms akimbo, glaring at him as she might at a recalcitrant boy of seven.

"Jesse Ford Billups," she says, "you gonna serve the man who beat you bloody all them years ago? Or you gonna help this girl do what's right?"

He sighs heavily. "Shit, Aunt Pearlie. I don't know what—"

"*What you say?*" The old woman shakes her finger in Jesse's face. "You know better than to curse me, boy! If your mama was alive, she'd knock you nekkid. You get your narrow ass in gear. *Now.*"

Jesse Billups, combat veteran and foreman of DeSalle Island, nods in surrender. "What about that one?" he asks, jerking his thumb toward Billy Neal.

Pearlie turns up her nose. "Leave that trash for the buzzards. They got to eat, too."

CHAPTER

63

"Tell me again about the teeth," says Sean.

We're sitting at the kitchen table of my house on Lake Pontchartrain, just as we've done so many times before. Spread out in a row on the table before us are eleven photographs. The women in the photos vary in age from nineteen to forty-six—the women we believe most likely to constitute Group X. We culled these from a group of thirty-seven women ranging in age from two to seventy-eight—all the female relatives of the victims of the NOMURS killer. We chose them while talking on the phone during my drive down from DeSalle Island. And lying in the middle of the row, with five women on either side of her, is the woman I believe killed the six victims.

"The teeth," Sean prompts me. "Are you awake, Cat?"

I turn from the table to the dark blue square of my picture window. Night is falling fast. "We all have large numbers of bacteria in our mouths," I murmur. The primary one is *Streptococcus mutans*, which produces the acid that causes cavities."

Sean taps a yellow highlighter against the tabletop. "And the culture of the saliva from the bite marks on Quentin Baptiste had none of this bacteria?"

"Right. At twenty-four hours, no growth. Very unusual."

"Could someone have made a mistake taking the saliva sample?"

"It wasn't some flatfoot who swabbed those wounds, Sean. It was the FBI's forensic expert. We have to assume he did his job right."

"I don't like assuming anything."

I look back at Sean and try to keep my voice even. "Me, either. It was an assumption that kept me from figuring out who the killer was yesterday. When Kaiser first showed me that lab report, the strep thing was a flag. A couple of possibilities hit me—like someone on antibiotics—but I was totally distracted at the time. I'd just learned that my aunt had committed suicide, and I was trying to escape the FBI building. I knew the saliva might have come from someone without teeth, but the possibility of it being a baby . . . I just automatically ruled it out. I mean, we're dealing with serial murders here. The image of a six-month-old just doesn't go with that. I feel like an idiot now. I've just been so out of it for the past few days. Alcohol withdrawal, off my meds, Valium—" *Pregnant,* I add silently. "It took me seeing that drooling baby at the funeral home to put it together."

"And this is what you came up with?" Sean says, tapping the photo at the center of the row. It shows a dark-haired girl of twenty-two. "Evangeline Pitre?"

"It's her, Sean." Evangeline Pitre is the daughter of Quentin Baptiste, the murdered homicide detective—victim number six. "That random meeting at the funeral home associated saliva and babies in my mind. After that it was simple elimination. I knew that none of the victims' female relatives had sons younger than eighteen months old. But Kaiser had told me one of Baptiste's daughters worked at a day-care center. The only question was whether that day care handled any male children under six months old, the age at which teeth erupt. I confirmed it by phone after I left the island, but I knew, Sean. I just knew."

"You can't convince me that this girl committed all six murders on her own," Sean says.

I study the photo, searching for signs of homicidal ability—as if such things were visible. Evangeline Pitre's eyes are deep set and dark, contrasting sharply with her pasty skin. She has a certain prettiness, but also a guardedness in her face, like the look on a stray cat that expects a kick before a scrap of food.

"Her father was a homicide cop," I point out. "There's no telling what kind of skills and knowledge she might have."

"And you think this girl is killing everyone's abusers for them? Punishing them?"

"It might be just that simple. Or it might not. Pitre could be killing them without anyone else in the group knowing what she's doing. But that's not what my gut tells me."

Sean makes a wry face. "My gut tells *me* that Nathan Malik developed the whole fucking plan. Pitre may have got the saliva to put into the bite marks. She might even have pulled the trigger, if she knows how to shoot. But where did she get the idea to use a human skull to *make* the marks? No, this chick didn't come up with the crime signature we've been seeing. Hell, she didn't even finish high school."

"I agree, okay? But that doesn't mean Malik was behind it. It could be any one of the other women in the group. One or all."

"You're forgetting Margaret Lavigne's suicide note," Sean reminds me. "'May God forgive me. An innocent man is dead. Please tell Dr. Malik to stop it.' Malik was controlling those women, Cat. Running them like robots, using their emotions to drive them."

"He probably knew what was happening," I concede. "That doesn't mean he planned it or helped carry it out."

Frustration tightens Sean's face. "Why are you so hell-bent on defending him?"

"Because Malik was doing all he could to help women in severe pain. Women that nobody else knows how to save."

Sean sighs. "We can debate this all night. What are we going to *do*?"

"I told you. I want to talk to Pitre."

"You want to go see this woman alone and—"

"Not alone. With you."

"Without backup."

"You're my backup."

He groans in exasperation. "You want to go in without backup and talk to a woman you think viciously murdered six men?"

"That's right. We won't be in any danger. She's only interested in killing child abusers, not cops."

"Margaret Lavigne's stepfather didn't abuse anybody, but he's just as dead as the other five victims."

"That killing was obviously a mistake, caused by a false memory recalled by Margaret Lavigne."

Sean nods like I'm making his point for him. "Yeah. And who

killed Dr. Malik? Who set that skull on his lap? The Hair Club for Men?"

"I'm hoping Evangeline Pitre can tell us that."

Sean doesn't reply. He's staring at me intently, but he no longer sees me.

"What is it?" I ask, knowing an idea has hit him. "What do you have?"

"Maybe nothing. Hang on." He picks up his cell phone and punches in a number. He's calling the Second District police station, where Quentin Baptiste worked as a homicide detective. He asks to speak to O'Neil DeNoux, a detective I've never heard of.

"Who's that?" I whisper.

"Baptiste's partner. Hello? O'Neil? Sean Regan. I need to know something about Quentin. Cop to cop . . . Yeah, I know I'm working with the task force. But this isn't going to the Bureau, okay? . . . Did Quentin carry a throwdown gun? . . . Fuck, man, this is serious. . . . Yeah? . . ." Sean nods at me, his eyes wide. "What caliber? . . . Thanks, man. I owe you. . . . I know you won't forget it."

He hangs up, his face pale. "Quentin Baptiste sometimes carried a Charter Arms .32 as a throwdown."

My cheeks are cold. "Jesus." I look down at the photo of Evangeline Pitre, suddenly unwilling to accept what I know to be true. She *is* the killer.

"What do you have against bringing in the task force?" Sean asks. "Do you have to be the one who personally breaks this case open?"

I look at him in disbelief. "Can you say *projection*, Sean? Shit. I don't want this case to break open at all."

"Why not?"

"Because I'm not sure the person behind these killings should go to prison. Not yet, anyway."

His mouth drops open. "You're shitting me."

"I'm not."

"Six men are dead!"

"Child molesters. All but one."

"The punishment for sexual abuse isn't the death penalty."

"Maybe it should be. For repeat offenders, anyway."

He slowly shakes his head. "That's for the legislature to decide. And a judge and jury after that, if it becomes the law."

"The legislature doesn't understand the magnitude of this crime.

Look, I killed Billy Neal a few hours ago, and you didn't have a problem with that."

"That's totally different! He was raping you. And he was going to kill you."

"Granted. But child molesters aren't just committing rape, Sean. They're committing murder. The victims keep walking and talking, so we think they're still alive. But their souls are dead. That's one thing Dr. Malik had right."

Sean leans over the table. "You're too close to this subject to make objective decisions."

Yet again, Dr. Malik's words come from my mouth. "You're right. This isn't something anyone should be objective about. It's the worst crime in the world. That's what Malik told me when I first met him, and now I know he's right. The victims are innocent children. Totally unable to protect themselves."

Sean holds up the photo of Evangeline Pitre. "This isn't a helpless child. She's twenty-two years old."

"You're speaking in chronological terms." *Still quoting Malik.* "You have no idea what's going on behind that girl's eyes. For all you know, she may never have matured past the age of six. Not emotionally."

With a groan Sean gets up and takes a beer from my refrigerator. When I see the sweating bottle, I crave alcohol for the first time in many hours.

"I've almost shitcanned my career," he says, wiping his mouth on his sleeve. "Over you and me, Cat. If we do what you want now, and we get caught . . . that's it for me."

I just stare at him. "You made your choices freely. You broke the rules on your own. I never asked you to do that. I'm going to talk to Evangeline Pitre tonight, with or without you. But be warned, Sean. If you try to go around me on this—if you call the task force before I'm satisfied that I've gotten the truth from Pitre—then I'll go to your wife and tell her everything we ever did. And everything we ever planned to do."

He goes pale. "You wouldn't do that."

"Look at me, Sean. I will."

He gazes at me as though seeing me for the first time.

"You have no idea of the intensity of emotions we're dealing with here," I tell him. "I know what an abused woman is capable of, okay? And before we throw Evangeline Pitre to the wolves, I've got to understand what happened."

He drains his beer in one long swallow, then tosses the bottle in the trash. "No backup," he says. "Dumb as it gets."

A surge of relief goes through me. He's going to come. "At least Malik is dead," I tell him, getting to my feet. "If he was Pitre's accomplice, as you believe, you have one less threat to worry about."

Sean slips his jacket on over his shoulder holster. Then he bends, takes a small revolver from an ankle holster, and checks the cylinder. "And if it's one of these other women? Or all of them?"

"Pitre lives alone. It's a weeknight. She has to work tomorrow, and she's not expecting anything. We go in forcefully, scare her, then show her a way out."

"And if someone else is there with her?"

"We take the photos with us. If we recognize one of the other women, we still go in. You take your Glock. I'll carry your throw-down in my purse. We'll be fine."

"How do I explain your presence?"

"The same way you always did when you took me on interviews."

Sean shakes his head, but a hint of a smile animates the corners of his mouth. "Shit, we were crazy, weren't we?"

"Certifiable. But we stopped some killers."

He nods. "Yeah. We did that."

"We're going to do it again tonight. Just not the way we used to. This time it's not about thrills or promotions or even personal satisfaction. It's about justice."

He raises one eyebrow. "You figure it's up to you to mete out justice?"

"This time, I do."

Sean passes me his throwdown gun, a Smith & Wesson featherweight .38. "Four in the cylinder, an empty chamber under the hammer."

I nod but say nothing.

"Could you use that on Pitre if you had to?" he asks.

As I feel the cold weight of the gun in my hand, an image of Billy Neal's bloody corpse rises behind my eyes. I can still feel his hot blood spurting into my mouth. Could I do something like that to a woman?

"Cat?"

"It's not going to come to that."

CHAPTER

64

Evangeline Pitre lives in a dilapidated white house on Mirabeau Street in Gentilly, a tree-shaded working-class neighborhood of one-story clapboards. It's full dark when Sean parks his Saab behind a beat-up Toyota Corolla at the curb out front—a car that Sean's partner just told us belongs to our suspect. Sean hangs up his cell phone and surveys the house with a veteran cop's eye.

"Joey talked to the detectives who interviewed Pitre after her father's murder. They said they'd hardly asked anything when Kaiser showed up and took over the interview."

"That doesn't surprise me," I say, trying to keep the tension out of my voice. "You think Kaiser sensed anything about her? He was a profiler at Quantico for a long time."

"He may have." Sean looks across the street, then back at the intersection behind us. He already made two passes along the street, looking for signs of surveillance. He saw none.

"We're way off the reservation here, Cat. Farther than we've ever been. If Kaiser already suspects Pitre, we could fuck this case up bad." He looks at me, his eyes sincere. "You don't want to call him?"

I give Sean a hard look, then get out of the car and hurry up the side-walk to the screened porch. I hear the fast clicking of heels as he catches up to me.

"Move out of the light," he says.

While I stand in the darkness under the eaves, Sean makes a quick circuit of the house. The main sound in this neighborhood is the steady hum of air-conditioning units, punctuated by the muted blare of televisions.

"Can't see shit," Sean says, trotting up to me. "Curtains closed all the way around."

Before he can bring up more reasons to wait, I walk up the three concrete steps and knock on the door.

Quick footsteps sound inside. Then the curtain in the window to our left flips sideways, and a dark silhouette peers out. Before I can get a closer look, the curtain drops back into place.

"Who is it?" calls a muffled female voice.

"Police," says Sean, all authority. "Please open the door, ma'am. I've got identification."

After a few moments, the doorknob clicks, and the door opens to the length of a chain latch. Sean flips open his wallet and holds his badge up to the crack in the door.

"Detective Sergeant Sean Regan, ma'am. NOPD Homicide. Are you Evangeline Pitre?"

"Maybe."

"I was a friend of your father's."

"I don't remember you. What do you want?"

"You are Evangeline Pitre?"

"Yes. What's this about?"

"Your father's murder."

There's a pause. "I already talked to some detectives. The FBI, too."

"I'm aware of that, ma'am. But we take the death of a fellow officer very seriously. We need to speak to you again."

"Well . . ."

The door closes, but after a brief rattle, it opens again, revealing the face from the photograph I studied under the vanity light during the drive over. Evangeline Pitre looks older than she did in the photo. And though her name is Cajun, she looks like a blend of Cajun and mountain blood. Dark hair and eyes mated with pale skin, and thin to the point of emaciation. Her lank hair hangs as if it hasn't been washed in days, and there's a purple suck mark on her neck.

"Sorry," she says. "I've been paranoid ever since it happened. How can I help you?"

"Could we come inside?" Sean asks.

"Is it going to take that long?"

"It could. You do realize we're dealing with a serial killer here?"

"That's what the papers say." Pitre looks doubtfully behind her, as though unwilling for us to see the squalor in which she lives. "Do you really need to come in?"

"We'd prefer it. You know how nosy neighbors can be."

A quick flash of hatred in the eyes. Evangeline Pitre doesn't get along with her neighbors. "Okay," she says finally. "Come on in."

She backs up, giving us room to enter.

The front door opens into a den. I've seen a lot of houses like this one in New Orleans. A door at the back of the den opens directly into the kitchen. Through it I can see glass doors that will open from the kitchen to a square cement patio outside. To my right is a hallway that leads to a couple of bedrooms—three at most—and a bathroom at the end of the hall.

The den is furnished with a flower-print sofa/love-seat combination that looks like it was bought at a thrift store. The sofa stands against the wall opposite the front door, with a rectangular coffee table in front of it. The love seat faces the left wall, where an old television shows the Home Shopping Network. A La-Z-Boy recliner faces the TV, and an old bureau of some kind stands against the wall behind me. Cigarette smoke hangs lazily in the air. I trace it to a cigarette burning in an ashtray on the floor beside the La-Z-Boy.

Evangeline Pitre has not once turned her back to us. She backed slowly into the den, then folded her arms and continued moving backward to the sofa, navigating around the coffee table without even looking down. She either grew up in this house or has lived here a long time.

"Seat?" she offers.

"Thanks," says Sean.

He turns the La-Z-Boy around so that it faces the sofa and sits. I perch on the love seat with my purse in my lap, barely able to restrain my curiosity. Evangeline Pitre bends her knees and alights on the edge of the sofa like a bird, as though she might take flight at any moment.

"Ms. Pitre," Sean begins, "we'd like to—"

"Angie," she cuts in. "Call me Angie."

Sean gives her his charming smile, but the official tone remains in his voice. "All right, Angie. My colleague is a forensic expert we sometimes consult on cases like this. She wants to ask you some questions about . . ."

His words blend into a meaningless monotone in my ears. He's following the script we worked out during the drive over, but now that I'm here, I think it's a waste of time. We don't need complex psychological tactics to get this woman to open up to us.

"Angie," I say in a familiar voice, "Detective Regan isn't telling you the whole truth."

Sean stares openmouthed at me.

"I am a forensic expert, but I'm not here to talk to you about forensics. I'm here to tell you what we know about these murders."

Pitre looks to Sean as though for help. She liked his officious fiction better than the frank tone of my truth. But Sean says nothing.

I set my purse on the floor, thinking for an instant of the revolver inside, then intertwine my fingers over my knees and give Pitre my most confiding smile. "Angie, have you ever seen me before?"

She shakes her head.

"I was a close friend of Dr. Nathan Malik."

Something has changed in her face. What? A tightening of the jaw? A new rigidity in the neck? Whatever caused the change, it's so profound that I feel as though a second set of eyes has opened behind the ones I can see. Eyes glinting with a primitive awareness whose only objective is survival. I've never met Evangeline Pitre in my life, but I know her.

She is me. I have that second set of eyes, too. The ones that watch in the quivering darkness, waiting for *him* to come—

"What is it?" Angie asks. "You're looking at me funny."

"Angie, my name is Catherine Ferry. Do you know that name?"

She blinks once, slowly, like a cat feigning boredom to a passing mouse. "No."

"I think you do."

She swallows.

"I know your father was a bad man, Angie. Other people thought he was good, but I know what he really was."

Her eyes have taken on a dull glaze.

"I know he touched you, Angie. I know he came to your bed in the dark. He probably hurt other children, too. That's why he had to die, isn't it?"

For the briefest instant, her eyes dart toward the back hall. Is she looking for escape? Or for help?

Sean stands quickly. "Do you mind if I take a look around the house?"

I expect Angie to bound to her feet in protest, but instead she settles back against the flowered fabric of the couch. "Sure," she says. "Whatever."

Sean moves into the hallway, drawing his gun from beneath his jacket as he goes. To keep the girl from panicking, I engage her in conversation.

"Were you one of the original members of Group X, Angie?"

A faint smile touches her lips.

"You're afraid to trust me, but you don't have to be. I know about Dr. Malik's movie. He wanted to give me the tapes for safekeeping, but I couldn't take them. The FBI was after me then. They're still after me now."

"Why would they be after you?"

"They think I'm involved with the murders. I don't mind that. They don't have any real evidence. I also killed a man about four hours ago. He was trying to rape me, and I killed him."

The hidden eyes probe me for deception, but they find none. "I don't get it," she says. "You're with a cop."

"Sean's not a regular cop. He's my boyfriend. I was molested, just like you, Angie. I know how it feels to go through that. And I'm not here to hurt you. I'm here to help."

Her eyes narrow in suspicion. I can only imagine what has been done to this girl by people who promised to help her.

"But for me to help you, you're going to have to tell me the truth."

"What about?"

"How it started. I know those six men were punished for what they did. But I need to know how it started."

Angie's face is as blank as the head of a mannequin.

"Did you ever meet a woman named Ann Hilgard?"

For the first time, I see fear in her eyes. Why should the mention of my aunt's name generate fear in this girl?

"Angie, if you don't talk to me tonight, Sean is going to have to tell the task force what I figured out about these murders. About how you're involved. And I won't be able to help you after that."

The fear ratchets up a notch. "What are you talking about? What did you figure out?"

Here goes . . . "I know you're taking saliva from a baby at the day-care center where you work and putting it into the bite marks on the dead men."

Pitre's eyes widen, and her bottom lip quivers like a five-year-old's.

"What I need to know is, have you done all this on your own, or is somebody helping you? Was Dr. Malik helping you? I know he knew about the killings. He told me that. He was going to talk about them in the movie, wasn't he?"

Angie's hands are shaking now, and her left leg is bouncing up and down. She's like a machine that has run reliably for twenty-two years, but is now about to vibrate to pieces. Sean was right: Angie Pitre couldn't have committed the murders alone.

"Did you videotape the killings for Dr. Malik, Angie?"

She stands so suddenly that I jerk back in my chair.

"This isn't right!" she cries, jabbing her sinewy arm at me. "You're not supposed to talk to me like this! You don't have proof of nothing!"

Sean races back into the den, gun in hand. "What's the matter?"

"Nothing." I motion for him to put the gun away.

He doesn't. "Bathtub's full of hot water," he says to Angie. "Why?"

"I was about to take a bath."

He points at the cigarette burning in the ashtray by the recliner. "Looks like you were watching TV to me."

"I was waiting to buy some earrings."

He studies her for a few moments, then holsters his gun and takes his seat in the La-Z-Boy. "What did I miss?" he asks, glancing at the hall.

"Angie was about to tell me who's helping her punish those men."

"What will happen to me if I talk to you?" she asks Sean.

He gives me a pointed look that I have no trouble reading: *It's time to Mirandize this girl and put her in front of a video camera.* "That depends on what you tell us," he says.

"Angie," I say softly, "I know it's hard for you to trust people. It's hard for me, too. That's one of the problems women like us have. But you need to listen to me now. Because I don't want to put you in jail. Okay? *I am the best friend you're ever going to have.*"

The guarded look doesn't lessen in vigilance, but there's confusion in her eyes. She's wavering.

"Take a deep breath, Angie. Take a deep breath and get it off your chest."

Slowly, Angie Pitre sits back down on the sofa.

"Whose idea was it?" I ask. "Who first said, 'We can't just sit around and bitch about this. We have to do something'?"

Her eyes flick back and forth like those of a crack addict. Then she says, "That's hard to say, you know? It wasn't really like that."

My heart thuds in my chest. I force myself not to look at Sean. "Was it Dr. Malik?"

She draws up her shoulders and hugs herself like a sullen child. "Sort of. I mean, he was always talking about how the men who do it never stop. You know? How none of the treatments work, except maybe castration. He said only death or prison ever really stop them from doing it."

"By 'it,' you mean sexually abusing children?"

"Yeah. Dr. Malik didn't think any of the old ways worked for victims either. They didn't make you well. It was all a lot of feel-good talk, he said. When you got back out in the world, it couldn't stop you from doing the bad things caused by what happened when you were a kid. You know? Sleeping around, or dope, or cutting yourself . . . whatever. Numbing behavior, he called it."

I nod understanding. "I've been an alcoholic since I was a teenager."

"There you go. So, that's why Dr. Malik started Group X. To try something new. It was like exploring a new world, he said. The dark world inside our heads."

"How many women were in the group?"

She shakes her head, the survivor's eyes glinting again.

"But all the members of Group X were repressed-memory cases."

"Yeah. Our lives were all fucked-up, and we didn't know why. I only got in because I was seeing this lady down at the mental health center, and she referred me. I don't have no money or nothing."

"I understand. So . . . Group X?"

"Yeah. What was different was that Dr. Malik did the delayed-memory work right there with all of us in the same room. And it was *intense,* man. If we weren't reliving what had happened to us, we were hearing somebody else relive what happened to *them.* And the way Dr. Malik did it, you couldn't hardly stand to hear it. When you're the patient, he makes you, like, become the kid you were when it happened to you. You talk in a little girl's voice and everything. It's scary to hear. I mean, some of the stuff I heard was really sick. Some people couldn't take it. Two or three times, people peed in their chairs. Seriously, man. And I think what happened came out of that."

"The decision to kill an abuser?"

She nods with sudden solemnity. "See, even though the bad stuff had happened to most of us years ago, in Group X it was like it was happening *right then*. All the terror and rage you couldn't express back then comes blasting out of you like an explosion or something. And it makes you *mad*. All of us felt that way. Even Dr. Malik. You could see it in his face. He wanted to hurt those men the way they'd hurt us."

"Did he suggest that you do that?"

Angie shakes her head. "No. See, as intense as all that was, it wasn't what started the . . . you know. It was that we got to talking afterward. We got to be friends, see? All of us. We weren't supposed to, but we started meeting outside Dr. Malik's office after group on Wednesdays. We'd go to somebody's apartment or whatever and drink Cokes and stuff. And talk. And it was there that we figured out the *really* scary thing."

I glance at Sean. He's hypnotized by Pitre's story. "What was that, Angie? What was the really scary thing?"

"That the guys who had done this to us were probably still doing it." She bites her bottom lip and nods as though talking silently to herself. "Not to us, but to other kids. You know? So we started watching them, trying to figure out what to do. But it's hard to tell, right? Unless you live in the house with them . . . and most of us had jobs or whatever."

"Of course."

"But I *knew*, okay? There's this kid on my dad's block, he's home alone all day—" Angie shakes her head with sudden violence. "Anyway, that's what it came out of. It wasn't just to punish them. I mean, that was part of it—to make them admit what they did. Because none of them will, you know? You get up your nerve for this big blowout, and then they just deny it. All of it. Dr. Malik had seen it a million times. They look at you like *you're* the crazy one, and then they tell you how much they love you and shit. It's sick. It makes you think maybe you *are* crazy."

"You're not crazy, Angie. I know that."

Sean is staring at me again, trying to get my attention. He's ready to make this official right now. But I'm not ready to call Kaiser yet. "So basically, you all agreed about what you were going to do?"

Angie nods slowly at me. She's transferred her allegiance away from Sean.

"How many of you were there, Angie?"

"Six."

"And now six men are dead."

She nods again.

"So you're finished?"

"Yep." She gives me a little smile.

"Did all of you help commit the crimes?"

She doesn't respond.

"'My work is never done,'" I quote, recalling the letters boldly drawn in blood. "Who came up with that?"

She gives me a conspiratorial smile, then shakes her head. "I can't tell on anybody else."

"But your work is done. That's what you're telling me?"

"Yep. All done."

Somehow, I knew this before I ever got here. That's why I didn't let Sean call in the task force. "Who killed Dr. Malik, Angie?"

Her smile vanishes, replaced by a profound fear. "I don't know. Nobody knows what to do now."

Is she lying? "This is very important, Angie. Who decided to make the crimes look like serial murders? Why didn't you just kill the men with one shot and make their deaths look like muggings or something? Something simple?"

"That was cool, huh?"

Sean clears his throat loudly, but I don't look at him. A strange light has come into Angie's eyes.

"You want to see one?" she asks.

"One what?"

"You know. What we did."

My pulse begins to race. "A murder, you mean?"

"We didn't call it that. We called it a sentence. Carrying out a sentence."

Now I glance at Sean. He looks like he's about to have a stroke. "Do you have a videotape here, Angie?"

She points into the corner near the television, where a cardboard box stands under a small round table.

"*Jesus,*" Sean intones.

"Is that Dr Malik's box?" I ask, feeling sweat in my palms. "The one with the stuff for the film in it?"

Angie nods, then goes to the box and pulls out a videotape. "This is one of the only ones on VHS. Most of them are on those little tapes. Those digital things. Mini-DVs or whatever."

"Cat," Sean whispers.

I feel a familiar buzzing in the back of my head. The tapes in that box could put my grandfather in jail for the rest of his life.

"Put it in the player, Angie. I want to see."

CHAPTER
65

Like a child about to show me a tape of her ballet recital, Angie Pitre pushes the tape into the VCR and waits expectantly.

Sean motions for me to walk over to him, his face taut with anxiety. By any legal standard, it's time to arrest Evangeline Pitre. But I'm not here as an agent of the law. I'm here to understand. Only then will I know what to do. It can only be my threat to tell Sean's wife about our affair that's keeping him from calling John Kaiser.

The TV screen goes blue. Then some numbers start turning quickly in the bottom left corner of the screen. I go to the box in the corner of the room and look down. Three rows of mini-DV tapes lie at the bottom of the box. The tapes are labeled with women's names in red Magic Marker. One reads, *Ann Hilgard*. I reach down and pluck it from the box, then slip it into my pocket.

"Look," says Sean.

A dark, jerky image has filled the TV screen: an exterior door. Someone is breathing rapidly, almost hyperventilating. A hand inside a clear plastic sleeve reaches out and inserts a key into the knob, turns it.

"What's that plastic?" I whisper.

"A hazmat suit," Angie says, her eyes locked on the screen. "Weird, huh?"

The door opens, and light floods into the lens.

The camera moves so quickly through the house that I feel like I'm watching an episode of *Cops*. A drug raid, maybe. But there's something familiar about it. *I've seen this house before.* It's one of the NOMURS crime scenes. The second one.

"Holy shit," says Sean. "Holy *shit*."

"Is that the Riviere house?" I ask in a stunned voice.

"Yeah," says Angie.

The camera stops at an open bedroom door. A paunchy, gray-haired man wearing white boxer shorts looks over from his dresser. Andrus Riviere, retired pharmacist, age sixty-six. Whatever he sees in the door terrifies him.

"Turn around!" orders a muffled voice. It sounds female.

"They can't hear you good in the suit," Angie says. "But it keeps you from leaving hair and stuff in the house."

"Cat?" says Sean. "Cat, we—"

"Face the wall!" shouts the voice. *"Put up your hands!"*

Andrus Riviere turns his back to the camera and lifts his flabby arms into the air. "Take whatever you want," he says in a shaky voice. "Money . . . you want money?"

A bright red flower blooms in the back of his undershirt.

"Shit!" cries Sean.

Riviere crumples to the floor like a spine-shot deer.

My heart pounds as the camera moves jerkily across the bedroom. For a moment I see only the ceiling. Then I see Riviere again. He's lying on his back, his face almost bloodless from fear. He tries to move, screams in agony.

"What did you do to Carol?" asks the muffled voice.

"I can't move my legs!" Riviere wails. "Oh, *God* . . ."

"Say what you did to Carol!"

"What?"

"Your daughter! Carol Lantana! Did you have sex with Carol when she was a little girl?"

Riviere's eyes bulge until I fear they'll burst from their sockets. For Andrus Riviere, the women in the hazmat suits are hell incarnate. "Carol?" he echoes. "No! No . . . *no.*"

"Did you rape Carol?" insists the voice.

"No! That's crazy! I never did anything like that."

The camera backs off. Then a plastic-encased hand holds the barrel of a revolver to Riviere's forehead. "Make peace with God. Admit what you did."

The old pharmacist is blubbering, saliva running down his chin. "Carol? Is that you in there?"

"Admit what you did!" screams the voice. Definitely female.

Riviere shakes his head violently.

On the screen, a second figure wearing a hazmat kneels beside Riviere and opens the jaws of the skull I found in Dr. Malik's lap at the motel. The hand presses the open mouth to Riviere's chest and clamps the teeth down on pale flesh.

Riviere shrieks in pain.

"Jesus," breathes Sean.

The figure is obviously using all its strength to drive the teeth together. Riviere screams again, and then the skull is withdrawn.

Riviere's weeping now, and panting as if he can't breathe.

"Bite him again!" shouts the voice.

"No! All right . . . all right! I couldn't help it . . . couldn't stop. You already know that, don't you?" Riviere's face contorts in pain. "I need a doctor! Please!"

"How old was Carol when you did it?"

Riviere closes his eyes and shakes his head. "I don't know . . . don't know."

The gun barrel cracks the bridge of his nose.

"Three?" he wails. *"Four? I don't know!"*

"Do you repent?"

The eyes bulge again, the fear in them absolute.

The muffled voice is relentless. *"Do—you—re—pent?"*

Riviere nods with sudden penitence, a desperate sinner seeing a way to redemption. "Yes! I repent . . . I do. I know it was wrong. I need help! Please help me!"

"I'm here to help you."

The hand presses the gun barrel flush against Andrus Riviere's forehead and blows his brains out the back of his head.

I jerk in shock, unable to comprehend that I'm witnessing the actual events I tried to reconstruct from evidence at the crime scene. No reconstruction could ever capture the brutality of this execution. And I know, suddenly and beyond doubt, that my idea of forcing these women to stop but not giving their names to the FBI was a fantasy born of my own pain and naïveté. It's true that Andrus Riviere will never molest another child. But what guarantee do I have that the woman who pulled that trigger won't decide tomorrow that someone less guilty than Riviere deserves a death sentence? Margaret Lavigne's stepfather already became an innocent victim.

"Cat, it's time to make some calls," Sean says quietly.

He's right.

"Cat? I have to—"

A muted thud cuts off Sean in midsentence.

When I turn, I see a naked woman with blonde hair holding a green plastic barbell in one hand and a butcher knife in the other. Half an hour ago, I was studying her picture on my kitchen table. She's Stacey Lorio, age thirty-six, registered nurse and the daughter of Colonel Frank Moreland, our first victim. She's knocked Sean unconscious with a single blow from a barbell. As I stare in shock, she kneels and yanks his Glock from his shoulder holster, then points it at my chest.

"I hid under the dirty clothes in the closet," she says to Angie, panting from excitement. "For a minute, I thought he saw me."

"Why did you hit him?" I ask, trying not to glance at my purse beside the love seat.

"Shut up!" Lorio snaps, straightening up. She's not much taller than Angie Pitre, but her rawboned body is mostly muscle. She has stretch marks and sagging breasts, but beyond that, she looks as hard as a frozen ham.

"We didn't come here to arrest anybody, Stacey."

She laughs, then glances at Angie. "I know better than that, you rich cunt."

Her face is bright red, her chest blotchy with scarlet marks. "Do you know me, Stacey?"

"What do you think? Your aunt was the bitch who screwed up my life."

"What?"

"Yeah, she came along with her perfect teeth, her thousand-dollar shoes, and her Southern belle voice, and he didn't know which way was up anymore."

"Who?"

"Christ. Who do you think?"

Suddenly everything is clear. This woman was romantically involved with Nathan Malik until my aunt took him away from her. Why should I be surprised? Ann had been seduced by one of her shrinks before. And when I spoke to her on the telephone about paying Malik's bail, she'd acted as if it were the most natural thing in the world.

"*You* killed Dr. Malik," I think aloud. "You're the one who knocked me out in the motel."

"He left me no choice," she says. "He was going to give us up to the police."

"Why would he do that?"

"To save himself from going to jail," says Angie Pitre.

"Dr. Malik wasn't in any danger of being convicted for murder."

"You don't know that," says Lorio. "But all he really cared about was his personal crusade. His master plan. He *wanted* us to go to trial. He wanted the world to see what sexual abuse had driven us to do."

"I don't care who knows," Angie says, suddenly upset. "We did what we had to do. God only knows how many kids we saved."

Lorio looks at Angie like a protective older sister. "That's right, Ang. But there's no need for you to waste your life in jail. Not to make old Nathan famous. The world's not going to understand what we did. And a lot of men would try to make sure we got the death penalty."

"I think you're wrong, Stacey," I say in the most submissive voice I can muster. "I think a lot of people would understand."

She laughs. "That's easy to say. But I'm not spending my life in prison just to be the flavor of the week on *Oprah*. We accomplished what we set out to do. It's over now."

"Is it? What about me?" I look down at Sean, who hasn't moved once. "What about him?"

"You two stuck your noses in where they didn't belong. I can't help that."

"Are you going to kill me? I'm just like you, Stacey. I was molested, just like you."

"You're like me?" Her eyes are cold. "You're *nothing* like me."

"Are you that blind, Stacey? You think being raised with money can protect you from your own father? Or your grandfather?"

Angie Pitre is wringing her hands. "Stacey, this isn't what we said, you know? Nobody else would go along with this."

Lorio looks sharply at Angie. "Nobody else had the nerve to go through with any of it, did they? They sat back while we did their dirty work for them. They watched the people who hurt them beg for forgiveness on TV, but did they lift one fucking finger? Did they get their hands bloody?"

Angie shakes her head. "I know, I know, but still—"

"Still *what*?"

"She's like us, Stacey!"

Lorio jerks the gun toward Sean. "And him? He's a cop. A homicide detective! He wants to send you to the death house. You heard what he said. *It's time to make some calls.* Do you want to ride the needle, Ang? Shit, you can't even give blood without puking."

"I know, but . . . God, I don't know."

Lorio's lips tighten into a white line. "*I* know, baby. You just go in the kitchen while mama takes care of business."

Stacey Lorio pulls a cushion off the sofa with her free hand, and I know then that I'm living the last moments of my life. I got away from Billy Neal. I won't be so lucky again. My eyes go to my purse on the floor, but it might as well be a mile away. Lorio takes a step toward me, puts the gun behind the cushion, and fires.

Everything registers out of order. A horse kicks me in the belly. Tiny fragments of foam rubber fill the air. Wet red blood washes down my stomach, and a muffled boom sounds in my ears. Then a woman screams.

"What?" I ask, walking backward, trying to stay on my feet.

"*Stacey, no!*"

Lorio is following me with the cushion, the black barrel of Sean's Glock protruding through the foam padding. She's two feet away when Angie Pitre jumps on her back and yanks back both arms. They go down in a pile of flailing limbs.

I want to help Angie, but instead I sit down hard on the love seat.

"*Oh, God,*" somebody moans.

It's me. The blood has run down my front and begun soaking my crotch. The gun explodes again, and somebody shrieks, but the women keep fighting.

I can see my purse on the floor, but I can't bend to reach it.

Stacey Lorio is sitting on Angie's chest now, screaming at her to stop fighting, but Angie keeps flailing like a crazed little girl. With a loud curse, Lorio turns the gun in her hand and smacks Angie across the face with its butt.

Angie Pitre stops fighting.

Stacey is climbing off her when Sean's hand rises from the floor and grips her elbow. He must be only half-conscious, because Lorio laughs and shucks his grip as easily as the hand of a little boy. Walking with calm assurance, she lifts the other cushion off the couch and lays it over Sean's face.

I look down at my purse, willing myself to bend at the waist.

Stacey presses the barrel of Sean's gun over the cushion, right about where Sean's forehead would be, and fires.

As I scream in rage, a tiny hole appears between Stacey's breasts. It looks almost painted on, but within seconds she is sucking for air as though steel bands have been locked around her chest. Sean's featherweight Smith & Wesson is shaking in my hand.

Stacey opens her mouth to speak, but a geyser of blood erupts from her throat.

Angie screams.

Stacey knees buckle, and she falls into a kneeling position beside Sean. She looks down at him, raises the gun over the cushion, then keeps raising it, trying to bring it to bear on me.

"Don't," I whisper, but the gun keeps rising.

I shoot her in the face, blowing a fine red mist into the air behind her.

As Stacey Lorio falls, all I can think of is the terrible irony that it was my grandfather who taught me how to shoot a handgun.

Then everything goes black.

CHAPTER

66

I spent much of the week after I was shot going to funerals. Two were expected, one was not. Two were postponed until I was discharged from Tulane University Hospital, and thanks to Stacey Lorio, I had to ride in a wheelchair to all of them. The bullet she fired from Sean's gun tore through my stomach and lodged in a muscle in my back. I lost a lot of blood and also my spleen.

But I didn't lose my baby.

Sean nearly drowned in his own blood. His head had been turned sideways beneath the couch cushion when Lorio fired, so instead of drilling through his forehead—as she had intended for it to do—the bullet punched through his right cheek a couple of inches anterior to his ear. It smashed five teeth, shattered his hard palate, and pulped part of his maxillary sinuses. Sean owes his life to Angie Pitre, who, instead of fleeing the scene, called 911 and stayed with us until paramedics and police arrived.

Stacey Lorio died instantly from my second bullet. I feel a deep sadness at the childhood trauma that created the hate-filled adult she had become, but I feel no guilt over killing her. She meant to murder both Sean and me in cold blood. Sean blamed himself for not cracking Lorio's "rock solid" alibis for the murders, but no one else had either. It turned out that her ex-husband was a drug addict. Because Stacey kept him supplied with pills from the clinic where she worked, he would have given her alibis for a dozen more murders and sworn to them all under oath. Lorio's other alibis had been provided by two women later identified as members of Group X. With hindsight all seems obvious.

Special Agent Kaiser spent a lot of time in my hospital room. The doctors tried to keep him out, but Kaiser can be pretty pushy when he wants to be. He demanded to know every detail of what had happened to me during the case, and of how I had solved the riddle of who was doing the killing. He was obsessed with determining once and for all whether the six murders in New Orleans had any connection to the events in Natchez and on DeSalle Island. Given the link between Ann and Dr. Malik—and in a way, Malik and me—it seemed inconceivable that they were not causally related. But they weren't. Not really.

Dr. Hannah Goldman put it best when she dropped by to see me and found Kaiser at my bedside. She patiently laid out the connections by drawing a line diagram on the back of a hospital cafeteria menu. The primary link between Natchez and New Orleans was sexual abuse. Nathan Malik first noticed me in Jackson, Mississippi, because I was sleeping with a man twenty-five years my senior. That relationship—a symptom of my childhood abuse—also resulted in my being expelled from medical school, which led me into dentistry and, ultimately, into forensic odontology. Malik's childhood abuse led him slowly but surely into work with sexual abuse victims. He became the natural end point of my aunt Ann's quest to find a therapist who could control the terrible fallout of *her* childhood sexual abuse. Given Ann's history—and Nathan Malik's sexual predilections—sexual involvement between the two of them was almost inevitable. Malik's childhood abuse also made him ripe for the countertransference that caused him to encourage vigilante justice among the patients in Group X. The murders committed by Stacey Lorio and Angie Pitre—and the decision by those women to use bite marks to mask the true nature of the crimes—resulted in my being called into the case. (The FBI's search of Stacey Lorio's apartment turned up a huge collection of true-crime paperbacks, filled with underlined sections about forensics and the psychology of sexual homicide.) As soon as Dr. Malik became aware of my involvement in the investigation, he became obsessed with communicating with me. Given his knowledge of my family's secret history—and what Ann had probably told him about me—he felt that my appearance represented some sort of meaningful synchronicity, and he could not ignore it.

"The simple answer," Dr. Goldman concluded, "is that sick people attract other sick people. Psychologically speaking, of course."

According to Hannah, though, my recent wave of nightmares about my grandfather and the truck had nothing to do with the murders in New Orleans. Those, she insisted, were the result of my pregnancy. The moment my brain knew that I was going to have a child, my subconscious realized that to protect my baby I needed to remember my childhood abuse. "Evolution at work," Hannah said. "Carrying on the species is the highest priority of any organism. Your brain decided that protecting your child was more important than protecting you from the trauma of your own past. Thus, the flood of nightmares and flashbacks. You were going to remember what your grandfather did to you whether anyone got killed here in New Orleans or not. Take my word for that."

But not even Hannah could explain what it was about the murder scenes that had clued me in on the true nature of the crimes. Like the FBI, I had been presented with classic evidence of a male sexual predator at work, and I had looked at similar scenes many times before. So what caused my panic attacks? What told me that I was looking at violence that was somehow related to sexual abuse similar to my own? Hannah thought it might have been the sight of naked old men. But in the end, I decided it was the smallest of clues. My first attack happened at the murder scene of the third victim. Eleven days before, at the home of the second victim—Andrus Riviere—I had seen a little girl who stuck in my mind. Her grandfather had just died violently, yet she seemed almost wild with joyous energy. She was racing around the house as if her birthday party were about to start. And knowing what I know now, I believe that it was. Andrus Riviere's murder had released that little girl from a living hell. And something about her face—something in her too-wise eyes, I think now—sent me a message without my knowing it. As Pearlie had known subconsciously about Ann's abuse when she was a child, I knew subconsciously that something was wrong in the Riviere house. Something that death had remedied.

Kaiser stunned me by telling me that Dr. Malik had willed all the videotapes and other raw materials for his documentary film project to me. These included his patient records, which were found in Biloxi, Mississippi, cached in the home of my aunt's third husband. As soon as these materials are released from the NOPD evidence room, they will be delivered to me. At some point I intend to review them all and begin working to finish Malik's film. I will include no footage of the murders, but I will do all I can to explain their motivation.

The day I was to be discharged from the Tulane hospital, I learned that Margaret Lavigne was also a patient there. I had an orderly wheel me down to her floor and leave me alone in her room. Margaret lay comatose beneath a white sheet, connected to an assortment of monitors and tubes. The insulin she'd injected into her veins had turned her brain into a useless gray lump. John Kaiser had told me that Lavigne's mother was likely to authorize the withdrawal of life support later in the week. I held Margaret's hand for a while, thinking quietly about the suicide note she'd left behind, and of the horror she must have felt when she realized she'd condemned an innocent man to death. Like me, she had been unable to believe that her father had raped her. She erroneously blamed her stepfather instead. I'm thankful that in my own case I was right, but I could so easily have been wrong.

The first funeral I attended was Nathan Malik's.

The psychiatrist had elected to be cremated, so it was a memorial service, held in a New Orleans park. About fifty people attended, most of them women. There were a few men, too, some of them obviously Vietnam veterans. A Buddhist monk chanted and said some prayers, and everyone laid flowers by the urn.

The second funeral was Ann's, and it was held in Natchez.

Michael Wells drove me to McDonough's Funeral Home, helped me into my wheelchair, and even drove me out to the cemetery afterward for the burial. While the minister gave a generic eulogy, I sat in the pews reserved for family and thought of the tape Ann had made for Nathan Malik. The mini-DV cassette I stole from the box at Angie Pitre's house had made it all the way to the hospital in my purse. I borrowed a camcorder to watch it, but I could only endure about ten minutes before I was overwhelmed. Ann had suffered far more than the rest of us. For whatever reason, she had not dissociated during her abuse. She had felt and processed and remembered every agonizing detail. Her primary concern had been protecting her younger sister—my mother. And though she failed in that goal, she tried her best. She did this by luring my grandfather to her room whenever she sensed his attention wandering to her sister. But Ann wasn't trying to protect only Gwen. The reason for her silence over the years was simple: Grandpapa had threatened that if she ever revealed what he was doing to her, he would kill both her sister and her mother. Ann had no doubt that he would carry out his threat. She knew better than any of us that he was capable of murder.

The third funeral—the unexpected one—was held one day after Ann's.

Today.

I didn't go to the funeral home. I had Michael drive me out to the cemetery to sit beside Ann's freshly covered grave. I stared at the mound of wet brown earth on the grass and wondered if I could somehow have prevented her suicide. Michael assured me that I could not, and I'm trying my best to believe him. A few minutes before the mourners were to arrive, Michael wheeled me up the lane to a vantage point from which I could watch the burial service without being bothered.

And here I sit.

The line of luxury cars behind the black hearse seems to go on forever, like the cortege of a slain president. I shouldn't be surprised. Dr. William Kirkland was a wealthy, powerful, and respected man, a pillar of the community.

My mother tried to keep the funeral simple, but in the end she gave in to the well-intentioned friends who insisted on a large production, including eulogies delivered by the mayor, the attorney general, and the governor of Mississippi.

Everyone seems content to pretend that my grandfather's death was an accident. That he drove off the edge of the bridge to DeSalle Island in bright sunlight at midday seems to escape everyone's attention. A few people have mentioned his "recent" stroke—which happened a year ago—and recalled his doctor forbidding him to drive. In fact, they say, it was the untimely death of his driver—Billy Neal—that caused my grandfather to drive down to the island alone to deal with some urgent business matters.

The truth is much simpler.

My grandfather killed himself. He knew that his life's foul secret was about to be exposed. That all of his power and money would be insufficient to stop one of his victims—me—from finally revealing his depravity to the world. And his pride could not abide that. He probably saw himself as choosing a manly death, even a noble one. But I know him for what he was. He was what he once called my father in front of me when I was a little girl. *Yellow.* When all was said and done, William Kirkland, MD, was a stinking coward.

I'm here today because I want to see him lowered into the ground. I need that closure. When you've lived with a demon all your life, and you somehow escape him, it's important to see him buried. If old Mr. McDonough would have let me, I'd have walked into the prep room and driven a stake through my grandfather's heart.

And yet . . . he didn't begin life as a monster. He began it as an innocent little boy who lost his parents in a car wreck on the way to his baptism. It was only later—I'll never know when—that the poison with which he infected me was passed into him. Decades ago, on some dark and silent country night, *his* innocence was stolen, and a transformation began that would transform the lives of countless others, including mine.

One mystery that will probably remain unsolved is why Grandpapa was buying up my father's sculptures. Was he driven by guilt over the life he had stolen so long ago? Or was he on some half-mad quest to understand the creative spark that he had snuffed out, creativity being the one talent he had never really possessed? Perhaps time or some as-yet-undiscovered document will give me an answer someday.

The burial service is mercifully brief, as the sky is threatening rain. The mourners quickly return to their cars, and the long line begins to leave the cemetery.

When all of them have gone, a solitary figure remains beside the grave.

Pearlie Washington.

She's wearing a black dress and a huge black hat, but I know her bony figure as well as I know my mother's. Probably better. Has she stayed behind to mourn my grandfather alone? Or Ann? Or has she stayed because she knows what's about to happen in the DeSalle family plot?

As Michael wheels me down the hill, Pearlie stands motionless, looking down at Grandpapa's grave. As we near her, a white Dodge Caravan with ornate silver trim appears in the lane and rolls slowly to a stop near the low wall. Two men in dark suits get out, walk to the back of the van, and unload a bronze casket. They settle it onto a collapsible gurney, then work the gurney across the grass to the corner of the plot, where a green tarp is staked out over a long hole in the ground.

The headstone above the tarp reads LUKE FERRY, 1951–1981.

As Michael rolls me through the gate, Pearlie walks over to me and touches my hand. "They doing what I think they're doing?"

"Yes."

I see pain in her eyes. "Why you didn't tell me about it? I loved that boy, too."

"I wanted to be alone with him. I'm sorry, Pearlie."

"You want me to go?"

"No."

The old woman watches the men strip the tarp from the ground. As they fold it up, soft rain begins to fall.

"Where's your mama?" Pearlie asks.

"She said she couldn't stand to bury her husband a second time."

Pearlie sighs heavily. "She's probably right."

Michael touches my elbow and leans down to my ear. "I'm going to give you a few minutes."

I take his hand and squeeze it. "Thanks. I won't be long."

"Take your time."

As he walks away, Pearlie turns and watches him leave the family plot. "He seems like a good man."

"He is."

"Does he know you carrying another man's child?"

I look up at the curious brown eyes. "Yes."

"And he still wants to see you?"

"Yes."

She shakes her head as though at some rare and wonderful sight. "That's a man you need to stick with, right there."

I feel my mouth smile. "I think you're right."

Pearlie takes my hand in hers and squeezes tight. "Lord, it's about time you settled down. We been needing some babies around that old place."

I take a deep breath and look toward Grandpapa's grave. "I think I was waiting for him to go first."

Pearlie nods. "Lord knows that's right."

Daddy's casket lies beside the open grave now, the rain pattering against its burnished lid. Strangely, the sound doesn't bother me at all.

"Could you open it for me now, please?" I ask.

One of the men from the funeral home takes a hex key from his pocket and begins unsealing the casket.

"What?" Pearlie gasps, her eyes filled with horror. "What you doing, girl? That's bad luck, doing something like that!"

I shake my head. "No, it's not."

As the man from the funeral home lifts the coffin lid, I reach beneath my wheelchair to the luggage pocket beneath. I feel soft fur in my palm. Using all my strength, I stand and walk slowly to the coffin. My father looks just as he did the other day, like a young man sleeping on the couch after a Sunday dinner. Gritting my teeth against pain, I bend at the waist and lay Lena the Leopardess in the crook of Daddy's elbow. Then I straighten up again.

"So you won't be lonely," I say softly.

Before I turn away, I take a folded piece of paper from my pocket and drop it in the casket near my father's knee. It's one of the drawings from the sketchbook he kept in the green bag in the barn. A charcoal rendering of Louise Butler, smiling at him with unbounded love in her eyes. Perhaps I should feel guilty for this, but I don't. Louise probably relieved Luke Ferry of more pain than any of us in those last years. She accepted him for what he was . . . a profoundly wounded man.

"Good-bye, Daddy," I murmur. "Thank you for trying."

I turn from the casket and walk back to the wheelchair, signaling Michael as I go. He comes quickly.

"I want to see the river," I tell him. "Will you wheel me up to Jewish Hill?"

Towering three hundred feet above the Mississippi, Jewish Hill offers the most commanding view of the river I've ever seen.

Michael can't hide his dismay. "It's raining, Cat."

"I know. I like it. Will you come with me, Pearlie?"

"All right, baby."

"Can you make it?" Michael asks her.

Pearlie snorts indignantly. "I may be over seventy years old, but I can still walk from Red Lick to Rodney and have strength left over for a day's work."

Michael laughs, apparently recognizing the names of two tiny Mississippi towns over twenty miles apart. He pushes me up the hill at a steady pace, and before long, we are staring over the mile-wide tide of river at the vast plains of the Louisiana delta.

"That's too big to look at," Pearlie says.

"I love it," I say softly. "I used to come here whenever I felt trapped in this town."

"I think you always been trapped here, until your granddaddy died."

"You know he killed himself," I murmur.

There's a long silence. Then Pearlie says, "I don't know any such thing."

I look up at her. "Come on. You don't really think he went off that bridge by accident?"

She looks at Michael, then back at me. "No, I don't."

A low humming has started in my head. "What is it, Pearlie? What do you know?"

She looks as serious as I've ever seen her. "I know everything. How much do you want to know?"

"Same as you."

She looks doubtfully at Michael. "Some things it's best not to know, Doctor. Why don't you go get the car?"

Michael looks down at me, and I nod.

As he walks away, Pearlie steps in front of the wheelchair and fixes me in her gaze with an old woman's severity. "After you left me on the island, I stayed with Louise Butler awhile. But I was nervous as a cat. I couldn't rest. So I took me a walk. I wound up on the other side of the lake. At the big house."

She's talking about my grandfather's lodge, the showplace designed by A. Hays Town.

"Before I knew what I was doing, I was tearing that place apart. I was still looking for the pictures, see? I knew they had to be some-where." She sighs and looks at the ground. "Well, I found 'em. They was inside a hollow book, just one out of hundreds in that library down there. And they were bad, baby. Lots worse than the two of you and Ann in the swimming pool."

"What did they show?"

Pearlie wrinkles her nose as though smelling rotten meat. "Every-thing. It made me sick to look at them. I went to use the bathroom, and I was crying so bad I couldn't stop. And then I heard some-thing."

"Grandpapa?"

"No. Jesse."

"Jesse Billups? He saw the pictures?"

Pearlie nods, her face filled with anxiety. "And they wasn't just pictures of any old children. Some of them were from the island. Jesse recognized them. Some of them belonged to people still living down there."

"My God. What did he do?"

"He cursed me. Then he took the pictures and left with them."

"What happened, Pearlie? What did he do with them?"

"He showed them to some other men down there. Some of the daddies of them children. See, the women had known about Dr. Kirkland, just like I guessed. Some of them, anyway. But they never let their menfolk know. But now the men *knew*. And they was killin' mad, just like the women worried they would be. Well . . . Jesse called Dr. Kirkland and told him somebody had busted into the big house and tore everything up. Said Dr. Kirkland ought to come right away."

I close my eyes, almost afraid to hear the end of the story.

"You sure you want to hear this, baby?"

"Yes."

"When Dr. Kirkland got there, Jesse and the other men put him in a truck and carried him round to Big Leon's house."

"Who's Big Leon?"

"One of the men on the island. He spent twenty years on Angola Farm. Jesse showed Leon the pictures and told him what Dr. Kirkland had done. Then he told Leon, 'You can have him for two hours. Just don't mark him up none.'"

"Oh, my God."

As Pearlie nods, her eyes glow with fierce knowledge. "Two hours later, they went back and got him. Then they did what that Billy Neal was gonna do to you and me."

"What?"

"Tied him to the steering wheel of his car and ran it off the bridge."

"*Jesus.*"

"After a while, one of them swum down and took the rope off Dr. Kirkland's hands." Pearlie is watching me closely, waiting to see my reaction. "You said you wanted to know."

"Did you see Grandpapa at all during any of this?"

"No. All I know is what Jesse told me."

My mind is filled with one question. "Did he beg for his life at the end?"

"No, baby. He cursed them till his head went under the water. Wasn't nothing gentle left in that old man. He'll curse the devil hisself when he gets to hell."

I suddenly feel exhausted.

"What you gonna do now?" Pearlie asks.

"I don't know. Wait for my wound to heal, I guess. The bullet wound, I mean. The other could take my whole life."

"I meant about the house. Malmaison."

"What do you mean?"

Pearlie shrugs. "Well, it's gonna be yours now."

"What?"

"I thought you knew. Dr. Kirkland always said Miss Gwen couldn't take care of her own self, much less the wealth she was born into. That's why Billy Neal hated you so bad. You gonna get just about everything."

Her words take some time to register. I have no idea what might be included in my grandfather's estate, but it's bound to be enormous.

"So, what you gonna do?"

"Sell it all," I say.

Pearlie makes an uncertain sound. "The island, too?"

"Why not? I don't ever want to see it again."

"If you sell that island, the people down there won't have nowhere to go. You own it all, the houses and everything. They just rent."

For a few moments, images of the island rush through my head. But the pain that comes with them is too much to bear. "They can have it, Pearlie. The whole damn thing. It's theirs anyway."

"Do you mean that? That island's worth a piece of money."

"I couldn't care less. I'll have the lawyers draw up papers first thing. You and Jesse work out fair shares for everybody. Except for Louise Butler."

Pearlie's back stiffens. "What about her?"

"Louise gets the lodge."

Pearlie gasps. "The big house? You're not serious. Those women down there hate Louise."

"It's her house, Pearlie. As of today."

The old woman makes several noises I cannot interpret. Then she says, "I guess you know what you're doing."

"For the first time, I think I do. Do you see Michael? I'm ready to go."

"We don't need no Michael. I can push this chair good as any man."

She steps behind the wheelchair and takes the handles in her firm grip. As she turns me around, I catch a last glimpse of the river, vast and majestic under the shadows of the rain. The water down there will soon flow past DeSalle Island, Baton Rouge, New Orleans, and finally into the Gulf of Mexico. Where I'll be then, I don't know. But the chain of misery forged through the generations of my family has finally been broken.

By me.

That's about as good a start as I can imagine.

Pearlie pushes me back toward the lane, where Michael's Expedition waits. As we approach, Michael gets out and waves. I lay one hand on my stomach and close my eyes. I'm not touching the wounded place, but a spot lower down. I don't need a drink now. I don't need anything. But for the first time in my life, I feel truly free to choose what I want.

"It's going to be different for you," I whisper, rubbing my tummy in a slow circle. "Your mama knows what love is."

ACKNOWLEDGMENTS

First and foremost, I thank the women and men who spoke frankly to me about private matters. For obvious reasons I will not name them here. Accounts of childhood sexual abuse are difficult to deal with, even on the written page. To recount personal experiences is nothing short of heroic. Few crime victims face the battles that those who as adults begin to recall childhood sexual abuse must fight. Far too often, family members and the general public refuse to believe their claims, even in the face of corroborative evidence. None of us wants to think about the harrowing crimes that innocent children suffer in their own homes. But we owe everyone who has such memories a fair hearing. Please don't ignore any child or adult who claims that she—or he—has been sexually abused. Listen, and contact a professional. Do not wait. Do not ignore your instincts. If you need more information about child abuse, visit http://www.gregiles.com.

As with all of my novels, I relied upon the knowledge of experts to add verisimilitude to this story. I warmly thank all of these people for their contributions:

Police expertise: O'Neil DeNoux, former homicide detective and a great writer in his own right.
Dental expertise: Dr. Carrie Iles.
Medical expertise: Dr. Jerry W. Iles, Dr. Michael Bourland, Dr. Tom Carey, Dr. Geoff Flattman, Dr. Andrew Martin.
Natchez City Cemetery: Don Estes, Maypop, Martin Anderson.
Mortuary science: Charles Laird, Dickey Laird.

Miscellaneous: Nancy Hungerford, Jane Hargrove, George Ward, Clint Pomeroy, Tammye Hoover, Lisa Bunch.

Early readers: Ed Stackler, Mike Henry, Betty Iles, Carrie Iles, Ann Paradise.

Special thanks to Geoff Iles, without whose invaluable help these books would be much less than they are.

Special thanks to Selah Saterstrom, for permission to quote from her hypnotic work, *The Pink Institution*.

Special thanks to Kim Barker, who first saw the blood on the wall. She's a wonderful writer with a great imagination. I'm glad she likes laughter better than fear. Woo-hoo!

All mistakes are mine.

ABOUT THE AUTHOR

Greg Iles is the author of nine bestselling novels, including *The Foot-prints of God, Sleep No More, Dead Sleep, The Quiet Game,* and *24 Hours* (released by Sony Pictures as *Trapped*). He lives in Natchez, Mississippi.